To a s...
and educ...
from a ...... writer.

CW00422187

~p,

Traveling True

Although this is an
unedited copy, I hope
you'll appreciate its being
one of the first.

VIVIANA IOAN

Ioan

December 12th 2018

National College
of Arts "Dinu Lipatti"
Bucharest, Romania

For the beautiful soul of my father, Tudor.

For the other heart beating for me, beautiful Virginia, my mother.

CONTENTS

ACKNOWLEDGMENTS

I wish my thanks could somehow reach the dimension where abides now the soul of the great Romanian novelist Fanus Neagu. He believed in me and back in 1990 took the manuscript of this novel, as it was then, to have it published. I hope to be forgiven for leaving the country without saying goodbye.

I thank my mother, Virginia, who kept prodding me into taking a break from writing to publish this novel.

My thanks also go to my nephew Adrian Ioan, for having suggested self-publishing.

1 THE ROAD

The road is an archway. They glide along into a new world, a lullaby ride on the back of a bluish serpent, among secret whisperings coming from the surrounding vegetation. The high canopy miraculously keeps them inside an endless tunnel-like corridor. Let's pull up! No, he says, I know a perfect spot, we'll stop there. Here, she shouts, isn't it wonderful! Not yet, babe, wait and you'll see what I mean, he seems to think, pulling his chin to his chest.

There are fantastically wooded hills — though some completely naked here and there — and dormant populations of wild shrubbery stretching up to them. Frames succeed one another. Majestic trees so dominant, close-cropped carpets of grasses, primeval colonies of fern ennoble static shadows in the woods. In silence, archaic mountains witness their passage. She is swept off by a childlike feeling of pity which she tenderly casts upon the bald bluntness of the oldest ones, hey you, bland old fellows, ever so gentle you. To her amazement, some seem to rejuvenate before her eyes, and garbs so fresh appear to be glittering in raw greens on their ancient shoulders. She marvels at this spectacular gallery and feels blessed to be here, but where shall one stop and which frame should they distort with their mobile outlines? Here, she shouts. He does not pull up promptly. Yes, here, do you like it? He stops the engine and turns to her, beaming, waiting for a reaction, has he not been right, as look what world he has brought her into.

They both draw in deeply of the pristine essence of the realm, and she would dart away to inspect those bushes, then farther on up to that row of trees, to see what is behind them, they are so stunningly tall — and she leaves on an impulse. Now she is running among the plants, which are indeed as wet as she had felt them from a distance. He calls after her, there is no time to waste, as he has found the place where they are going to lunch, next to a milestone.

It is there that she is hastily unwrapping the grub, she gets clumsy, could she possibly meet his expectations, and they start to swallow down. He has finally given her a rest, they are hungry, aren't they. Now and then a car whirs past and she feels like calling out her happiness, look, people, I am with him! Yes, they are cozily camped next to this dear milestone, what a feeling! She is packing things back now, hurriedly again, yet take care, dear girl, he is watching you. Done, the pit stop is over and they can well resume their ride, it is boiling hot inside the car, and he starts off.

He pulls up. Not at their milestone this time. She had been desperately praying for him to stop there, with all the inner powers she had been able to summon, all her love, and their spot did call out to them. Mim recognized it, but he did not push the brakes. Dark, unperturbed, he viciously squashed the yell from the woods. He stopped the car much farther away, the place is as beautiful, but some poisonous liquor starts dripping into her heart. Their two young companions are smiling, they are together. He and Mim are not. He tries to patch up some joke, but words and gestures come out artless and awkward. The artist is a prisoner within his own boundaries. She feels like breaking him free, there used to be no boundaries. This is their last ride and at the end of the road nothing but darkness awaits her. Mim has the picture of a lurid hole gaping wider and wider for her soul to agonize in there, wounded and dumb. There is not a glint of light to send the image of her grief to the world. Her soul is rolling on end in poisoned blackness, rubbing its heat off on the margins of endlessness, a putrid void. All Mim feels is dizziness, with her poor soul lost like a cub in the wilderness, ceaselessly letting loose its grief and gathering it back, doomed to languish in the hole with its own grief forever.

He and his two younger friends have been making jokes. This time genuine laughter strikes her ears and although she admits the wheeze is worth a laugh, she cannot unclasp her darkness. The sun is going down now and fields of flowers turn their heads after it. Life seems to be happening somewhere in the distance, wonderful life, Mim breathes in… Deep down a bubble bursts open splashing her unaware with an insolent taste, yes, life! Let her dive after it in limpid waters, she starts, she had better take the plunge, but no, not while Anton is here. Grim, his lips seem to taste bitter and sour, and stay clenched. This used to be his flower, oh, where has his flower gone? Poor wretched girl gone mad, there is no one but she who has ever seen *his-flower*.

They set off again, Mim in the front seat near Anton and the two youths together in the rear. None of them says a word. The car gulping the dark-ash gray of the asphalt sweeps her senses away and she flaccidly lets herself go down the slide of the road, her ears throbbing, her memory whizzing and swaying to the cadence of the elegant swan-swings on which her mother used to push her as a child. She feels her stomach to be nothing but a thread, a piece of thread thinning away. Her wanderings… Her teenage wanderings come back to her.

When she got upset she used to leave home to amble lonely in the streets and her parents did not object. She would come back enchanted by what she had seen: houses, people whispering outside their gates at sundown, hushed streets with her gliding along as in fairy-tale infinite halls, and no pain at all. Now, though, there is a huge canvas sewn out of sorrow, so tightly sewn. It has caught her inside and there is no way out of this gigantic balloon filled with her own grief. Strip of asphalt, where to? Let something happen, something must happen, let the ground crack, let the planet tip, let them hit something and not know, let someone hear Mim's tiny wretched cub! Nervous spasms convulse her brain's commands to each and every fiber of her body, yet the whole construction which is her body remains still. Now, let it be, the ultimate act, jump! What if she opened the door and flung herself out? The car skids onwards neighing like a bitten mare then comes to a stuck halt. Horns, brakes, a ragged doll thrown away, the three of them running, the girl covers her eyes, the boy is puzzled, Anton: let someone call for an ambulance, let someone do something, for God's sake! He is bellowing in terrible anger. His supple nostrils sniffle in vile spasms, frightening shadows pump rhythmically at the angles of his jawbones and Mim finds herself irradiated by the foul frown he had involuntarily cast over her that very morning — her eyes in his eyes, at last. 'It is a pity you never look into my eyes, that's bad, Mim,' he would chide her. Oh, how many times has she not tried! She did not dare, she feared what she might feel. He has several times caught her in the act, 'you're sneaking glimpses, aren't you?', 'why don't you look me in the eye, why are you hiding, come on, tell me'. Childish embarrassment would rush screaming up to her cheeks as she asked herself how real her guilt might be.

His merciless stare earlier this morning, look how she lies impaled onto its deadly ray. She had been waiting for him to come, shrouded in a splendor of all-embracing light,

4

dressed in a white gown and brimming with shame, yes, she had been utterly ashamed at the thought of his imminent appearance, and there he was, his frame in the slit between the two tall buildings, then out in the flood of sunlight, and the moment he clapped eyes on her the sun went down. Mim had seen the dark shadow descending from his eyes to his mouth and the skies had gone dirty hanging like rags, with shreds of old photos and dead birds.

A putrid deluge has rushed over, leveling all her memories into stench: boundless beaches splashing myriad aromas into the sun, lips drying out into perfumed vapors, blue breezes stealing through silvery shrubs to caress her cheeks. A black tide has paralyzed her life into a foul-tasting gelatin, why her, of all people, whence this unearthly torrent against life? The noxious lymph has now filled in all chambers, poison, spit it out, a last spasm squats her memory and everything gushes out of her toxic and stinking, let someone throw her away, please. The stench also gushes out through Anton's nostrils and mouth and his glassy eyes stay transfixed. He is mumbling something, he is scolding her. Yes, she has misbehaved yet again.

2 BEYOND

Her strolling through the city, her outings… Yet it is so cozy and agreeable in here. And is it not wonderful to wake up in a crème master bedroom, with everything around you crème, the clock on the wall, the bed lamps, the wall-to-wall carpeting? And your own paraphernalia among all these, there they are on the bedside table, scattered among someone else's books. Will she ever finish reading *The Nuremberg Process*? She does not think she will be able to, as she has a work of her own to write. But why not have some fun, meanwhile, with the unexpected *Guinness Book of Records*. She had never imagined herself with the famous Book in her lap, yet here it is, the latest edition. Why reopen it though, it is nothing but trifles and she already knows the Romanian names in there. How she rejoiced in discovering them. Besides, she felt she was privileged to share Stefan's yearly routine. But it feels enough for her having done it just once.

It is a novel day, everything is new, exploding into the sun to light away all sorrow in the world. She will go out to breathe in the day accompanied by people, to walk the streets which stretch white for everyone to advance. She will come out into the light.

Anton must have crossed beyond at daybreak, and he surely is among congregations of fishermen now, and might be having a drink in the coolness of the grocery shop with its keeper. What pleasure could men find in sitting in the dark pouring liquid down their throats until their bellies burst, Anton's, the shopkeeper's, the schoolmaster's, and who knows whose other belly? And what about that contemptible helping hand, or assistant, of Anton's? A stub of a man as red in the face as a boiled crab — they say he is a drunk. She recalls him carrying luggage from the pontoon into their boat, their luggage, Anton's and hers, as they were crossing the river for the first time together on that day. 'Take this, come on, hurry, this one too.' Anton does it strong with his subordinates. He might well be in command, but he should not treat the poor man like that, as if he were a servant. She cannot accept that and she felt like giving the hapless fellow a hand then, but it would have been stupid to have Anton watch her doing that. She noticed his ironic glance and wondered what kind of a person he was. Why should your assistant carry the baggage for you, and why should you yell at them like that, she wondered. 'Dirty drunkard, I can't wait to get rid of him, I've had pity on him so far only for his kids' sake, but I've had enough.' Mrs. Arvinte was somehow filled in on the subject, and how could she not be, when that was the star topic over the chicken soup at the Arvintes' dinner table every Saturday. Smilingly, Mim recalls how Antonush was going to get rid, once and for all, of that wretched guy whose surname had a strange resonance which always made her think of a hen's claw scraping earth.

Oh, yes, Mrs. Arvinte's chicken soups, bountiful, teeming with home-made noodles and whole yolks from the wombs of fat hens brought by Anton from across the river, soup as they make in Moldova, prepared by a dark-eyed housewife from up there. 'I'll give the bastard the sack, you'll see, I'm only waiting for…,' 'let me tell you what he did today…,' or yesterday, or 'listen to this…,' Antonush would begin, and then go on to have a good laugh by himself only at the thought of what he was going to tell the whole table. They were all ears waiting for him to unreel his yarn, soon finding themselves infected by his peals of laughter and splitting their sides above the plentiful plates. God, how Anton's eyes were sparkling, sincerely unveiling two rows of perfect small white teeth, and this probably out of heartfelt gratitude for everything awaiting him there on that table, to which he was about to treat himself, the hot dishes, his preprandial anecdotes that were going to set the table in roars, Mim herself. He was flashing glowing looks at her. A drunkard — would conclude Mrs. Arvinte. Well, duh! — her husband would exclaim implying that he had lived it all, and so he had. Mim could not possibly know what Mr. Arvinte knew, and except for few, nobody had the faintest idea what it used to be like 'in olden times in Moldova', when he had put things right with his horse and gun. Mim has still not understood whom exactly he had put in fear in those remote times, but has formed an impression that he had been some sort of chief over a whole county, or region, and now, yes, she can figure it out — Mr. Arvinte used to be one of those responsible with the collectivization of the villagers' assets. She can hardly accept the idea of his having ever been evil at heart, and she cares about the person he is now. She even used to secretly pride herself on Anton being the son of such a powerful man.

The man by a chicken's claw name lies at the other extreme. That is why he has become a heavy drinker and Anton's wharfie. Mim tries to imagine what he might have felt on that day, deep down in his soul, a soul clad in a man's flesh. His shredded manhood must have felt like a rag waded through mire, all the more so given the presence of a young lady. If only he had known that she was all on his side and would have carried those bags herself, had it not been for Anton.

They had lots of baggage then, including a couple of fishing rods. Only that their fishing-across-the-river expedition got them lost with the current, and nearly lost for good. God, how they were lucky. And, God, how Anton tormented her, yelling and grinding his jaws, while casting wild looks at her: steady the helm, what the hell are you doing? Mim was crying. She could barely strain herself, tightening each and every fiber of her body around that bloody stick, hoping for him to stop yelling. But Anton was growing darker and darker, and she observed his face turning blue with paroxysm, when all of a sudden he would thunder again: hold that thing properly, you hear, you're driving me mad, you can't do anything right, you're good for nothing. Then he lowered the pitch to a continuous mumbling in the same key. She felt like giving everything up. She was losing her strength and Anton seemed to be ceaselessly throwing her towards a filthy periphery of the world. But what if she could prove to him how adept she was. What if she could finally make him understand that it was not up to her? She was wholly dedicated to the helm, body and soul, not Mim anymore. Anton, look at me, I am the helm itself, all of me, aren't I but a helm, she imagined addressing his better reason. He was bellowing, perpetually bellowing, chasing disoriented tears on her cheeks, hold the helm! Amid her despair, an impish thought struck Mim: what if she burst into laughter at his next yell? And was that really a helm or a rudder? No way, it was nothing but a shovel, an old short-handled spade which God knows how had got into that boat. Right, how come there was a spade in there? It proved handy, though. Now she could barely help bursting out into roars of laughter every time Anton, as a true sea wolf in a storm, roared about her steering the boat. Nonetheless, she kept struggling with that silly spade against the current. The more vehement he was, the less could she help the thought of a dement blast, only that she was the helm, and the river was not joking, not at all. Everything was real and tears were streaming down her face. She had reached her limit and all that was left for her to do was laugh. All she wanted was to be free to laugh. It was then when she understood why people gave in to the monstrous limbs of the river. People die before they can feel any pain, drowning is bearable.

At the very climax of the calamity, the two poor fishing rods fixed at the stern were the last thing they needed. The counterweights piled chaotically upon their ends were invariably standing in Mim's way. Not before they finally reached the pontoon — their seemingly unreachable destination for an admittedly long while, despite their having it in sight all along — did they, completely worn out, mussy, and groping their way, as it had got dark, come across the valiant rods. For one second they suspected each other of a common thought: at the end of the whole ordeal, a pleasant surprise was awaiting them under the water. Mim was filled with joy as she sensed Anton hearten up. At the end of the road, she had done it, and Anton was at her side again. He proceeded to inspect the lines and Mim was praying that he would not find anything out of order. He did. The nylon lines were gone. "Didn't I tell you to take care, what have you done?" No, she could not bear it any longer. Had he already forgotten what they had been through? What more could she have done, she, the rudder that had been steering, from noon to dusk, the lights and shades on his face. He is definitely not human. This man is something else. And that wretched drunkard is his slave. Downright horrible.

Stefan is no different. She still has the image of that lanky shy man who would not dare come into the house. "I've brought a parcel," he said from the doorway, looking down. As soon as she had been announced that man would come, Mim went to check the dining room, and then made some coffee. The chauffeur of Stefan's father was bringing some delicatessen for them. The new lady of the house had to make a first impression: kind, warm, totally different from the former one, the spoiled frail blonde in the photos, so beautiful, yet how cold. "Come in," Mim ushered him, to his utter bewilderment, "please come in," but he got stuck in the doorway. He simply would not go past the threshold. Later that day when she told Stefan about it he laughed at her: he's never come into the house, and there've been many times he ran this type of errands. Mim could not believe her ears, never, never in the house. A solitary cup of coffee was awaiting him on the glossy black stretch of the huge table, while the man might have been wondering who that woman was who wanted him to go into the house. He may have found it bizarre, and so it may have been, Mim did not know, but then Stefan said not even his best friends had benefitted from the honor of stepping into his ex-wife's sculptured sanctuary. The dining room had been reserved for special occasions. "Well, that's the way my wife was, my friends and I had to gather here in the kitchen." Mim, too, likes it better here, not in that heavy, far-away room, at the other end of the corridor, right opposite the entrance door. It is nothing but furniture, all table and chairs and very serious sideboards. 'I want to sell that furniture, but who the hell buys furniture worth 60 000 lei, and I'll sell the bedroom, too, to get rid of anything reminding me of her.'

Awfully must he have behaved with that girl, which could mean he did not love her? Was this her place, or on the other side of the bed? She would light her bedside lamp, read, laze, 'she hardly did anything, it was in bed that I used to leave her in the morning and also find her upon returning home.' 'All she was interested in was her attires,' 'the lady had to be rested,' 'she never used to stay with my friends, and she hardly ever even noticed their presence.' Well, this caps the climax. On the other hand, well done, she is a person whose guiding principle is rest, and Mim admires her for that. Stefan would cheat on her — true, before they got married, or did he do it after that as well? 'She didn't like to join me at parties, the pure maid had to be home early, so I took her back to her parents and then went to parties alone.' Had he, or had he not loved her? 'I had to get married, didn't I, and whom was I supposed to marry, if not my girlfriend for so many years?' She was a mere child. Stefan, a student at the time, would wait for her every day at the gate of the high school. 'There was nobody else for her, she didn't know what to do unless I told her, I meant everything for her.'

Mim would like to see scenes with the two of them together, she perfectly blonde, with plaits perhaps, and what did her schoolmates think about her being seduced by a university student? Stefan was a handsome guy — she saw him in some photos. What was it like to be in love with Stefan? It was so hard for Mim to penetrate that girl's inner world, to have a taste of what she may have felt. But no taste came to Mim, she felt nothing at all. She would like to put herself in that girl's place and look at him through her eyes, a schoolgirl's, and then the wife's. She must have looked at him once and been caught. Just like the moment Mim first set eyes on Anton, in a flash and so up close. Mim never had time to step back and have a second look, her union with him took place that very moment, deep, and maybe this is what counts, the encounter, the first scene.

Years ago, when Mim was taking an acting course, this was what the teacher told them, that the first impression counted. Mim was not so sure and kept wondering which really weighed more. The last one, she thought, as you have time to convince the audience, who will remain with the last still. The finale is definitely what one takes with them. All the same, what if your first appearance does not impress! It is difficult for you to conquer them, no matter how lovely you might tease their souls later on. Yes, you have to get into their hearts from the very beginning, and even though you may lose power on the long run, they cannot get you out of there. They will wait for you to shine the next time. It must be the same with love, it does not approach you, but strikes and shines and dazzles you.

Mim saw this light when Anton's image crashed like a flash upon her. That was just a single shot, but what Mim did at the time was start to make up a whole story out of it. It was later on that she realized that story was, in fact, her own life. There was a moment when she simply knew. That weird man, and Mim bending over his body, his voice coming from long ago, from his childhood, those uncommon sounds making her own vocal cords tremble and at the same time freezing her chest, as she was waiting, caught in astonishment, lips chaste and eyes closed, waiting for that man to reveal his secret, what he was meant to do in this world, whence he came and where to: I need someone to love me. Crouched below her on the floor, with fists clenching forcibly, Anton then uttered: I am with you now, Mim, I need you.

Anton is beyond now, he must have crossed the river as the sun was rising raw and cold. Wild horses running free on the green meadows, he, Anton, did yet again not find his hunting rifle, while the horses would not relent their race to let him catch them, not even one. The horses are running and their manes are luring him with brazen lush waving: catch us. It is no use chasing them now, the horses are there on his territory, 'look, Mim, those are my domains,' he would tell her full of enchantment, with eyes and soul vaulting across, to the realm stretching on the other bank of the river. He is there now, the master of the realm, which he is every day, till the afternoon crossing back to town. He is happy. Or might she only think that because she is not there herself?

She remembers that weird night in the tent. It had been raining heavily and the sea was moaning faintly close by. Fantastic vapors were distorting their bodies' magnetism, their thoughts, when Mim sensed in the air a fleeting aromatic whiff. It was instantly gone, a scent from the past that she started to trace, crouched in the moist sand, her hair hanging down like a curtain to blind her eyes against reality. Her memory was insinuating itself like a nymph among the subtle energies all around Anton's luscious body, those furtive vapors nestling lime fragrances and her perfume. Mim had brought a perfume bottle she had used during that first summer with him, but it was empty. It was in her mind that the fragrance persisted, and she had caught that whiff and was now weeping, smelling and weeping, tears washing her down towards the ground, where she stared and where she saw darkness. The darkness got foggy and turned grey, then grey became white, her shy white dress. That was when Anton started to speak — a man who no longer had a reason for living. "I have wronged many people, Mim, and look where I am now." She began to quiver silently. The old play of shadows on his face that she recalled made her eye globes stop still. His jaws were grinding, she knew. All he could utter after that was these words: I could just well do anything. Despair, this is what despair was. This cannot be, no, Mim was begging him embracing his knees with her arms, straining her head downwards between her shoulders, stretching her vertebra toward the ground, then draining her arms, which had somehow become aquatic, into winding limbs on either side of her body, to finally coil them around something and stop still to hear: it was myself that I have wronged, Mim. Then the thud of a fist in a palm was heard. No, Anton is not happy.

3 THE INSTALLATION

They got there at sundown. The tents were pitched on the beach, right near the sea. Mim liked it there. She was savoring the welcoming campsite atmosphere, with so many people gathered together, the cool fresh breeze, the vibration of the sea and its enigmatic blue green. Nonetheless, she did not know what to do and where to turn to in order not to make any mistake. What was hers there, after all? Neither the tent nor the friends, not even the mute man with opaque eyes and heinous motions. What was she doing amidst those strangers? Any place on earth seemed to be more legit for her than their territory. They were going to pitch their tent there.

Roxana and Dan were now and then trying to enliven the atmosphere with a little humor, the three of them were talking together and their bodies were incessantly moving. Mim felt as though she were a lifeless object, some kind of useless pole they were all seeking to avoid. If she had been able to, she would have dug herself deep into the ground to make room. Anton was certainly swearing and calling her names, she could hear his thoughts: what was that pale-cheeked, sad-mouthed nag doing there to spoil their holiday? Tears and begging were what he least needed. Each person should shift for themselves and mind their own path. The two youths had to be thinking Mim was Anton's latest date. Away with the other one, who had acted so childishly as to try to poison herself. Mim was sure they were curiously measuring her from head to toe in order to compare her to the other girl. Above all, they looked plainly confused by her sadness.

That first evening Roxana spoke to her: ever since we met Anton we haven't seen him with anyone else but Ioana. What bounty of thriving life went extinct once those words were uttered, how many words and how many silences between Mim and Anton. Anton and Mim on the road — come on, let us take off. It was ten at night and cold, they loaded the car with blankets and some food and off they went. The same familiar windings of the roadway and the same rocks, only that frozen that time, and covered in dark. Then in spring, when the sun is most beloved, milky fields, warm sunrays charging at them from all directions, green-scented puffs and barely awakened zephyrs, air-born emanations of sun-touched skin, freeways seeming to open their long strips for them. What was space, they were conquering vastness: in the city where she was studying; on the realm where he was working, that fantastic land bordered by waters; at his parents' place; at her parents'. How could she possibly witness the installation of the tent, she was ashamed to look, ashamed to hear their words. They were busy: it's the first time I've pitched a tent, I have no idea how it's done, I know, I've seen that before, let's fix this in, step aside, easy, where shall we…

It was late dinner time on the camp, laughing could be heard, while the newcomers were being stared at by a circle of nosy audience. How cool and invigorating it must have felt. What about Mim though? She had obstinately insisted on coming here to make a fool of herself, so she was now gazing unperturbed at the sea, awkwardly standing among the congregation, arms dangling lifeless on the sides and feet gawkily dipped in the sand. She had fled from home, Stefan's home, and it was only now that she had realized that. Yet, that was not the object of her concern for the moment, she would explain everything to him when she got home. What bothered her now was being an alien, surrounded by alien motions, the reason why she was focusing the horizon, feeling that it was only the light in the distance which could empathize with her. She was floating away towards the zenith when it came to her that she might try to give a hand with the construction. She wondered what Anton might be expecting of her. What was she supposed to do: mingle in or keep aside? His inner thoughts seemed to resound in her mind again: look at her, people, I have brought her all the way here and she won't lift a straw.

With time, she had come to realize that Anton was expecting her to join him in no matter what kind of work he did. She always remembered the first time he had reprimanded her: pull your finger out, what are you waiting for, this car deserves a wash, doesn't it, it's the car that took you to the seaside. She had thought she had better not interfere with whatever he was doing. No sooner had she found out what Anton really wanted of her than she got frantic to please him. It had got dark by then and the car, devoid of seats and mats, was lying solitarily on top of a moundy area not far from the river. She took a broom, then a duster, changed the water in the bucket, but to no avail. He had already started to speak mean words to her, while furiously scrubbing the mute barren car. Mim stood at a distance and heard everything, imagining wire brushes galling her from the inside. She kept standing there to receive blow after blow, she stood the scratching and the bleeding speechless, staring in the distance. There was a bright light at the pontoon across the river, and she was hearing everything.

This is what she tried to do now, give the three of them

a helping hand, make herself useful. She passed a metal rod, joined in her hand to fix something, harmless petty chance jobs. Not a single glance did he cast in her direction, not even when working together required it. He kept himself the farthest he could from her and even the faintest prospect of a touch brought a disgusted grimace on his face. Even so, Mim still thought it was better to make a contribution. At some point she got hit in the head, badly, but kept quiet, in shame. Who was she to whine? Roxana dashed to see what had happened to her, Dan asked if she was all right, no, it was nothing, but she got dizzy and they both helped her sit on the ground. Anton did not even look, but she read his distorted profile: this is exactly what I needed, work accidents.

Mim's thoughts went back to the other girl, wondering if he might have loathed her when he heard she had tried to kill herself. He could not stand imbroglios, anyone or anything that got things complicated in his life had to be rapidly shed out of the away, irrespective of degrees of his attachment to that. His own well-being was all that mattered to him. He had this extraordinary power to discard feelings and routines that no longer served his purpose. Or had he? What if he was weak, what if, who knows when, some time in his past, something happened that made him choose this strategy for protection? Why did he keep all the letters and postcards from women, why did he collect all those tokens? Mim had seen them amassed in a corner in his room, on undissimulated display. Hers were there too, but they stood out amid the lot of triviality and melodrama. Some of those puerile phrases had even caused her to laugh heartily by herself. What was life, after all, since Mim could proudly walk through the crowd, defying that pile of nonsense. She still could not believe her eyes. Anton, the man who took delight in the most refined art, the adorer of painting, poetry, music, the man who shed tears at the passing away of the great poet! Finesse, this was what he most appreciated in Mim, he had told her so. Had he never come across that before meeting her? Or had that happened to him just once before, and Mim reminded him of that woman? 'When I saw you glued to that pillar in the train station, you reminded me of someone.' Who was that woman? Could she possibly be the sender of those short lines on postcards from around the world, the woman who no longer lived in the country and whose name had a freezing cold resonance in her mind, cold and sticky? Mim had always restrained from touching that strange glue, his past life. And he had never bothered to hide that evidence, as he was living the present, was he not. Well, she was nauseated by this present.

Although she knew how terrified Anton could get at the thought of ever being with women his age or only a few years younger, who would one think signed the most embarrassing of the latest letters? Shock and terror: the public servant at the city hall, 'the lady with the house'. The moment she saw her in a photo Mrs. Arvinte showed her, Mim despised him. Anton had been tormenting his body and mind, gritting his teeth, as he had brazenly used that poor woman, corpulent and obviously older than him, bespectacled and boasting a castle of rigid locks on top of her head. She was the epitome of what he most loathed, of what had always sent flying 'the citizen of the asphalt', as he enjoyed calling himself. The silly creature possessed absolutely all the elements of Anton's worst nightmare.

What he was after was a woman whose green tender body ruled out any prospect of ever gaining weight. With this purpose, his girlfriends' mothers always made the object of his thorough inspection, as Mim's own once did. Anton believed in genetics, that was his Bible. The women's fathers were also closely observed, for him to envisage how their daughters' skin would stretch on their muscles and the muscles would be positioned on their bones in the long run. His own image trapped with a consort whose evolution was unclear seized him with horror. This horrific image had been literally chasing him all along, in a race with no end in the real world. He would have taken this madman's chase beyond the boundaries of his country if that had been possible, but no, he had been early on predicted to die of gunshot once he crossed the border. 'Ask Mom, if you don't believe me, she knows everything.' So there was nothing left for him to do but put up with being circularly chased by an army of future-to-be buxom females within the boundaries of his native country. He would take in the length of the women's tibia, the muscles of their shanks, 'a woman's most beautiful muscles, Mim,' and, alas, there was no hope for the ones who hid femurs joined to a too wide pelvic bone. This was what his new home had cost him, enacting his own nightmare. With the unique purpose to possess, to have what others could not afford, which was well worth a spit: I did it.

The tent was finally pitched: large, two-roomed, cozy. They ate in a circle on its veranda, with Mim hardly swallowing anything. It was their victuals. She was embarrassed to admit she had brought some food herself, how could it be laid next to theirs, so she had left it in a hidden spot and none of them even noticed the package. He was devouring the meal, what could possibly hinder his appetite, when the long ride there and then working to install the tent had used up his tone. He was a strong man who needed proper nourishment and care. He deserved to be given everything his vigorous frame, kept in perfect shape through body building and lawn tennis, required. Nothing was allowed to interfere with his cult for his own body, of which he was so proud. 'There's no better exercise than this for the calf muscles, see how easy it is to do at home?' Mim was practicing it too, against the wardrobe. This one, look, is for the back muscles, and he would beamingly show her his beautiful muscular assets.

Roxana and Dan were the only ones who addressed a

few words to Mim. They both were evidently intrigued by the curious barrier between their friend and his new girlfriend, shrunken, shrouded. Until Mim fleetingly explained to Roxana: it is the end, not the beginning.

4 TOMORROW

How wonderful, all on her own, with the kitchen awaiting her, cozy and bright, where she can make herself a cup of coffee or a sandwich. The radio set will connect her to the world, and if she wishes she may well blow away the cobwebs and go out for a stroll in the streets, any time she fancies, well, not right now, let her drink another cupful.

Then she would start to prepare herself for the world outside, eventually left the apartment, shut the door relishing the action of turning the key into the lock, and, door locked, let herself scamper down the stairs, and then into the light. She felt love, the sun covering her in its glory. As soon as she escaped from among the apartment buildings, stretching in front of her were the roads in the valley, the river bank, and the land beyond. Gentle wild breezes would open her nostrils to aromatic herbs and elfish secret creatures, and she felt like flinging herself towards the wide milky green realm across the river, where she yearned to laze under yellowish willows.

But she was headed to town now, free to get lost in the crowd and window-shop, as she had all the time in the world until Stefan was due back from the office. What about her paper? She still had nearly two months to work on it, and she had gathered absolutely everything she needed. Was it not pure delight to get information about trends in art, aesthetics in our everyday life, street aesthetics, relational aesthetics, oh, how happy she was with nobody telling her what to do, and with having to do exactly what she enjoyed. That was why she was strolling on the streets now, as she was not supposed to isolate herself indoors, was she? In just a while she would make her retreat to start preparing dinner for Stefan, just like the female character she had seen in an almost silent movie long ago. Mim had been mesmerized by the slow neat artistic twists and twirls the woman was pulling off while preparing salad for her husband. Another man was sniffing for her former presence in the house, looking for traces in her bed, among the books she might have read. He was determined to reconstitute her existence out of snatches of impressions left by her on the objects around. Yet it had not been him she used to wait for, but the one she had got used to laying the table for, and with such exquisite femininity. That was nothing but the right thing to do for a woman, and Stefan was surely the man for whom Mim could exercise that.

She pictured herself chopping vegetables in the kitchen of the apartment which Anton once showed her. He simply took her by the hand and said: come on. Up the stairs in a building completely unknown to her, in a select neighborhood in town where white prevailed, they toured a home that day, kitchen, bathroom, bedroom and all. He was seeking a home for the two of them. You like it, he kept asking her, but she was at a loss for words. She was not sure what he was up to. Do you like it, he insisted, yeah, it is nice and bright, why shouldn't I. Abashed indoors, she could only feel happiness once they got out in the street again, hand in hand in the crowd. So Anton was intent on purchasing a house, driven by the same ambition that had made him buy a car with money made through his own business. He had the money, but the law did not permit him to buy a flat in town, since his registered residence was in a different county, the one across the river. 'I am determined to have a house of my own and I will, you'll see.' I know what I have to do, he would say, looking valiantly ahead.

During the following months Mim sensed he had something cooking, some kind of surprise for her. But Anton would rather keep her away from his wheeling and dealing, so she did not need to know much. A real man knows how to get what he wants, for both himself and his woman. He had altogether brought her to live with him and his family, almost sheltering her from some kind of vile influence. He liked to find her there when he came back from work, or from some afternoon business meeting. He had started to often rush out to solve something 'for the house', but would hurriedly come back for them to resume living happily in their nest. Mim could feel he was concentrating all his resources on accomplishing his goal. An assertive smile had alighted on his lips, and it would not leave there. She was waiting for it to burst into the triumphant grin of the man who has got it all for him and his woman. A bitter-sweet net of secret telephone conversations had started to weave itself in the atmosphere of the house, like those ethereal spider webs you sometimes get into in spring time, you stop, do not know what it is, then go on with your day. Anton used to watch her intensely, maybe conceiving the moment when her joy would fulfill his masculine pride. In all truth, Mim could also perceive in him a note of genuine wish to make her happy. If only you knew what I know, this is how his eyes spoke to her. You will soon see the surprise I have in store for you, they seemed to say. In spite of all this, early that summer, at the very peak of those elaborate workings, they had to split. 'Only for the summer, Mim, please understand me, it's all for the house.'

What does she care about the other man now? She has

comfort, she can play with the salad right there in Stefan's home. What else should she look for, anxiety, the hell with anxiety, she can make herself a fresh cup of coffee and, savoring its invigorating flavor, listen to the world on the radio. She can go out if she chooses to, she has the whole day to herself. And when she feels like it, she can resume working on her diploma paper, or she can well read a book. Some day she will escape beyond the river to see Anton again. She can do so whenever she pleases. The very window of her bedroom looks out to the realm so dear to her, and who could stop her from spending her mornings there and dreaming, enjoying the sunrise.

5 THE MISTAKE

She has to work, yeah. Seated at the huge oval table in front of the typewriter, surrounded by an array of sheets and scraps of paper covered in her notes, which she does not yet know in which specific order to use, the mug of compote on one side and the cup of coffee on the other one, and daylight right in front of her, the window that looks out to the new district of apartment buildings in town. Somewhere ahead of her lies the block where Anton has recently moved.

Where has her strength gone? She is willingly working on disparate bits and pieces, but simply refuses to envisage the moment when she will logically put them together into a whole. Well, it will come, there certainly is a plan hidden somewhere in the recesses of her mind, as she knows for sure that her subconscious is more powerful than her. Yet, how could she eventually vacuum clean the entire mess on that table into a meaningful bulk? This is sheer anarchy, with Anton so close by in his new flat. Their cowardly furtive encounters, crammed between his friends' visits, brand new friends. Their silences, by-now-routine, and their partings, and the gangrene, Stefan. Stefan is missing. She had so long been waiting for his error, and he finally erred. How come, then, she is so indescribably miserable.

Is that dust, or an illusion? Dust lies in mute silence on the furniture and she can taste its squalid dryness on the palate of her mouth, in her throat, between her fingers. Oh, this oppressive medieval dining room. But she is mistress here now, the sole dweller of the whole house for two long days. Gazing out the window, a sense of power has begun to grow in Mim. She resumes typing. Stefan had found someone to do this job for her, but she refused the service. It was a pretty slow operation, yet it kept the final moment, the climactic demonstration of force, away from her. Let her bide her time and peacefully type whatever she has handwritten so far.

God how it is hot. She makes herself some more lemonade, and gets back to typing. This is what she most enjoys, experiencing something new. Why would terror creep through her senses every now and again, spoiling her state of well-being? The moment will come, her work will have to be born, and eventually it will rise high, anointed with all her knowledge, studies and research work, she will somehow take it out of this boiling soup, and dry it out into a beautiful, levelly shining sphere. Her perfect work will definitely take shape. Although this logic appeases her, it is a short-lived tranquility, as who on earth is going to summon up strength and make the supreme effort, if not Mim herself. She will do it, undoubtedly, but when exactly this is going to happen is yet unclear to her. She has other things on her mind right now. She is lonely and Stefan has committed a mistake. He must be laughing, conversing, dancing with his former classmates. In circles around ornate tables, they are laying down achievements, adventures and incidents, past and recent, spouses, kids, jokes.

How unexpectedly bitter the drop had been, and how bulgy it had surged, expanding like a stain in her chest, day after day, little by little. Mim prayed Stefan would change his mind and say: you are coming with me, a two-day break is no big deal. The next moment she prayed he would keep quiet, let him keep quiet and leave. She was waiting for his inaugural mistake, so that she could finally be free to despise him. The stain had been continuously growing, no, he did not believe in her. That is why it gaped like a canker the instant Stefan meticulously took out from the wardrobe a black suit she had never before seen — if she had ever seen anything in that house — then a pair of black patent shoes from the drawer below, laid a bow tie and a pair of gold sleeve buttons on the dressing table, all there before her eyes, she perched on top of the precious crème matrimonial bed, head stuck to the seemingly damp limy wall with the crème lamp at her temple and an open book in her lap. Head bowed, he kept performing stealthy motions about the house, laden with guilt, a big guilty tomcat. He would light a cigarette, leave it to burn itself in on an ashtray in the kitchen, and then come back to fumble in the wardrobe again. He was leaving. He turned on the bathtub faucets, therefore he was now running his ceremonial bath, and Mim could imagine the foam soaring.

The foam in his bath was so inviting, foam she had never experienced before, which she simply adored. The sole thing in his home she was in love with. What seductive fragrances as the water rose, a cascade that dispelled thoughts, worries, memories, only herself and the waterfall, and the foam inflating, smoothing her glossy skin and luring her to indulge in daydreaming. She would caress herself and a perpetual smile would stretch her facial muscles into something absolutely wonderful, she could feel how wonderful she was, with her sleek pinkish skin so warm. Foam is happiness, she felt like crying out loud. Now she could hear the water roaring and see Stefan roaming about, ready to immerse himself into the tub. When he does, as soon as Mim hears the bathroom door shut with him inside, the stain will turn into a ghastly gape. He is now bathing and will soon leave home and Mim will remain stuck to the wall, stunned in disbelief. He has implacably got in. Stefan stirring and splashing the water makes it clear to her that she has been sharing the beatific properties of the bath foam with him all during their cohabitation. She pulls her face in disgust, no, that foam does not become him. The dark curly hairs on his chest and the scented foam are completely incongruous, and the very moment he leaves, she will unleash her hatred.

Now the dressing up. Each move he makes gets the stain deeper and darker, soon to envelop Mim's entire consciousness. Now, his last cigarette. He is in the kitchen, all lustrous and perfumed, plucking up courage to cross the threshold outward, beyond Mim's space. Now, he is coming over to her, sits on the margin of the bed, and does not ask her to look him in the eye, since he is about to err. "I'm leaving. I have left some coffee for you, and some cigarettes. Go to bed early, as I might pick you up in the morning for the river cruise, OK?" He dared not stand up and leave immediately after. More, he took her chin in the palm of his hand and gaped sadly into her eyes. It was then that she thought he had been about to send her into the bath. He subsequently told her what an ordeal that whole ceremonial had been to him. He loved her. "You're not mad with me, are you?" he continued, thus admitting to being culpable. He then rose to his feet, and shortly Mim heard the front door shut behind him, clunk, and flung herself in the cavern he had been so meticulously digging, with a sharp scream: God, how I hate him!

She promptly got out of the bed and turned on the radio, lit a cigarette and started a furious race to and fro on the dark green hallway, between the kitchen and the dining room. She dashed to the fridge and proceeded to absurdly unload it of all kinds of goodies, then to the bathroom to run herself a scented bath, and came back to light a second cigarette. She was in charge now and was going to feast on his exclusive delicacies, French cheese and Sibiu salami, caviar and butter, American cigarettes and the richest Cuban coffee.

The storm is over. In the silenced house, Mim, the mistress, seated at one end of the oval dinner table, her gaze straight ahead out the window, pushes her hatred gliding away on the glossy surface, as now nothing can disturb her anymore. She will work. She imagines Stefan across the table from her, where once he stood erect facing her. She was writing, and he was staring, well aware of his imminent departure. Therefore Stefan had once before left her, but then he had asked her permission and she had agreed. He kept his eyes glued on her like a madman. Time was ticking by, Mim was typing, and Stefan was standing stock-still opposite her. Not the slightest shadow moved on the other side, and it occurred to her that he had stopped breathing. She got scared and clung to her typing, fearful to look. But she heard something. He was lighting a cigarette, thank goodness. Yet he would not give up the gape. She could feel it like a hot tide coming for her, engulfing her, what on earth was the matter with him? He put out the cigarette, still keeping her trapped in the fiery beam of his eyes. Mim decided that only words could release the tension, so she stopped typing and asked: why are you staring like that? Her words seemed to have awakened him, or well offered him an unexpected aid: would you mind if I left tonight? Oh, that was all there was, Mim told herself with a sigh of relief, but there had to be more to it. She said she did not mind, but her voice sounded uptight and her aloof smile was tainted with perplexity. Stefan was still fixing her, she saw his eyes, there was sadness in them, heartbreaking sadness, as though he was never going to see her again. His eyes seemed to be two pools of melting gold, trickling down flows of despondency onto his cheek bones, while the glow reflected by the long lacquer finish of the surface between them revealed dramatic depths in that inert man, a sphinx which stood for grief, a hieroglyph for grief. Whence, Mim wondered. "I've been standing here for an hour to decide whether to leave or not." His voice sounded gruff, as though coming from some age old subterranean world. Mim listened on: I simply don't want to leave, Mim, I can't. He came over to her side, drew a chair, sat right next to her, and from so close, his gaze fixed into her eyes, he asked her again: would you mind if I were to leave tonight? Mim could make neither head nor tale of that, so she said: well, if you say you don't want to, then why are you insisting on leaving? "I'm going to leave. But if I know that upsets you, I'll stay." "Oh, for God's sake, why are you tormenting me like this? Tell me, what is this all about?" That was when he started to explain: a woman is waiting for me, at her place, she desires me; would you mind if I went there? He had got hot. The more passionate he got, the more he needed her consent. He could not possibly join that woman without Mim's blessing. "What about me, am I going to sleep alone tonight?" Yes, came his quiet answer. "OK, go." Abandoning her in his home to spend the night in another person's house, well, that was pretty funny. That seemed absurd, but Mim suddenly remembered that he loved her. And despite all that love, he was intent on deserting her. At first she refused to believe he would go, but he genuinely wanted to. Was she not a woman herself? No, not for Stefan. He had all the right in the world to go, Mim really wanted to be able to let him go, although the prospect of remaining alone for the night scared her, and against her awareness that something had fundamentally changed. Till when this mock-marriage game? Until she got over her love-sickness, which Stefan had been persistently stalking that far? "You may leave, Stefan, I don't mind."

She remembers working late into the night that time. She would now and then pause to recall his eyes, how he loved her completely, then resumed the quiet enjoyable night typing, perfectly reassured. But this time he is in error.

What that hateful clunk of the door stirred up in her is streaming in one single direction, which Mim cannot yet define, although she can feel her pores opening toward a grand liberation.

6 WINE

Chilling dry autumn. She is waiting there, prey to the harsh wind going through her body. Vacuumed of people, the town is ready for dusk to set in. He will eventually turn up and Mim will get to see his newly acquired apartment. She had declined his previous invitation, but look how Anton had been seeking to find her again. Why had he?

Only a couple of nights ago, another man was meeting her at the railway station, a warm kind man, Stefan. She got off the train, it was evening and the platform crowded, there he was, next to the newspaper kiosk. What a sheer bliss to have such a good-looking man waiting for her. He was always waiting for her, wherever she came from. She had been jokingly in love with him once, without him even being aware of her existence. Their ways had crossed a few times, but he had never noticed her and she histrionically mimed defiance. Well, it was her that man was expecting now, look at his deep, welcoming eyes, Mim approaching him — hi, he leaning against the glass door and blocking the light: Anton came to look for you. When? Last night. Mim froze. Yet she asked, "How do you know?" "Well, I looked for you too. Your roommates told me you were still at your folks'.'" She wanted to say something, but words would not come. There were no words but muteness cauterizing her throat. She should take off right away. Anton had come to see her, and that in spite of her having acted so cold when they first met after that unjust summer. Let her flee to him, now, there was not a second to waste, now, and she would be with him all the way. But Stefan was right there waiting for her reaction, how could she possibly let him down? No, she definitely had to contain herself till the next day.

She did not dare utter a word on the way, and neither did Stefan. That night they went to his apartment, Mim for the first time there. Together with another couple, they were celebrating the patenting of Stefan's latest invention. Mim and the other girl cooked the meal together, soup and pilaf. Watching in silence the dismemberment of the chicken, the rice lying under the nacreous water, Mim had the impression the vapors in the room were the only obstacle between her and Anton, whom she was imaging alone in his apartment, waiting. Here potfuls of food were boiling nicely on the stove, in the adjacent room the boys were playing cards and listening to music, the four of them ate everything up with gusto, and then played a seemingly endless chain of canasta games.

Far into the night, Mim remained alone with Stefan and they endeavored to talk, surreptitiously getting closer and closer to each other, until she buried her head into his chest, concealed from his sight. His beautiful mouth started to grope for hers, while her mind was plunging deeper into darkness. Life and death were clashing into her fragile throat, which was yielding helpless moans. Secluded in the dark, she was hoping the pain would go away. As Stefan began to undress her, she felt all her innermost screaming and shrieking were about to burst, splashing him harshly. But no, he did not deserve that, it was their first night. What if she revealed herself though, and told him the truth, yes, let him know. Tears started moistening her face inaudibly, but soon she was shuddering, which made him ask: are you OK? No, she broke out shouting.

She was waiting for Anton now. She would not be, had he not looked for her. She had finally found the spirit to call him up, that very morning, and there she was, almost freezing. What should she say when she sees him again, what will it be like? It is him, look how Anton is getting near, until he comes right over to her and asks: how are you doing, are you cold? Mim nodded, shaking. He held her in his arms to warm her up. "Come on, you'll be all right, let's go to my place and I'll make you a nice mug of boiled wine." Never before had he addressed her so considerately. They walked almost hugged together to the parking lot. "Look at you, you're all frozen, come, get into the car."

The smell of newly built construction is striking. She is finally going to see the justification of their breakup for the summer. He unlocks the door, and Mim promptly finds herself into a spacious entrance hall that looks more like a storehouse: concrete floor, car wheels, petrol cans, canisters, that kind of stuff. The living room is unfurnished yet, he explains, so he leads her all the way to the farthest end of the corridor. She is taken aback by the sight of what passes for a living room: his old room relocated here. As she is still shivering with cold, Anton gives her one more paternal hug, then hurries to the kitchen to light the burners of the gas stove and get the wine boiling. "It'll be ready in a bit and it'll do you good. You may take a hot bath, if you want."

She had already started to lose her stiff feeling when she walked into the bathroom. With the running of the simmering water, she came to flush deeply, and, little by little, her lips drew a contented smile, what with the bathing and with him preparing a beverage specially for her. It was the same Anton, no doubt, so she went out of the bathtub a little more confident, wrapped her body in a white fluffy bathrobe of his, came back to the room, and sat on the edge of the bed, near a stool he had placed there as a makeshift table. He brought large teacups and a pot of steaming aromatic wine, poured some, and they locked eyes, somehow without seeing each other's pupils. There was only a dim light coming from a lamp in a corner and, feeling at ease, she took a sip from her cup, then another one, and with each sip she took she better realized how detached she had become, and she came to imagine that no, maybe she no longer loved him. The man she loved was lying on far-away radiant beaches in her memory, and how proud she was to be able to carry on an exchange with Anton as with an old pal. This was what she felt he was now. Mim, the girl he had found in the train station two years before, was now as mature and undaunted as she could be, and that certainly was a nice feeling. "So, tell me about you. How are things going?" Anton asked. He was obviously proud of his new home, and they both were relishing this new type of relationship between them, all the more so due to their managing it fairly well in spite of all expectations. Then the discussion came to his house. Why all that mystery, Mim could still not understand what he had been doing all summer. Why had she not even been allowed to see him? "You gave me up for this flat." The wine had by now got through her whole body, that pungent reek of paint had gone, it was hot and music was playing, and Mim almost began to adore life again. Happy with her newly gained confidence in Anton's presence, she thought she was able to have a detached look at things now. She was in the house which she used to hate so much, and for which she was beginning to develop a kind of strange fondness, rough as it was, and filled with heat and music. He filled her cup again, and in that atmosphere scented with savory cinnamon and citrus fruit essences, she felt she had spectacularly rose to his level of maturity, leaving far behind shy, wet to the skin little Mim. She even felt sadness, thinking of that Mim.

They went on to talk about news of the world. She uttered words sluggishly, swaying her neck to their rhythm, now smiling with her head backwards, and the next moment leaning down with her elbows propped on her knees. He was there on the bed, safely at a distance, as they were supposed to be at table. The windows were by now hazy with the vapors coming from the gas fire in the kitchen, bringing the music too close to her soul. She was in a kind of delirium, no longer distinguishing between what she was imagining and what she was actually saying, fancying herself to be aloof, and ironic, nice apartment you've got, she smiled, the wine invading her she experienced an impression of power, she was powerful, she once loved a man and so what, she could go on with her life, it was not as hard as she had thought, and that man was a person just like anyone else, why had she been aching so severely?

Her mind drifted back to their first night together. Music flowing in the air, they dancing in a tight embrace in the parking lot, and the two glasses cut out of plastic bottles filled with piquantly dainty liqueur, lemon and sugar. They were enjoying themselves amidst the rows of mute windows behind which the citizens of the town were sleeping away the day's routine, snoring citizens, maybe. Their weird night, the mysterious man, look at him now, he was her equal, or at least so it seemed.

Could it have been the woman who helped him buy this apartment in the city? No, no way, that was one of his family's connections, whom Anton sometimes used to telephone with Mim sitting right next to him, good evening, and then issues related to the purchase. Mim remembered answering her call once. The phone had been ringing several times that morning and she was the only one at home. She dared not answer it first, she had never before done that, but then she thought it might be Anton calling from work, he might need something, so she picked up the receiver and heard a pleasant female voice at the other end, oh, 'the lady with the house'. Anton got mad when she told him, why on earth would he react like that? He asked at one breath: and what did you tell her? "I told her nobody was in, and that she should call again in the afternoon." He lashed himself into a fury. He went straight to his father: listen, Mrs. What's-her-name called this morning, haven't you talked to her today? "Sure, I went to see her at her office, and she asked who the girl on the phone was," Mr. Arvinte said. "And—" roared Anton demanding a quick answer. "And I told her: Anton's girlfriend, who else." Anton raised the roof then, why?

He must be punished for that, no matter the consequences. He will definitely not be happy in this house. You will never be happy in this house, she heard herself say. But it was all an act, she was not taking anything seriously anymore, and he was watching her from the shadows. Although she could not make out his face, she could feel his grief penetrating her like a thrill. Why was darkness so profound in this man's soul? Thence he struck: Mim, what am I going to do if you fall in love with another guy? She leaned forward to leave the cup on the stool and smiled at him, confused. She caught a glimpse of his eyes, and that very moment he flung himself like lightening over her, snatched the homey bathrobe off her body, and started kissing her mouth wildly. Yes, him, she will remain with him. This thought pervaded her like a leveling wave. She was being made happy again, that was why he had looked for her.

She was leaving the following day, going to her parents' home, as it was the weekend again. He saw her to the station, assisted her in getting on the train and remained speechless on the platform. He just stood there focusing his gape on the steps of the train car, well aware of Mim's infectious spell, which was overpowering him. He would rather fling himself in a comfortable armchair and doze it away. Mim even fancied he was praying he could fall asleep right there, standing, praying the train would glide secretly away, drain away from him, together with that girl, her smiles and games, her laughter and all, what the heck, he is a grown up man. 'You are a child, Mim, what do you know about life?' Let her drain away on the sly, he is whispering, so that he can feel no pain. But Mim is there. What can she say, when there is nothing in the world of words, or gestures, nothing in the world of secret waves, nothing that could bring him back among people? This is what Mim felt then. God if she had not struggled to see him live. Her whole opera was being destroyed, as Anton was going back to his lair, back where she had found him. That was his decision. The train is moving off and she says nothing. She is drifting away from him, stone-still. Anton is a boulder left back in darkness.

7 THE MIRROR

You would say that her gauzy dress was purposefully created for this stifling indoor heat. So large and long, with a simple straight cut and high slits on both sides, for her to lift her legs and prop them up on the chairs under the table or bend them under her bottom, a garment that facilitates her quick peregrinations to the kitchen to fetch more lemonade. The balm her moist skin is exuding smells just divine and she can perceive it oozing from the flimsy fabric. She could not possibly stand the touch of anything black, black woolen fabric would simply suffocate her pores, so she would definitely rule out any accord between black wool and her skin now. Stefan must be sweating like a pig in his dramatic gala costume, seated at some table to converse, looking back on his high school years, buried in thoughts. The photos she saw in his old room at his parents' revealed him as a handsome adolescent and young man. Thick straight dark hair falling in a fringe cut just above his eyebrows, and those huge dewy eyes complementing a sensuous mouth with bounteous well defined lips. It was his mother's mouth, which Mim thought no longer suited him. It was completely incongruous with his present haircut, his logic and deep thinking, inspiring a sense of the grotesque in her.

Stefan was thinking too much and he was too patient, which was getting on her nerves. She sometimes had an overwhelming feeling of being stalked by him. Mim had become the object of his research work. She pictured him, in relation to her, as a researcher in the true sense of the word, who would meticulously plan his expected results. The fact that it had not been his soul but his reasoning that pushed him to err confounded and at the same time disappointed her. On what grounds had he not taken her to his graduation anniversary? Was he keeping her indoors to recover, as if she were a convalescent, or could he have been driven by a purely base motive, namely the consideration that she might not rise up to the occasion. Well, little did he know that her wardrobe at home was packed with splendid exclusive garments she herself had designed. She turned heads whenever she made her appearance at an event, so that was quite a ridiculously unfortunate misjudgment, which fully deserves retribution.

She has never really been much into casual clothing. Shimmery décolleté attires have always been at the center of her creative endeavors, dazzling garbs for the ritzy evening parties to which, ever since a little girl, she has pictured herself going. Over the whole year she used to gear up for the summer season by putting together a trousseau complete with beachwear, evening wear, dancewear. Years had once been to her but units of measurement for these time lags, in expectation of the train which would take the entire family towards the sky line, and into the world. All year round she would exert herself, by day being a good hard-working schoolgirl or playing with the other kids, and by night planning her life, starting with the following summer, and through all the successive summers to the top, to success and celebrity. Each and every such nocturnal session would end up in impending disaster, irrefutably accepted, as she had lived it all, had she not, and there was nothing left for her to do in this world. Without a goal, there was no point in going on, this was what knowing meant. As a student she once had to write an essay in French about wisdom, *la sagesse*. Well, when you have done it all and reach the end of the road you become *sage*, composed, quiet.

Each outfit was a world in itself, whose spirit was carried, through Mim's intermediary, wherever she went. People gazed wondering where she had come from. She looked just like one of those beautiful people in the glossy magazines. Stefan could not have done anything funnier. He had been out in his mean narrow calculations, and by miles. They will now turn against him and against his much flaunted love for her. She will punish him. She will leave home too, and will go to see Anton. Everything makes sense now, and the two days ahead of her have revenge written all over them. She rises from among the piles of papers, gets dressed, takes one final look in the mirror, equips her purse with the minimum things she may need, opens the front door, locks it behind her, and flies away.

In no time she is at Anton's door. It was such a beautiful day outside, for absolutely everyone. So she presses the doorbell button. "Mim," he exclaims. He is all white and confused in the slit of the door and his features start all at once when he sees her. But he does not seem to be angry. "I've dropped by to see you," she says all in one breath. He lets her in and sees her across the storehouse-hallway to the main room, where she regains some confidence and feels pretty again. Anton is pleased to have her as a guest. She remembers how amused he was by her using the local word *musafir* for guest, quite common in the region she comes from. As he is to-ing and fro-ing about, Mim decides to sit on the bed, but hardly has she done that when he says, "Will you make some coffee?" Yes, she starts, sure, and off she goes to the kitchen. Here three stools make up a provisional table and there is a bast mat on the rugged concrete floor. She recognizes the transparent smoky Jena cups in the old house and tries a feeling that she likes it in here. The tender moment is ruined though as Anton walks in. He has come to grind some coffee beans for her. The two of them together in that close space tastes somewhat familiar. She would hate the smell of burning gas if it were not for the cozy aromatic heat that is permeating the whole interior. He walks out and in again, getting two cups ready to receive the lively, spiced hot drink on a Saturday afternoon, when everyone should enjoy themselves.

She remembers how he used to observe her attentively in the kitchen, with alert exigent eyes, making anything she did difficult for her. What a relief now to be let loose. She removes the hot pot from the ring and as she tilts it to pour coffee in the first cup she is presently startled by his approaching voice: let me do that for you. Well, he knows everything while she is childlike and inexperienced. She was in love, but he had never seen the causal relation between love and awkwardness. Love meant for him a woman drilling about like a machinery for her man, cunning and dexterous. 'Quick on the trigger, that's how she should be if she loves me.' She could not help it. Had she insisted, he would have probably thought she was dying to make a wife's demonstration in front of him, and that was the last thing on her mind. Plus, the word 'wife' is not in her vocabulary and it sounds so vulgar. Therefore she stepped aside and let him pour the coffee, hurrying notwithstanding to take the tray from him, carry it to the room and place it on the two joined stools beside the bed.

To break up the embarrassing silence, Anton asked how things were going with her, well, nothing much, she was working on her diploma paper, and, oh, she was staying in the city for the time being, she had told him that before. Yes, he remembered. Mim began to feel sick, nauseated by all those flat words between them. How could they be chatting in the same way pals do over a glass of wine?

To keep up the palaver he asked, "What about today, how come you haven't gone home? It's a Saturday."

"I just haven't."

"I imagine you didn't do that in order to come and see me."

"No, I was working and, as I was sitting at my writing table, I don't know what got into me. I got dressed and left. I live nearby," she added after a brief pause.

Anton was obviously trying to do his best to be neither too cold nor too warm toward her. That was a lot more subtle than his usual histrionics, that vile condescending vein that at some point in his life got into his blood, that off-putting barrier of sudden decisive gestures and bluntly jerked words, or sometimes quite the other way round, long strings of words uttered sluggishly in his phlegmatic capital-city accent.

"I've taken up painting, you know?" she then ventured to say.

"Painting," he repeated, and his face brightened up. He was smiling a secret smile to himself. The enchantment that concept triggered in him put him right off on a different track and turned his attention to the paintings he had on the walls, his dear assets. He raised one arm and pointed to the white horse painted by a friend of his when he was in university.

Mim twisted her torso to look at the bluish maned phantasma neighing from above the bed. You could perceive several horses there, it was a beautiful hypnotic representation of racing. Her spirits sank at the thought that it would be very difficult for her to ever impress him.

"Look," he said making an exalted conclusive gesture, then he emphatically articulated the word 'painting' again. "You like it?" he asked fastening his eyes upon another painting.

It was nothing but a sort of twig fence that gave you the

impression you were looking at it right from amidst the very twigs. A set of violently drawn strokes in drab brownish tones, cutting through a vaguely outlined dark violet brume, which conveyed nothing to Mim but brutality. Gross, impotent barbarism, rather than pure violence. Mim almost felt the lashes coming upon her from that spot on the wall in a ridiculously offensive animation, activated perhaps by the apprehensive side of her mind, debris from the past.

"I've only just bought this, you haven't seen it before."

Appreciative words would not come to her, so she was keeping her mouth open in a fake contemplative gape when he asked, "Do you like the idea?"

God knows what he made of that piece and she would not dare let him know what she did. "It is interesting," she lied in a barely audible voice. She would rather have told him about herself, about everything she had to show to the world, about the tangle of shapes and colors swelling in her in a frenzy of sensuous dances she was ready to splash out on blank canvas. She was now ripe to unleash the forces she had been suppressing since a child.

Never ever had he been interested in discovering the child in her, since for him Mim was wholly a child, *l'enfant parfait*. He would reproach her with that: you can't understand, what do you know? But had he ever been at least curious to meet that child? No. While Mim had been permanently searching for his childhood. She would imagine him playing in his grandparents' yard in that far-away northern land, him being dressed up by his mother, him having his hair combed, and being coddled by her. She had even arrived to recreate his grandmother's picture in her mind, or his father's, mounted on his horse and ready to set out to solve vital matters. Mr. Arvinte used to be a man of deeds and strong will, who his wife looked up to in veneration and would zealously wait upon.

She once tried to reveal to him secret games she used to play with her brother when they were kids. Mim had always had a passion for tramcars and their silent glide along shiny infinite tracks. Wherever her parents took her on a visit she used to lock herself in the bathroom, sit on the throne and maneuver the arms of the towel stand buzzing and fancying she was driving a rail vehicle. Not even the stories about her entrepreneurial game of the greengrocer's stall had he found entertaining. He was probably recalling his own toys while Mim was exposing her child's self to him.

How she loved exerting herself as a *borsh* seller. She would earnestly fill big milk glass bottles with water from the tap and place them on the sill of the small square window of their summer kitchen in the backyard. When she got tired of that she upgraded her trade to selling potatoes, her favorite merchandise. She was intent on soiling her hands to perfection, and the amount of earth under her fingernails could hardly be enough to satisfy her standards of dirtiness. She would rub the palms and the back of her hands against the bottom of the tin basin which substituted for the dish of the imaginary counter-scale, but she could hardly be a match for the young women sellers she used to gawk at while their hands were wading through heaps of vegetables. She would diligently load up the dish with the vegetables stored in the kitchen and empty it in shopping bags, trying to imitate those girls' mannerisms and laconism. She had a fascination with the market place and the young vendors' dirty hands, and was keen on tarnishing hers in the same fashion, just in order to have sufficient ground for making herself pretty afterwards and stun everyone, wow, is that the greengrocer?

She would clean up, then go into the house and take a bath, put on one of her mother's dresses and walk into her pair of pink stiletto pointy toe pumps. Once she chose a *pochette* to match and hung pearls in her ears, she was fit to proceed with her habitual parade to and fro the long courtyard, her eyes brightening with delight at the sound of the heels clicking on the bluish-grey flint slabs. That was still not enough, so she went on to lock herself in the house, where, in front of the tall dressing mirror in her parents' bedroom, she began to lower the neckline of the dress and put on lipstick, looking admiringly at her own image. The next step was to draw the table to the right focal distance from the mirror so as she could initiate one of her mock professional photo sessions. What followed was a frantic display of costumes, make-up, hairstyles and jewelry, with her as the focus of attention perched on that vintage piece of furniture. Snapshot after snapshot she went from an ingénue through star to diva. She ended up spread almost naked on the top of the table in various poses and God she was beautiful. She adjusted herself to a most glamorous pose and remained transfixed, literally knocked out of time, staring into her own eyes until tears came to them. That specific shot would soon be lost forever, and this ached in her chest beyond shrills of pain. Transience was, for her, unbearable. She would rush to her mother's wardrobe to dig for black garments which she then put on crying. Back to the mirror, she would stare at the bitter traits of her face for a while, after which she used to distort them into a series of grotesque grimaces, with pouched, cleft, or stretched wide cavernous mouths and either squinting or awestruck bulging eyes. The moment the clown in her came to life she stirred up a frenzy of make-up being rubbed in gross quantities all over her face. She delighted in this ludicrous operation which made her ugly and finally free to put her mind to rest and laugh. She felt powerful, there was nothing left for her to lose, ha, ha!

Before long, exhaustion would bring her down to earth, back to dignity, so she fancied herself as a calm, perfectly serene mature woman, hardly likely to be touched by anything anymore. And when she could no longer find her way through the chaos she herself had created, she abruptly went in a fit of rage against the heaps of entangled dressing gowns and nightgowns, lamé dresses and tops, gauzy curtains and strips of velvet drapery, swatches of chiffons and satins, lace and scintillant sequins. So she set about grabbing them one by one, folding and putting them back in their places, all this time bickering and calling them names like an old hag. On top of everything she got seized with panic at the thought of her mother's imminent coming back from work to witness the mess.

Quite, her mother had never really seen the looks of the house at the end of such a debauchery session. She would arrive, Tomina was as good as she had always known her, Mum's quiet obedient child, and family life went on duly. That was why her mother did not know her. That was why Mim gave her a shock when she designed her first outfits and went out to show them off. Little did her mother know about Tomina's vast life experience within the very walls of their house. She had already been a fashion model, a dancer, a musical actress.

All the less did Anton have any idea about these talents of hers. On two occasions only had she revealed herself to him as a dazzling diva. She had not had the time to and, anyway, it would not have counted, and it did not matter any longer. Therefore, why bother do it now? Why should she tell him about herself, when it was facts he wanted. Even if he were to see her paintings, he still would not believe. For him, Mim was not an artist. She was just a classy girl, fairly well-educated and bright for her gender. But this was not the truth. She was a repressed voice struggling to be heard. There was a slight possibility that he had perceived that but refused to admit it, either for fear of spoiling her or simply because the artist was him. No, nothing coming from her could ever reach the heart of this man, who was now sitting with a cup in his hand, gazing at his beloved acquisitions.

He rises to his feet and goes to the closet in the hallway to pick up some clothes, disappears from view, and soon reappears ready to leave. She feels it befitting to stand up herself, if only he said something. And he says, "Mim, I have an errand to run. Play yourself some music, I'll be back in a bit."

He took off with her sitting there aghast in disbelief of having been left alone in the house as in the old times. "I'll bring over two friends of mine, Roxana and Dan, you'll like them for sure, you'll see," that was what he had said. She played the songs Anton had once referred to as the best duet singing there could be: Streisand's voice and Dylan's style. What could sustain life in a more troubling manner on a Saturday afternoon, among his coffee cups in this room featuring two massive old pieces of furniture and original paintings on the walls? Mim went back to her crouched position in her place, still trying to figure out a meaning for his leaving, when he would return, why he had left her waiting there.

Her visits were now brief, as she had to hide herself from his new friends, so what on earth was she doing there alone, a stranger? Yet, what a pleasant feeling of contentment, Mim still being his old same dependable friend. He had asked her to stay. What a relief she did not have to rise to her feet and go, she would have felt sent away and utterly hurt. He really had not wanted to get rid of her. And how could he have done that, when he had once been running after Mim calling her name, as her quick small steps on the asphalt were killing her soul the farther she got from his voice. He, who had once asked her, pressing her body against a recess in his car: who do you love, Mim? Nobody, she had whispered guiltily. "Nobody? That's my name, isn't it?" He had stalked her into a corner and was holding her in a tight grip, kissing her mouth in order to drain the whole truth out of it.

8 AUTUMN

A sleepwalk back to town. Was there anything? Only streets and dozens of speeds, numbers, continuous walking on the curbs and spindly jets lashing at her cheeks, all sorts of speeds, either humid or cool, the last warm breezes, the first silent fragrances, quietness, the town is muffled. Mute citizens are bustling the evening into night, lighted number plates of cars, that was all there was, and between crowded sidewalks and trails of light speeding past, on the borderline between the two worlds, Mim, strands of hair blown with the wind, blind listening and tracing the essence of her shelter, the interior where she had first smelled the scent of her man. Her shelter might be hovering somewhere along the way and Mim, her long slender neck stretched forward, was ready to meet it with a kiss.

Nights and days were a continuous flow of perceptions, a river which she hoped would drift her shelter back to her. Mim did not laugh, she was walking. Sometimes she would stumble over some impediment, the surrounding world was not completely smooth, but she would rub herself against any asperity, thus nicely glazing them away, along her hypnotic slide. Mim did not cry, it was night and she almost wished to go blind, dazed by the array of odors. A myriad of scent-laden gusts and whiffs were playfully whizzing around her, but she had not yet gone blind. Mim did not scream, she was arduously pursuing her quest. There were the others, whispering, legions of drifting souls would cross their ways nearby. A new man had emerged, his field would hang out close now and then, and soon she came to feel him like a warm cloud hazing her delirium, permanently lagging behind her. Mim did not speak, there were the girls, and she would curl under the blanket to continue her slide. It was the same in the mornings, when she would walk up and down steps in a huge cold building, a building she knew. One summer Anton had been waiting for her there seated on the large steps outside, and when she got out he sprang to his feet and they went away, he holding her by the hand, taking her with him, here, it is right in this spot that she senses the glim of his eyes, the tracks of their steps. In other places she viewed herself with piles of books in front of her, listening in on the street, he has come!, and she flies off, footsteps of hers walk in and walk out over and over again, or climb down stairs and the two of them meet and depart as one, they are forever departing. Mim was gliding on their trails throughout the city. Whenever she turned around the new man was there behind her, she recognized his breath at her each and every passage back home before the tucking in for the night. Stefan had begun to follow her on the streets. But Mim was waiting for the stroke of blindness to occur. Her shelter would burst bright to engulf her.

Day after day, the smoky haze above smells more and more of autumn. The evenings though, she would still be stirred by some chance late summer waft. Shoes on the asphalt muttered in cold decent tones echoing flatly towards the barren branches of the trees. Imaginary vendors lining the streets and alleys seemed to be offering her regally blushed, rich-flavored apples as she was passing. She had got used to feeling that man accompanying her but, amidst car lights and breezes, she was still tracing smells. Mim no longer cherished her body, yet this body of hers was carrying her along, hair billowing back in the wind and pores whipped by the autumn chill. The body stopped. An electric arc thrust her from head to toe and her body darted into the driveway. Currents were whizzing and whistling all through her, causing her neck to elongate and protrude forward. Mim sent her innermost powers to fetch what she had so long been seeking, her beloved shelter. Her nets had been thrown to enmesh the object of her quest and now it was coming to her. The car pulled over right there at the curb next to her body, the door opened for her to get in, Mim let herself loose and slid inside with a loud inaudible scream as though she was then inaugurating her lungs with air. She was finally blind and let herself fall, fall to the end gulping in her own perfume blended with his, their bodies together and the old field of secret particles swarming around without any definite outline, one single membrane which, oh my God, bursts open, and here they are one next to the other. Now Mim sees. Anton is gripping her shoulders as if she were some kind of oddity. "Mim, what's got into you?" he says. The autumn outside creeps in and sets between them. She came to her senses and heard: I'll give you a lift. He turned the car around and headed back to where he had been coming from, the student campus. The shadow — Mim recalled, then said, "There's one other person." The car came to a steep halt. On the opposite sidewalk, Stefan was drawing back like a shadow.

She started to pour it all, the raving story of an absurd summer. Anton had got a home in her absence, but every evening drove his car on that very road hoping to find Mim again, what was he doing there anyway? How could he, how could he live a whole summer without her? What was he going to do lonely in his large apartment? He had traded the girl in the rain for four walls, how could he have done such a thing?

"Mim, you are..., a puzzle I'm really into." An awkward, gross way to put it, one night at the disco. He had taken a good grip of her long hair and was pulling it backwards whispering in her ear her name, Mim. Curving her neck in an arch he kept interrogating her: who are you, Mim? The haze of cigarette smoke and the music were surreptitiously ebbing away in larger and larger circles. Anton and Mim were gaping an abyss all around them, in the middle of which her uneasiness tasted uncanny, what on earth did he want of her, was he crazy or what? For long months she had been waiting for him to say something clear, and now this? Nothing but silence, and now brutality. Quite strangely, her fear gradually gave way to a state of expectation again, she was definitely curious to find out, once and for all, who that man was. Fixing her stare on his wan mouth, she was determined to wait. She wanted words, real words. But the performance of that silent freak was puzzling her mind, caught in the fogginess of his ominous netting. She feared she would get lost in the darkness to which he was luring her.

"You," he uttered, then continued in a cracked voice, "you mean two things to me..." Her heart stopped beating to let herself listen. Ever since, those words have been murmuring into her mind: *rain* and *train station*.

How could he have the heart to wipe that girl out of existence? Mim had changed over the summer and would avenge her. No, there is no point in her seeing his apartment. An icy gale was blowing stone-hard determination into her heart, so she continued her account in a sinister note. "It's too late, why should I visit your new place? I've been sick, real sick, day and night I sat at the dinner table like a monument waiting. For two whole months, and my parents didn't know what to do." It seemed to Mim it was not her talking anymore, as she could not feel a tinge of anything. Another Mim had sprung up next to Anton, making the girl she was before completely disappear, as if melted down into the ground. The stern pride of what Tomina had once been had bloomed unawares. All her past anguish was turning into circus on her lips and all she wanted was a good laugh. But sarcasm and terror were growing side by side in her mind. She was terrified by the deadly coldness of what she was saying and at the thought of calamity looming. Even so, the torrent had to gush out at all costs and nothing could possibly shun its flow now, not even the apprehension of losing him for good. Tomina was in charge now and she felt nothing but contempt for Mim. An animated picture of her shivering somewhere in a dark corner was flashing back from the margins of her memory, only to irritate her more. So she could not help it. The least she could do was pray.

9 BALLET

"What are you crying for now?"

Mim twirls around to face him. "If I cry, I do it out of pity for her, for Mim, that's why."

Her eyes stop issuing tears abruptly. As much as she might enjoy indulging in their alleviating dampness, they have simply dried out. She searches for Stefan's eyes, as is he not supposed to be her caring mock husband? She really feels protected here and no evil can harm her any longer. As anxiety is ebbing off, it gives way to a warm comforting feeling. She is relieved to have got rid of that man and to be here with someone who inspires anything but apprehension to her.

"I talked to the manager of the theatre in person today. He's expecting us to drop by his office within the end of the month. He'll be out of town until mid-August."

This is exactly what she most desires. Why, then, does talking about this position leave her cold?

Stefan insists. "You have a copy of the scenario, don't you? Have you read it?"

Why would he pry into whatever she might be doing? "Yes, of course," she answers. "What? Are you afraid I won't manage?"

"I was just thinking you lack experience, that's all."

"It was not me who insisted on this, remember? I can't deny I'd love that, though. Still, think of it, taking someone else's place, well, I don't know how I would feel. I don't like the idea of people keeping a place warm for me. I'm still thinking whether to accept it or not."

"Tomina, you're not taking anyone's place, the position is vacant. True, it's not public knowledge, but—"

"OK, I understand. We'll see."

"There's nothing to think over, everything's set."

"Not yet," she concludes.

"As you wish. I'm done with this topic." And he picks up where he left off with his reading.

In bed. The two of them spend the sultry afternoons sprawled on that broad platform while people breathe in the breezy air along the quay. And if they ever go out, it is invariably as far as the summer terrace across the block and back home.

Stefan seems to have second thoughts and resumes his interrogation. "Did you finally manage to get hold of that course book?"

Mim prays he would leave her alone and answers languidly, "Not yet. But I've talked with the library and as soon as they get it they'll let me know."

He surely could make a good detective, she says to herself. You should never breathe freely thinking he is done with you, as he will come up with another one-off matter he needs to clarify when you least expect. This makes it so difficult for her to slip in her issue, that of going out. What more to ask of this man?

She does, though. "Shall we go out?"

"Patience, Tomina, I've just got back from work."

"I didn't mean now, a little later."

"All right, if you really want to, we'll go."

"I do. I'm fed up with staying indoors."

"Why? I understand you go out in the morning quite often."

"Yes."

His remark put her off balance and she keeps mum. Is he getting somewhere? But why should she bother her head about that? She will recline back against her pillow and will lie there bored stiff. She is off it, anyway. Tomorrow everything will be fine, she will be on her own again. She fancies herself preparing breakfast while listening to Mozart, then reading. But when will she set about finishing her paper? And when will she expose to the world the deeper, most wonderful things inside her? She will dedicate herself to that back in her home town. She might as well accept her governmental appointed position and take everything she needs to wherever that is going to be.

Stefan starts up the TV, then lounges himself back on his side of the bed and resumes reading. Why should he have done that if he holds the newspaper spread wide right between his eyes and the screen, she scorns him inwardly.

Ballet. Tchaikovsky. The flickering light from the screen is reflecting now, Mim knows, in Anton's soul and hers alike. She imagines this music is for the two of them, and it soars and soars, swelling into an elated spirit larger than life that they both breathe in, making the world become too small. With each pull of a fiber muscle, there is a twitch in their chest, a sensation of strength, or hatred, and the next moment the dancers' willowy arms caress them with appeasing strokes. Look how the human breast is triumphant, and shoulders clasp life in, bending towards the womb. Soles stump orders, calves elongate to beg, or swell to curse, and thighs make love. Man rises, the beautiful human being. Does Stefan not hear the music? He is slouching unmoved, nose dug in that ugly sheet of paper scribbled all over, only to work her into lather. Mom, Dad, come and take a look, this is Stefan. I cannot love him.

It dawns on her she should stir up a kind of conclusive

duel between Anton and Stefan. So she dares him. "Stefan, look what they're showing. It's ballet dancing."

Stefan draws the paper nearer to his nose with a sudden jerk, as if wanting to bury his face into it, and gives her a flat response. "I'd rather read *The Sport Magazine*."

This is alarmingly horrible. Stefan and Anton are oceans asunder. But she needs further evidence.

"I can't believe you don't like ballet."

"I don't."

And she asks, "You don't?"

And he answers, "I don't."

Stefan is a sterile heavy blank mass, in spite of his breeding, his erudition, and the superhuman intelligence that has always amazed her. Stefan lies heavy beside her, suppressing her aspirations toward worlds yet undiscovered. He knows everything, so nothing could enrapture his attention anymore. The fantastic ballet movements on the screen stop to a still and Mim feels like grabbing him by the shoulders and giving him a good hard shake and pictures herself pulling at his inert limbs. She can see his feet sticking out from under the flimsy cover and images his ridiculously plump alabaster soles.

She flings herself upon him and snatches the paper off his hands. "Look!" she cries out.

His bland matte eyes, his bitter mouth with the lower lip drooping towards his chin. This icon of disbelief sends a chilling wave all over her. What has she done to Stefan? The man who takes care of her and is patiently nursing her through her lovesickness, the good man who wants to keep her protected from 'that beast', 'that man is not human, Tomina.'

Silence covers the bed. Twilight will settle upon their uncomfortable grief and tomorrow she will be expecting him in the bright kitchen with dinner laid on table. From its window she will see him coming home and will be filled with joy, and they will celebrate. They will eat together.

10 THE CAMPSITE

Green tents, yellow tents, blue tents. Stern-looking bearded men clad in rainproof capes, hoods either on or off. Humdrum camp vibration. High boots. Clusters and tents. Everyone sticks to their business, flat smiles and countenances. Long-haired men in robes walk in and out of stark yellow or deep green tents. Illusory green ground. Float. She is here, dissipated into the faint hustle, sensing the essence of the tribe vibe. The green float is receding slowly into the background, with her left behind, on tan ground. Is this a painting? Tinged lethargy. No woe, no bliss. It is peaceful there. Green. Illusory green.

She is alone with the tent ceiling hovering above her. The perfect tranquility in that vision is lingering on her mind. It must be the impression left on her by this campsite. It is her wanderings among the tents, it is the crowd and their whisperings that have all mingled in that elusive tableau of the alien green island. Nothing feels alien here, though. It is hot and the people are laughing, all amassed together to form a kind of clan, so close to one another, so close to her too. Whence then that strange vision of an island beyond reach both in space and in time?

Whence the clenched lips, as yes, those lanky beings seemed to have them all glued up. Oh my God, it is him. Anton blew his iciness into her sleep, pushing life toward the brink of the universe. Anton is stern and cold, and it is him who walks in and out of their tent with clenched lips. Mim dare not let herself speak and the two youths whisper between themselves. This is where the faint hustle comes from, yes. Mim keeps herself away from Anton. Her eyes are here, but her soul is soaring in the distance, mute.

The canvas of the tent is filtering the light from above and raspy green needles, coruscating, are gently chipping away the coldness around her body. It is sunny outside, it is a new day, there are another two left. She begins to stretch herself out, but her muscles are too shy for that. She is no longer happy, spoiled Mim. No, there is no way she could relax her body here, that is an indecent gesture and an ugly thought. But look at her lithe figure, at her muscles beautifully elongated on the bones. This is what keeping on the go can do, and the swimming, and hardly eating anything, wow! She is back in her former shape, so gracefully slender, and that gorgeous wasp waist of hers. Why, oh why had she let things slide, abandoning herself to the exhilaration of being with him, so heavily and so literally heavy? Anton had not got a ghost of a chance at seeing her body at its best. She stopped taking care of her body the minute she laid eyes on him. Being with Anton was enough for her. They used to wolf down copious meals and then loiter away the afternoons, together and carefree. They would retreat in his room to read and listen to music completely naked. She had let herself slide through a kind of magical tunnel, tempted along by something as tricky as the mirror which pushes you to sacrifice your freshness for a moment's glory.

Strange were the workings of her body, and of her facial appearance for that matter. She could be as attractive as she could be ugly. Who has ever heard of a thing like that? Was she perchance magical? And when the spell dissolved, Anton saw her for what she really was? Paralyzed with disbelief, he would rave and storm against her charms, against himself, against fate. The threads of her magic would weave back and then unravel again for him to wonder. But it was not the witchery he was afraid of, poor fool. These thoughts which haunted Anton were once laughed off as ridiculous by Mim and her mother, my goodness, what nonsense. Even so, that vital spirit which breathed life into her, extending her spinal cord, elongating her limbs, stretching the skin on her cheek bones and her eyebrows towards the temples, felt like magic. Her hair too was sparked into lush life and her lips filled with vital sap and natural color. That life-giving breath which was glittering in her eyes was indeed magic, the magic of euphoria.

Now she has exactly the physique to meet Anton's feminine ideal: lean and long-haired. But her lips and cheeks are veiled in sadness and her eyes are in mourn. And as much as her figure might be to his liking, there is no Mim. For him she no longer exists. She will get out of the shadow to remove the numbness away of her trunk and limbs. There are so many people outside and she can hear them talking. The farther away she walks the younger she will get, as she feels old in Anton's proximity, a woman who has lost her man, hollow-eyed and crouched at heart.

She got instantly old when she saw him coming from between the buildings. No sooner had Anton come into the open than she wilted and shriveled right there before his dirty glare. Their last time together. That was what they had agreed upon the previous evening. Theirs was going to be a decent farewell celebration with congenial mature smiles over champagne bubbles, for a new life. Therefore she had come to meet him all dressed in white. Despite the inappropriateness of the attire, despite her bashfulness to wear it, that was the drive she had felt before leaving home that morning. It was him who had invited her, only that he may have thought she would not take him seriously, or who knows what might have happened in between. That other girl had tried to kill herself. And look who died, Mim. She wished so hard to die on the way here that she still has a feeling it has happened for real.

Mim, who would once wait for him to come home swaying on the swing in the front garden of the block, or sitting in the warm kitchen with an ear to the street, so close to his dark-browed mother forever bustling about, Mim who used to gulp up the flood of clear radiance coming from his eyes for being welcomed in such an innocent, immaculate way. No, the rending sound of his voice that morning was beyond all bearing.

"I have to go now, Mim, I promised."

"But you promised me, too."

"Why can't you understand I'm leaving, everything's already fixed."

"Then take me with you, I won't disturb you in any way, believe me. I just have to be with you, that's what I've set my mind to. That's what we alone decided, please."

She reads irritation on his lips. Or could it be hatred? No, it is repulsion. Well, she is not sure what it is. All she knows is that he wants to brush her off. Oh my God, no. "Please." She seems to hear an old hag's groan and pictures herself embracing his ankles with wrinkled arms and binding his calves with her gluey sick slobber, prostrate at his feet like a pool of dirt. Try as he might he cannot toss her off. With the hag weighing heavy on his feet, the poor man still has to dash off, run away, he is running away from something, in his car and off, on the road with his new company, the boy and the girl. "OK, I understand, you're going with your friends, but why can't I come too, is there anyone else?"

"Just for your knowledge, no. I want to be alone, to enjoy myself." Then he goes in a fit of rage and starts to bawl. "Leave me alone, you hear? You're all driving me crazy, all of you."

It is better like that, Mim says to herself, one cannot get that mad at someone they loathe. Then she is at it again. "If you are alone, then why can't I come, what can I do to you?"

He answered back with a vile, omniscient sneer. It is better like that, a whole lot better, she said inwardly.

Mim does not think it was the blatant, bold resonance of the words 'what can I do to you' that had brought that malicious grin to his lips, but something somewhat different. She used to conjure all the secret energies in her to turn her body into a kind of medium that diffused music into his body. An inaudible transmission took place, feeble yet steady, from her skin into his skin, from her pores into his pores, so private and so basic, delicious, through waves of pure animal feeling in harmony with the rhythm of life, that innermost visceral rhythm shared by everyone. Her body felt like a heart bloomed open and somehow spread all over him, swaying, throbbing, as she used to travel her own inner life on the surface of his milk-white skin, so soft, so elastic. Her nostrils were running like wild creatures on fields of bliss, vast, balmy with primeval herbs and dews. Hundreds of bashful tiny springs were there for her lips to water themselves freely and they did suck in pure life, prostrate on the sweet membrane stretching on the plateau between the blades of his hips. She would rest her ear there and pause to listen in to the thriving of his warm entrails. This expanse of wonderful skin was breathing to the rhythm of her own breast, which she felt with the sharp sensors of her nipples. And it was not the sound of viscera that they carried deep down to her female essence, but the power of life, which then propagated and diffused throughout her body. This flow of stirring messages in perfect accord with the music which was playing swept through her brains, and what she did was send it back to him. As simple as that. She passed the music through her body.

The image of her body enwrapping him comes to her mind and she dares a smile. Yes, that ravishing body of hers, aching to channel love for life, wanted to be everywhere: at his mouth, on his neck, with her arms and hands and abdomen, with her delicate ankles. She would gently slide her ankles around his, then up on his shins, and ended up playing in the circle of his palms. Yes, almost like a live heart would she enter him, beating rhythmically, a tentacled heart that would glue itself in there to pour out the elixir of life. Mim aspired to perfection. And she had managed to touch him deep down in his male core on the way. Art, this is what lovemaking meant to her, every time almost getting there, 'I want more, Mim, I can't feel you,' so she tried harder, bringing the modulations of her body into harmony with the music until the crudest, rawest membranes came in tune and turned into symbols of beauty.

It was this exaggerated aestheticism and her desire to please him that had always kept her own inner beast in check. Quite right, Mim had never freed it up to howl, bite, and die. She was proud though when Anton unleashed his hounds, knowing something deep down in her had turned his key. But maybe her artistic endeavors were not just it, were not the real thing. What lovemaking really meant to him seems to be above her bend now. What she knows is that Anton always felt something was missing. 'Do you know what I want real bad,' he began once, 'I wish I took you on top of a mountain and fucked you there in total silence.' Did his words penetrate her with a new thrill then, never before experienced, yet somewhat familiar? 'All I want to hear is your shrills rend the skies when you come.' Could he have felt that she was doing nothing but laboring for the sake of art? 'Can't you get real just for once?' No, to be sure, he had completely misunderstood her: Mim's art was deceitful. Therefore she had sinned out of too much pureness. But are they not, all those we no longer want in our lives, always blameful?

And when she thinks how she had been following him to heel. Up the stairs and then everywhere he walked about the house, keeping after him to say yes. He raced out through the door, locked it emphatically and hurled himself down the stairs with Mim shadowing him like a ghost all along and then up to the car. And before she knew where she was, he got in the car, ready for off. The engine let out its first grumble directly into her heart and her heart sank.

The car is still in place, purring. That once exhilarating taking off sound is now beyond all bearing. No, this is not what she has come for. The engine is working itself up into a menacing vroom and Mim flips out. The hell with her love and the old hag story and all. She is going, too. Were she to cling to the rear of the car and be dragged along, she will go. She wants away, period. She keeps standing on his side of the car facing his window. Stupid. He can pull out any moment. Well, if he does, she will jump right in front of the car. He has two options: either take her along or not leave at all. What a pathetic picture. The man had started the engine minutes ago and she was still begging at his window. Nothing could bend his determination. What was that frightening about her? He would rather have killed her than take her with him. Why?

If only she had not felt tears in his eyes and a gulp in his throat no earlier than one month ago. His face caught light when he saw her. "Mim!" It was him again, her Anton. But that, maybe just because he had been drinking. What was this man hiding in his soul? Mim figured she was there too, buried deep and forever. She had miraculously come to surface and he had eyes for her again. He was beaming with happiness. A seat at table for Mim, fruit juice and coffee please, this is Mim, he kept introducing her as though that damp country joint across the river was filled with customers. And he could barely keep his pride in check.

With his head bent down over the table he was fidgeting with the tablecloth. "Mim…" But he relapsed into silence, unable to speak. She had, for one split second, a sheer sense of belonging to him. What he was keeping within his lips did not need telling. She had always longed for Anton to speak up about whatever he felt for her and was now surprised to see him trying to disclose things so deep that they were beyond words. "I spilled earlier a drop of coffee on the tablecloth and this reopened some old sores. I thought of you. The spot is right here." He was hiding it under his palm and was somewhat reluctant to expose it. "Yes, a mere coffee stain." She leaned forward to see it, but he placed his hand back as if wanting to keep her off his grief. "You know nothing, Mim. Yes, this brought you back to my mind." He was speaking with his chin thrust into his chest, a man who had lost his woman irremediably. This was what his guttural voice told. Frustration swelled within her and she wanted to say that she was there, but her words went unsaid. Why she was not Mim anymore she could not understand. Then she was hit by his true penetrating eyes and an enlightened smile. "Telepathy, Mim."

It was telepathy that had sucked her out of doors. She had simply felt an urge to fling herself over the river from right there at the window. Her frantic running down the valley and the crossing by ferry and her first step on the land beyond had felt like one single vault toward him. And in spite of the glaring sun, a few drops of rain coming out of the blue had given her a sign that he, there, was thinking of her.

They had been really happy together that day, blown by the wind. She is Mim, he proudly introduced her to the ship captain — an old almost toothless river wolf of a ruddy face, whose eye wrinkles dashed from under the peak of his cap as cheerfully as the silvery strands of hair did at its back. They spent all the trip back across the river with the captain, high up in the bridge of the ferry boat, the two men drinking vodka and laughing themselves sick. This infectious atmosphere rubbed off on Mim. What with Anton grinning and with the sun shining, she was laughing too. Well, sunshine is different up there in the middle of the resplendent river. And how happy they were later together in the car, then at his place once more, all that, after so much suffering and after he had forbidden himself to see her again.

Mim had been all along in his thoughts, if only she did not know that so well. But she knows. Then why will he not take her with him this time, why would he rather run her down? She will embark on this journey and that is it. This has no longer anything to do with Anton. All she desires is to have her frame transported to the seashore in his car, so she is simply cadging a lift.

"I no longer mean to go with you, believe me, I won't even talk to you if that's what you want. Only give me a ride. Once I've left home, I simply can't go back like that. You give me a ride now and we won't meet ever again."

The engine stopped. He wound down the window and offered her a deal.

"Look, Mim, I'm giving you this ride on one condition only. You come along now, but you have to promise you'll never come to see me again. Deal?"

"I promise." Never to see him again, reverberated in her mind, never. For a fracture of a second she was seized with panic, then her brain hastily reconstructed hope — she will sure as hell be able to see him if she wants to, without him being aware of it, why not. All she needs now is take this ride.

Her disquietude made him soften a little and he said, "Look, how about we meet ten years from now, if you want?"

"I'm not allowed to see you, true?"

"Come now, this was our deal, remember?"

No, there was no way she could bargain for that, there was too much gloom in that deal.

"But how can I promise such a thing? Do you think I can foresee my future urges? If I feel like seeing you, who knows what I might do? I'll come and see you, just like that. From a distance, don't worry." And she lapsed into a smile.

"All right," he said.

To him, she seemed to have regressed to her child self. He opened the door for her, she got in and they left.

Why had she been dead keen on coming here with him? She may have felt everything depended on that. Three days with him and love would conquer. Besides, she knew perfectly well that Anton was aching for someone to love him truly. 'Leave me alone. You're all driving me crazy.' All of them. It was not only Mim that he was mad with. Ioana too, and who knows who else. What a stupid childish thing to do for one who is in love, which must have left him cold. Still, that girl had wanted to die for him, but no, it is definitely tactless to wish to die when you are in love. Mim will live, she has a lifetime ahead of her to fight for him. Poor Ioana, you could have died and in vain, death cannot breed love, and desperation, my dear, scares people away together with their love as a whole package. How could you think that your tormented soul could have won him over? More, Mim, I want to see more, I still don't think you love me, he used to tell her often times. And had she died at his feet, he would have thought she deserved it, as dramatics gets dangerous when your performance is too true to life.

She has two days left, but she has not so much as dared admit her love to herself. She even feels uncomfortable carrying that love about her and would do anything to put it away. No, it is not for him. But what if the cause of his sulkiness is Ioana, not Mim? Maybe he is really in love with that girl, or simply feels pity for her. How could he bear the sight of Mim when the object of his love is far away, on a hospital bed? No, Mim has nothing to do with this, Mim is no longer the present.

A lovely girl, Ioana was, with long straight hair parted down the middle. And she would pull the side strands together back towards the top of her head with one hand only, like this. This is how Roxana described that girl the previous night and Mim pictured her seated on the margin of his bed, bent forward and resting her elbows on her knees, gazing down at the floor, holding that posture as she talked or kept silent. Flashes of her came to Mim, of Ioana in the silence of the pervasive odor of lime paint.

They're loafing in there playing chess all day long and once in a while come over and play rummy here, Mrs. Arvinte had disclosed to her. So this was what they were doing, as he and Mim had once used to. She remembers how they would invent funny games of their own, yes, the stern somber male had sunk in his second childhood with Mim beside him, and how overtly happy she was with her triumph. If Anton and that girl were playing, then that was sad for Mim, utterly sad, sad beyond her wildest imagination.

11 THE RIVER

The grand river. Beyond, a realm where mustangs roam at will. It is from across the river that he comes here every day, back to the warmth of home. The room is glaring with sunshine. The silent woman foibles about in nitid silence, thick-browed and wordless, her plumpish round mouth clenched shut. A far cry from her mother's exuberant mouth. How incredibly beautiful her mother is, younger, and irradiating such lively brilliance from her green eyes and sprightly cheeks. Not when she is angry, though, God how bitterly dour she can get. Her mother's eyes can laugh and her mouth can bloom open with joy, but what about this woman? Really now, has Mim ever seen her laugh? No. Anton's mother does round her lips, but Mim has never seen them split her face. True, she barely ever exposes her teeth, whereas her mother's gleam, light always sparkling on their immaculate enamel. A picture of her mother, so young and beautiful, seems to come to her mind now.

Mrs. Arvinte is also beautiful, this is what Anton says. She surely is, with her black buttony eyes and the thick black eyebrows perfectly, yet somehow timidly, arched above their glinting darkness, so much different from the stylish expansion of her mother's eyebrows. It is him, it is his eyes and his eyebrows, but his limp blond hair creates such a stark contrast, so disturbingly and totally alluring. Mim is sure his mother dyes her hair. It cannot be naturally coal-black and so dull. Even so, the oval of her face definitely belongs to a beautiful woman and her thin short nose, despite its rather bizarre shape, does not interfere with its harmony at all. On the contrary, her proud nostrils seem to add a bit of provocative spice to her countenance. And her forehead, it is only now that Mim takes in its flawless line and realizes she must have been attractive in her youth. Quite curiously, in pictures with Anton as a little boy she hardly looks any different from what she looks now. Mr. Arvinte loved her. These dense dark brows must have bewitched him. Anton has the same round mouth, but it is his father's, with opalescent white lips as if blown dry by strong Tundra winds. And his fine bladed Slavic nose, it comes from Mr. Arvinte too. Yet a strangely beautiful inner stream gives life to Anton's features. What an exquisite work of nature his mouth is, so perfectly contoured in its stiffness and also so fresh and mobile with pale moldable lips, oh, his Slavic lips. She wonders what true Slavic teeth look like, are they small, even, deep rooted teeth like his?

Anton will turn up any minute now. Mim will first see his frame in the doorway, the whole of him in flesh and blood, and his mouth will break open into a boyish smile. What if his face gets dark when he sees her? She can already hear his jaws grinding in her head, eroding each other in a manly clash. It is about time for him to arrive, let her hide away. He may have got used to being without her, who knows. Work, home, car, music, work, home, friends, Mom, and no Mim. What has it been like without her, what has it been like missing her? Her thoughts are at once strangled up in a whirl. What if nothing has missed? But there is glaring light outdoors and children are playing. The river is candidly following its course, playing with fulgent rays of life on its shimmering back. Highways are stretching as far as the seashore whizzing of rides Anton and Mim have experienced together, so how difficult can it be for them to get over the breakup? One leap is enough and they can be as happy as ever. Even the grasses on the lawns downstairs feel invitingly warm and there are benches lining the quay, vehicles speed to and fro, housewives are fretting about in their kitchens to get dinner ready and it is so hot in here with the gas burners all aflame and the dark-browed woman, his mother, her apron, the greenish blue tiny flowers bouncing and twirling, now they have taken refuge behind the pantry's door, but here they are coming back again.

Is it really possible that she can hover above the ground or not? Mim would quite often address herself this question after a night dream. She sometimes almost thought she could. If she walked quickly-quickly, ran, if she really wanted to soar and folded her whole body like a skirt trail in her lap and then hurled it up in the air, she would be instantly free, only inches above the ground. You did not need more to enjoy the feel of flying. Or was it just a dream? Now she knows she was dreaming. Almost every night, then with gradually diminishing frequency. There were times when she was so convinced it was real that she would scold herself for never giving it a try. She could well do it on her way to school, so why did she not, what was she waiting for, why would she torture her mind like that, night after night, when it was so easy to try and find out the truth. Now she realizes all these lecturing sessions came in the aftermath of the dream itself, sometime between sleepiness and wakefulness. Wakefulness and sleepiness, this reminds her of her passion for physio-psychology in her early teens and of the scientific books she used to read then. All that vast knowledge seems to have gone into thin air. But she could take up psychology again with Anton.

They enjoyed reading together. She read, while he dug

up for books. Or she was the one to ransack the book storage on top of his wardrobe for something new or interesting or appealing. Sometimes he was listening with his head lying in her lap, other times he would look up some place on a map, a word in a dictionary, a name, or a poem to give her to read. They were listening to Tchaikovsky — no, you don't like it, you have to feel it, Mim. How unfair of him. Of course she felt, but in a way somehow different from that in which she did modern music. It seemed more like a private matter to her, which required tranquility. Well yes, he would wave his arms in ample grand gestures stirring the air all around him in the room, eyes floating high in a kind of trance, while Mim would stay mum in her corner, until it got dark.

The sun has set. Vapors creep up through the surface of the ground and billow sluggishly to the skies. When they walked out onto the street the earth had already subdued the day's sultriness and Mim would inhale the remains of those faint breezes, relishing the dizziness. She would get back to Aunt Ana's, light-headed and bemused. This was in the beginning, when she had only just met him. Another day had passed, a day with him, and the offerings of the day would dim her consciousness and thrill her to pieces. Those days smell all alike in her memory. The vapors are long gone and you feel like crying, you could gather all your cells and wring them out and cry to madness.

She would plunge back to those vapors, but not now when he is going to turn up in the flesh, right here only a few steps away from her. He is her man now, her man for a fact. And will he smile, will he be joyous? She will not dare, but wait for him to smile first. "He's here," she yelps. "It's his car, have you heard it, Mrs. Arvinte, I can recognize its sound from here." She panics — run or had she better stay put? What will he say after such a long while? What if he takes no heed of her, cold and merciless as she has so often before seen him? She has got past it, and it was so tough and painful each and every time. And each time, she went through the hoop until she dared touch him again, although she knew only too well that was what he was expecting of her. There he was lying in wait while she was raking her brains for resources of courage, absolutely motionless, motion-less. She has so many times got away with that and look at herself now in his mother's kitchen. When Anton comes to his mother he cannot be other than a mere son, he is someone's child, after all, nothing more, so why should she bother her head so much about it. 'Mum, give me something to eat,' 'I've had such a hard day today, God how I've been scurrying around like mad.' And she is right next to Mrs. Arvinte now, how reassuring.

He rings the doorbell. Mim jumps to her feet in a fright. She is shaking. "What shall I do?" she asks staring in the light from the window. "I'll hide myself in the living room," she announces the woman and dashes away. She crouches down on the couch there without having enough time to shut the door. I will feign sleeping, she tells herself, what if she had been waiting there till she dozed off? Mrs. Arvinte opens the door for him. Mim should pretend being only lightly asleep so that when he comes into the room she can freely wake up and bide her time until he smiles or not. She hears his mother's voice saying jokingly: come on in, we have a guest. "Who?" He is playing fog, fakes naiveté. Could he have guessed it is her? But here he has already entered the room and she springs up from her scheming cogitation. The numbness in her body is real and she cannot react in any way, as though she was awaking from a genuine slumber. He is radiant. "Mom, fetch some glasses, will you," he calls towards the kitchen then takes a bottle of red wine out of his briefcase. "A man has come! Let's celebrate the event, shall we?" Never before has she seen him triumphant like that, his eyes, his lips could not help exploding, just like her mother when she bursts so easily into laughter. Therefore Mim makes him happy and he has finally betrayed his feelings. It is she who makes him happy, not music, not Dostoyevsky, but the girl who has just returned.

She has returned after so many days. She had left, vanished, slept far away in a desolate frigid long room cast somewhere in the fields. Anton does not know what happened there one night, the most gruesome night in her life. But she got over that too. Curiously, evil always lets go of her at the very last minute. Just before the final blow, when she expects darkness, a kind of somber plaque ready to crash her, catastrophe ceases. The eerie clanking of a key being nervously twisted into the lock so close to her heart, almost glued to its hot convulsions, only her heart and those sinister sounds, she and they at the core of the quiet, a quiet expanding as wide as the planet, the universe, absolute emptiness. Please let her at least hear a dog growl, she prayed, if only a dog barked somewhere. But it was some men's mischievous sniggering that began to wriggle right into her heart. She and the other two girls were now counting down together the blast of the evil outside. They were doing the summer practice session on an art camp and everyone had left for the weekend except for the three of them, now prisoners locked in there. There was a long squat window running almost the length of the room, but it was so high up and hardly had they started to even picture themselves escaping like that when they felt the evil increasing at the door. New sneers, sounding more and more shameless, lewd, forward, and growing impatient. A whole new bunch of keys seemed to have recently arrived. Heavy, macabre, they were alternatively jangling upon their deadlocked hearts. The girls had all turned into a compact clot on the inner side of the door, like a sort of threshold against fate. "Come on, open up, we know you're in there." There was openly declared attack now. Weapons, or better let them get in defensive formation, push something against the door to bar the brutes' intrusion. This is what they did, they finally broke the clot, dragged two iron beds and propped them against the door, but there still was a long while until daybreak. Time, only time was going to save them, God please let time pass by.

Only now does she realize how lax and malevolent time seemed to her then, when in truth it had been racing to save them. Likewise, Anton's malevolence has now proved to be nothing but pretense. Look how joyful he is and she had no idea. That night could have been less dark, white maybe, which means as tormenting, oh God, black and white akin. White nights imply hordes of contrasting meanings. Mim did not know she had to escape just in order to make him happy.

The three of them clink glasses. "A man has come back," he toasts with the corners of his lips pulled high up by his earlobes. This is a shot of happiness, Mim thinks. She took a snapshot in her mind then, and as she did so, the ruby wine stood still for her to catch a spark from the light which was flooding in with the river.

12 GREEN

Green, copious green, dark-green, teal, Persian green, blue-green, aqua, fuzzy celeste commotion. The sleek windings will take shape into light, they will not only embody but be light, a long stare aimed at the world as a whole, and at everyone's core. After that she will finish the wild flowers, deserted in a clay pot, with no wind or rain. She will load more violet into the background shade to make it gleam wet with the calling of the woods. And that race, a desperation of leaves amidst nebulous gleaming, the crimson rush away. She will delineate her mother's flawless profile, the outline of her nose, her chin, purely perfect, and the effulgence coming from her emerald eyes. The black eyes of the quiet woman from Moldova, she will paint them too someday. God how much work for her to do. All these visions are hers, and there is no way she could ever lose them, yet they all have to come to physical life for people to mind them. The scene painter has seen her landscapes and promised her a few canvases exhibited at the autumn exhibition housed in the theatre's foyer. Well, she has to study hard if she is to turn into a scenic artist. That position is more likely than not hers, so what more could she ask from life. It is going to be her dream come true: costume design, scenographic views, she will be at the heart of showbiz, from where she will shine, she will impress. She will prevail and the whole world will be hers. People are already gossiping in town, sure, they are keeping a place warm for Abrasu's daughter-in-law, and Stefan's colleagues have started to drop hints, yeah, they will soon be able to admire her art at the theatre, at least that's how the story goes. Do not be so sure, she would retort, and they would throw alluding sneers at her. Yes, Stefan told her, everything had been taken care of. And how long is it still till first September? It is the town of her dreams, her beloved town with her name written on billboards, and Anton will see them, he will come to the theatre and be overpowered by the stage itself. It will be Mim looking him straight in the eye from amidst canvases and folds and columns. But how on earth is she going to cope with her wild impulses to flee, to escape across the river and plunge into the bounty of living she once enjoyed with Anton? And how about Stefan? He will hurt like sin.

Where was his pain hiding that night, what was it like for him? She had only wanted to see Anton, just have a quick look at him, nothing more, as was is not normal for acquaintances to see each other? Her love was by then long dormant, tame and harmless, so nothing could be that wrong. When she had passed by that block that morning she had seen Anton's car parked outside and simply took a detour up the stairs to his apartment. But she was not allowed to step in. She, Mim, can anyone get that? She was forbidden to enter that damn house. Anton was expecting that girl and he wanted to keep out of any imbroglio. What imbroglio, for goodness sake, Mim was just an old acquaintance. People who know each other so well are normally happy to meet again.

That very afternoon they went out for a stroll, she and Stefan and another couple, two tranquil decorous families on a restaurant terrace, with beer and small chat and smiles. Sweltering urban summer afternoon, sterile, hollow, desolate. Mim, all locked in a stiff statue, was drifting in a sort of unworldly desert, her desperate inner conscious wailing for the whole world: there exists Anton. She was being kept prisoner. Look at them writhe and smack their lips, look at them swallow that jaundiced liquid of such a bitingly sour taste, and one more swill of fetid air, and against all this: there exists Anton. These people will carry her along, they will shuffle their lazy feet on deserted Sunday streets, and they will escort her past Anton's home again, with Stefan firmly gripping her hand.

She was advancing petrified in this strange procession when, right at the end of the block where Anton's parents lived, she broke herself free from Stefan's grip, looked him straight in the eye and started to explain. "I have to talk to his mother tonight. I have to see her."

"Are you sure you want to do this now?"

"Yes."

"Still, I don't get it. Why don't you go tomorrow morning, or any other time you wish?

"Stefan, I really don't know how I could possibly make you understand, I must discuss something with Mrs. Arvinte and I need to do it now. Wait for me at home, I won't be long, please."

"OK, if you insist—" He avoided her eyes, trying to keep up appearances and play it cool. But vowels weighed as heavy as lead in his wracked throat. "Are you sure you don't want me to wait for you here?"

"I am."

The other pair parted with them, then Stefan went on home alone, leaving her standing there like a rock, her back turned to the building she was supposed to enter, and to the other one, farther ahead, she had actually felt a sudden urge to enter. She had to go into the former one instead, where the Arvintes resided. After climbing a few steps up, she turned around and went down again, pausing to ponder for a few seconds. She would not dare gate-crash those people's house like that. Might Stefan have already got home? Captive in the ground-floor hall, she pictured him lying in ambush for her outside, curious to see if perchance she was going two blocks farther down the street, to Anton's place. What a shame to be seen by Stefan like that: a liar, a sinner, and in love. This thought gave her the creeps. Fortunately, it was not in his nature to act behind her back. If he said he would wait for her at home, then he had to be there. And her heart was pounding like crazy pushing her to get out of there and run to Anton, to see him.

She half-opens the heavy iron door and slips out. Her mind is struck with terror. What if Stefan, suspicious, is somewhere outside? In the dark, her back plastered to the wall, Mim is creeping along the warm building keeping into focus its far end and praying to reach it before someone pries into her urgent business. She is finally there and cringes at the thought of getting into the open. But she has to, so she shoots away in a scamper hoping Stefan is not watching her, poor silly her. Whew, she is again safely glued to a warm wall, a wall on whose other side families are lounging nonchalantly in their homes, people who have children, and supper is being cooked. Sounds of crockery are coming from inside kitchens, husbands are loafing in front of TV's, while she is shivering like a lunatic outside, where Stefan could hide behind any shadow. How degrading of him to be tailing her, if he really was. But just before she almost reaches the front door to the building, Stefan's sharp mind spikes right through her own: of course he knows. In the silence of his home, smoking, he sees Mim grating herself against rough strange walls and grieves deeply for her. Pictures are flickering in his mind, of her straining, of her hiding away her shame, and the cigarette smoke impassibly spiraling to the ceiling fails to blur her, fails to veil her.

She runs up the stairs and rings the doorbell. Faint noises are coming out through the door. There are several of them inside. There he is approaching. The door opens. But who is that in the slit of the door? What she sees is the pretty head of an astounded girl. "Is Anton in?" Mim asks. "Yes, just a minute." The girl leaves the door ajar and disappears in the semidarkness of the vestibule. Some spells of chatter and laughter, then directly him, right there facing her, tall and pale, blond strands dangling. "Mim, what happened to you? Come" — and he guides her down the stairs, outside, then around the corner and to the back of the building, incessantly asking her what has happened. Wordless, she is wordless and cannot control her tremor. "What is the matter with you?" he insists, this time sounding truly worried, but then her teeth start chattering uncontrollably with an inner chill. "Tell me." The worry and warmth in his voice move her so deeply. He grabs her by the shoulders and searches for her eyes. "Mim, tell me what happened."

The two of them together and nobody else, this is all she needed. She could just lie down and die. The two of them alone, it seems the people in his flat no longer exist, not even for him, their host. It feels like that in the air.

They are back on the evening when she ran away and he ran after her down the stairs, down the alley, on the street, calling out: Mim! — he did not want life without Mim — Mim! Or on the evening when he grabbed her shoulders just like he did now, in the parking lot among the blocks of flats. "Mim, you know what this place is, you know perfectly well where I've brought you now; this is our place, isn't it?" He had been hurting her with incredible words and she had stood listening to each and every one of them. He was receiving no answer and was obviously in hot water, left to patch things up on his own. In spite of his lingering hope to get some reaction from her, that time Mim as he knew her had simply vanished. "You think I don't care? I do care for you, Mim, I care a lot. You don't believe me?" And he looked her in the eye like a madman. "If I spoke those words to you, it was only because I want you to be like my mother." He was holding back tears. He, of all people! "Exactly like my mother, do you understand?" He could either strike or cry. There was nothing in between.

Now her response is not coming for the simple fact that there is no need for her to articulate anything. All she wants is this, Anton and Mim alone for a few moments. He says, "Look, if you want you can come up with me." Yes, the tone in his voice holds the same consideration — alien and cold — as on the evening she first visited his flat. He only wants to spare her feelings, which he overtly expressed that very morning: Mim, come now, don't make me be rude with you. "Get a friend and bring him over, and we can watch some movies on the video." Quite instantly she fancies she is able to talk, now that she can get into his home as a friend, which sounds decent enough. Everything gets settled in the end, so she says, "I have a friend, yes, I'll come with him in a shot, I live in the neighborhood." They will all be friends, she thought, Anton and Stefan will talk together and thus, little by little, she will finally come around. "But no—" Something is lying heavy at his heart. "I don't think I'll be able to do that, I'd feel kind of odd." He and Mim had to remain intact, it would hurt him too much otherwise. And so would it her. Anton and Mim lives on. "I just wanted to be a minute with you. It's hard to explain, it just came to me and I needed to see you. Just a whim, I have to dash." And she fleets away back between the blocks of apartments. It no longer matters whether Stefan sees her or not, tears are literally washing her down the neck, washing her with pure renewed life, while she is gulping back the life that was.

She only stopped when she got to Mrs. Arvinte's door. She rang the doorbell and cast a desperate glance at her from the threshold. The next thing she knew she was sitting in the warm kitchen peeling cloves of garlic with the mother who kept on about Mim aiding her son to get rid of all the evil forces around him. "Day in and day out he's hanging out with those kids staying up late every night. Oh, I don't know what's got into him. You shouldn't let go of him, Mimi, don't give up." And what was she doing there, was she not supposed to be at her parents'? No, she had rented a flat a few blocks away to work on her diploma paper. She was boarding with Stefan, she thought all covered in shame, she was treating him like a landlord. And she instantly felt sheer disgust with herself. This jerked her from her agony. She should go home, her place was there with Stefan. She rose to her feet, said goodbye, and left.

She will forever treasure Anton and Mim. She will paint effulgent light on her canvas, a glinting blue-green stare arrowed at the world.

13 PEACE

Quiet had reigned for quite a while now all over the house, in the women's room, and in the men's room. Mim just existed, apathetic, within the globule of tranquility suspended between her and the two women seated motionless on chairs nearby. She was lying numb in a kind of void, an inner void merging into the surrounding one, her palimpsest for future ventures of recharging. All she could hear was the faintest rustling of inner voices telling her of new life, back from square one again. Her dear covert energies were there for her, ready to help. She seemed to have expanded herself like a balloon and was somehow floating within this strange physical representation of herself, above the paraphernalia in the room — pies on a platter, TV-set, napkins and glasses, above the souls in there and above their blanched, timorous carcasses. She contemplated her own body, molded in the armchair as it was. She would gladly give it up for a while, with its physical mass as a matter of fact.

A shadow stirs in a corner. It is moving in from the other room, Anton's figure holding two transparent wine glasses. The next moment, a sketch with limbs sprawled over the carpet on the floor as he gets down on his knee at the bottom of the armchair. In the silence of that confined space, he is extending his arm holding out a goblet for her. But Mim, up there, remains unmoved. And as she lies like a statue on a pedestal, she becomes aware of his face in the corner of her eyesight, a face which slowly comes into focus, red-eyed. Pure aqua is glimmering at the bottom of his pupils. He, Anton, has been crying, is crying. Then sounds come to her ears: Mim, please, will you forgive me? She comes back to her senses, concentrating on hearing — why was Anton crying? He does not seem confident she could hear him. "Mim, Mim, can you hear me? Mim, I'm crying because I want you to be like my mother. I want you to be like her, Mim." Mrs. Arvinte, she thinks, the woman from Moldova tending day and night to the needs of the men in her family, the woman who worships them. But what had Mim done? What had happened earlier that night?

She was not allowed to greet other male persons, not even her fellow students, nothing was supposed to relate her in any way to a male, and that also included objects. A mere book, yes, Anton had forbidden her to study on a course book borrowed from one of her colleagues.

"In half an hour I'll be back, and I don't want to find you reading from this book. Return it to him right away." The more he was imperative, the more the implication that she had to call up that boy was driving him out of his mind, so he decreed, "Wipe his phone number off your notebook if you want to be with me."

"Yes, but I first have to call him if I am to return the book."

"You'll find a way. It's not my business how to deal with this."

How on earth could she give up that course book when she had an exam to take? He will have to cope with that, one way or another, and if he does not, then—

"Can't you really understand? I'm sitting an exam in a

few days and this is the only copy available, we're all in our class using it in turns, not just me, and when I'm done I'll pass it on to a girl, isn't it better that way?"

But no, he won't reason with that. So, aiming his index finger at the wretched book, he announced, "I'll be back, all right?" And he raced out, banging the door shut behind him.

Her only roommate who had witnessed the scene remained agape and crossed herself as soon as he had left. Holding back tears, Mim did not give up on the book. On the contrary, she turned on the steam, promising herself never again to fail an exam because of him. She had deferred one the previous summer.

Anton came back later that evening, pushed the door wide open, and halted in its frame keeping a straight face. She broke off her reading and lifted her head, only to see him stand rooted in his stance and observing her. He cast a fatherly glance in her direction and pouted his mouth with mock child-like peevishness which he presently developed into a grin as broad as the span of the doorway. His subsequent advance toward her seated at the table near the window was quasi paternal, as was his arm rested on her shoulders and also the warmth in his voice when he asked her, "Are you studying?" The father was content to find his daughter in her place, plunged into study. She felt him markedly proud. Had he managed to consider things reasonably in the meantime, she wondered, or had he simply put on an act earlier, in order to see her reaction, or test her resilience?

The icy touch of glass makes her unclasp slightly her hand, rested as it was on the arm of the armchair, and she then cannot help turning her palm up to take the goblet he is holding out for her.

"Please clink with me, Mim. This is all I'm asking of you. This time I won't ask you to forgive me, I don't deserve it."

He has drawn nearer and is keeping his own glass at the level of her eyes, so close to her face, fixing her from above its hem with a persuasive gaze. His ivory lips begin to take a bulky grotesque shape through the liquid and Mim, contemplating this mouth beyond the wine glass, so incongruous within the context of the collage, is struck by the bizarre thought of a fourth dimension. Ha, she is using Anton for an experiment. He is nothing other than an ordinary human being, a boy who has this obsessive desire that his woman take after his mother. Listen here good people — and Mim places the image of her hands on her hips, he wants me to take after Mrs. Arvinte. Well then, some investigation is needed here, has Mr. Arvinte ever beaten his wife? Involuntarily, her eyes focus again on the element in motion of the collage and an inward impetus prompts her to giggle. What she does though is say, "Clink!" And she actually clinks glasses with him, what the hell.

His mouth brings to her mind a sense of austere gayety, the image of a weird Venetian mask, vitreous and elusive, now stern, the next moment gracious and beaming, and true, he no longer can keep his lips together, they are now sliding one upon the other until they finally come apart, closing in on her face. It must be his beautiful mouth, so she sneaks a glance at his eyes to make sure. They are swept in penitent tranquility of a tame tint of bole. Oh Asherah, the mother goddess from Levant, she prompts to herself.

He only says, "Cheers!" in response.

Mim still can make neither head nor tail of this and of what happened. She does not want to know. She feels like leaving everything behind, all of them and herself. But where have the women gone? She did not see them leave. Everyone had retreated to various corners in the house to make space for their peace, Mim and Anton's.

14 THE STREET

This is the little street, but she passes by looking straight ahead. Not a mere glance along its mute quietness. It is anyway dead in her soul, so let it rest in peace. But does she really not hurt at all? It feels as though never in her life has she walked this way, no rustle, no whisper, nobody, nothing.

In truth, this little street was once thriving with sweet-scented life. Fragrances were lolling on the sidewalks and would invade her at the shiest motion, broil her senses at the most secretive whisper. Her illusory swing hanging between lime-trees, where thoughts used to lavish love on her, Anton's alabaster presence and, radiating silence, the tunnel of his mind. The front gate and the flowers, the interminable passageway always swept in darkness, and then the little camouflaged patio where she would wait for the sun. The windowless room, damp and cold, and the door, wow, the portal of light through which she used to travel into the blue, with the branches of the apricot-tree framed within. It was through that glass door that she had seen the thunderstorm and it was beyond that glass door that she saw infinity, everything. She lived here for one year, at Aunt

Ana's. One whole university year and the whole ensuing summer.

As a little girl, she would come here with her brother and parents. Each summer she used to look forward to it, knowing that, after a troublesome night of expectation and the click-clack of wheels on the rails, there followed the hidden little courtyard. She would coil her legs knees up to her chest, enclosed in the middle of that patio as if inside a hot womb. From that posture she would sniff in bewilderment for the pulse of the universe, relishing the intimate relationship she was establishing between her tiny soul and the expanse — what might have been and what will be, whence, how further away. Everything might have existed for a long, very long time, and that was marvelous. How many kings and queens, and naked people ripping off with bare teeth hunks of meat unknown to her, eyes glinting around a bonfire? The glimmer in their eyes reflected huts and stone dwellings, houses glazed in sunlight, parched blue walls, palaces painted in sumptuous damp colors, stones amassed indomitably at the crossways of sand routes. How many vagrants and how many toilers, strings of burnished slaves leaning forward their naked pumped up chests? And a wan-looking girl exiting the darkness where she had laid an endearment bouquet for her gold-plated man, a child. Tomina had burst into tears at reading about that flower bouquet, her mother saw her and Tomina shut herself into the bathroom to shed tears freely and try to understand time. Oh, how many young girls clad in straight linen gowns and how many ruthless men had seen exactly what she was seeing from the courtyard, staring at the skies. There was an instant, nothing but a split second, when she felt a sort of communion with them all, the sole spark of a scintillant blade cutting instantly through the same meat, time.

The family would call her to dinner and they would enjoy together the rich tomato salads, forks bustling about in the bowls. There was congenial chatter and clatter and her mother laughed — she would turn beautiful beyond measure, her beaming mouth and eyes appearing to make everyone even more cheerful. That was why people looked forward to seeing her and they, at home, were joyless without her and could not wait for her to come back from work, she brought light and beauty and well-being. Aunt Ana would laugh too and recount all sorts of stories from times past, when she was young, about men and women. They were young and they loved and they fought. There were times when Tomina could barely grasp the meaning of what the grownups were saying, and she gathered they were keeping things from her and her brother, so they left out certain words, key words, and it was then that she thought men and women was the topic, those things children could not understand. Some things, she knew — she would chuckle. They were so secretive and cautious, not knowing that Tomina had so many times cried with understanding. Yes, she could feel that age-old consuming longing to comprehend infinity, man and woman together.

What is *infinity*, she would ask Mom and Dad. Of all the words she had heard, this was the only one whose meaning she could not understand. With time, she came to realize on her own that it was a question, a question gaping in brusque waves, wider and wider, larger than her mind, up to a point when it blasted and she could no longer draw in air. She would arch her neck upwards and indulge in tears, then quickly hide herself in front of a mirror, where she reveled in distorting her own flushed features. She would smudge moisture on the cheeks, the neck, with palms stretched as if for a magical ritual, calling forth inner springs of felicity. She waited in silence for the growing flow to invade the flesh of her cheeks, inflate her lips and uncover her teeth until it spattered her with light from the mirror. That was a flicker of happiness telling her that she was blessed to be born in this world and that she had a long,

long lifetime ahead till old age. She who could perceive the infinite would strike the world with her flashes of love. She continued to bathe like that in happiness and her own fluids, staring at herself, until she froze in the depth of her pupils. Despite her urge to run away, she stayed there seduced by the darkness inside, imagining that something terrible would happen if she broke the spell. So she waited and waited to flee from the face of death.

The little garden was her miracle and her secret, as much her mirth as it was her distress. She was only a child, she was well aware of that and she would sometimes rebuke herself out loud in a mature condescending voice. What she needed was patience, which was sad, but who should she turn to? And she would give in to smiling. She smiled like an old woman thinking that people would laugh at her if they caught her doing that. And how about her Mom and Dad? They would get into a fright, as they had no idea what Tomina was doing in the secret garden. They would be dumbfounded to see on their child's face such mature sadness or delight, such tormenting questioning. This was what she would be after, a partner for her quest. When she grew up she would look for someone like that.

That explains her exuberance that summer. She was perpetually happy because she was perpetually waiting for him to come, and everything she felt or guessed in her soul and everything she knew then and from then on would imperceptibly vaporize into him and vice versa. And were they not to find the truth, they would at least be happy to share the same knowledge, as one single body and mind. She used to spend the mornings with books on her lap, sacredly seated in the heart of her garden, but she could not bring herself to rivet her mind on them. As hours swept by she was living as she had never lived before or imagined one could live. Before long she would have to initiate the going out ceremonial again, she would put on nice clothes and do her hair to meet him. She thought of all the people who had been, multitudes whose existence her mind had the power to hold, which made those course books and the exams appear ridiculous. Her mind could cut through the essence of timelessness, so why should she attend those funny meetings where people like her would wait to hear what she had to say and assess her knowledge by scribbling things on their sheets of paper? She could bone up all those books and assimilate everything if she chose to, but those precise exams were insignificant and she would laugh them off in only a few years from then. Time flies by anyway and she would lightly find herself 'after years'. Discouragingly enough, though, time was made up of instants. Be they sharp and painful or happy and large, be they minute or lengthy and oppressive, it was in one of these instants that life could get shut off, and yes, she had to pass successively through them all, one by one. No matter how easy it could be for thought to fly years away, it was you with your body and mind that had to strive and endure. But she would ponder these things later, as right now she was in such high spirits. She woke up every morning facing the sky and realizing, yet again, how fortunate she was. That was why she would stretch her body, beaming and whooping with happiness, hidden from anyone's view. Yet, she felt like breaking her secret wide open for the whole world to know. She would fidget about in and out the house until she ended up again into her spot in the middle of the garden, course books piled up on her lap and thoughts drifting, either slipping back to what had been or leaping forward, and featuring Anton all over. He would regularly make his appearance in front of the gate outside. As soon as she heard the car's horn blaring, her heart started racing and she rushed outside. They met and went away.

And that little street looks so distant now. Mim seems to have forgotten about Aunt Ana altogether and, the very moment she met Anton, it seemed it was even her own parents she dismissed from her mind. She will not brood about Aunt Ana right now. She was her mother's aunt and Mim had never been that close to her, but has lately started to become obsessed with her image as a young woman. She wondered how beautiful she could have been, young Ana all her life in love with one man only, her first. Mim had been hearing that all through her childhood, the most important thing, which Ana would forever repeat. Now and then her mother would commence to sing the praises of her beauty. 'Aunt Ana was beautiful,' she would say, lost in a brown study and strengthening in high arches: beautiful. How beautiful? Tomina had several times studied photos of her, who is in this one, and who is here? She was looking for young Ana. But only late did she come to appreciate the perfect features, the proud plump mouth, and the immense, vitreous black eyes. Ana's aged face comes back to her memory and it strikes her that Ana was neither old nor young. The face Tomina was familiar with had always merged into the youthfulness of the one in old pictures giving birth to one particular image of Ana. That is why Tomina never understood her mother whenever she said Ana was beautiful. For her, Aunt Ana remained Aunt Ana as she knew her, and she could also never get over the word 'aunt', which weighs heavy enough on a child's mind. Whence did she get the idea that 'aunt' was against youth and beauty? But just when Ana's youth and her love were about to come into focus, Tomina met Anton. There has been no Aunt Ana ever since, her exaggerated attachment to her parents has slackened, and so has the flame of her love for her mother.

Aunt Ana passed away without Mim feeling any emotion at all. She saw her lifeless body laid on the long table in her house and left, she left with him, they left with their friends headed for the seaside and laughed and had fun. It seemed as though Aunt Ana had never even existed. And after so much time she dreamed about her. And in that dream Ana urged Tomina to be happy, as her place was there beside him. She advised her to set aside her pride and return to him, to forgive him. Go after him, that is the right thing for you to do, she seemed to be telling her in a peaceful voice, from amidst a nebula dimly lit by the glow of her love, her first love. Ever since she woke up the following morning she has been looking back upon Ana trying to ask for her forgiveness, but no, there is nothing to repent about, Ana understands everything, she knows. Why should she sneak a glance back at the green gate now, there is nothing there. What Mim knows is the only thing that matters.

15 COMMOTION

"Isn't he handsome? Look at him," Mim insisted.

"Yes, I guess so," acknowledged Costin.

"And isn't he happy!"

Mim existed in the light of Anton's serene beam. Yes, the exultation he was radiating had stretched his skin with such surprising plasticity that the light it reflected simply dazzled everyone around, making him shine like an Apollo at the head of the table. Mim was overtly delighted watching, from her side of the table, those lively ivory lips, thinking that was the tint she would choose if she was ever going to put on foundation makeup. She fancied gushing about him with her nearest table companion, their friend Costin, their witness in the train station the night they first met. She figured Anton would thus hear her above the excited chatter of the others and understand it was no one other but him that existed for her. Although Costin was cold, a near stranger to her, he just happened to be seated there right between Mim and Anton, like a welcomed medium. The glaring gusts in Anton's eyes, now deep dark and glossy, were engulfing the entire room, but Mim could feel it was on her they were focusing their power and it seemed all the walls around were reflecting fire on her, without mercy.

"Happy birthday," the whole table cheered in chorus.

Mrs. Arvinte held up her glass. "Happy birthday, Antonush, and whatever you wish may come true, dear Mom's darling—" Then, breaking her shyness, she shot the latter part "—I wish you to be happy and well with Mimi together."

Mim's heart dropped. What if his eyes lost luster and the walls got dull and even the glass bottles stopped glinting on the table? The brightness in the room may have dimmed, but just for a heartbeat, for Anton went on reveling and laughing, and his eyes seemed to be searching for hers. He thrust two arrows right through her pupils. His pupils were so wide that she was all absorbed through their gaping blackness. The clamor lulls. All the souls around them soar away in a hushed cloud, while only the image of Mr. Arvinte's lips linger on her retina, voiceless — happy birthday, they may have uttered. If only she dared let herself in, now that the passage is wide open, look how he is ushering her in from the head of the table, all-powerful and buoyant. Mim fluttered her eyelids just once and it was all gone. "Mimi, shall I pour you more wine?"

It was Mr. Arvinte, who was attending to her, and here came Mrs. Arvinte with a platter of pies.

"Look here, these are the cheese pies you like most, Mimi."

"Ah, Moldavian pies!" Mim rejoiced politely.

She was clumsy to receive this attention with Anton there, overseeing the table. The more so, since he had not addressed her a single word when they clinked glasses. Cheers, and that was all.

Yet it was him who had picked her up from the student campus. She had been waiting for him since early afternoon till dark and he still was not coming. But it was his birthday and she was sure he would turn up. She knew his mother had made preparations for his party and their friend was coming too, the one in the station, accompanied by the girl he had waited for then. The ballet dancer, blonde and large-mouthed, with big white front teeth. Her legs, although pretty thick and shapeless and looking like two straight pipes, were exceptionally long and there was damn much sex-appeal about the way she bent her torso forward in a perfect right angle, or arched it backwards, her thin mane dangling loose to the ground. Now and then she would give you a ballerina pose and spin her frame in a gracious pirouette, which Mim reckoned could inflame any man's curiosity.

They were once both on the beach, Anton and Mim, staring in the horizon over the expanse of hot sand, over the strip of wet sand just before the water, the furrows of white foam gently sweeping up the shore, flickers of people's ankles, calves, children's skinny torsos and limbs, that girl's high legs, the outline of her body advancing toward the water against the blue-scape of sea and sky. They shared the same picture and knew they were both watching her, when Anton broke the silence.

"She looks pretty good, doesn't she?"

"Uh-huh," she agreed leniently.

"Yay! She's got those long legs, man!"

Mim could not afford to throw herself into such an exchange. She should not be there, in the first place, as was she a man to respond to that? So she made efforts to keep mum, afraid she could just let the cat out of the bag and embark on a cold analysis of another woman's figure with him. This would alter her femininity, would turn her into a male, which she was definitely not, and Mim in the train station would vanish. So she kept staring, speechless, as the ballerina was slowly disappearing under the water. She was waiting to see though how far he was going to carry that put-on.

"But no, you are a totally different build."

Mim's body was therefore no foil to hers, so he had given up contrasting them. Although Mim lacked something he admired in that girl, her body was beyond compare, a body he favored and relished without any specific reason. Mim now wanted him to continue speaking to himself, as though she were not there, which he did.

"You see, she doesn't have your waist and your curves, that delicate shape of yours. She is flat, that's it."

Mim was still sometimes wondering whether he had added those words then just in order to draw a conclusion in her favor, to spare her the hurt. There were times when she felt Anton was someway angry with himself for fancying Mim. He desired her in spite of some obscure principle of his. Only God knew what. Likewise, there was something in that blonde that intrigued him. They had met several times lately with her and Costin, and Anton would sometimes gage her by the eye, always from behind, occasionally sharing impressions with Mim, maybe when he felt he had been caught out. Or was he trying to turn Mim into his accomplice? Accomplice in his lust for life he was so proud of and loved japing about. I would die to watch the lips between a woman's legs while she does the splits, mmm, how I love to picture them fretting each other and contorting, he had once whispered in her ear while they were watching a ballet show.

Mim had started to be obsessed with that girl's style, the easiness with which she offered ballet demos wherever and whenever, sometimes with an overt dedication, to Anton for example, regardless of Mim's presence. She had a peculiar way of keeping her trunk erect, her long neck always stretched in perfect line with her spine, no matter her position. And she took great delight in throwing her legs up in the air when you least expected. However, her grace had something brazen about it, not outright licentious, but rather foreshadowing in a tonic, sportive way the humors of sin. Mim secretly considered the prospect that some of that girl's attitude might rub off on her, the more so now that she found out cheeky girls appealed to Anton, as they did in fact to all men. But why should she copy a style that was not in her nature when men felt attracted to her own? Mim was not cheeky and she did not need to do anything special to have men come to her. Had Anton not done the same? Still, she felt that her inner will to attract, that innate brashness which characterizes any true woman's movements had started to lessen. She had met Anton and her instinct was no longer sharp on the prey. The ballerina girl had jerked her back to reality: a woman should never stop seducing her man.

In each gesture and any look men saw hidden clues women would not even dream of. They gauged and compared them and inwardly animated their bodies at will in all sorts of positions, just like in a puppet comedy, either to indulge their fantasies or simply for fun. Mim saw in men's minds monstrous caricatures of female limbs, in Anton's mind and in Costin's as well. She even figured the latter having visualized her in God knows what obscene or funny stills. Was it not true after all that man first erred in his mind, where there was infinite space for sin to accrue? *Homo ludens, homo sapiens ludens.* With evolution, the play had been gradually transferred to the mind, men's intellectual playground. They, the artful creatures, the foremost in everything, yet stirred up by females. Them, females, the static, the sluggish and the fat who tended to their chores within reach range, around the fireplace. On the one hand the heedful women jabbering to themselves about today's and tomorrow's needs, and on the other hand the playful men, the gamers, devisers of their own mental nights. Ah, little blonde lady, you and the likes of you are walking the world just in mock of male play, aren't you? Whatever might be spinning in men's heads has been passed down to your genes. Although Mim had not given her much attention that day at the seaside, it had been a while since the girl started to haunt her consciousness: women like her among us were the necessary squeaky toys that foregrounded the ludic world of men, the artists of mankind.

The guests are dancing in the adjoining room, which has ceased to be theirs. It is now a dark hall filled with perfect frigid discotheque sound. The old record-player is shut in the closet together with the lofty music in the now silent grooves, since the boys have installed the latest hi-fi sound and light technique, the same they recently tested at the community center in the village across the river. Maybe this is where her feeling of frigid coolness comes from. The night ride to the pontoon; then the silent crossing of the river, only they and a couple of other cars on the ferry; the others, Anton's friends who were of her age, some good years younger than him. She was so cold and hungry and sleepy and thought she would rather be cuddling in her warm cot in the student dormitory to fall asleep early so that she could feel good during courses the following day, look beautiful and turn heads in the university's corridors.

She would give impromptu performances in those huge halls, cabaret scenes in which she mimed throwing an imaginary feather stole over her shoulder, waving willowy arms in the air and moving lasciviously among the chance audience, brandishing an elegant hand from behind a marble column and then appearing herself in a vamp's pose in front of one or another of her colleagues. She would hoof her way up to the balustrade of the sumptuous upper gallery and glide rolling along while stroking its cool luster, her gaze hovering over the palatial central hall downstairs or lost across, to the opposite side of the gallery. Her whole play seemed to call out: look at me, I am throbbing with impetuous talent all dedicated to you people, I love you. She and her student mates would enter a room to attend the next seminar class and she could barely wait for it to be over, so she could make her grand comeback and perform again.

And look how she is wilting now waiting for a glance, a gesture, a mere word from Anton, to see what Anton wanted, to do whatever Anton suggests. She is back in the darkness of the dancing room. There is a faint play of glimmering lights from the technical paraphernalia and her eyes are also becoming aware of the dim glow of the night light outside, probably the moon and the street lamps in occult fusion. There are five of them in here, the very same party at the community center. It is the fifth one who has brought in the hi-fi, as this is his passion, to mix music and lighting for events. All the other four mock auditioned for DJ that night in the village, including Mim. All through her adolescence did she keep the want to do that, in spite of being well aware that it was only the offspring of party potentates with connections abroad that could succeed in ventures like that. Just like those boys. She was at least being offered a chance to put herself to the test and exorcize those latent dreams. Much to her disillusion, the timbre of her voice lost vibrancy over the microphone and she sounded lifeless. She realized she should give up her femininity in order to sound good, which was out of question, with Anton staring. She knew that performing on stage was all about exaggerating, about training your voice to shout on low notes, to beat at beastly rhythms, or to utter words in a firm masculine tone. No, that would not suit her. It was not for her, it was for men, as were they not the first actors in history? A feather flew off Mim's mind that night, leaving her in perfect balance with herself, yet she can still feel its trace — an apostrophe telling her something was there once.

"Well guys, that's it," Anton said rubbing his palms with satisfaction, once he had unlocked the door to the community center and let everyone in. Minutes earlier he had been at the steering wheel with Mim in the front seat next to him. Below the tan velour driver cap, Mim knew, there lurked his powerful square Tatar-like jaw bones, framed by strands of fair hair, and his lips, when he kept quiet, pushing one into the other to help him make out the road ahead in the dark. The other three were crammed in the rear seat with items of technical equipment carefully held on their laps. There was readiness for a lot of wheeling and dealing in there, e-hey, the villagers, who were all fast asleep at that hour, did not have a clue, not even in their dreams, that the car speeding across the village in the quick of the night was carrying loads of gear meant to entertain them, and that a threesome of determined associates were rolling up in it, lured by the bundles of banknotes under their mattresses.

"Are you cold?" Anton asks shortly sneaking a peep in her direction — to check on her looks, she thinks.

She perceives herself ugly, her skin heavy with dust and her hair freezing dry. She answers, "No, not very cold."

"Just say it, and I'll turn up the heat. See how warm it'll get in here." He dedicates her a smile, with the same purpose of warming her up, then raises his voice and addresses his friends in the rear, "Hey you folks back there, how are the gang doing? Shall I turn the heat up or not?"

"It's OK," Costin's reply comes promptly.

"How long is it still?" the blonde lingers on her vowels in a charming drill.

"Here we are. Look, it's right there on the left."

The community center. A long rectangular military-like bunker, sad and desolate in the night. Petty dark windows. There alight the entire carload of city folks into the gelid atmosphere, all stretching their limbs to remove the numbness and smoothing down their clothes and hair. Anton adjusts his cap over his brows, ready to do business. Every Thursday and Saturday night they will organize a disco in the village. Costin and his other friend possess state-of-the-art equipment sent over from abroad, as well as cassettes with the latest club music and hits, while Anton has had everything set with the mayor and the party secretary, who agreed to rent out the big hall to them. Subsequent to this try-out session they will fix a business appointment to discuss details together.

"Aaah," Anton gasps, "I don't think I have the key." He is eyeing Mim waiting for her reaction.

"Uh-oh," she exclaims with a start. "I don't believe you."

At which his mouth goes into a smug grin, while he carefully takes the object out of one pocket of his sheepskin coat and, brandishing it through the air, calls out at the whole group, "Look what I've got here!"

They are stamping their feet to keep warm, as in an odd kind of chorus cheer for Anton to manage to unlock that old board door with drab paint peeling off all over it. Finally it is done and they get in. Right on their left is the stage, perked high up. To their right there spreads out a seemingly interminable empty space whose cement floor and bleak walls emanate an icy cold sensation. After figuring out where to place the equipment, the two boys go repeatedly out to fetch the hi-fi compact system, the amplifier, the floor-stand speakers and all the other necessary devices and leads. The table on the stage and the couple of odd wooden stools come in handy. The ballerina girl is frolicking about the place on her own, while Mim is staring farther into the dark void trying to imagine it crowded with young village folks. She envisages a mass of dull-colored synthetic winter jackets and above, a sea of dark-haired heads interspersed with glowing cigarette butts, hands raking back sleazy hair, drooling grins wobbling on top of Adam's apple necks that jut out from between the wings of their squalid, flat opened collars. Yes, they could fill up a hall like that, she concludes to herself, if only the music was going to be loud enough to reach as far as its other end.

She is snapped from her reverie by Anton's sprightly

voice. "Well, what do you think?"

"Uhh… I don't know, well, I think we could do it."

"It's freezing in here now, but wait until you see these folks flock in, they won't feel a thing." Anton gives her an omniscient snigger, in eager expectation for his buddies to return so that the threesome can poke fun at the crowds they are going to summon to the disco.

Mim is trying hard to feel at ease, as aw, is she not downright boring. The boys have already installed the equipment by now, put out the electric bulb above the stage and turned on the music and the lighting system. An electronic French Can-Can fills with vital energy that wretched hall, which, ooh, possesses excellent acoustics, due probably either to the cold or to its bareness. Mim instantly has a feeling of belonging with the group, herself manipulator of the body movements, grimaces, and emotions of the hordes of youths that are to pervade the entire cement floor. The blonde girl is now dancing down there, while Mim, up on the stage, has got warmed up to the atmosphere and, all ablush with excitement, is techno frolicking on the wooden boards. She keeps an eye on the two boys who are exerting themselves on the electronic equipment and at the same time gives Anton scenographic instructions about where to best place the lights. He is beaming with satisfaction that Mim is cheery, that things are going to work out well, and that this discotheque idea was damn good.

It is his birthday anniversary now and the same two boys are busy doing the exact same thing, right now tending the lighting system. Costin's girlfriend is dancing alone, twisting and wiggling her torso, bending it backward and forward, and now and then hoisting one leg or the other as high up as her jeans will allow. And all this time Mim is waiting seated in the darkness. Anton enters the room, encompasses it with an observatory glance, and gets out, leaving Mim to wonder what other chores he has to do still.

She dare not call after him, waiting for him to come to her instead. Just like she had been waiting all afternoon to be picked up.

She was leaning on the sill of the dormitory room window when loud bangs in the door startled her upright and she twirled around to see the door wide open, the stale flat white of the corridor wall, nothing, and then suddenly Anton's frame filling up that colorless background. He was posing for her in the door frame, eyes glowing and sending fulgid daggers right through her, his mouth writhed in a bizarre smile under the tan corduroy cap pulled low over his forehead.

"Mim..." he uttered her name in an undulating pitch. What he meant was he was there for her. "Come," he added after a brief pause. She had sensed something unnatural in his voice and the word 'come' had popped like a cork out of a bottle neck. He pushed the door shut and made for her direction in an ungainly prance, grinning. "Today is my birthday, Mim, you know that. And I'm here to take my girlfriend with me, come on."

Mim had watched stiff-silent his dramatic entrance, keeping a bewildered smile on her lips. Realizing he had drunk a bit too much, she pictured him seated at table in somber little rooms in the village across the river, joining big-bellied and ruddy-faced men, happy birthday, one more drink and one odd glass to Anton's health, over sadness past, and memories, and joys to come, all there laid on a white tablecloth, or a green one, among bottles and glasses more or less full. He must have been drinking with nearly all the people he had been visiting that day, all this time with the anticipation of coming here to take her away. Trying to figure out the right wishes to make, she could not find a way out of conventionalism, overwhelmed by a strange kind of clumsiness she had never experienced before. Taking Anton in with eyes full of affection, she felt like telling him how much she loved him, but she did not know how to begin.

Anton drew her close to him, pushed her chin up with his index finger, and asked, "Mim, what's the matter?"

"I'm happy, that's all, I'm happy you've come. Happy birthday!" She could not bring herself to give him a kiss.

He pushed her face higher up to his mouth and Mim touched his lips lightly, with her eyelids half closed. Then he said, "Are you ready?"

"Can't you see me? I've been waiting dressed like this since three o'clock."

"You thought I wasn't coming, eh?"

"Maybe I did…, but thank God you've come."

He stretched out his arm in a courteous manner, inviting her to the door. They managed to lollop their way there, Mim dizzy with emotion at the thought she was going away with him. Happy birthday, have fun, her roommates wished them smilingly, each perched up on their beds. Anton slung his arm over her shoulders, weighing heavy upon her body, and started to gush about his girlfriend, mmm, and how he had come to carry her off, aww, and they were flying off. They finally got in the car, wait, I have a gift for you, no, not now, later — and he dumped the clutch and the car shot out screeching.

"Hey, take it easy!"

"It's my birthday today, you get it? And I'm damn happy."

"OK, you're happy, I understand. We're headed to your place, aren't we?"

"Wait and you'll see."

He was speeding through a maze of narrow, cobbled side streets Mim had never even heard of. Although the car was jolting and shaking like mad, it kept floating bravely, pitching and rolling like a boat on rough sea. At some point she got really scared, with him apparently plastered and crazier every minute. The deeper they got into that tangle of streets, the firmer he was in stepping on the gas pedal.

"Anton," Mim kept shouting, "Anton, what are you doing?"

"It's my birthday," he repeated with growing enthusiasm, "and I do whatever I want."

She found a reason to make him stop, so she said, "Pull over, I want to give you my present."

"Not now," he whispered, "when I tell you."

Oh, my God, was Mim imploring inwardly, pressing her palms against the glove box as if that was her last resort. He is insane, she thought. Never before had she seen him that crazy and she had no idea where he was taking her and what he was up to. For a second she was thrust with the same fear she felt on their first night in the parking lot, when he began to pull her legs apart like crazy.

They were now at the upper end of a street which sloped steeply down to the river. As the car sped downhill, Mim did not even feel the jolting, for fear it would only stop once it plunged into the cold dark water. At first seized with panic, she then gave in to acceptance. Her brain was swept by a kind of leveling beatitude that they were together. The car soon jumped and stopped still. He had pulled over halfway down that street.

"What's here?" she asked.

"Nothing, just a street."

"Then why have you pulled over?"

"That's what I wanted, it's my birthday, remember?"

"You gave me a terrible fright, you know? Now, here is my present for you," she said as she took a package out of her bag and held it up for him to take. She read out the birthday card she had written for him, then leaned forward and touched his lips.

Anton stopped her. "Mim, do you call this a kiss?" He crushed her to his chest and they kissed full. Then he said, "Mim, I just wanted to be alone with you for a bit tonight. The others are at my place already."

"They are? What are you doing here then?"

"Yes, they're all there. Shall we go?" he asked sobering up suddenly and turning his palms up matter-of-factly.

He drove in his usual manner all the way to his parents' place and Mim kept wondering how he had managed to ride at such high speeds on those narrow meandering lanes. As it seemed, drunkenness had sharpened his reflexes and, wow, what a man he was, and all hers. Never ever would she be afraid with him beside her.

Mim gets herself a full glass to fool away her loneliness and sits again on the margin of the bed. Holding the glass like a candle in her hand, a wave of sickness surges through her body, from the venter up to her constricted throat, and she can feel madness slowly spreading all over her brain at the thought that Anton is no longer coming. But the light from the rest of the house flashes through the slit of the door and he is right in. He stumbles on the blonde girl who is dancing, then keeps groping his way to where the boys are, seemingly taking no heed of Mim. He plays at wanting to make sure everyone is having fun, then twists on place and makes back for the door, this time purposefully bumping into the girl, whom he holds into his arms, and they start revolving embraced, dancing together. A sensuous slow melody starts playing as they are swaying tightly intertwined in the middle of the room. Taking a sip of the liquid in her glass, Mim feels pain writhing in her chest against her will. And she is struggling hard to drive away the damn evil foe. Keep heart, Mim, she encourages herself, nothing bad is going to happen, this is just fun. She thinks she may have done something wrong and that is why Anton is avoiding her. Why has he brought her here then? She rises to her feet and slinks out of the room.

There is a boom of light on the other side. The dinner table laden with sweets and Mr. and Mrs. Arvinte's cheerfulness welcome her, making her really feel at home. As she sits down on a chair, Mrs. Arvinte's bland high-pitched voice gives her a light start.

"How come, Mimi, you're not with Antonush? Go there, dear, and dance with him."

"Leave the girl alone," her husband chides her.

"Come, have some dessert," the woman then invites Mim.

She takes a cake and bites, but her eyes well up and her jaws clinch, so she places it on her plate, leaps to her feet and makes for the bathroom forcing herself to swallow the bite on the way, leaving Anton's parents perplexed at the table.

When she returns she finds them still sitting there, the woman eyeing her questioningly.

"What's the matter, Mimi, what on earth happened?"

"Oh, it's nothing. Something just came to my mind."

"Is he dancing with that girl? Hmm, I've seen her."

"Yes, he is."

"You go back there and act cool, as if nothing was the matter. Don't take it to heart, Mimi, that's what people do at parties. Come on, don't leave him alone, go."

When she enters the room she finds everyone seated, glasses in hand.

Anton bounces up asking solicitously, "Where's your glass, Mim?"

She promptly retrieves it, still full. "Here it is."

"Cheers!" From under his brows, he fixes a cruel stare on her, as though he was expecting some token of weakness from her part, some proof of love, a desperate embrace, or maybe tears.

But no, Mim pulls herself together and sparks as their glasses clink. "Happy birthday!" she says, then clinks her glass around and comes back next to him.

There is an intermezzo, as the boys are cueing up the next tape. The blonde is struck by a brilliant idea and says, "Let's bring in some cookies."

"That's right," Mim agrees, giggling inwardly at

herself being as smart. So she takes the opportunity and dashes out succeeding the girl.

As they reappear, each with a full platter in their hands, a rhythmical beat is playing. The girls place the platters on the table by the window, done. Now Mim regains lust for life and starts moving her body to the music. They are all dancing, Anton gets out of the room, Costin invites Mim to dance with him, Anton comes back with a bottle of wine, puts it on the table and leaves again. Why is he not coming back, Mim wonders, all rigid and devoid of vital energy again, but the door opens and she knows it is him. She cannot see what he is doing. The track has switched to a slow song. As she turns her head to the side, she sees his back disappearing again into the light of the small passage-hall and bang, he slams the door shut. But here he comes immediately back, unleashing his fury on the door again. She only hears the dreadful bang. Still dancing with her partner, Mim gyrates and is now facing the window. In the dim light coming through it she can distinguish Anton pouring himself a glass of wine and then drinking out of it, his glance somewhere in the ceiling. As she and Costin keep gyrating slowly on the carpet, Mim loses sight of Anton. The next thing she knows, a powerful blow nearly wrecks her back. She cannot tell what he has hit her with. The blonde and the boy with the hi-fi are rotating embraced, unaware of what has just happened to Mim, nobody seems to know anything, not even her dancing partner, Costin. She is in pain but, out of shame, keeps moving slowly like a marionette, pleading God for this song to end, so that she can speak to Anton. Her heart is pounding like crazy in her chest, scared to death, why is this happening, what on earth is happening, and what is Anton going to do next? Anton's back, the light in the slit of the door again, he is gone, blackness, but the next instant she is blinded by a blazing flash, his face, his jaws, the wings of his nose flapping in a rhythm of raging fury, the manic glints in his vitreous eyes focusing her. She rotates with Costin losing sight of him, but just as she does so she receives a terrible kick that almost rips her body apart and she staggers on her feet and the pair shakes and is finally demolished. Mim bends down, and the dancers freeze, or at least this is what she believes. Somehow they are all behind her, while she is desperately searching for Anton's eyes, her face turned up to him.

She pushes herself upright to beg for an explanation. "What's happened, please tell me!" She has no time to get scared of his grinding jaws, as she instantly finds herself punched fiercely in the face. She figures out it must have been his fist, since her head jerked backwards and she simultaneously felt her lips full and fleshy, wet. They are bleeding. Blood is trickling down her chin, dripping on her hands. "Anton, please tell me, what have I done?"

"What you have done?" he snarls. "Come with me."

"No," Mim screams. He grasps one of her hands and holds it firmly, and because she struggles to pull herself away from his grip, he starts yanking her arm like mad and twists it. She stubbornly thrusts her feet into the ground, hollering out to him, "Let go of me, please!"

"You're coming with me now."

"Where?"

"Come and you'll see."

"Help!" Mim starts begging for the others' interposition, but no one seems to budge.

Eventually, Costin dare say, "Anton, I insist, please let her ease off for a while."

"No, she's coming with me now. This is between me and her."

As he drags her out through the door, her hand clasps its outer handle pulling the door shut and she holds tight on it, questions flickering in her mind as to whether there really is no one in the dining room anymore, and might Mr. Arvinte have made his retreat for the night, and must Mrs.

Arvinte be doing chores in the kitchen as usual? They are fighting in the narrow space of the passage to the bathroom, Anton grimly pulling at her, and she still hoping to reason him down. She no longer wants any trace of Anton in her life, all she wants is him to relinquish his grip on her, let her go away to get on with her life. Her life is in danger now and she is determined to fight for it.

"Where are you taking me?"

"To the bathroom. I want us to talk alone in there."

"No," Mim shouts, thinking of her life. Her eyes into his eyes, she asks, "What do you want? Kill me?"

These words stir him even more and his bull's rage blasts out his flapping nostrils, and his jaws crush, and he jerks her from place while with the other hand opens the door to the bathroom, trying, in a rabid delirium, to pull her in there.

"No," she cries, "help, please help me, he's going to kill me, help!" She musters up so much strength, that in spite of his almost inhuman force, he cannot make her move an inch. "Leave me alone," she snaps at him, gaining confidence.

He releases her the very moment the door to the dancing room bangs wide open and the three youths burst horrified through its frame, all at once. Anton shuts the bathroom door and goes into the dining room, where he pours himself a glass of wine, then he crosses his way with all the others, going back to the room he took Mim out of only seconds ago. Exhausted, Mim plops her frame into an armchair. Mrs. Arvinte has got out of the kitchen and is now standing stock-still, a hand over her mouth. The blonde girl comes near Mim and strokes her shoulder lightly. She asks Mrs. Arvinte to fetch a bandage soaked in ice water. As the woman hurries away, the two boys, speechless, go the opposite direction to join Anton.

They stayed shut for a while, men and women, each in separate rooms. And there was absolute silence, as none of them understood what had happened in the house and why. Mim felt relieved to be in that armchair, thankful she could breathe, thankful she could still reason. She was being granted a respite to indulge herself with her newly acquired lips, so big and soft, and with that confident feeling she had often imagined people with large mouths had. Now she knew she had been right to presume that the way people perceived each feature of their appearance influenced their behavior toward the others. Look at herself now, for instance, how self-reliant she felt with these gross plump lips, which could have well served her as a bastion against any outer hazard, had they always looked like that. It was flat clear, life was a lot easier for people with large features. They had enough flesh laid aside in the face of adversity, or harsh wind, or some chance fright. And maybe this was where brazenness stemmed from.

16 THE BELT

The folds of the crème drapes have turned into glowing shafts of amber. She slept with Stefan last night. Stefan covered her with his hot body, his voice radiating waves of fire, and he melted upon her, making the sheaths sink, and she was sinking with them down to the core of the bed, with that scorching torso burning hot all over her. Stefan was melting into her. His big, lubricious lips, so mushy, his teeth, the puffing rhythm of his breath and the wheezing, his voice coming from intimidating depths to vibrate so close into her ear, Mim. His dripping mouth leaving slobber in her ear, trailing saliva on her face down to her lips, the lapping and the slurping, and the slobbering on her teeth with his teeth, big and keeping the heat inside. Those teeth came apart and she was sucked into the vortex of fire, his beefy soft tongue, which she felt deep red, luring her to the heart of that furnace, their tongues sliding in hot waves of drool. His trunk was rubbing against her white breasts, against her venter, and she could almost hear the bristle hairs on his chest rasping her bosom, while his arms were coiling like a halo around her head, his palms pressing against the apex of her head as if begging, then down on her temples, her ears, her shoulders, which he was meaningfully clenching in an effort to let his fire get into her, down through her throat to her navel, her womb, and her warmth. Yes, her uterus was bathing in a sea of hot embers, crushed between the claws of his short sinewy legs. She felt him pressing hard unto her as he was struggling to get between her thighs, and further down into her, all ablaze and trembling. 'Mim, I love you.' How that felt good, burning hot and so good!

But it is pretty hot and it feels nearly as good now, as she stretches her body as long as the length of the bed, yippee, she did it! Stefan is at work now, and his woman lazing in bed. God how that heat overwhelmed her! The bed is still like an oven, she chuckles. Let her fondle with herself and remember. She is so sultry down here between her legs, ah, Mim is hot and delicious, so tender and creamy to the touch, smelling so dewy and a bit flowery and a bit milky, and a mild piquant spice she senses too, that is still her. Mmm, the essence of her skin turns her fickle and lecherous. She wonders whether Stefan had felt the same. Oh my God, what exquisite shapes, the woman is a wonderful creature and craving for a female body must feel maddening, then crushing a woman between your arms, teasing and fondling her, torturing her then holding her tight, and the big thrust, thrusting your manhood forward into sweet her like crazy and leaving here, crossing to the other side, going beyond, bye!

Beyond, that was what they used to call their largest room back home when they were kids. They would tell one another to go *beyond*, would look for things *beyond*, take this or fetch that from *beyond*, let us go *beyond*. She used to think *beyond* was just the name of that room. Later on did she come to understand the actual meaning of that word. If only Anton knew that what *beyond* means to her now is the realm across the river which he treads every day. He knows nothing of little Tomina. Stefan, quite differently, is inquisitive, forever curious to find out more, irritatingly curious and on the watch, just like some kind of researcher. But last night he simply conquered her, she is a woman, after all. Why should she not make love to him, roll this lovely feminine body of hers with his between the bed sheets and try it out. Look how this milky-sweet entrance into her is stirring her desire, and oh, why is Stefan not here right now to take her. Here, search me thoroughly, Mr. Analyst, squeeze my nipples, twist them to hurt me. Ah, if only Stefan dipped his thick fingers into her to play! Oh my God, is she crazy or what? Yep, she is a crazed woman, all by herself in this house, free to do whatever the fancy takes her.

She climbs out of the bed and turns on the radio-set by the window, the absolutely fantastic massive radio-set, the old-timey real thing which can tune in to any station in the world, right from this very room, BBC, elegantly pronounced with phonological accuracy, Voice of America, with seducing consonants touched by a unique tinge of luscious masculinity, other languages racing the planet surround. Well, let these sound waves pass right through Mim, who thus becomes one with the whole world. Many people just like her are playing crazy at this very moment, as yes, people do whatever they feel, venturing in all aspects of living, totally free. She tunes in to a language whose saccharine sibilants have ancient flavors about them — ah, it is Greek, then on to an Italian station, no, back to Greek, let them speak in Greek as she is preparing some special treatment for herself. What shall it be? Her brain waves are scanning around in search of the perfect fancy. Let her find something to play with her own breasts, some sort of utensils from the kitchen, yeah. Already feverish, she rushes to the kitchen and starts scouring drawers and cupboards. She soon finds two small transparent shot glasses which flash pretty promising signals at her. They are so tiny as to let only the tips of her breasts in. She tests one, ah, it feels amazing. Mesmerized, she watches the left nipple swell to incredibly bold cockiness, then, already wet between her legs, rushes back to the bedroom with the two gadgets in hand.

All these preparations are driving her crazy, crazy like anything. The hell with love and the hell with Anton, it was all bullshit, histrionics, falseness. And when she thinks how she used to sweat her way to perfection, how she would die to be perfect for him. Here, this is what real pleasure is, to tremble with lecherous craving and drip, not dry out for fear you might not come up to his expectations. She sits herself at the end of the bed and, gazing in the large oval mirror on the opposite wall, starts brushing her nipples gently with the palms of her hands, cunning prospects of future debauchery etching in her mind. She gives them some good squeezing next, only to set the ground for torturing twisting round, back and forth. She wants so badly to inflict pain on her own poor breasts that she keeps wrenching until she gets genuine screams out of her throat. At this point she starts rubbing the reddened buds just with the tips of her index fingers, ever so lightly, keeping the silence to feel the thrills of pleasure tingling her down there, under the mound of Venus. She comes to her feet and draws closer to the mirror, thinking of Anton. He used to enter her right under that mound like a sharp dagger hurting her, then would play with her for minutes on end to Bach's music, back and forth, delicately, to that crisp ludic rhythm. 'You like that?' he would ask. She sits back on the bed and cups the tips of her breasts meticulously, two nice suction cups with her nipples inside and her flushed face above, leering lustfully. She is shameless, an obscene creature defying the world from an apartment by a river in a country. She reclines on the bed with her hands intertwined right in the middle of her crotch, one from the front rubbing on her clit, and the other one from behind, thus wrapping herself in a kind of depravity belt. If only a man were here to abuse her. Stefan will only be home in the afternoon and they will have dinner together, whereas Anton must be across the river now.

The peoples' tongues surround the globe, the crème room with Mim curled on the bed being part of this circuit, and the only reality she is aware of now is the point where her two hands intersect. This brings back the memory of what Anton did to her when they came back from her friend's wedding reception and she just fancies playing that movie in her mind again. That may have been the only time when she had acted like a real woman to him, bold, unabashed. Her body dressed in that dark blue finest velvet, breasts draped in two simple folds running from her waist up to a string around her neck, her back completely bare and legs flashing out from between the thigh-high central slit of the long straight dress. She had been dancing all night with her fine legs on display and he had been appreciatively watching her from a distance with lickerish male eyes. She had once been little Mim for him, a soul and a body both in his possession, his toy of choice.

They got in front of his door long after midnight. He unlocked it and ushered her in reverentially, with a telltale grin on his lips of what he was going to do to her inside. His eyes glinted with mischief from under his brows as he stretched his arm histrionically, with a trace of derision, making a mockery of her not being his anymore and of his not wanting her anymore. He sequenced her in the obscurity of the vestibule and, as soon as he locked the door, grabbed her brutally by the hips from behind, bent her over a pile of car wheels and snatched up the skirt of her dress. "Wait," she said, knowing that the dress would not slide off unless the tight waist belt was unclasped. Staggering on his feet, he kept tearing at her diaphanous garment, angry that it stood in his way, until the belt snapped open and the dress ripped at the side seams. Victorious, he pulled the garment off her and tossed it away, unbuttoned his fly and pushed her back forcibly, bending her down, face crushed against the top wheel. The next thing she knew, he was cupping her breasts pulling her tight to him. As he was squashing them to destruction, he suddenly thrust himself into her, in mock play that she no longer belonged to him. "Now I want to fuck you. Tonight I'm going to fuck you for real." He had been right all along, she was a conventional *bourgeoise*, a social aesthete who deserved to be 'fucked' truly for once.

There followed a night of unrestrained physicality, their last love night together, or maybe their first. You're driving me crazy, he kept whispering, you're driving me nuts when you move like that, completely nuts. It was the night he talked. Quite understandably, he could afford to reveal some thoughts now that she was no longer his date, at least about her body if not more. She had always driven him crazy. Therefore her musical efforts had not been in vain, ha, that, at least. They made love freely that night, she was free, Mim, who had nothing left to lose, knowing that the following day he was driving her to the train station again, back to where he had picked her from.

She will never forget, she will reel that night in her mind whenever she pleases, everything is still in her head and not one single picture is lost. Let those silly sucker cups pop off her breasts and her hands unclasp from her crotch, the hell with this nonsense. Gutter, this is the word, she has let herself drop into a dirty pool here on the bed, come on up, get those silly things off your nipples, Mim, and plunge yourself in the bathtub to make clean, let things be clean again.

17 THE TENT

She would like to paint that deep green evening, the second one, and the greenish light in the tent. Despair as fathomless as the sea, that malachite irradiation tending to enwrap her soul and seemingly stealing light from there simultaneously. She had this strange feeling everything around reflected her own soul. It was hot with everyone gathered in there and something boiling on the stove. An icy gale had invaded the campsite all of a sudden and the sea had begun to roar. It was now struggling nearby telling them of vast spaces and uncontrollable forces which were keeping time by their terrible gusts. There was no other measure and no beginning or end. Inside, the ticking of their tiny hearts was barely audible, people looking forward to their hot meal, in the shelter.

Mim and Roxana knelt on mattresses scouring through their luggage in the darkness of the dorm. Mim was pleased to hear the girl's childlike voice utter the name by which Anton called her — Mim — then quietly say, "He asked us something today..." Mim was waiting, and Roxana said, "At noon, while we were playing cards, remember? You'd left to wash the glasses and then he asked who was prettier,

Mim or Ioana?" So this was the man she was in love with, Mim thought, letting the girl continue. "And we told him: Mim loves you so much." Mim had told Roxana that that was the last trip together for her and Anton and that they had agreed not to see each other again in at least ten years. "But please, Roxana, I beg you, keep it dark, act as if you didn't know who I am. I don't think you and I will ever meet again, so promise you'll never bring up my name." Mim was not allowed to tell who she was. 'Keep your lips tight in front of my friends, OK? No stories,' Anton had ruled. But how could she? She stretched her neck upwards in front of that girl and let out a whispering shrill. The truth had cut through her a harrowing wound. "Roxana, I love him." She could now make out the girl's eyes, round with astonishment. Somebody had to know, this was nothing but humane behavior. Mim lowered her chest and bent on the mattress stretching her arms as far as she could, letting her eyes water in silence. There had to be a place on this earth for her love, so she would bury it there, deep. But again life, struggling inside her, wanted out in sharp shrills, higher and higher, so she raised her arms to the ceiling, her neck again, in a kind of monument of despair, and up there was dark malachite green.

Back around the fire, Mim cuddled at his white feet, so beautiful, he sipping wine. She could see their feet together from down in the sand, where she was swaying her head like some sick woman. Time had lost her among columns, sandy caresses were confusing her, and right in the middle was the fire. It was she who was keeping the fire and shadows were praying all around in a maddening dance, the columns gyrating: Mim was an ancient priestess. Had he not told her once she was using magic? He believed in witchcraft and was afraid of her — 'Mim, you must've put something in the food.' Although she had smiled then, she was not sure that was the right thing to do, so a tinge of bewilderment quickly wiped her smile off her face. Yes, he really believed so. Magical powers were coming to her now, oozing through the greenish canvas walls, insinuating through the shadows, and radially charging her poor fragile body, which was continually swaying. What namely did the world mean? Anton was there, all glossy in the dim light, there for her to dance her arms toward him, her eyes shut and hair sweeping incantations in the sand. 'Why don't you look me in the eye, what are you hiding, huh?' He sometimes addressed her as if she were some kind of sorcerer and, in spite of his apprehension, was trying to show he could outplay anything. Mim had caught his look several times and had seen nothing but a glassy wall beyond which he was wakefully lurking. So why should she have looked into his eyes? She had never found there the warm delight he expressed in front of a painting or an artistic body movement, or when he listened to music. Either vigilance or nothing, no expression at all when it came to Mim. The raw truth was there beneath the sand which she could now penetrate. He had never beheld her with pleasure, he did not even like her, no. She was simply something he needed, that was all. Yet, Anton was somehow intrigued, terribly tormented, this thing he needed so, *Mim*, was it by chance toxic? She could now feel him without even looking. The limbs of fire she was sending were reflecting in his liquid eyes, she knew, she was feeling him through the plasma among the columns of heat, so fantastic, rising unsparingly from the earth. Yes, she was the enchantress and she would insinuate herself through Anton's open pores. Now she saw he was not happy.

After the meal was over she found herself alone with Anton by the fire. With her body fallen in the sand, there was nothing else but Anton, so she laced her arms around his knees, defeated. She finally sneaked a glimpse at his sad liquid eyes.

18 THE CHAIR

"Stay put, I'll be back in a minute. I want us to do something special today." To her relief, Anton smiles openly. She knows she can feel at home here, so she starts roaming at ease about the room. Children's voices can be heard outside, and sunlight gushes through the window with reflections of the river, which is languidly indulging in the sun like a benign serpent.

In all this flood of gracious light, Mim would have liked to give Mrs. Arvinte a hand with the washing up, but he said no, he took her by the hand and pulled her away from the rest of the house. "She is coming with me, we have things to do." "What important stuff have you got in mind," mock-wondered his mother smilingly. Mr. Arvinte adjusts his eyeglasses on his nose and retires on the sofa with a newspaper. "Antonush—" his father calls at him meaning to start a businesslike discussion between men. As they are whispering together, Mim feels awkward. Anton seems to have forgotten he is holding her hand. Meanwhile, Mrs. Arvinte gets herself busy with clearing the crockery away, and Mim is downright embarrassed, swaying her body from one leg to another. "OK, off we go," Anton announces the end of discussions and pulls Mim toward his room.

He opened the door and let her in. The stacks of books in the dark corner, and farther on, the window, a wall of aqua in the afternoon, beyond which anything could be. He left her there and shut the door behind him. She wonders what Anton's mother might think about her, retreating like that immediately after she has been regaling herself on the food the woman had been working on all day in the kitchen. It is in that room that Anton's mother leads her existence till late into the night, when the men of the house are already fast asleep to regenerate their bodies, to be whole men the following day again. Everything for the men, the masters, so much loved in that household, and whose words are regarded as sacrosanct. But is that rather feeble woman enough to tend to such a proud household of men? She is the girl of one of them, Anton, Mim shivers, and she is completely subdued. She is waiting for him now, he who has slyly taken her from the dinner table — thank you, mother — and has laid her aside in his room.

She hears the now too familiar tune of the door, followed by the willfully discreet, yet never so, sound of the tiny latch, no matter how smoothly Anton's hand would operate it. That gives her a thrill. What will his game be today, and what is she supposed to do, shall she say something? "What are we going to do?" "Shh," he smiles, bringing his index finger to his lips. "I want us to read. But what we are going to do is a different kind of reading," he announces, getting down to preparing the set. He takes three chairs from near the window and places them next to each other in the middle of the room, after which he comes right to her, bends down, and gives her a long caress from the knees upwards under her skirt, both-handed and utterly intent. Her breasts bounce in panic and Mim can feel their rock-hardness, the sharp nipples scratching against her large T-shirt. Her heart starts racing in preparation for something she knows nothing about, but he has definitely in store for her, something only Anton and her heart know of. Never before has she yearned for his palms cupping her breasts to appease them, true, has she ever really wanted anything from him? She just kept lying in wait for his next move, and once this done, got into a trance with the sole purpose of serving him. He pays no attention to her breasts, leaving them to ache under the scorching fabric. Instead, he tells her to sit on one of the chairs. What on earth is he going to do to her? He had once before told her to sit on a chair, in that same room, right under the window. It was evening then, and there were no thrills, as she was completely unaware of what was going to happen.

They had many times made love in that room, but always to music, always on the vast spread of the bed, that liberating campo of the mind, on which she could roll her body in total release. The chair, an item whose name made her smile when Anton uttered it — *chair*, had a simply ridiculous resonance in her mind. The actual contact with the coldness of the sheeny piece of wood gave her frissons. She had plastered herself to it obediently though, waiting for what was to happen, feeling her thighs heavily dilated on the insipid object. That was the first time she had somehow glimpsed a kind of humorous arrow head in her, aimed at Anton and his doings, a tinge of mature superiority. It was as though she had been for the first time able to contemplate Anton with motherly condescendence then. Only that the arrow turned against her the moment when he, flexing his knees, began a prolonged ralenti downwards until his head reached the place where her thighs had earlier been so cold, just like a tomcat face to face with its prey. Her heart was ticking like crazy, and her thighs were by now on fire. She would have wanted them off that chair, she would have wanted them muscular and supple, but they kept stubbornly glued to that stupid piece of furniture as if melted with the seat. It was too late, anyway, as his eyes had already got there — Mim could see the top of his head, the point from which his straight blonde hairs spread radially, that blondness she was so fond of, yet unrelenting now in such a dark manner. Underneath she could visualize the horror of his eyes looking through her thighs, at what she kept hidden there, on the slightly concave palm of the chair. He slowly pulled her skirt up, with just the tip of one index finger, and then began to spread her thighs apart, inch by inch. What she felt was panic, tumult, a chaos of exasperated, impossible commands. She knew she could not resist him. That was why she felt a kind of contraction of the brain, from the nape to the top of her head. She was nothing but a knot, the knot at the end of the rope, waiting to see what was going to happen to the body hanging below. That time her breasts had been lax all the way until something triggered them to life, a wave starting from her conscience: she was eager to know, she wanted to feel something new. So be it! — was the order she gave herself.

She eventually managed to unglue her thighs, with his help, as they both came to want them to come apart, in spite of Mim's weakly play of resistance. He got his both arms busy now: they were graciously working like two pistons, seen from above as a sort of funny ballet on both sides of his head, from where the power came. And what she had now on the seat was feverish and crude. Concavity seemed to have turned to flatness, a plate on which she wanted to offer herself to his fingers, to his eyesight. He pushed her panties aside and introduced his finger into her secret world, a world not even Mim knew. But he had a right to it, he had dared and won this right for himself. She pictured his white long fingers, with beautiful rectangular fingernails, and imagined feeling herself with the skin on their tips. Ah! — curt, as silence was required, her hot interior was confessing itself right there and then, next to the window, the perfect place for Mim to listen in to her own inner life. She was not aware of Anton straightening her legs, one after another, in order to help her panties slide down. One could think he feared wakening her up, and that was why he had conjured up his highest artfulness on that very offering plate. The way into her was free now: he had spread her legs completely and was looking. He then started a tender movement of his head, drawing nearer and nearer, until she felt what she knew was the coldness of his lips. He pulled her body closer to him, on the edge of the seat, and Mim began to feel him stronger and stronger between her thighs. He got himself busier and busier, almost on his own. She was fully awake by now, wondering what his senses might be telling him. And, God, what could she possibly do? Terror was amassing on her brain, when he gently slid his palms down her thighs and whispered: relax. She loosened up, and a wave of contentment washed over her, contentment for what she was passing through, a kind of pride that her mind was trying something completely new. But she wanted that over now, enough, it had to end, and end right away, so that she could check whether it was still the Anton she knew. She longed to see his face.

This time, he is intent on finding a book. He has drawn a chair next to the wardrobe, climbed up on it, and is searching for one. It is the Russian authors he is inspecting, as he is fascinated by the Slavic soul. He has found the right one and, delighted beyond measure, puts the chair back next to hers and places the book on her lap: *Crime and Punishment*. Immediately after, he goes to play some music. It is Tchaikovsky, the sublime piano notes they both recognize, since they once admired a human body in a quasi-spiritual extension of muscles to that music, a body that seemed to be aspired by some divine forces and, at the same time pushed upward by powerful human will, some secret belief that you can physically soar in the air, a body sliding up on a rope in an avant-garde ballet show. "You like it?" She says yes and feels glad, while Anton rejoices at the prospect of his own pleasure. "Look, I'll sit here, and you have to sit like this." He arranges her in place with his hands. "Read to me whatever you want from this book." While Mim goes over the contents, he bends her torso until her head reaches his lap. "Are you OK," he asks. She tries to cuddle up in a more comfortable position — "Hey, what are you doing?" He has pulled her skirt up and is pushing her panties off her. "You keep searching while I deal with this." "OK," she agrees, and resumes her perusal, until she has found where to read from. "Shall I start?" Mim's mind is proud again; let it be, let this be, too. Yay, she would like to read like that as long as possible and relishes this new experience. He hauls her buttocks up and brings them closer to his lap. "Wait," she says, "I need to adjust myself." "Is it better now?" "Yes," she cajoles smilingly and resumes reading, quite comfortable with the thought that particular part of her body belongs to him now. She is pleasantly surprised at herself being able to read at ease in those uncommon circumstances and does not mind at all Anton's eyes feasting on her naked buttocks. Her breasts have long got quiet, so nothing more could possibly spoil her relaxation. Mim is reading, while he is delicately playing his fingers between her buttocks, ever so slowly, to the music and to Dostoyevsky's words, and to the shiny waves in the window. Mim envisages their glitter on the smooth skin of the two halves blooming brazenly from her tiny waist. But this dear waist of hers is by now being tormented upon his strong thighs, so she has to adjust her posture. "Don't stop," she announces, "I just want to find a better position." Although she no longer feels completely relaxed, she inwardly decides this curious recreation is worth continuing.

When the play of his fingers grows into a perceptible rhythm, she entreats, "Let's keep it like this a little longer." In spite of his curt agreement, she senses his reluctance, and the flames of his ardor go right through her breasts to pump them back up. Anton grabs her buttocks with his both hands, ready to tear them apart as though he was hungry for the hot middle of a fresh loaf. Mim pushes herself toward him, thrashes heavily against his lap, until he turns her around and the book drops to the floor. The music has stopped and Anton is torturing her lips with his beautiful mouth, yes, she has been unconsciously longing for that pain, she thinks as they slide together down to the floor. On the generous expanse of the carpet, Mim finally stretches her muscles unrestrictedly free, and this against Anton's extreme urge to spread her legs open. She also gets desperate, let her open them, but it just does not seem to be wide enough. Anton wrenches his torso high above her. He is hovering over her, all-powerful, yet so intimately close. "Mim, this is how I feel you are my woman, and you know it." Her mouth and body give completely in to him, so she is lying in wait. Let her be united with this man.

19 VACATION

Boo, she looks horrible with those sunken cheeks and spent sunken eyes. She herself is spent like a consumed, yellowish candle. But the summer exam session was over, gone, and she is free to repose her poor bones on the large stiff mattress in her tiny chamber: just the wide glass panel of the door looking like a tunnel of light focused on the crown of the apricot-tree, the wooden cross dividing its four panes against flooding light — boom, and, at the distant end of the room, crammed between the wall and the bed, the small vanity with its miraculous mirror, timid and round, which treasures within its frame the decent pride of some truthful, wholesome, genuine times, times long past.

Even such vane things like beautifying powders used to be different once, so very fine, faintly sour-scented, elegant, seductive, unforgettable. The naturally carnal pinks, so sincere, or the deep red batons-rouge women used to spread thickly on their lips, woman-fragranced rouges, so much intriguing as they were soothing, whisperers of caresses and of floating petals. As a little girl, she would play with her mother's extraordinary tiny boxes at home, clad in arabesques of pastel colors, and old rich perfumes dried immortal into the paper wrappings. Once you opened one such box, a sublime, unearthly matter was disclosed to your senses. They belonged to my mom, her own mother would tell her, this was the kind of things there once existed, not the run-of-the-mill stuff nowadays. There was one particular lipstick whose full red, quite curiously, had the power to lend almost godlike light to a face, to Tomina's, too. Her whole face caught brilliancy when she put it on, and the loftiness on her lips sparkled in her eyes and on her child's forehead.

Well, that lipstick could bring some life to her features if she had it now, but she had lost it a long time ago. Why does she not lay her body on the bed, and let her also get some pads with chamomile infusion ready at hand, to press them on her exhausted eyelids, as once in bed, she knows her body will not be capable of moving again too soon. Anyway, what else could she do when she could barely even walk? She is going to repose on her back and, who knows, she may even fall asleep in that position and keep those pads on at length to see if the end effect is really as written in those beauty magazines: no more circles, no more bluishness, no more tiredness. She will get up from that bed feeling miraculously well, the skin of her face refilled with vital saps, and that around her eyes flawlessly white, thus restoring her youthful mien. But let her place the cup of infusion at the head of the bed, let her soak the pads in it, and lie down at once, then reach for the bloody pads and cover her eyes with them.

But what, it is him. She has heard the door catch and the feeble trembling sound of its glass panes so close. Why on earth must this happen now, just as she was, for the first time in her life, going to lapse into lengthy, complete relaxation? She has promptly removed the chamomile pads off her eyelids, as who else could it be but Anton, yes, in beige corduroy jeans and with pale lips in the semidarkness, he is advancing towards her. Halfway to the bed, he pauses in his course. "Hey, what's with you?" he asks, then starts frolicking in the middle of the room.

Mim rises from her reposing position, gah, how she would have liked to be let alone, for that one time — did he not say he would come over later? "I'm tired, that's all there is; I'm just lying down with these eye pads on to recover," she explains forcing a decrepit smile.

He inspects the chairs in the room with inquisitive eyes, then goes to the wardrobe and pulls its shabby doors open. Mim observes him negligently grab her red sack by one handle and throwing in clothing. He is carrying on his activity in silence, now and then hoisting an item up for examination before tossing it in the bag.

"What are you up to?" she finally dare enquire.

"We're off," he announces bluntly, then resumes his job in a more cheerful manner.

"Off for where?"

"The seaside."

"Well, but I don't have anything appropriate for the seaside here. Plus, I was hoping to be able to rest for a while."

"You can rest there. We're going with my friends, come on, get dressed, we're already late."

"Wait, I don't even have a bathing suit."

"We'll buy one."

Mim has gone into a frenzy of thoughts: her methodical preparations, the assiduous work on shaping her body with aqua gym, the early sun-tanning at the women's naked spa, imagining and sketching new garments, modeling them in front of the tall mirror at home. And look at her now, a mere wreck, compelled to let her frame be born there without any suitable clothes, in a gathering of unknown people. So she has to do something and get over her fatigue, if not now, maybe on the way there.

"What are you going to wear on your feet, these?" he enquires, dangling a pair of ecru sports sandals before her eyes.

"Well, yes. So, you don't understand, I can't go like this." As the large cotton bag is being loaded with stuff, the thought of the imminent effort she will have to make is growing in her head like a tumor. "I just can't," she repeats in a pleading tone.

"Ooh-la-la, you can't — are you ready?"

"No."

She cannot recollect that specific ride to the seaside, nor their way back, or the stops they made, if any. All she remembers is that she had put on a long denim dress which made her look tall and thin, and that it was only when they had got into the hotel lobby that Anton eyed her lengthiness from head to toe and reproved her aside, away from his pals' ears, as if he was embarrassed with her: couldn't you find something else to put on, this is the sea coast, Mim. The ecru sandals on her feet were her only salvation, super pretty and downright casual. And what on earth could she possibly retort to that; had he not seen her upon departure? He may not have had the courage to draw her attention and had plucked some up to tell her now. Mim images him grumbling in his stomach all the way there: her dress, her damn dress.

She also remembers that as soon as they got into their room her complexion caught fire and she turned beautiful — her long wavy tresses would stand on end with inner living force. She has the image of the triumphant reflection of her face in the vestibule mirror: pink-flushed, incredible, stunning. She recalls Anton go out of the bathroom — their roommates had only just brought their luggage up and were already gone to the restaurant downstairs. She sees him drawing near, yet not venturing to do what he had in mind. He cups her head into his palms, turns her to face him, kisses her hard, then pushes her over the edge of the bed, unbuttons her dress up to the waist — wait, she says, aren't we supposed to join the others downstairs, what might they think? "They think nothing," he says and plunges his hips between her legs and they make love under the stress of both time and passion, after which they promptly rise to their feet. He pulls his jeans back up and fastens his fly while Mim adjusts her garment and hair in front of the same mirror, that long lush hair of hers, like an aura around a face uplifted by high spirits. Knocks on the door are heard. "Yes." "Hey, aren't you coming?" It is their friend Costin.

They were all accommodated in that two-bedded room, three pairs, it seems. Mim and Anton's sleeping quarter was on a blanket on the floor, between one of the beds and the doors of the built-in closet. During that first night, there was no way she could stop him from making love to her again, both of them hidden like two moles under the thin cover, and holding their breaths like sinners. Oh yes, they sinned in a terribly adventurous manner that night, with so many souls all around them. She also remembers that chain of hotels lining the shore had used to be her favorite place on the coast before that summer, where she would make an evening appearance as on a sort of catwalk, pleasurably thrilled by the murmurings trailing behind her: she is an actress, she is a dancer.

There was a guy in their group who, at some point, started to harass Mim with minor mischiefs, probably following the first night, when she and Anton had shamelessly made love under everyone else's eyes — that flimsy, almost immaterial linen sheet had barely been able to conceal their sin — and obviously, in everyone else's ears. And it had all been Anton's fault. This is what she felt then, which makes her laugh now, when she is comfortably reclining on a wide bed with a French *policier* in one hand and the other one plunged into a paper bag of fresh crunchy peaches. She could not care less about her looks, so she does not wear any makeup. Stefan is lying beside her with his book in hand, trying to feign aloofness. She allows nothing more than light kisses and mild strokes from his part. He has to wait a little longer, he has to be patient. But has she considered how much more difficult this must be for him here by the sea, with all the heat exuding from loads of naked skin? No. She does nothing but munch and read, experiencing the ultimate relaxation, something she has always craved for. Until now, the salts in the air, the sultriness, the surrounding multitude of souls, and her desire to be perfect had invariably interfered with her freedom. She no longer uses makeup in the daytime and with every day that passes she becomes prettier and truly fresh. She preserves herself for the evenings, when she wants to turn heads. She knows Stefan loves and desires her, he keeps telling her that. In spite of this, all the fibers of her body remain mute and she even cringes at the idea that something, someday, might stir them. She will definitely not want another Anton beside her. She feels just fine being free.

The incident with the beefsteak comes to her mind. She cannot quite remember when that took place, but figures out it may have been on the second day of that unusual holiday, during dinner. Well, if Mim had had the mischance of being allotted a knife with a dull blade, why would anyone blame her? The mean guy, and his wicked moustache, wanting nothing other than to embarrass her, attacked her in front of the whole table with a demonstration on his own plate: look how you should cut the meat, dear. What he was after was in fact finding fault with Anton, who had allegedly brought a child along. Anton caught presently on, but, with grinding teeth, took it out on her. However, he was kind enough to offer Mim his own knife — here, try this one — but still in an irritated tone. Well, this is more like it — she uttered stressing each and every word, in an attempt to redeem herself, after having hopefully gathered all her physical force and adroitness in that bloody blade, and impeccably sliced off an insipid morsel of meat. Although she had no wish to eat that shoe-sole-like matter, she stubbornly carried on, meticulously cutting it bite by bite and putting those in her mouth one after another. Well, that was a damn awful meal. Why would such a thing happen to her, of all people? She, who had turned the art of eating into a hobby ever since a girl and had been practicing all along, taking it to perfection on every given occasion? Well, she had fallen into that villain's trap. Why would he not leave her alone? Little and scrawny, he was nothing but a cocky moustache above a foul, foul mouth. Now she remembers, yes, he was about Anton's age, if not a little older, and he had no partner, so there were only five of them. How could they have otherwise got into one car only, sure? God, how terrified Mim was at that time that Anton would put an end to that situation by disavowing her, would give her up only to shut off that man's constant scoffing. She already pictured herself driven back home and never phoned up again. She prayed they would leave that place soon and get outside the venomous range of the mustachioed man.

Quite contrastingly, everything feels so good now, when Mim reads on the beach all morning unaware of the crowds around, taking delight in cheap detective stories with *poules* and *flics*, her belly and thighs lolling in the warm sand, the pores of her skin delicately kindled by the sea breeze, with the recurrent prospect of a new peach crunching between her teeth, and the comforting proximity of Stefan, her guardian. His presence does not constrict her serenity and he never scolds her. He credits her with absolute trust, as he considers her a normal, whole person. What he does is maintain a protective mesh of affection around her. She wishes really hard she could show some lenience when he kisses her, when he embraces her from a distance with his unquenched desire, longing to stick his body to hers and feel her. At moments as such, she gets blocked by some unexplained impediment and she begs him to wait. In spite of this invariable response of her body, Mim has not lost hope and keeps confident in his patience.

Stefan is a very wise person, who has reached *la sagesse*. Whereas Anton is the artist, on a perpetual, insane search for the truth. As to her, she thinks of herself as being alternatively both, a kaleidoscope of living experiences, a mosaic of all feelings possible. Although Stefan loves her, he is not insanely and brutally jealous of her, as Anton used to be. She is well allowed to talk to his friends, as she did with the members of that rock band. She was so enthusiastic to be able to talk about Pink Floyd, the gods of rock she worships, to exchange impressions about the unique sound of their music, which transcends galactic margins, although it stems, without fail, from feet treading the earth. This is what she imagines when she listens to their music, a sort of Gopo's little man, his tiny soles gravitationally stuck to Mother Gaia, his cosmic arms reaching for infinity, and boasting an ubiquitous ovoid head. Those guys played a tape of Al di Meola's music to her: maddening jazz-rock, patchwork of styles and rhythms either rejecting or attracting one another, getting a jungle growing on metropolitan streets. Mim danced all night to that wildly overwhelming music on the terrace of the boys' bungalow, while Stefan chattered with them indoors about mutual friends and past episodes.

Anton and Mim on the long terrace above the sea, facing the head of a beautiful brunette against the distant aquamarine background. The girl seated right across the table from Mim features heavily made-up eyes, a mass of teased hair on top of her head, and big gold circles at her ears spanning all the way to her deep-tanned bare shoulders. Crowds of souls are crammed inside the bar, everyone busy watching the final of the Football World Cup. A man comes out of there now and then and joins them at table to check on the girl. Each time he makes an appearance, she starts fawning languid gestures upon him, sometimes perched on his knees, other times getting up and looping her arms around his neck from behind. They are on their honeymoon, which Mim only deduces from what they are saying to each other, and which seems to make the young woman feel really proud. There are others seated at that table, some from Anton and Mim's group, others from holidaying parties coming from the same town, and also chance companions who just sit for a while to exchange a few words, then rise and resume their passage. There was such a hustle and bustle to and fro, especially from inside the bar and back there. Mim occasionally turned her head and could see the mass of people indoors through the huge glass walls. They looked like a drill team all leaning forward and staring open-mouthed at the screen which dictated their reactions. The customers on the terrace were permanently kept updated by means of messengers who came out to report on the score at fairly short intervals.

Anton did not seem to be impressed at all by the show-off of the brunette tease, despite her super sexy aspect. The seascape was not a favorable background for her to play off against Mim. Her beauty looked rather wan in contrast with the glory of the surrounding blue, glory from which Mim was drawing miraculous powers. That girl was commonplace and vulgar, and the loads of black eyeliner made even her happiness appear faked. There came a moment when, all of a sudden, some sort of imaginary wave washed everyone away and pushed them inside the bar, everyone on the terrace except for Mim, quietly seated between Anton and the wicked mustachioed guy, with the vamp facing them from the other side of the table. Words started to float, on smiles with bizarre connotations, across the table between the vamp and the ogre, the latter sitting in state, legs wide spread and cigarette in hand. Come, Mim heard. Come on, my husband won't tear his eyes from the screen now. Mim wondered if that was not just her imagination. No, the woman had begun to plead out loud, bending forward across to where the ogre sat, as though Mim and Anton were nothing but chairs, columns, hedges, some kind of inanimate décor. Where? — inquired the ogre conspiratorially and promptly got an answer: in our room, we'll make it quick. As at a sign, they jumped to their feet and disappeared. Mim and Anton looked at each other and burst into laughter. She was stunned, how was that possible? Anton said he had not seen that much oddity in those people's behavior. What, during your very honeymoon, Mim insisted, in an endeavor to open his eyes on other women's shamelessness. "If the husband is dumb, let the woman take action, it's not your business anyway, so why should you get your claws into her?" Before long, Mim understood the reason why Anton had not taken to that girl, he knew her kind well.

On another day of their short vacation, they went to a different type of bar, simple, tiny, and vintage. There, both Anton and Mim silently admired a beautiful tall woman, with shiny jet-black hair pulled in a tail at the back of her head. She moved about graciously, modest in her straight, floor-length dress, to fetch cups of coffee and long drinks, which she would quietly place on tables. She was as absent as only an apparition could be, speechless and smileless. The only words that her head, ennobled by a high ballerina forehead, uttered, were to explain that she and her husband were working hard tending that café every summer season. "You see, Mim, this is the kind of woman I like." Anton's words hurt her and in that instant she wished she had been in that woman's place, but just for a split second, as there was no way she could trade down her youthfulness, her lavish wavy hair, her euphoric lust for life.

Nothing else does she remember of that trip. What comes to her mind, thinking back at it, is her own image with a black veil on her head. There was an instant when she really looked like that woman. It is time now she picked her book back up from her lap and carried on with her reading. She sank her teeth into a new peach and took a bite — crunch. Having Stefan beside, she slips into the petty world between the covers of the *policier*. Something must definitely be happening there.

20 THE VEIL

She is the night itself, like a veil upon the city. The car comes to a halt and he is about to get out of it. She will, too. She is a woman, a woman in the deserted station, prepared to get on a train. As in a dream, they walk side by side toward the ticket office — I'll buy your ticket.

She standing before the tall wall mirror in the entrance hall at home, just before going out of the door, for a hundredth time, to see him, gazing at her own pristine face: arched eyebrows, thinner traits, somehow more mature, and her eyes, disturbingly unfamiliar. She will enshroud herself in black, all black, what an exhilarating relief to think that black becomes her. She is beautiful, and she is woman. She will leave home on another trip to see Anton. She perceives herself as a nun about to embark on a pilgrimage to appease his intricate soul.

Silence, Anton met her eyes in silence, his words had been scarce, and she was speechless. The train will bear her away. Serenity has apparently started to lift, like a veil of fog, and will eventually dissipate into emptiness, above her own veil. What will happen to her then? He is approaching, head bowed, ticket in hand. Her steps, his steps. There exists, in the darkness of the night, lining the dry platform, the heavy shadow of the train with its gloomy railcars. Then Anton's voice, which does not give her time to wince. "Why have you dressed yourself in black?"

She shrugs her shoulders. Therefore he has noticed, he has been reflecting on her veil. She knows him so well; they used to be one. The truthfulness of this belief of hers flashes over her like a veil of light, then suddenly billows away, leaving her mind bitter. Shall she tell him? She should, and she has to do it right now, or it will be too late when she has made her first step on the train car.

"I am invited to my colleague's wedding reception next Saturday, you've met her before. I can only go if you join me." Nothing comes from him, so there is nothing left for her but the darkness of the train. "I beg you," she insists.

"I don't know what to say, Mim, I can't promise you anything."

"I won't go without you. Can you not just escort me there, and I promise we won't stay long. It's more like a festive supper."

"I don't know, Mim."

Oh, God, let him not turn her down. And he will not, look how ill at ease and disconcerted he is, look how hard it is for him to say no.

"Do not say no. I'll come to pick you up next Saturday."

She finally did it, got it off her chest. Feeling her body somewhat lighter, she gets on the train, intent on finding a secluded corner where to nest her thoughts. He standing on the platform, Mim anticipates returning to meet him.

21 SOIL

Illusory impressions of brass, agleam in the background, alluding to a mind rich with spirit that sprinkles filaments of lucent green ideas into light. Liquid breaths of air — desires stirred by whiffs from the fields. Cheerful daisies splashed on canvas in eager expectation, a carpet of thick grasses to pacify all souls, rootstocks turned colorless with secret yearnings, slender stalks longing for the sea... These all are rustling in a chorus talking to Mim, dizzying her with cool bitter-sweet aromas, swaying her imagination to distant skylines which suck her mind into the big wheel of awe. She always gets lost in front of her own canvases, through stunned, hugely dilated pupils. As much as they are telling her things, it seems other people are also fascinated by the miracle of her paintings, so full of restless, thriving life, and incessant murmuring from the core of the wild. Her first exhibition at the Municipal Arts Center had been a sheer success. Look, good people, how could it have been otherwise, when the artist herself gets lost in the realm of her own creations? This is why she forgets about eating, about living, about traveling.

Important people from her native town or from the

capital city had wanted to meet her in person and talk to her
— where have you been hiding until now? Little did they
know that Mim commuted every day to the countryside,
where she would hide in a school which was forever cold
and damp, horrendously so in the winter, when, fur cap and
winter coat on, she would dare take off her gloves only in
order to handle the paintbrush of one child or another. She
also pitied the poor kids, whose hands coarsened with too
much work in the field looked so aged so early. They were
uncouth, noisy, and totally unskillful, though some of them
were not that reluctant to go to the trouble of doing
something with a brush in hand. As to the older pupils, they
could not care less. They would sneer and snigger, and give
one another nudges with their elbows, or sling words that
hardly made any sense. There was a detached building
containing two enormous halls, where the high school
classes were held, in which the students' voices resonated
three times louder, even ten times so in winter, when the
noise banged on the ice-cold walls. What Mim tried to do
was guide them toward a world of colors and light, toward
themselves and whatever was valuable in each of them.
Nonetheless, she had a sense of absolute helplessness. The
more so when it was freezing cold in the classrooms and
they all tried to keep in check the violent chattering of their
teeth and stomped their feet in an involuntary,
monotonous, hushed drill. Mim simply could not envisage
those children's hands, reddened and numb with cold, able
to draw long gentle strokes of a brush, against the
resonance with their huddled up souls. It was their souls
that Mim could not reach, which she did not virtually mean
to, as she had from the start encountered an amorphous
wall of apathy and lack of response. She had been seeking
to find the passionate essence of her country's nature, once
laid lavishly on countryside natives, who would in turn offer
it generously to the traveler. Such were the memories from
her childhood, when she would range across various

regions each summer with her folks.

They would hike up mountains and over hills, climb past waterfalls in the heart of dusky woods, visit monasteries, or go rowing on lakes which kept amazing legends locked beneath the mirror of their surface. All the paths on which they treaded were strewn with love and hospitality, sprinkled by Mother Nature, one would say, upon the homes of the local people. The spirit of the realm would reveal itself to little Tomina in their eyes and their gait, in the hands which had painted the façades of their dwellings so cheerful and sunny, those hands which had planted the flowers outside their gates. They spoke in a tongue as sweet as the land they inhabited. What beautiful footpaths and lanes, what fairy tale-like abodes lining them, only to lavish upon travelers whisperings of endearment! And what a suite of flowers to cheer both dweller and passer-by! The spirit of the country where she was born and of its people simply enthralled Mim. She felt love for those simple, upright, wholesome people, legend tellers and dance stampers — she used to think that was why they called their house yards *bataturi*. She felt love for those well-scrubbed, law-abiding peasants who would glance in the distance over valleys and hills, earnestly tending to the livestock in the yard and the crops in the fields. And what fabulous forests there were, which would transiently creep scraps of primeval secrets into her child's ears, and the chorus of birds chirping in response to one another, tuning in to the chorus of light which sieved through the canopy above, reaching down to the moist darkness below. What a wealth of pure water springs and lively brooks running down with fresh tales to be told. Where is the cleanliness of foretime? Or was it that she perceived everything through a child's unspoiled senses?

She also misses the traditional old time farmstead of the plains of Baragan. In spite of having grasped its essence only once, that feeling would not leave Mim's soul. Barren, battered earth yard, a solitary leafless tree stock with all the branches chopped down to stubs for the poultry to perch on, a squat mudbrick hut painted in a stark azure, so spotless and pleasantly cool inside, a boon against the sweltering heat. The amaranth coated wooden floorboards and the walls were covered in hand-woven rugs, shaken clean every morning against the tree trunk in the yard. The simple wooden cot, so high and absurdly bulgy in contrast with its narrowness, priding on an array of huge plump pillows in white starched linen cases, displayed a colorful bedspread woven by the wife on the loom, with pure wool thread spun by her very hands from the fleece of sheep taken by local shepherds to graze on the bogs by the great river, on vast moorlands up north, on the fat grasslands at the bottom of the mountains.

Mim tends to physically lean forward, as though longing to join that fascinating world now gone, with women bent over their weaving looms and men waging their daily simple wars, longing to revive the feeling of joy this idyllic way of life once gave her. She herself stems from those peoples' existence, and she wants to revisit them through her paintings. Every day, she comes back from the remote school where she teaches art, and immerses herself into painting, avidly seeking to reconstruct the spirit she would have liked to find in that village. She could faintly discern it, true, while she was waiting for the commuting coach towards evening in summertime, on the rare occasions when she did not hurry to catch the noon one to get home sooner. The quiet courtyards with all the necessary goods and chattels, the tall poplars, the fruit-trees, the livestock with their pungent, mind-invigorating odors, which boosted one's sense of the soil and of what God created to walk on it, the sense of one's own yard. The soft breathing of the zesty breeze coming from the fields, the peace of the small wooden bench at the gate, some chance careless mulberry dropping from its leafy nest with a shy smile, the languid dancing of the road dust thirsty for rain, her own thought of God's water, of the fertile broth in the soil, of sprouting and of fruiting. Once seated on a rustic bench like those, she could no longer bring herself to leave it, immersed in contemplation of the balmy tranquility around, of that simple, honest way of living. It was only in such moments that she realized that village meant more than the bleak, unwelcoming classrooms of the school. Then, how could she explain her heart's beating with joy and her body's almost involuntary jump to the margin of the road when she recognized the front of the approaching bus in the distance? How could she explain the sense of victory she had every day when the vehicle transporting her entered the town? She understands it was simply because that was where the fire of her family's household burnt, that was where her mother cooked the meals and would wait dinner for her, and where her father would bid her welcome by shaking out his smile before her, inviting her with his eyes to step in — come in, Daddy's dear, to bless the home with your presence. Her father was full of love for his wife and children.

Back then, the immediate purpose of each and every day of her life, starting with the very moment of her getting out through the apartment's door, was to return home. She often felt indescribably wretched, cast away on the outskirts of the world, treading on either dusty or snowy lanes, frozen to the bone, not able to discern the least sign of movement on the road which led to the city. She would reflect on her wasted existence, on what she could have achieved if she had chosen to live her life beside Stefan instead of reliving the memory of her life with Anton. If she had not traded the world of the theatre, offered to her on a silver platter, for the depiction on canvas of her love for Anton, concealed in her small room, so close to the sky. There was a period of time when Stefan would follow her about, to the train station, even to her parents' town to talk to them, and would ask nonplussed: what is wrong with me, why is she running away from me like that? At that very time she was wandering in the footsteps of Anton and Mim as they once were: along the river bank, over the gentle greenness of the area across the river, up the tame hills on which his town stood, on alleys among apartment blocks where they had once reveled, on the sunny gravel around the lighthouse, to the ferry pier, down wide slanting avenues, along the side of freeways. She had decided to keep wandering on her own, to go to that faraway rural place, amidst populations of grasses spread on vast fields on the way to the sea. There, she thought, she would be able to draw inspiration for her art, searching at leisure for the earth's perfumes, taking in the spice and the rustle of the wild vastness of the lowlands. There she would find the proper shades and tones of green on which to plant her raving love and grow it, then let it loose into the world, and hopefully back to him, to Anton. 'Stefan, I simply can't' — this had been her decision — 'I can't accept that position at the theatre; I will go to that village and I'll think everything over.' That was when Stefan finally understood her, he let go of her. He has never so much as given her a phone call ever since, nothing. Comprehension had cut through him like a sharp blade.

With time, it had got into her head that maybe commuting was wearing her out. Waking up before daybreak, then all that anxiety and daily feeling of extreme apprehension at the likely prospect of missing the bus and not finding another four-wheeled vehicle to take her back to town for the night exhausted her both physically and psychically. Therefore she soon hit on a beneficial solution: she would stay there over the week and return home only on Saturdays. She had started to speak heartily about her new scheme to her parents — you'll see how I'll turn fresh as a daisy again, and that clean country air will do me a world of good. Uh-huh, yeah, absolutely — her mother would hum in a skeptical, omniscient tone, while keeping a compassionate smile on her lips. Why do you say that, would Mim counteract in outbursts of passionate conviction that she was right, and subsequently lend credit to her plan by reminding her mother how pretty she always looked in autumn, after the harvesting season, when both students and teachers had to work in the field.

Each September, with the beginning of school term, it made her sick only to think of the harvesting drudgery, what with the marching of the whole army of school staff and pupils all the way to the distant field, and with the toiling under the roasting sun till dusk. Hours seemed to stop still, days to last forever. Then the exhausting footslog back to the village. And what with the waiting for a lift on the margin of the road and with rolling back to town in a chance old jalopy or a wreck of a van, her home seemed to her so distant in space and time. In spite of her constant grumbling and sighing, once she found herself reunited with her family she looked her very best, with blooming roses in her cheeks and eyes sparkling with robust health. She ate with appetite and slept like a log, and had a teenager's agility and briskness of mind. Very well, then, Tomina, let me see you at it — her mother would smile in disbelief. Let the girl have a try — her father would break in. 'Why, do you think I will stop her, I won't.' Her parents had always let her choose for herself what to do, whatever made her feel good. 'Indeed, Mom, you've always told me that.'

So said, so done. Mim made arrangements with an old woman who lived near the bus stop to hovel her over the week. The woman did not have a dreamlike courtyard like those Mim had seen as a child in Moldova, nor did she boast a homestead as pretty as the other ones in the neighborhood, but what counted for Mim was that she was no longer going to spend each moment of her life with an eye to the road, that she would no longer have to wake up at the crack of dawn, nor would she waste so much time on commuting.

"All right, mother dear, I'll be waiting for you. But I'm telling you, dear — as I reckon you should know — you'll have to sleep in the same bed with me, there's no other."

"Er…, yes, it's OK, I think I can put up with that. I'll have a try tomorrow night just to see what it's like."

However, the following evening, once she found herself into the woman's yard, a wave of extreme loneliness came over Mim. The time inevitably came for her to be shown that which was going to be her night quarter.

"There you are, mother dear, that's the bed over there. But get this, dear, I wake up rather early, to work on my loom, can't help it."

"What time?"

"Well, to speak truth, mother dear, that'd be at fourish."

First came the weaving loom, at the window, crammed between the door and the bed.

"I'm afraid I might cause you a little trouble, dear, as the bed shakes every time I pull the batten," the woman explained.

This time a dark cloud descended upon Mim's conscious, definitely ruining her contentment about a new beginning. Will she be able to cope with that?

While waiting for the night to fall she imaged the long grey course of the road, the apartment building where her family dwelled and which rose tall on the right side, as soon as the line of poplars ended and the bus rolled into town. She visualized her mom and dad quietly seated in the kitchen mentioning her, what might their daughter be doing right then, and would she be all right? She got overwhelmed with a deep sense of pity for herself, seated as she was on a little stool outside the tiny cottage in utter desolation, wishing for the dark to send her right in that ridiculous bed, where she could finally stretch her slouching body on the side by the wall. Meager words were exchanged, but what conversation could she make with the poor woman. Mim had turned minute and insignificant, a mere squirt on the face of the earth.

All night long she did nothing but wait for daybreak, for eight o'clock, for the classes to begin, for two o'clock, and finally for the commuting coach to pick her up and take her straight home. If only day could come sooner, she kept praying, nose pressed against the coarse wool of the wall tapestry. Where have you cast the poor soul of her, dear God, with no one beside, no akin soul to turn to. She retraced images from her gratifying life up till then: fabulous her sparkling her way along the shoreline on balmy summer evenings or turning heads at parties, arms linked with Stefan; her Bovarism in the all crème apartment of a faint luxury tinge, that apartment she so much yearned for now, from where she could look across the river in the distance any time she wished, imagining Anton was there; her last cry for Stefan, her lenient, ever so gentle Stefan — she was blind drunk, had been grimly vicious earlier, heartsick before that, and only a few previous days she had been paralyzed in shock.

It was on a Sunday when she felt like traveling again, so she set out for their town, Anton and Stefan's, thinking she might dare pay the latter a visit, as this much he had last said, that whenever she pleased Mim could call on to pick up the photos taken of them at the party in the theatre's foyer. Despite her stern, arduous hopes, suspicion was growing in her mind that something terribly ironic might have occurred inside her body just as she had made a final decision and left Stefan's place. Well, it was this feeling that prompted her to see him again.

She on the staircase climbing up toward Stefan's flat is imploring each and every step to accommodate her feet, her mounting emotions covered in shame, shame for being, this time, for him. Once she finally comes to face the too well known door, she takes a deep breath and presses the knob of the doorbell for just one tick, prepared to wait. She is praying he would be at home, and God it has already got dark, and she hears the clank of the door catch. There he is in the slim opening of the door, mellow and warm, making her think of a ripened fruit, dark eyes lucent under his embrowned brow. He is taken aback by the sight of her: wow, Tomina! His brow brightens all at once, yet too ripe, heavy-eyed, it is too late. Mim can sense a shadowy presence in the house, Mim is too late. He takes her in, faint-heartedly it seems, and she makes a cautious step into the vestibule, then she follows him into the dining room, the room of the subdued gleams where she had written her diploma paper. They both seat at one end of the oval table. "How are you doing?" Rather tepid and clumsy. His embarrassment masks a mix of frigidity and warmth, as he keeps his big watery eyes glued on her. He remains like that just for her to send, to his pupils as dark and woeful as the top of the table, an equally equivocal answer: I've just run in to see you. Stefan seems to come back to his senses and lets her know how happy he is to see her again, then excuses himself: wait a minute. The shadow which had perturbed her intuition earlier has been stealthily expanding within the house, and she can by now feel it like a constant pressure on her temples. As the shadow is secretly closing in on her heart, here reappears Stefan, sequenced by a young woman. In plush house slippers, Mim recognizes the short-haired girl of a quick roving eye — aha, that one.

Some night that woman was seated at a table in the white restaurant downtown and Stefan had pointed to her with a malicious grin saying, "See that girl over there? Never a night passes that she doesn't come here, I gather on the lookout for men to join her." Not many minutes after that, he invited her to their table and Mim was surprised to see she had a foot cast in plaster. "I simply like it here, so what can I do?" she addressed Tomina. Then, exposing her stiff bandaged leg under the table in a gesture of blunt frankness, she continued in a proud voice, "In spite of this, I'm here all the same, aren't I?"

They greet each other now, curtly and dully, after which the girl immediately disappears, with Stefan on her heels. Mim is contemplating her own chin as it is reflected by the murky sheen below, her lips, her nostrils, the sockets of her eyes — ugh, she looks ugly, and what the heck is she doing here? Whereupon another question enters her mind: what is that person doing here, of all people? Her screams get to Mim from the bedroom. Bawling and squalling interspersed with hysterical sobbing are rasping in her ears like mad. Mim has the impression the woman has climbed up on top of the bed, whence she is hurling pillows at him, with every throw emitting harrowing wails laden with hatred and anger. Stefan's husky voice travels the lengthy corridor in such low timorous waves, as though trying to tame one woman and appease the other one at the same time, to restore peace in the home. Mim can no longer witness this pathetic domestic show, so she rises to her feet and makes for the front door. She pauses in the vestibule, hesitant, wishing to say goodbye. Stefan shows up at the other end of the hallway, distressed, worried, yet teeming with benevolence — forgive me, he says. "I'm on my way, goodbye." "I'm sorry, Mim, I don't have the photos here, they're at my parents' — you came out pretty well, you know — I am really happy you've come, believe me — we haven't even had time for a chat." Contented without any apparent reason, she waits for him to open the door for her, gets out, scurries down each flight of stairs with light cheery steps, and lets herself out into the kingly September atmosphere, inhaling greedily, oh, this beautiful life, how fascinatingly complicated it is, and Mim has already made her debut on its winding corridors, long, crisscrossing, infinite. Sucking in strength from the rich autumn air, she is swaggering to the train station. Oof, if only it were not for that nasty menace which keeps biting at her mind, prompting her to start praying. She should entreat nature it were not true, and that providence had not left any mark of Stefan's in her womb and it could bring her back to life completely liberated, back to herself. Solely once has she made love with him, one single unique time, and — curse strikes. Why, oh why was she fated to suffer in the wake of them men?

No later than one week after that take-leave visit she gets ready to attack — be it or not, she will not wait a minute longer. She is dead set on putting into practice what she had had a mind to, were Anton not going to inject into her that killer serum two years ago. She will do what she thinks could not allow any form of life survive, and will persist in putting herself to torture, even though she will have to die in the process. She had started to apply herself to the ordeal the previous night, by heaving the bed in her room ad nauseam, and she resumed that routine first thing in the morning, laboring with such grimness that she felt the arteries in her head almost burst and her eyes pop out. She had bought a bottle of red wine, vermouth — she had heard it was toxic enough, and she would drink it till the last drop: half of it before the searing-hot bath, and the other half afterwards. A still from a movie had lingered on her mind, of a dead-drunk young woman immersed in a steaming bathtub. Everything fitted in well — it was a Sunday, and a hot-water day on top of that. She let the water scald her for as long as she could bear, while she concentrated her mind and senses on tracing the effect of that hotness inside her body, right beneath the pubic mound. Every time she stirred the water with her hips, there was an unsparing sensation which not only sent all her blood on simmer, but also caused the local neural network to panic. That was when Mim felt the effect of the procedure at its deepest, like needles being cruelly plugged into the flesh inside her. Cruel, nothing short of cruel was Mim on herself that time, savage and barbaric, swaying on her feet intoxicated as she kept telling herself she was powerful and would make it, she would prevail over Stefan and any of his traces on her. She headed out of the steamy bathroom back to the safety of her own room, eager to get hold of the bottle and finish off its content. Her folks were in the dining room, confident she was either painting or reading. She slit the door aside and, as cautiously as she could, took the telephone from the small table in the hallway inside, placing it on the floor. Now she was ready to start forcing that liquid down her throat, which she reluctantly but with unflinching determination did, continuously asking herself what might those men feel, who drank their bellies full. She found that out not long after she drained the last solitary drop, when the walls began to swirl around her and she dropped flat down beside the telephone. She had nearly lost control of her limbs, which she would hoist up in the air and then let drop heavy in a most absurd, awkward manner, but why, there was such cool refreshing blessing on that red carpeting, with the yellow telephone between her legs, as was she not in the center of the universe, was she not unique and craving for the world, which she knew would be hers. Oh, yes, right there and then, she had the world in her pocket and everything she had to deal with was just a mere bagatelle, including this histrionic crying of hers for Stefan, despite the longing thrusting through her like a searing iron rod. Her eyes welled up — well, let her have her cry out, let her indulge in her dramatics, caressed with her own humors, prostrate on the ground. In the silence of twilight, the wide world was humming Verdi's *Marcia Trionfale* to her. Although she ached for Stefan, she was stronger than life. She phoned him — I just wanted to hear your voice. God knows what else she said and how she said it, and what the man might have imagined. Anyway, she does not think she unveiled too much of her grief, as she did so once the handset was back in its cradle. On a notebook she had found blank at hand it still stands scribbled in large, loose, barely legible handwriting: *Stefan, I love you and I want to be your woman,* with numberless variations on pages and pages on end. The following day she was again free and all by herself.

She was all by herself now, forgotten beside an old woman in a shack of a house in a village which had gone pitch dark with nightfall and would not see light before the first gleams of the day. How she wished the sun would rise at once. She was counting the plump lazy seconds one after another and this is how she must have eventually dozed off. Bam-wham-zonk, bam-wham-zonk — the cot went, jarring with crack and thunder. It yawed and rammed against the wall and pitched, and just as she thought it would snap, it brusquely came to a halt. She had been roused by the beating of her own heart, and it was dark, still night — darn, whenever will dawn crack here? When she turns on the other side, the peasant's wide behind clad in dun-colored bafta meets her sleepy eyes. She is pounding in stern commitment against the beater of the loom by the dim light of the petroleum lamp. In mute amazement, Mim is gaping at the woman's elbows butting the air hither. Now, stillness — she is passing the yarn across, yeah, this is what she must be doing. There is an interlude of silence when the peasant keeps her upper body bent over the loom, working with her hands, then — bam-wham-zonk. By now Mim's heart jolts in apprehension just a moment before, as soon as she sees the woman's elbows getting ready for attack. She abandons herself to the torture for hours on end, as where on earth could she go?

That was Mim's only night in the village. On the following day, the nearer she got to the town, the more thankful she felt for its kindness to have her back, wallowing in deep feelings of love for its people and the stores, the lighting, her comfortable bed, her family. For some time she had been trying to read the envy of the village folks, but it was only during that night that she got to the back of it. Why, them city folks had water running out of the wall, as it were, and if they cared for some refreshment or some ice cream, they had only to stop at any corner and buy it. Oh my, they could even have a seat at a table if they wished to and gape at the passers-by, or they might as well go into a cinema hall and watch some movie.

In spite of all these, that village is the place where she smelled the herbs of the earth, where her soles felt the ever so lovely tolerance of the soil, where she used to get lost in the distance feeling the world as God made it. Time was slow in the fields, there was humiliation, as sometimes teachers were also required to do their allotted stint, depending on the party's directions of the day. They were supervised and there was even lecturing and loud admonishing for leaving behind some unpicked potato or who knows what other vegetable. At times, there still flickers in her mind the image of a former primary school teacher in the neighboring village turned party activist — erect in her red high-wheeled sulky — who would turn up unawares to check on them, blowing hot coals on their tracks. The lunch hours, however, were a real gratification for Mim. Enchanted, she would listen to the call of the grassland, to the swish of the wind, to the insects. She would gulp in the scent-laden air, trying to discern smells and aromas and tell them apart, her eyes gaping in the radiance all around. It was there that she fell in love with soil and where she envisaged her future paintings, so enthralling, stemming from some kind of orgasmic loneliness. Mim understands she had been fatally cast there to be united with the earth. Without this, her love would have remained voiceless, and her paintings maybe too watery. The earth is the substance of everything she has displayed.

22 THE SEA

It can be no other than him — why, at this hour! The dorm room was quiet, with all the girls reading themselves to sleep. "Come, Mim." He must have come straight from the road to see her — Mim knew he had only left that morning for the capital city on business and expected him to stay there for two days at the least, as he had announced. "You've come back so soon" — should she pitch it as a question or an exclamation, well, she is happy he has returned on the selfsame day, hurrying back to her. "Mim, I've been missing you badly, come." He drags her into the glare of the corridor's neon lights, and shuts her out of the coziness of the room, that long room of theirs lit by a sole joke of a bulb. "Bye, girls!" Mim somehow took pride in leaving them in there to squint their eyes at leisure, if they pleased. Bye, I am being carried along by him, she wanted to tell them every time she left with Anton. But what, has he got a Tatar's puckered eyes now? His round hazel eyes, proteanly warm or glassy or gloating, are now darting blazing glances at her, from irises turned so hugely globular that she wonders how come they do not leap out of those squinted eyelids which, yes, seem to be squeezing out want, hunger — he must be hungry, she muses. He squashes her against his chest, crushes her small face into the wooly fibers of his sweater — it smells of road. Hidden between the flaps of his jacket, Mim rejoices with a feeling of shelter, as if in an interior that is both cold and warm, since the autumn air is also there with her enjoying the comfort of the male protector, of her man. When Anton slightly pushes her back to take a look, she comes out dizzied. "Mim, all the way here I've been thinking only of you, will you believe me? I tore along to reach you sooner and drove directly here. I didn't even stop home to change or eat something." The creases in the corners of his eyes — Mim sees them clearly for the first time, maybe he is tired now, but this is what he might look like in older age. The sudden realization that Anton is already a fully mature man sends a pleasant thrill up her spine. He is at least more mature than her, with those Herculean shoulders of his which had arduously carried whole carcasses of animals over and over again, entire fleshy pigs and huge cow legs, to sell them on his own account and make money, piles of money, as few were able to earn at the time in the country, and buy himself a car. 'It took me only a year's span, Mim, and I got directly to the factory with a bag of cash and purchased it' — and his face would burst into a smug grin. 'Well, my old man has dough, loads of it, but I wanted the car to be solely mine, Mim, so I worked double tides and sweated and slaved like a Trojan and got it, that was my ambition.' He pulls her along behind him until they reach the somber front door, all made of iron. The janitor is dozing in her chair behind the glass partition. Mim tosses one more oblique glance in the direction of her window as she creeps hastily out after Anton on the coda of her string of remembrances. 'Many a time I was within an ace of being caught, Mim, but I never stopped, I could have been put behind bars for life, you know.' Alas, he looks just like an escaped convict now, *el fugitivo*. And with the heavy clang of the iron door still echoing between her frozen ribs, there falls upon her a hail of parched lips, famished and fumbling, and no saliva would come out of his dried out glands — her mouth is caught unawares. "I'm drained, Mim, I can't take you to my place tonight. It's already too late and I know you have courses tomorrow morning, but I want us to spend a little time together."

Mim has never seen him like that. You might think he is running away from something or someone, back to Mim, it is only Mim he hungers for and he seems fearful of losing her. What on earth might he have met at the end of that day's trip? He takes her by the hand and leads her to the road border where lies in waiting, in a similar pitiable condition, splattered in mud, the car in which they had spent so many beautiful times reeling out their happiness like a ribbon over hills and valleys and into the wide world. "Come into our car, Mim, it's our car, right? Everything that belongs to me belongs to you too, you know, just like at home." He opens the door for her and she gets in, then he eagerly goes round to the other side, his door slams shut and the next thing she knows, his lips are rubbing against her mouth in a wild, random manner, and they keep doing so until they moisten — the roof of his mouth smells fasting, aha, it is him this time, Mim thinks, another memory coming back to her.

Being permanently enthralled by thoughts of Anton and the prospect of meeting him, Mim would simply neglect her meals, and there were days when she did not have a single bite of food until late into the afternoon, when she would often wait for him to return from work at his parents' home. Once, he had no sooner come through the door than he told her to open her mouth in order to have her breath checked: blow your breath toward me, Mim. "Why?" she asked. "Blow your breath out, come on," he encouraged her. She had immediately realized her stomach smelled empty, so she would not open her mouth, ashamed.

Blow! — she could not help it and did so at last. "Do you know why it smells like that, you haven't eaten, that's why." That once, embarrassment poured down through her like liquid, all the way from top to toe, and she swore she would always put something in her stomach before she met him.

Without warning he grasps her nape and pushes her head down, nose between his thighs. He is bulgy, his corduroys give out a heady reek of road dust and gasoline, and he keeps pressing her mouth against the incredible beam apparent under his fly zipper, smothering her against its copper teeth as though inducing her to pray they would uncouple at once and rid her of their strange, ferruginous taste. He was entreating her, Mim thought, to slide the zipper open and disclose the swollen heart beneath, enveloped in warm human membrane, for a change. Then he suddenly jerks his hips upward and unzips his fly. "Forgive me, Mim, for coming to you unwashed like this; say, will you forgive me, I would've been too late otherwise, but it will never happen again, I promise." It is feverish, breathing sweet mildness against her cheek. Anton forces her lips apart with that virile bold heart of his, Mim prides in its hotness, and his strong hand on the nape of her head spurring her is giving her frissons, except that she is suddenly faced with an unfamiliar taste, acrid and pungent, miasmic, rancid, and fetid vapors of an unknown kind creep through her nostrils up to the sinuses — no, this is not him. This is not the hygiene freak she knew, who would take a shower ten times a day if needed, who would check up for smells all around him, sniffing people, sniffing her, yes, he enjoyed her smell. No, this is not him. And yet, it was still him, 'I've been waiting for this moment since morning,' the man simply wanted his woman, he wanted her, Mim. She is hard put to it though to satisfy her man like that. In the dead silence she is struggling to find a way within herself. "Come on, Mim," he pleads.

Late in the middle of the night, he is parking the car

on the narrow strip of ground between the long building of the students' dorm and the tall neighboring concrete fence. "It is better here, Mim, no one can see us." He was aching for her, "You know well the way I can best feel the woman in you." He sat her on his lap, and all along his virile strive, when he assumed he was making her feel woman, she did nothing but picture herself as if she were a rat doe, miry and scared-stiff, and there was mire under the car's voiceless wheels, and her almandine eyes turned round, two red vitreous pinpoints scanning from the darkness one lit window or another of the dorm building. Impassible students are lying under their bed covers whispering, reading, playing cards, while she has to endure, for fear she would wound his pride and he might fly into a rage, and she could lose him. 'You should never turn me down, Mim, if you want to keep me.'

They kissed and she came back to herself again, and she felt she had won her Antonush back too. He was soon off, leaving the poor rat of herself to open, at that godawful hour, the heavy iron portal, head hung in shame, praying she would not meet the janitor's eyes, however sleepy those might be, only that Mim's eyes could not help stealing a peep, which, damn it, once shot, seemed to have purposefully clutched flat under the woman's drooping eyelids. A venomous jet spattered from there and got to the marrow of her bones. Trembling in a pool of shame, that was how she waded her way through the corridor that time. Marrow wallowing in shame, veins wallowing in shame, she left long trails of guilt all the way to the warm wooden door, then once on the other side — blackout, and finally under her quilt, sacrosanct comfort.

He had been finally away, therefore, but not in August, as written on the back of that postcard. They were already in October. It had been in her soul rather than her mind that she had been counting the moments until that date, waiting to see if he would go to meet that woman. She was dating him in the capital city on August 23rd. Mim's heart was telling her the truth — they both knew the sender of those lines had been the one important woman in Anton's life And if he left town in August, then Mim would find out how important that woman still was for him. Contrary to her gloomy expectations though, right in the heat of August he took her on vacation to the seaside. "It's just the two of us this time, it's our holiday," Anton announced. He had put her through so many tests, and their first travel there had been a sort of pilot-study on her, as had all their dates that summer, for that matter. Or at least that was what she felt. He would keep a close watch on her with his utmost observant eye, while Mim simply rested in wait for his whatever next move. Poor fool, not a day passed without her praying for him to call her up, to collect her from Aunt Ana's one more time and take her with him. She may have not been sure whether or not she had passed that test, but he choosing to spend that summer's vacation with no other than her was a fact.

Loaded with Mim's red flabby sack and her traveling bag, he walking ahead of her to the car parked at the opposite curb of the little side street, with Mim, a little confused, closely behind — "Oh, they've left the lid of the trunk ajar!" "Who are they?" she asks, stopping in her tracks. "Some thieves, who else?" He takes a peep inside and concludes: they've stolen my bag. Which one, well, there was a plastic bag with some ewe's cheese, come on now, why should they steal somebody's cheese, of all things? She gives him a show-me look then gets nearer and pokes her head under the lid of the trunk, only to meet a sight of exquisite tenderness, which makes her lips round in wonder: bashful, three delicate rose buds of a deep pomegranate hue lie in there alone, like a godsend. "Wow, roses, how beautiful," she exclaims. "Who laid them here?" "Why, them thieves!" he scoffs, shrugging his shoulders. "They've left roses behind, how nice," Mim marvels to tears, "such wonderful thieves they are, aren't they!" Lips still apart in disbelief, she starts to have a good look around the car, under the beam of his smiling gaze. "Oh no, nothing of this is true," she decides, and even if she is shy to consider this, she lets it out in the open, "It was you!" Indeed, that Anton should have done such a thing is even harder to believe, but whoever the rose angel was, her soul is already flying ahead of them on the road. He denies firmly: it wasn't me, and I really don't know who put them in there, cross my heart. Too late, she has already gotten into her head the idea that the roses are from him. The mental image of him bending over to place the rose buds in the car trunk, with a thought of her, and for her, will not leave Mim. Why then should he persist in exculpating himself? He could not bring himself to convey open signals to her, or maybe he felt uncomfortable with that, or was simply maladroit.

Mim took the roses — each had its stalk wrapped in tin foil, and laid them by the rear window of the car, and her heart kept hurting through the whole ride for fear they would wither in the scorching sun, but she was too bashful to let her love feelings for them show, as might they not be love tokens from him? Never mind, she kept telling herself with a shrinking heart, if they did dry out then she would keep them for life. He never avowed authorship of that gesture. Those roses, however, which she keeps confined under a glass cylinder, still are the most precious things she possesses, with so much love concealed in their petals.

The month of August was gone, September days had passed one by one, Mim had moved from Aunt Ana's to the student dorm, from where Anton would pick her up every evening to take her to his parents' place, then back to the dorm around midnight, and this until each weekend, when they would stick together for one whole day and a half. And he had not been anywhere away from town without her. It was only now that he had gone to the capital, whence he had brought himself heaps of new clothes. Of course, to her he had not shown them all at once. Instead, every day he would nonchalantly put on yet another new garment. They all suited him well and there was no other man in town dressed like him, this was his newly acquired attitude. 'Do you like this, Mim? You won't see the like of it on anybody else here.' There were sweaters made of fine soft wool, pastel-colored cardigans, denim jackets and overalls, and many other items which were obviously coming from abroad. She remembered he had one other time been away for a day alone, before the date mentioned in that postcard, when she had also noticed an upgrade in his wardrobe. Those secretive escapades of his remained a mystery for Mim but, with their exception, she knew everything he did, she accompanied him wherever he went, be it on business or personal. 'I suppose you've seen that postcard — tell me, Mim, did I go anywhere? I'm one woman's man, and that woman is you now, period.' Therefore he had left that card on display on purpose, for Mim to see it and, when the time came, be convinced of his faithfulness. Was this his only way of showing affection? As for that woman, Mim felt she must have upset him deeply and wondered if maybe she had betrayed him in some way. Aha, she had betrayed him by leaving the country, by going there where he could not possibly follow her. The image of a living figurine was taking shape in Mim's subconscious, of a ballerina who had left her native country to make a career in the free world. 'As long as I can't go abroad,' he had once told Mim, 'I am determined to be as well off here as I could be there, and I will.' He must have suffered immensely, Mim thought, and decided to settle a score with life by making a fortune. Lurking at the back of her mind, however, was the dispiriting intuition that Anton had also vowed to himself never to fall for a woman again. All he needed was a woman to love HIM. And it so happened that he found Mim, and Mim was trying hard to give him proof of her love, only that it was damn difficult to bring him out of his shell. Women deal in histrionics and are hypocrites. They must have become the epitome of evil in his mind, therefore he would go out there to take revenge and punish them, try them out and torment them until he got to the very core of them: their true love or nothing.

In his student years, Anton used to act with a well-known youth theater group. Mim was stupefied by his improvisation in a restaurant during their vacation on the sea coast. He had put on his act so well, that she really believed him then to be an authorized official of some ministry, wondering why he had never told her that before. On their way out of the restaurant, still thrilled with astonishment, she asked him if he actually worked for that ministry, and his answer came in a tick: no. He took her once to see a performance of that theater group when they came on tour to their town. Ophelia was meandering mad, genuinely mad, among the audience seated in circles in the stageless grand hall all aglare with light from the arc lamps, muttering a tune in the darkness of her grievous condition, so heartbreakingly aloof in her ignorance, puzzling Mim and opening wells of despair deep down in her heart. She had somehow brusquely grasped the irreversibility of that disorder of the mind, which made her cry inwardly. Madness was like death. When one goes mad, you cannot have them anymore. They may breathe in this world, but they do no longer belong here. All the other characters were shouting their vindications or rending the mute air with their perorations, they were worrying and brooding and mulling things over, and would trot about and wobble among the concentric rows of spectators. Anton, in a pensive mood, would steal a glance toward the VIP area, and whisper into Mim's ear something like: see that bearded man over there, he is the manager of the company, great theater personality. Anton was engrossed in profound admiration for that man and in memories of those fabulous years when he had been involved with art. "Why don't you go talk with him during the intermission," Mim suggested readily, but no, there was no way he would do that, he said, and she insisted on a variation of the theme, wondering whether or not that man would recognize him if he did that. "I'm blessed if I know," he said with a shrug of his shoulders. He was pretending. He was again keeping her in the dark with reference to his past life. But what with a word here and what with a whisper there, Mim gradually came to infer from Anton that the famous producer was an eccentric, that kind of bizarre *monstre sacré*, maybe a gay, and without doubt, a giant in the theater world. He was literally crazy, according to Anton, as only an insane personality like his could devise and stage such productions. "Well, what do you think, Mim, have you ever seen anything to match this?" She had not, true. That show had left her dumbfounded. Never had she imagined *Hamlet* staged that way, shocking and at the same time so unaffectedly humane, sublime, so disturbingly close to your soul. That Ophelia haunted her for nights and days on end. The breath of her voice, the nacreous sheen of her skin, the airy veil of her blonde locks and those vacant eyes, her madness, had all impregnated Mim's mind, and for life, she thought. She assumed that hallucinatory amalgam featured him, the producer, the brilliant director, the magus with his tangle of warped sexual instincts — God, how fiercely handsome all the boys in the troupe were, and God how fiercely handsome Anton himself was. It must have been impossible for the maestro not to feel drawn to a still more handsome Anton, un-mellowed, white, and so sweet-lipped. Had the master's hand perchance patted him on the shoulder, had he ever whispered in his ear or breathed against his tall nape, had he, for any random instant, glued the pupils of his eyes to the wild raw smile between Anton's teeth? If so, what might Anton have made of it — the pores of her skin could detect a strange emotion breathing around her man like an aura. What had his instinct told him, she wondered, had he or had he not been at the threshold of a different taste, on the borderline to the unknown, to another beyond. And had he made at least one step across?

There was no way of finding an answer to that. She might have just as well taken up voodoo to shed some light on it, or on such obscure issues like the lady in the postcard, Anton's road trips to pick up western stuff — and, above all, did he care at all about Mim?

Mrs. Rosu. What on earth did Anton do with Mrs. Rosu on the very first day of their vacation by the sea? It was almost evening when, out of the blue, he announced Mim he had to go and see that woman, who had helped them find accommodation on the overcrowded seaside. "Just tell me why," Mim went on and on keeping an ambiguous smile on her face, "why do you say you have to go?" "Listen, Mim, I won't be long, it's just that I promised her, and you know better she's gone to no end of trouble to help us." It so happened that he let slip a string of some most nonsensical, ludicrous words: I'm just doing the curls for Mrs. Rosu. Hmm, what might he have meant by 'doing the curls'? On a first impulse, she could not think of other but pubic hair, since that was curly with everyone, right? But she held back that hunch, for heaven's sake, no, what in God's name was Anton? Sakes! — he never meant to tell her that he was going to trade a quickie with a stranger for a hotel room? She scoffed that off as preposterous, only that the smile on her lips was wane enough when she questioned him about what exactly he intended to do with that woman, and it could not shake off the bitter taste, and soon her senses were presented with the delusion of some viscous pool of a mephitic stench — slops, her mind flicked away to slops and pictured her own smile writhing its way out of there as if it were a soggy rag, yes, this is how her smile was dripping toward Anton that evening, their first evening at the seaside together, just the two of them all alone, plus that thorn in Mim's side: Mrs. Rosu and the doing of her bloody curls. Her whole soul rose against this. She would not let him go, tears ready to drop off the lip of her eyelids, slops dripping and splashing her, such nasty defiance, Mim of all people, who had come here with her beloved man. The two of them on the road, alone in the cubicle of the dear car, he blazing the way for her, solely for her, through the archaic world on the other side of the grand river, up to the seashore, the two of them abreast facing the sunrise on the winding strip among mounds and hills. Then on the straight line of the highway cutting through endless fields of sunflowers, prostrate slaves to the king of light, through golden crops of wheat, past Tatar homesteads and groves of peach-trees, the two of them together, free in the wide world. "I hate you to go. If you go, then I'll go too. I'm going back home, I'm serious." He was still smiling and she wondered if the way his lips moved and came apart betrayed any guilt or not, since they appeared to be exceedingly elastic. And were those white powerful teeth he revealed to her view now in all their splendor, and next in a most discreet simper, lying to her or not? "Just tell me why you're going, it simply gets me." By and large, he repeated the same nonsense as before, tagging it: haven't I told you? The thing was that Mim could not make head or tail of that specific locution, *to do one's curls*, at least not in the context including Anton and that dame. What on earth did that mean, her overheated neurons kept searching. Well, he could not choose but go, only because he had promised, and that was flat. And he was laughing. Was he laughing at her childish fit of jealousy, which he probably found cute, was he poking fun at what he himself presumed the said lady might be happy to perpetrate with his aid during their brief business meeting, or was he simply considering the irony of the de facto situation, when he had to *do the curls* for one woman in order to be able to make love to another. Or still, he might well be laughing at Mim having misinterpreted his words, laughing at her, maybe because he enjoyed teasing her. And what if his laughter was nothing else but a nervous outburst, a guise for his own gaffe, when he had spoken out his mind and said out loud what he guessed that woman was after. God only knew why he was laughing, and insisting to go, and explaining, it was high time, and that one was waiting, and they were going to need her all through their stay there, as that room was only for a week's time, and he wanted to offer Mim a proper, long holiday. Mim got dark at heart, questioning the kind of man she had gone on vacation with. In his place, she would rather have left the seaside altogether and come back some other time maybe.

And when she thought of their arduous preparations and of the childlike enthusiasm of their packing for the road, and of the gusto with which they had gathered all they needed, and of how they actually flew off. They dropped by her parents' place first, with whom they ate out at a restaurant in the center of the city. They all sat at a table in the spacious glass-walled room, so dear to her as the eyes of the people she loved were all drowning in the same light. As they were about to leave there, he went to buy a bottle of whisky from the bar — 'Mim, I'm not taking my girlfriend to the seaside as any other man.' She was going to see how pure that drink was, all natural and premium quality Scotch, she would definitely like it. He also bought two cartons of cigarettes he knew she was fond of. Although they were not smokers, they would delight in lighting those wonderful long fine tobacco slims, which would give any interior an elegant misty touch, so magically soothing after their love making. And then, there was something else about those cigarettes that she knew they both equally relished, namely some kind of connection with the western world where they came from. They also had packets of high quality ground coffee for mornings, and lots of chocolate, wahoo, all the delicatessen stuff they could possibly need to indulge.

When they parked the car outside the hotel, Anton hurriedly fetching afterwards the key to the room, both loaded with luggage, going in, and the door — clang — shutting them inside, Mim plunged herself irrationally on one of the beds and he on top of her, for the very first time free in a room, incognito. It was there and then that they openly demonstrated to each other the long hungry yearning for that moment, for being on their own at last, free to throw themselves into each other with thudding and thumping and smashing and any other kind of noise, undaunted and loud, mouths opened to crack, limbs loose, forgetting about the pestering routine 'shh!', and about fingers tenderly manipulating the latch on his door, and even about music — just they and the music of their bodies. What wild excitement. They told each other their variants of that ride's story, and they were identical. He at the wheel focusing on the road ahead had been eagerly anticipating this, and so had she, playfully laughing beside him, and lavishing innocent caresses on him. They pulled at each other as though trying to catch up with all the frustration and cool down the urge. The bed linen was of an immaculate white, starched, sheet perfectly stretched on the flatness of the bed, as if to match the way they were, two plain bodies, two honest minds, united in one color. And after all this, why should her heart grow dark, why should she go back home? "I won't be a minute," he announced and went straight out of the door, leaving her alone in there, to turn purple with rage. The air inside weighed heavy on her, it turned lead in her chest, unable to nourish her brain. She felt it no longer received oxygen, she felt she was suffocating. He had therefore chosen for Mim to leave. Hardly had she reached that enlightening conclusion, when he turned up again, face as quiet as a blank sheet of paper. He seemed eager to see whatever he might put on it — was Mim really mad with him, was she brooding? "What, you're back already?" she expressed her surprise. "You can see me, right? I haven't had time to do anything you suspected. Is that clear now in your mind?" He had just told that woman he had to be right back. His girlfriend was upset.

What might Mrs. Rosu have made of Mim — a girl picked up by that handsome man and brought to the seaside for a bit of enjoyment, a docile bimbo, rather modest, plain, unattractive. That was what she had really looked like on arrival at that tourist agency, way-worn, skin dried out on her, hair wiry with dust, almost faint for lack of vitality, just hoping for Anton to find her a resting nest. Except that the dame got stunned when her eyes alighted upon the other facet of Mim — tall, elegant, a beam of distinction flaring from her lips up to her temples, due probably to unexpectedly regained happiness. That was when they both went to see her later that first night. The impact was downright physical on the poor woman, as though whacked in the head by the frame which encased this other, untouchably beautiful, image of Mim. As she was calmly seated in her office, the woman actually jerked her head backwards, and with such sudden violence you could expect her to lose it, expect her all-curls head to drop to the floor somewhere behind her desk, and Mim instantly visualized the beheaded possessor searching for it on all fours. Forget about Anton, the woman must have told herself, abruptly realizing, as it seemed, that she could not even dream of laying a finger on a man like him. Mim was the only kind of woman he would ever flaunt at his arm. Due to the shock, she even admitted sincerely: I could not imagine, when I first saw the young lady, that she could turn so pretty, she must've been awfully tired, well, I don't know how, but I just couldn't picture the two of you together; but now I've changed opinion, I'm amazed. "She is beautiful," she ended in a definite tone, addressing specifically to Anton. She sure would find them accommodation for another two weeks, they should feel free to contact her any time, and did they mind if they were to move to another resort? She waved them goodbye, then formed her fingers in an OK sign and said through the improvised circle: you are a million dollar pair.

They spent the latter part of their vacation at a luxury hotel on the beachfront, they once made love on the balcony, Anton did not care if anyone saw or heard them, let us *épater les bourgeois*, he said, let them get sick and green with envy. The evenings they would sip whisky, read naked, lick themselves, make love to each other until they got exhausted, then they would start the whole love ritual over again, with the sea moaning all around in a spherical murmuring wave which kept sweeping over the tourists, interwoven with whispers and cries and ripples of laugher, and a colorful shower of music, melodious sprinkles here and there, either lively or languorous, some alluring shrill of a saxophone soaring to the skies like the spout of a splashing fountain, some chance phantasm of a roving car taking some girl to a reveling venue, or to bed, or back home, but above all this, universal silence, their peace on the sea shore together.

By day on the beach, he would rub thick butter from breakfast all over her skin, mmm, you look damn appealing like this, he repeated, and she surely did, as she had lost weight and was getting back to her former shape, just like she was when he first met her. The evenings, she was slim and sexy, incredibly attractive, but he would not utter any flattering word from his mouth. One evening, however, he could no longer hold back words and told Mim he had never seen her so ravishingly beautiful. Sleek deep garnet satin clung to her slender curves enhancing her stature and setting off her narrow waist, lush auburn hair flowing low into the back V-shaped décolleté.

Against all the peaceful love sharing, it happened during their stay there that Mim beat him. In a fit of fury she went up to Anton and started punching him randomly. They were going out, and she had decided to look her best that night, so that he could finally get to see her. She therefore positioned herself in front of the mirror in the bathroom and embarked on beautifying her face meticulously. What she saw reflected on the evenly lit silver surface was a plain portrait which deserved completion, and the amount of love she had to put in made her forget about time. Never ever would she have finished, if it had not been for a moment when she thought she might have been stringing Anton along. She was nothing but a work of art, hardly willing to move or walk, reluctant to make any gesture or grimace, or even to speak, for fear she would spoil that image of herself. As stiff as a painting she transported herself to the bedroom, where he was lying in bed. He had been waiting there for almost two hours without saying a word, neither pressing her to hurry, nor reminding her it was late, was she not aware what time it was, or something of the kind. When she got near him she timidly called his name, suspecting he had dozed off — Anton! She was ready to reveal herself to him as never before. To her bitter frustration, he pressed his forearms heavier over his eyes in a resolute gesture, as if loathing it to see her, as if determined to ruin her hopes. "What are you doing, Anton, sleeping?" Completely blindfolded, he just tossed bluntly, and in the harshest tone possible: we are not going anywhere anymore. She had not worked that hard on her oeuvre to receive this, to let him shatter it to pieces by not having a look. In her naiveté she still asked why. "You are asking me why!" he blurted out. "We just go for a short walk and then come back here, please." She was free to go on her own, he would not budge. Mim went back to the bathroom. She could not bring herself to start chipping away at her *objet d'art*, not before someone had seen it. Eyes staring into the portrait's eyes, she kept standing there until a tide of suppressed resentment pooled up within her chest, when it overflowed into her blood system and rushed to clench her fingers, strain her muscles and her nerves. So she went, with clenched fists, straight back to him and poured punches over him to get his head to pop out at once and look at her, cast one single glance at her. She stopped, walked back to the bathroom, silently removed the garments off her body, and got under the shower head with the makeup still on, with a painful wish to delay demolition. Water raining down was as pacifying as a balmy tranquillizer, when he turned up right in front of her, thirsty for revenge, she knew. She is afraid to remember what she felt in that instant, as she stood embraced by the hot streams, facing that Caliban of a male livid with fury in the frame of the door. His nostrils announced thunder and his mouth raged: as long as you live, never again dare strike me, as I myself fear what I am able to do. Then his fists bore down upon her, and one hit her clean in the eye, and so she got a shiner to take back home.

They soon got past it, but her mother never forgot — a *belfer*, that's what he is, she would say at times. I beat him too, Mum, in fact it was me who started it, Mim would try to explain her whenever she recalled her daughter's black eye. *Belfer*, what in the world would that mean? That was yet another word whose meaning remained obscure to her. Her mother could not clarify its meaning either. All she knew was that she used it in a derogatory sense with reference to Anton, as though he was a vile brute. Mim put it in relation to some French expression, maybe *belle faire*, probably similar to the Italian *dolce far niente*, and would smilingly tease her mother, telling her that was not as bad as she had intended it to be.

Having him beside, Mim gave up her former avid frolicking with the sea, forgot about the unbounded enthusiasm with which she used to yield herself to the sunshine and the sand. She did not as much as flinch as they left there, got in the car, Anton started the engine, and all she was aware of was being with him, nothing more.

23 THE PAINTING

Oh, my beloved and dearest of all, eyes impregnating one another in a hallucinating vortex of colors, it was out of my soul that your frayed corner was torn away. I am crouching with pain. Worlds are collapsing within me as I listen in wonder to voices telling of my becoming, how the building of me had long ago started, and how the one I am now, in all shape and mind and soul, could not have been born outside that interlude of madness when I created you, languidly snaking eyes of colors, forever drifting, forever fusing, forever parting...

Wherever you are, tiny shred from my painting, I bemoan your absence. I have begun to falter. Could this anticipate a grand change, are my lines and shapes going to bend and wriggle, will I leave any ballast behind and rocket away, or will I contort into new inconceivable configurations? That terrible thunderstorm of earthshaking proportions, the sense of its pristine power is coming back to me, am I about to close something? I do not know. What I know for sure is it is all thunder and lightning in me right now, I can feel glassy fires splattering hot blood against my inner walls, hallucinatory projection of splashes and thoughts chasing, smearing one another, sliding one against the other.

And what about us, rebellious, unruly projection of floating blurs drifting apart. Shall I hurt through the same shrill, the same spasm of my soul? Ah, as you were tearing yourself away from me, billions of capillaries taught to feed together within the same contour broke — the still of a fetus prematurely snatched from a pulsing womb. The cruelty of the act still makes my flesh and bone wince. Why should we have let so many shadows and gambols, fluids and cells scatter away? Look how we are still drifting unenclosed, in separate membranes, meandering about with oozing gashes in this soothing oil which, alas, cannot, would not heal us. Not in a thousand billion years will our blood vessels be sewn together again, and so we keep floating burdened with this added weight, wiser, lower and lower down, to lie.

24 SKIN

They are now lying next to each other, traveling high in the violaceous gloaming of late twilight, toward a free, audacious world, full of passion. Yet the truth lies right here on this wide bed: Mim and this man. The music has stopped, and there is nothing but the silence of the wide window panes.

She had slipped her skirt up on her hips and put on her blouse and had tiptoed to the adjacent bathroom, hearing Anton go out too, surely to fetch something from the kitchen for them to enjoy in their den. Once locked inside the tiny room, and thank God nobody in the house had seen her, she had rushed to have a look at herself. Light flared back at her from the mirror, her sparkling eyes, God how she was beautiful. She pulled her hair to the top of her head leaving a few undulating strands to fall loose down her neck, her wonderful, fragile, long neck, only to think of the pleasure he felt when he kissed it, or when his long fingers tenderly encircled it. And look at her tiny rosy ears, so happy now, so exquisitely set high toward the temples, to which the arches of her eyebrows also seemed to aspire. Just telling by the way her hair looked, anyone could see she was feeling great, and her eyes promised even better things to come, yes, she would walk in wonderland from now on, passing her fresh body, undismayed, through everything there was. This dear body of hers with its slim waist, she climbs up on the edge of the bathtub to get a glimpse at it, wow, what might he be feeling when he slid the flat of his palms over her delicate soft skin, along the shapely curves of those hips, or when he clutched her waist tight.

She had stood under the shower for a pretty long time, running the soap on her body over and over again and enjoying the water at leisure, to make herself clean again, young and pure for him. If she were a man she would be crazy about Mim as she looked right then. Unblemished, she had returned to his room and, with that narcissistic sweetness still on her lips, kept elongating her queenly neck either forward or backward. But could Anton not see what she had seen in the mirror? He had, anyway, pronounced the word 'woman', and that was reassuring, he had referred to her, his woman, Mim. Only after the first try-out, followed by the first douche, did Mim feel really at ease, when this other, new person was born, the woman who would lasciviously undulate her body before her man's eyes, the woman who felt a desolate sentiment of longing trailing in his absence, and would stretch her body along the lines of those insubstantial trails, as if trickling in his wake. Face to face uncomfortably reclining on their sides, on the margin of the bed, with darkness only separating them, they could hardly make out each other's glinting irises, while she was praying they could get closer, which they surreptitiously did somehow. She could not explain the way they eventually found themselves one next to the other, skin to skin, burning and just waiting for minutes to fly away sluggishly through the window, one by one, waiting for Mim to pull herself together, spring to her feet, primp herself up and leave, back with him in the car, rolling down the street, he eventually pulling over in front of the gate, where she would disappear on the other side.

If she were him, she would caress Mim, would gather her up to him and once again merge his mouth with hers. Only minutes ago she had been so incredibly beautiful, but it seemed her charm had secretly seeped underneath, deep inside the thickness of the mattress, to leave her like a staring doll there next to him. She should rise at once maybe, and go. He was inwardly entreating her to leave, yes, this was what might be rolling in his mind, but she would not budge, let him think what he might, she simply wished she were transported, in that exact stance, up to where her bed was, in the tiny chamber at Aunt Ana's, and let fall asleep. "It's high time," she ultimately said nonetheless, as how longer still should she keep lying withered like that, 'we have to go.' OK, he says — aha, therefore he had been looking forward to that, there you are, dumb girl, get a load of that, he had to bring it home to you, and you damn well deserved it. So they would both scramble to their feet, ready to shoot off in the night.

Other times he had second thoughts: wait a minute, what are you doing? Why, it was not that late, and they resumed meditating on their own feelings in muteness. Skin to skin, with every sense would they explore each other's inner life, involving a kind of oppressive, astute physics. Their skin acquired a peculiar gift, awake to the voices of their insides which came out in a unitary irradiation of signs. Skin to skin, a magnetic dance would arise, the skin of his palms, the skin of her contours, her writhing waist sending forth heat from her womb, her small pointed breasts swelling up to full roundness for him to cup and squeeze them, the sweet skin of his lips wincing at her hardening nipples, each bud on his tongue tasting the limpid warmth of their nubs, a simple touch, pore against pore, a tender touch at her woman's core, ah, that is the woman in Mim, let him torment the woman, yes, his tongue is feeling her skin, 'do you like it?' Mim moans, revealing herself to him, her essence coming out into the wash. She finds herself swept up into his arms, sprawled onto the bed, and he is licking her breasts. She draws him to her mouth, mouth to mouth he is raising his torso but she aches to kiss him, his shoulders, his chest, she clings to him and they roll over embraced, with her sliding along his whiteness, up to his neck, his temples, the pale eyelids and again his mouth. As she was, entranced, trailing her mouth across his smooth skin, he kept pushing her down toward his midriff, and she could not understand why — she remembers the first time when that happened, I can't, she mewled and whined continuing to kiss him there right above his venter, arms stretched high on his trunk, fingertips tasting his wet lips, while he was pushing her dangerously lower.

Mim panicked then, she had to wake up to the situation. "Please believe me, I cannot do this, I don't know what this is." "The fuck you can't," he said. She was at panic stations, whatever shall she do? Distraught and still in hopes of salvation, she just kept begging him to believe her. "How in hell did you use to make love with your boyfriend then?" he jeered with malice. "Would you believe me if I told you that for me it was like a surgical operation that I wanted to get over with? I simply could no longer bear the thought of having to pass through that someday." He snapped at her, "Mim, I won't have you lying." 'I'm not lying. Maybe I'm not right in the head.' He lapsed into silence. Dull waves were heaving his chest as he was trying to choke back the terrible forces which she felt were clashing within. Poor wretched being, she continued to plead for her truth. "I've never had a single look, I've never touched him, I didn't even think such a thing was conceivable." "All right." He understood she was foolish, but sincere. He brought her head near to his again, where she felt just fine, back at his beautiful mouth which tells her, "It's still me down there, Mim; it's me, OK, this is what you have to know." She did, she knew it was him all over, and she wished she could liberate herself for this whole new world that was him, a different world which was opening up for her to explore, if only she could let go of herself, if only she could let herself in. He steered her again toward his lower abdomen. Mim's mind saw the world zooming out from the window to infinity, lights swept across the night sky, lights gleaming, beacons flashing, cars speeding along highways, reflections on the water, ships slicing dark stretches of silence, airplanes blinking high above oceans, thousands of them bore travelers over the world every night, thousands might be crossing the skies that very moment, trails of colored lights were whizzing in her head dragging her along into the spread world, into the high world, on Anton's chest, she was back trailing kisses of love on the flat membrane of his venter. She glued her ear to it and listened, the palms of her hands traveled up his muscular thighs, she was getting near, it was warm and pure, embalmed in some secret sugar, sweet vapors, sultriness, and her mind rejoiced in the fragrance of life spiraling down into the whirl of their fluids, thinking baby, clean, moist, intimate.

He holds her head in his hands, caresses her dearly, and brings her mouth back to his. Lifted in the air by strong fingers clenched around her middle, laid carefully on her back, Mim finds herself between his legs, with his frame dominating in silence from the ceiling. He is about to come down onto her. His contours hovering above like a field of energy shutting her off from the rest of the world, awareness of his willful mind sends her heart pounding with apprehension — now. Now everything turns quiet, shh, the furniture around stares still, the bed sheets, time. She is awaiting the thrust with a cringing heart. Now. She is on the other side of the world.

25 THE FIRE

She would invariably find Aunt Ana in her spotlessly clean kitchen where everything sparkled, where everything was fixed tight into place including the rugs on the floor, pinned down with thumbtacks. 'I can't stand tripping on them,' Ana would say. Mim had got stung by one of those thumbtacks when she was a little girl. That instant she saw Aunt Ana as ugly and mean. 'You are wicked,' her tiny round mouth grumbled, and her aunt and Mom and Dad burst forth into laughter. Why were they laughing so heartily, Tomina wondered totally baffled, when she had called the woman names? Why would Aunt Ana answer back with a blaze of whiteness, all her teeth suddenly bared and above them, luminous eyes joyfully crinkled toward her temples.

Everything was neat and well-defined about Aunt Ana, her perfectly rounded tan lips, the high cheeks, the imperceptibly humped edge of her short nose clad in smooth flesh and impeccably tipped above those intriguing, slightly flared nostrils. Everything was rounded about her, her black eyes forever glinting below her clear high forehead, gracefully curved out, stretched upward by her sleek dark hair, which was always pulled firmly into a knot at the back of her head. Not one single hair was misplaced, and Tomina could guess the delineation of the skull bones under the glossy helmet of her hair, as black as tar. Only the bun above her high nape told she was a woman. Aunt Ana seated on a stool in her kitchen would draw the ashtray and the packet of cigarettes with a matchbox on top near her, take out a white stick, put it between her lips and light it, to then relax in her favorite pose, leaned forward with elbows propped on her knees, with her left hand continuously caressing the opposite knee. She would drag heartily on her cig with a glint in her eyes, those deep eyes which cast a long steady glance forward in the distance from the middle of the room, the heart of her hearth, and tiredness and all sorrows would dissipate. Mim would sit and calm down beside her, amazed by the tact with which her aunt fed her craving. A broad smile lit up her pensive countenance whenever she saw Mim, come, sit here beside me.

"Well, I've got the cooking done, mashed a couple of aubergines too, cleaned up a little. What about you, dear, how are things going? You should get your nose out of your books from time to time."

"Don't worry, Auntie, I've not been that much of a bookworm lately."

"Now, really? You're an awfully clever girl, I know you."

The thought that that day she again had done nothing at all made Mim smile inwardly. "Clever, right, but if you don't study you can't possibly get to know things," she said in mock self-reproach.

"Quite so. But I am not to worry about you, no."

"I'm simply not able to see my way to doing it, Aunt Ana. I sit with a book on my lap and I cannot bring myself to rivet my eyes down on it, and if I do, I can't make any sense of whatever is written there."

"Now I know. Your thoughts are slipping somewhere

else. Tell me, is he a good boy?"

This made Mim wonder if there was any way in which she could explain to her aunt what was happening to her. In the first place, the word 'boy' sounded awkward with reference to Anton. She found herself at a loss to define him in any way.

"I don't know, he is a difficult person. There's no knowing what plans and ideas he has in his head."

"You don't say!" The woman swerved round to face her. Fixing her eyes upon her, she asked, "How old is he?"

"Umm, around thirty, I guess, that's what he looks like. He's a grown man proper, I should say."

"Well then, dear, this one's gone through the mill, he surely knows a thing or two. So take heed."

"Yeah, I know, through the mill," Mim repeated, drawing her lips into a wise child's smile. "But, Aunt Ana, would you believe that there are moments when he breaks into such pure laughter you would say he was a mere boy? That's incredible. Except that he's tight-lipped most of the time. He won't say a thing, and when he speaks, he tells me the story of his would-be life. I feel like I was some kind of tape recorder he plays to record his own voice."

They would go to his home, enter the narrow vestibule, with Mim so shy, wondering where his mother could be. Each time, she heard noises coming from the kitchen, whose door he would quickly shut if it happened to be opened. That was where Anton's mother always was, be it when they came in or when they left. They would tiptoe through the living room, where his father was sometimes resting lying on the couch only to deepen her shame, Anton would open the door to his own room for Mim to steal in and he hastily went in after her, sliding the latch in place for safety. He then set up the record player and chose a record. "Today, I'm going to play some divine music for you, let me see if you can guess what it is." Wonderful, Mim mused, only if it were not for that trial she had to pass through. He lowered the tonearm on the vinyl disk and the music began, but Mim could not enjoy it, anxious for fear of failing the test. She was raking her memory for anything she had listened to until then which might help, but nothing from the past seemed to come to her rescue, and if it did, she brushed it off as a misleading clue. And he was there in wait facing the window, halfway between this and the bed, where Mim was seated. Straddling a chair backwards, arms resting on its stark wooden back in a solemn expectant posture, he kept his gaze lost in the twilight. Mim's conscious presented her with a most weird picture of herself as being a statue incongruously placed on the edge of the bed in that man's room, some lost wooden idol with both woodworms and spirits squirming inside, crazed by those sounds, her eyes fixated on his wide nape, on the soft straight blonde hair she had not thought to be so cold and callous. "Well—" he would execute a ruthless spin to face her. "Don't you know?" She was cold trapped, and those eerie restless specks would keep scurrying and blaring within her. "No, you do not like this music," he would resolve. It was *Sheherezade*, it had to be *Sheherezade*, she thought, as the spirits were easing off and swaying a mesmerizing waltz, inducing her dormant anima to ooze obscure little waves of life out through her eyes. She was evading the room through the window, interwoven in a gauzy lacework with all the spirits in the world, which she curiously seemed to know, as though it was her Sheherezade was telling about. "Oh, yes," Mim snaps out of her reverie and stands up for herself and her passions, "I love this music." But there was no convincing him. She could see that in his frosty forbidding eyes, on his stern blanched lips. God, please let those lips part to say something.

When his lips finally did so, Anton told her about the three things he wanted in this life. He began with the library, a library of his own with thousands of books to encompass all the great literatures of the world, which he could read and reread at ease. "I'd like to lie down listening to music, music to suit each type of book, and have women read out for me, read whatever I fancy. What can beat this?" His eyes would turn warm, would burn with delight, and his mouth would extend sideways in contemplation of pure pleasure, showing the girl he was actually on his own, that he wished her anywhere except there. Yet, there still were two wishes left, so he continued to speak. A horse, that was what he also dreamt of, a stallion for him to range on horseback the fabulous realm across the river, sometimes swampy and fertile, other times dried and barren, those lands saturated with fish, trod by people who drank their water and ate their meals out of the grand river, peasants who watched over their melon fields and, farther away in the hazy distance, over flocks of sheep. He would ride there where Mim's glance could not reach him, among sheepfolds, to taste fresh ewe's cheese, to take some for home and return loaded. But he was to unfold one last wish, so the girl was waiting, her heart beats floating on the muffled sea of violins between their ears — a rifle. His secret desire was to be a hunter, to go shoot wild ducks and stop mad hearts of dumb hares and that was all. He did not need a person, Mim was unwanted. What was she doing there then? As they left, neither of them spoke any word. Speechless, they climbed down the stairs, walked the pavement, rolled in the car, Anton fantasizing about his books and horse and rifle, and Mim feeling uneasy to distract his reflections by her presence. She just wondered why he kept picking her up every afternoon.

They came to avoid talking completely. They would enter his room, listen to music until it got dark, and when they could hardly make out anything around, they would get up and leave. Mim hoped that maybe the music could bring them together some day. While he was listening, either motionless or waving his arms in the air in a fantastic play,

Mim, from her silent nook, was sending wave after wave of herself to soak into his heart, into his mind, and make him turn his face to her. And this until one fine afternoon, identical to all the other ones before, when he shouted at her out of the blue: undress yourself. She had heard him well and clear, that was what he had actually said. Some odd, perplexing anguish got hold of her as something indescribable was at pains to come to the surface, so she had to open her mouth and do something about it. There was no way she could take her clothes off in front of a man, just like that. Puzzled, her brain had to come up with a solution, and it was not her subconscious or anything like that, this time it was really her, with her dear body. And it was about the man she had so long and so many times been waiting for, the man on whose path she had decided to walk, no matter what, the man she had gone through so much inexplicable suffering to understand and get close to. There was no way either she could give everything up, not now. She remained mum, while he was looking daggers at her, his jaws pulsating steadily.

"Take off your clothes, haven't you heard me?"

"I can't see what you mean, how can I do that on command? I just can't…" she bemoaned.

"Huh, I'll be damned if you can't." A cruel, knowing sneer cut across his face.

Her body started to tremble — the enigmatic man, the long days of waiting, the music, and now all this ugliness, Mim asked to undress as at the doctor's, Mim so ashamed in front of this man.

He un-straddled the chair, sauntered out of the room, and soon came back holding two highball glasses in one hand. No sooner had he placed them on the table in the corner by the window, than he hurried out of the room again. He came in with a jug of some brownish-greenish beverage. Wheels of lemon were decorating the bottom.

"Iced tea," he said. He poured both glasses full and

came up to hold one out for her. "Here, hold this."

It might do her some good to sip that ice cold beverage with him, no, she was not going to give it all up, she would stick with him regardless of what happened, until the day she understood him.

He drew himself a chair and drank alone by the window. Life was gently flowing back from his past like a shuffle of cards and sat before him on the table. It seemed as though he was considering the display melded on the deck, chin drooping, elbows propped on the edge of the table, to better weigh each imaginary card on both sides. Maybe it was Mim he was searching for among those figures, what kind of person she was and where from she had come his way.

A few minutes later she saw him rising from his chair and coming toward her. He sat on the bed beside her and remained there gazing at the dim sky. Mim could distinguish his calm profile, dark shades still pulsating feebly in his cheeks at some nerve's quivering. The girl was waiting, just as she had been all along. But this time, he was well aware of her. He turned to her all of a sudden and sprang to her mouth — he was kissing her, he was kissing her in the same way he did on the night they met, when he did not want to let her go unknown. She wondered if perchance he could only get close to people by means of leaps and jolts. He was ashamed with his own feelings, yes, maybe reluctant to reveal himself to the others as weak a human being as anybody else. He kept kissing and hugging her, and she was on cloud nine, as what she liked most was him kissing her on the mouth, and she was after all celebrating a victory. Minor, but real. He was a person just like everyone else and she could draw closer to his secrets. Quite. As simple as that.

They went on like that for an indefinite number of moments, until he stopped, eyed her gleefully, and said, "You see, Mim, this is what I want."

He had found somebody, and that was Anton's major wish. That night's image, of him lying on the floor, of her embracing his head and loving him, comes back to her, of him totally abandoned to the new person he had found, of her holding him and calling his name in her head, my man. There was an instant when she knew Anton, and no other, was her fated man. Why then was she having that intense feeling of loss and wretchedness? Was it life, pure and simple, with what had been and what would be? Would it be Anton?

He drew her so near, clasped her with wild desperation, and hissed her name right into her ear, Mim. He was about to disclose his deepest secret, untold to anyone else before, and she had to mind that. "Mim, what I need is a woman to love me truly. Truly," he repeated grinding his teeth and pulling her hair backward to hurt her. "Love for real, understand?" He pulled harder — no one else knew. "For now, I reckon that's you."

"No matter how hard it is, Aunt Ana, I still want to decipher this man."

"Does he behave nicely with you?"

"I don't know."

Ana smoothed her hair back with both hands, exhaled the smoke in her chest, and asked, "Do you feel happy?"

"Yes."

"Then go on with him." Her aged hand decidedly squashed out the cigarette. She rose to her feet and emptied the ashtray in the dustbin, wiped it clean, then raised it up for inspection in the sunlight to make sure it was spotless.

In every house she went, she was attracted to the kitchen. That was the room where she always found Ana or Mrs. Arvinte, and it was also there where she would impart all her doings to her mother, both things that pleased her and things Mim knew would upset her, but which she had a right to know. She sometimes wondered where her penchant for kitchens came from, and thought that was maybe because home was the place where the fire was burning. With the passing of time she has come to fully comprehend. Those large black eyes are indeed beautiful, Ana's eyes, the fire in Ana's eyes, which she must paint. She has to find the blends of colors to depict fathomless depths from where a lurking light can call out.

26 THE CHILD

"Mom, come and see." Mim's enthusiastic cry subsided to a whisper, for fear she would scare away the pigeons. Their whiteness was lining the window sill on the outside, their round breasts poking out in pride, small heads eager to perceive the soul on the other side of the glass panel, in the fresh quiet room. They must have felt there was a new life inside and seemed to have flocked over to bestow auspicious gifts on the baby.

Mim had been living some euphoric months. She was practically spending her life by the crib watching the baby grow, inhaling the pristine balm of its skin, keeping the beats of her heart glued to its peaceful breathing, praying it would open his eyes and see her, recognize her, give her a sign from his world that he could hear and understand her, that everything was fine for him to exist in this world, as look, there was love, breathable — nearly unbreathable love, all around. Mim was waiting for the baby to grow up, watchful of his every sign and signal, offering her whole self as a globe, bending her own existence on itself into a motherly sphere where he would feel secure and well. Inside that sphere she also expected him to wonder at the beauty of the world in which he had come. Therefore she would sing to him, talk to him, toddle about the room holding him in her arms, she would sway him to sleep and was always there when he woke up. Using her arms and hands, mimicking with her face, she used to enact fragments of the outside world for the newborn. And everything was on the beat of music. The child was continuously presented with an endless sequence of scenes and suites as of operettas, musicals, rock opera. But it was mostly jazz Mim improvised, wriggling her hands and fingers, twisting her joints to the frantic rhythms of life. She believed the child had to be early on aware that life meant a whole lot more, that it was nothing but restless movement.

And he was joyful, Mim felt he was looking forward to whatever awaited him, with her forging his curiosity from tumult to ecstasy to absolute quietness, easy baby, be patient, now you will get to sleep, and upon your awakening, we will resume our journey. He had started to brighten up whenever he saw her face or heard her voice, more so when she had the train of little men of her fingers dance above his crib. But Mim was at the same time seeking to convey other things to him through those undulating exertions, more subtle things like the joy of existence, the splendor of the world, the baffling immensity extending beyond his tiny cot, the sense of harmony and roundness, the intriguing luminosity of the spiral, as her improvised shows would spring up timidly with a chanted rhyme, soar in vigorous rapping to the ceiling, to then subside to a mere sigh, and stop once the baby boy fell asleep. And they would come to life again and again, in cycles timed in with the child's biological rhythm. That was how his days and nights would succeed, adventure, patience, and adventure again. He would have a won-der-ful life, Mim was sure, just by noticing how he heaved his little chest in utter delight of what was awaiting him. The Prince of all Princes, Wonder-on-the-World, Light-of-the-World, this was what Mim called him, you are the prince of the world, she would say to him putting her pointer finger to his forehead for emphasis, and he understood. Mim felt he could understand everything she told him or acted out in his face. The two of them communicated. Her wish had come true unexpectedly soon, so her prays had not been in vain. And now look how white pigeons gathered at his window, as if to confirm Mim's predictions: an exceptional human being had begun his earthly journey.

Out of breath, Mim stepped out of the baby's room and this time called out loud at her mother, "Come and see, let anyone dare tell me now I wasn't right."

Her mother strutted her way along the corridor hardly able to keep a straight face.

"Well, let us see the wonder my girl has to show."

"Look, can you see them?"

"Wow, dear me, yes…"

"See how they are lingering at the window? They aren't flying away, right? And you know how they usually pop off when someone approaches."

"Quite true, dear," the woman conceded, remaining *bouche bée*.

They both stood still goggling at the pigeons. These seemed to be readjusting their occult senses to the new presence inside the room, but would not leave all the same.

"They are here for him, I can feel it, Mom. Do you get it now why I call him the Prince of Princes? You'll see. It was not for nothing that I'd been waiting for his birth with so much eagerness. You know well how I'd been waiting for him."

"Yes, dear, I remember too well."

"Have you seen anything like this before?" Mim insisted.

"No," her mother said turning to Mim. "I haven't." A smile arose on her lips all of a sudden, then she did the complete spin and made for the door.

"No, you do not believe."

"Why yes, I do, of course I do. Come on, Tomina, I've got pots boiling on the stove. I have indeed seen something rare," she concluded, to assure her of her conviction and at the same time to get herself leave to return to the kitchen. Flaunting her smile back along the lengthy corridor, Mim could still hear her saying, "You may be right, I hope to goodness you are."

To help the baby sleep peacefully, Mim exerts herself to channel love into his dreams, in case he has any. Quite so, what kind of dreams might the baby be having, shadows, lights, Mim's fingers — she bursts into subdued laughter thinking of the child's perception of the probably hilarious image of her fingers writhing and waving to various rhythms. Or maybe quite the other way, who knows what weird representations were setting in his brain, a blank slate thirsty for data of any kind.

Alex is almost a year now, and holding the terrestrial globe in his arms, he understands how it hovers in the universe spinning and spinning, he gives it a spin to enact this for the grownups around him, and tries to show them there are other such globes, many of them, which are all spinning just like that and do not fall for this very reason. He then breaks away with the globe, pacing the house, coming back to rotate around Mim, who agrees to substitute for the sun, and so on and so forth, she the earth, he the moon, here, take this ping-pong ball and show us how the moon goes. At barely one year of age, he gazes in the sky with Mim and comprehends. He is quick to understand, seeming to make sense of everything he sees, and will soon figure out how really difficult it is to get to the bottom of things. He will be intrigued and grow curious and will find answers, only to be puzzled again and resume questing. Mim is utterly amazed, Alex has already taken this path and he will surely reach wisdom earlier than normal. Full of pride, she imparts this to everyone she knows, she tells them of the pigeons which used to come to his window each day, of her beatific impatience to welcome the baby into this world, and of how she felt, the very moment his conception had been announced to her. He would be the human being she had so long been waiting to communicate with. It is exactly so, she explains to them bringing forward lots of arguments. 'No matter in what language I speak to him, he understands what I am saying.'

27 RAIN

They finished eating, the girls cleared the table and scrubbed the dishes in the sand and washed them, the boys seated themselves comfortably on the veranda, the girls made coffee, then the four of them set down to a game of cards. Each in turn dealt the cards and Mim was inwardly admiring her own grace at handling them when her turn came, putting a faint but easy smile on her face. Roxana and Dan were really friendly. A card fell to the ground between Mim and Dan and they both dashed to pick it up, the boy was faster and gladly offered it to her. They had touched shoulders. "Careful, you two," Anton ruled. Mim unwillingly caught his eyes and noticed his discontent brow, yes, he was jealous. What could she make of that?

But the sky turned suddenly dark and the sea grew slate-gray and began to boil. Will it rain? Mim was secretly blessing that likely prospect. It rained whenever she came to see him. She remembered the day she was waiting for him at the ferry in a scorching sun, and a few rain drops sifted down with the blaring rays. Sometimes it started to drizzle just as she left home, other times the weather changed the following day, but not a single time did it forget to rain.

There was a certain kind of light, there were those lapses of muteness which dissolved her existence into a sort of sickening longing for sorrow, which she could not explain. She thought that maybe too much happiness resulted in boredom and that was why, motionless, she often let her mind travel away. Why do people rarely mind the passing of time, she wondered, why do they drift apart on random paths and way too late awaken to reality, only to find themselves astray and lonely? People mill about after whatever strikes their fancy, but it is exactly what they most love that they cannot possibly benefit from, as their truest, innermost desire rises victorious from among the mind's wearied chimeras not earlier than the very end when, finally enlightened, they wish they could start life all over again. People will not listen to each other, people will not merge. Too bad, she mused, and she and Anton were people, too. What forces brought storm into her soul, followed by deathlike waste-ness? What forces had always made her glimpse, from the zenith of happiness, that visual elegy — the image of Mim and Anton sliding off each other and drifting apart shrouded in rags torn off one unique thought, the two of them embodied in a splotch of honey slowly gliding on a surface into two separate languid tongues, long and mute, to divide them, to hide them from each other.

She was wet through again in her mind's picture, Mim in the train station who caught a glimpse of an ageless man in the crowd. That was the only meaningful instant, when she could not discern what exactly was weird, when she did not yet know him. She used to brood and yearn for that, where had that instant gone, what was left for her to be in love with anymore? They had begun to part the very moment they both set out, enchanted, on the challenging road of deciphering. They had all along been out for finding an answer, solving the puzzle of their apparently fated encounter. She still cannot put her finger on what was strange and why it had felt so. Maybe it had been nature itself, that terrible storm which had swept along grasses and trees pushing people to cluster for shelter and bringing them face to face. Maybe the rain, which had soaked her through and turned her into an unearthly beauty. Or still, maybe his eyebrows, which seemed to belong to another face, the two thick arches that could have traced a circle together, his fair hair falling down in straight strands below his earlobes, and the light-colored lips taken from a Greek statue. Or was it her hair, heavy with water and falling in wavy trickles down her shoulders, the phosphorescent radiance which cascaded into her eyes under rain-laden lashes, or maybe her isolation as she stood plastered to that column in the middle of the platform. And they proceeded to discover each other, but they meant nothing compared to that miracle. What they had fallen in love with was the miracle. What forces would induce her mind to visualize rain pouring and they walking away, each straying without aim, sodden to the very core with longing for that lost first instant. What made her cry so often and dream of herself without him in the rain, then tell him it would be raining when they eventually parted? It was only now that she could make some sense of all that. A shameful, despicable wish had been stealthily growing inside her that they should become separated, only for him to see and give her right, only for Mim never to die and stay forever. It would inevitably rain, she mused, and whenever it did his thought would slip back to her, there was no way out for him.

Now thunder was rumbling in the distance and they both winced, their secret connecting their eyes across the table. It was celebration in Mim's soul, which was going to revel with the rain. Anton would irrevocably acknowledge the miracle, with Mim herself as witness. As the rumbles were drawing closer, a violent gale whirled through the campsite lashing everyone inside their tents, and although it was early into the afternoon the sky got suddenly pitch-dark and there was only petrifying lightning and thunder. A strange satisfaction sprang inside Mim, a feeling of queer happiness she had never before experienced, aware that they were both prisoners to the storm, he and she taking shelter together just like on the day they first met. It felt as though she, Mim, had sent this thunderstorm upon the camp, and her soul was jeering with inhuman pleasure seeing how Anton was squirming in the claws of her messengers, yes, he was being executed. There was nowhere his thoughts could escape and they both knew that.

As they were all lying amassed on the mattresses, Mim's eyes transformed her into a glowing idol which was connecting to the light, that strange light thrusting through the heavy downpour from far, far away. Hard as he might struggle, against his will, Anton let himself glide silently in, so that the others could not see, so that Mim could not see. Enveloped in a hot halo, the girl in the train station was staring right through his eyes, the wet girl he had been running after and had received then, shouting with joy, as a gift from the rain. She could now see how his eyes and lips were finally tamed, more, they were victims, she could read apprehension, she could read truthfulness in his eyes. As she was listening in to the rapping of the rain on the coarse canvas, she realized nothing could ever separate them, no, they were connecting through the bond of rain, and it would always rain.

Before long the wind calms down and eventually ceases. It is drizzling faintly as Roxana announces she feels like taking a swim, 'the sea must feel wonderful in the rain.' They all get out into the vestibule. Through the slit of the tent Anton and Mim watch the two youths running toward the waves. They will lie in waiting here, for the first time alone, which is not easy at all. To break the embarrassment, Anton walks out into the veranda while Mim remains rooted in a lulling stance, eyes gaping into the rain light. When she feels she has had enough, she goes back in and sits onto her mattress to enjoy the aftermath of the storm on her own.

She is meditating with legs crossed when she becomes aware of his presence in the other room. He, too, has been into the water. He will seat himself on one of the camp chairs to guard the tent, waiting for those awkward moments to wear on. What shall she do but keep herself quiet in there, as though she did not exist? Anton thrusts inside his head dripping with water and casts a mute glance at her, then swivels away and sets down to fumbling with the kitchen things in the vestibule. He comes back again and stands in the doorway for a while just to make up for words, after which he sits down on the adjoining mattress facing her. They remain like that, wordless, listening to the water constantly falling above. Mim feels the radiance of her own eyes so powerful, that she is put to shame, and does her best to keep him out of its ray. She is staring right past him into a dark corner, hiding from his eyes, although now she feels he is trying to tell her that he knows. Why has he come to her, is he no longer avoiding her? It is the rain that has cleansed him of that vile venom, yes, only the rain and the insidious workings of the wine manage to reveal his true self and bring Mim back to him. Only that, as soon as he sobers up, he no longer wants to see her in his face.

"It's raining," he eventually deigns to say.

"Yes."

She still cannot look him in the eye, especially now that he bends down toward her and clasps her shoulders, glues his cold lips to her scared mouth, kisses her — Mim being kissed by the monster who had been willing to get rid of her as if she were a leper woman. He is embracing and kissing her, he is kneading her breasts with the palms of his hands, as she is considering the chilliness of the water which is trickling from his hair onto her cheeks. His palms slide down toward her waist, to her bewilderment, to her horror. It is so hard for her to slip off that old hag's camouflage at his touch, she feels deeply ashamed. Still, she will take it off. She is a woman after all. But alas, no, the two of them together have been lost forever, this driest of all perceptions overwhelms her and the rain has stopped. He will soon come back to his senses and be sorry, he will regret inducing into Mim the wrong idea that he has changed his mind, no, Mim belongs to the past.

Dan and Roxana make their appearance in a cloud of noise. Wrapped in large bath towels they pop their heads in the mattress room one after another — hello! Mim gathers her body more safely together, against the powerful wish to run out into the open and breathe in some fresh air. She would like to wander through the campsite to free herself, purify herself. The man who had tried to approach her in the intimacy of the tent makes her physically sick. The man she loves no longer exists. Who is she in love with then? She has a strange vision of a bitch rolling over in pain before the weak ripples on the shore but, try as she might, the yells would not come out. Something has implacably collapsed with a thud inside her, blocking all exits. She will come out among the campers and smile, she is young and has noticed people turn their heads at her passing. As soon as she departed from the tent the jaundice and ankylosis disappeared by magic, her movements regained plasticity, and she was her own hopeful, ample self again. So she will definitely get out of there.

You might think that morning she had for the first time seen the sun rising above the sea, with all the people bustling and trotting about and Mim one of them, among the crowd at the market place, gloating at the colorful merchandise, watermelons and plumpy green peppers, of which she herself bought some. Men were looking her up and down, she must have looked nice, if only she had not been tormenting herself in the monster's car first and then in his tent. She rejoiced in the glorious sunlight and the tenderly embracing heat, coffee was being sipped almost everywhere around, kids were chasing one another in the sand, husbands were tinkering beneath cars, women were busying themselves over pots of food, chopping onions, peeling tomatoes, just like Mim herself had done and forgot about Anton.

It is the last camping day, tomorrow they will leave here. But she will probably cook again. She had never imagined how enjoyable it was to prepare meals on a campsite, with grains of sand crunching between your teeth. Well, she would not cook if it was not necessary, or Anton would think she does it for him. She cannot find a reason why, but this man suspects every woman of a sly hidden wish to get married, as if it were some kind of sin. He is haunted by the prospect of himself being cajoled, bewitched into it. He is living each minute of his life in fear that someday a woman who does not love him will get hold of all the riches he has amassed with so much sweat, threatening, using, and trampling on others. She nearly feels pity for him, realizing the nightmare he is constantly living. Maybe this is where that inhuman cruelty of his stems from, which Mim has always sought to understand. She felt like howling at the thought of Anton's impossibility to ever get to know someone for what they really are. This handicap of Anton's was driving her out of her wits. She had so long suffered next to him, and there had been times when she glimpsed some kind of opening in him toward people. She perceived Anton liberated then, yet always against his stone-hard will, which dictated him to remain on the guard. He must have made a crucial decision sometime in the past, a past completely unknown to Mim. What had happened to him, what had he gone through? 'Please don't dear me anymore, and stop calling me Antonush, this is my mother's blandishing only — and will you let up on me with all your endearing caresses and so much laughter — you're always laughing and I'm not going to play into your hands, period.' He had seemed to have something against her lively manner from the start, and her childlike shyness and clumsiness would often get on his nerves. 'You sometimes laugh when you should be serious, really.' She had not taken him seriously at first, but with time she came to realize that the man was not kidding at all. Who knows what malefic intentions he saw in her innocent screams of laughter? Maybe just some womanly cunning scheme. Or even negligence, possibly ugliness. Gradually though, without any of them being aware of it, Anton came to join in her gamboling and jolliness, he became as free as a madman, as it was clear to Mim he had once been. He would play cards with her while driving, with her in the back of the car and the front right seat turned into a provisional card table. Only playfully had she once suggested that, as in spite of fearing angry outbursts she still could not resist teasing him, and when he said yes she could hardly believe her ears. Anton himself came to invent all kinds of odd games which they carelessly played together, and they would run and tumble in the city grass and cry with joy for being together. But for some time he had been aware of the change in him and smoldering, lying in wait to charge at her, which he soon did. 'I have to be my own self again, I cannot be like you. I want to be myself.' She got stunned. Was he afraid of happiness?

They were leaving the campsite the following day. Mim did not know what exactly she would go back to. What she knew for sure was that she was going to paint the shimmering beach and the sea ceaselessly beckoning to people from indefinite distances, milk-white children thoughtfully pushing sand into castles, naked Mim standing tall in a mountain handcar, gliding on shining tracks out of the wet darkness of woods into sunlight. She was leaving Anton in search of the world. She knew she had some explanations to give back home and could not think of anything reasonable anymore. How could she possibly reason things out with Stefan this time? That well of magic power inside her had dried out and her eyes would no longer impress him. And why should they, after all? She would see about that tomorrow, now she was going to enjoy the sunshine of what was left of this wonderful afternoon by the sea and the lively bustle of the colony, whose pulse she would soon cease to feel. She should have relished every minute of it. But there was still at least one last meal to cook and they would all make a feast of the forthcoming supper, and she would swim in the sea extending the muscles of her body clean and free.

28 BIRTH

Mad with happiness, she is scampering on the sidewalk
riding the burning embers of her cheeks against the icy
currents, the lissome, pouting traits of her face nearly
bursting. Fresh and vibrant she is frolicking her way on the
thin layer of beaten snow at her quickest pace. Her soul is
way ahead, beckoning her constantly forward. Petite and
pretty, that was what a passer-by whispered to her as they
crossed their paths, and that was exactly how she perceived
herself to be, at her prettiest, not beautiful, dramatically
beautiful and mysterious as she had created her woman-
about-town self, but burning like a flame down the pristine
snowy path to him, the one who has just arrived into this
world. The most beautiful day in Mim's life.

People like shadows, walking chimeras into the crude
light of dawn, she felt like shouting the great news to them,
she actually did shout, inwardly, to all the early risers
around, like a passionate messenger who was flaunting her
duty across town. That was what Mim was, that particular
morning, the personification of a heart which was shouting
with its every throb, a petite vibrant heart which was
beating at an increasingly higher rate as she got closer to

where he was. Happiness was teeming in the streets, and Mim still wonders if the town folks were really all happy that day, or maybe that was her impression, or if it was not her who was throwing happiness about like confetti. Petite as she was, Mim was able to train a whole procession down behind her, filling the streets with good cheer, hey, the baby was born!

What she saw that day was just a tiny bud of life wrapped in a bundle of white diapers, up at a window on the seventh floor of the maternity hospital, the rosy smile of his mother governing above. It was freezing cold, but this gave Mim energy, it served as a kind of invigorating invisible prop for her powerful emotions, the perfect background for her existence that day.

"Let me give you some advice: you should never bear children." Mim froze, staring vacantly at the sea froth, fierce, freakish, boiling white among the rugged breakwater boulders, mourning white. Inveigling, poisonous, slithery, the putrid green was so deep. Mim strained herself like a grave chord and burst bitterly on the rocks, between her and Anton. "Why?" But she did not want to hear any answer at all, as nothing more mattered. Anton then whipped up a trap scenario: Mim's own imaginary child down there. He was scanning the water for a most frightening whirlpool, the poisonous tip of his pointer finger punching her backwards into her own existence, back before she was even born, in her mother's womb, more backwardly still, into unknown blankness. He was mercilessly sending her into the depths of the sea, while she was supposed to go there and see what it felt like. "Tell me, if your own baby were to be now down there, would you jump in for it? Give me an answer, come on." Mim had already vanished beneath the foaming terror, into an ocean of darkness, the mighty unknown, cold and boundless. Try as she might, she could not see the baby. Despite her mind's desperate exertions, life from her life, pulsing life drowning was unconceivable. She would have probably succeeded, had she continued, but her mind hit the rock of his dictatorial voice. "You would not jump." At hearing this, she laid the image of her own body on a stone slab and let her muscles, head, and heart drain into the pores still emanating the day's heat. This mark of the sun reminded her of the world's brightness and of tomorrow. The following day she would be blessed with sunlight just like everyone else.

It was only later on that she felt the pain, like a knife swiveling into the flesh of her heart now and then, that very night, in the nights that followed, then more and more rarely, more and more feebly, yet still there inside her, like a diamond thrown upside down into another dimension, an opposite dimension, anti-matter insinuating itself as the very idea, twinkling scientifically, philosophically, cosmically, of the existence of anti-matter. There was a swarm of whisperings, willowing down into her soul, about her own existence: anti-matter. A wound, a hole widening its tenebrae against life itself: you should never bear children.

Mim and Alex, tiny and white, his rosy rounded lips agape in the sun and green eyes squeezing the dazzling light in with discomfort. They were up on the embankment, him lying in her lap high above danger, protected against the gigantic depth unconsciously fretting after prey, whatever prey, alluring with lascivious froth to the secrets below. "My love, you do not really know how much Tomina loves you." She squeezes him to her breast. The time had come she resumed her trial. Maybe Anton had been right to put her through that. It could be the litmus test for motherhood. Just imagining the child…, oh no, she cries inwardly. Yet, would she do that, would she throw herself among the rocks after him? She cannot possibly tell, as people transform themselves when there is immediate urgency, when there is need to. They say God gives you strength. Mim keeps struggling in her imagination, would she give her life for him, everything she is for him to live? Yes, she has an answer to this way of putting things, yes, she would definitely do that, and thank God she can finally clear things out and get on with her life.

She wishes Anton could see her now as she is watching over the little body on fire. She can feel the heat sending her own brains scorching mad. Let her die, if this could help Alex get better. Yes, she wishes she could trade her life for his, if this were possible. But for now she is strong, she has grown stronger than she ever could have imagined and has been running about — to the doctor's office, to buy medicine, back to the baby. "My love," she is trying to breathe in his fever, the illness in his body, through the pores of her miraculous skin, in such an intense concentration that she practically transcends despair. There is power beyond despair. All you have to do is step over the threshold. As the half-light of dawn is insinuating into the hotel room, the ardor is decreasing and the baby, red hot just minutes ago, turns pink. Mim keeps pressing a wet tissue against his lips, the sweet lips of his little mouth. The image of Alex on the night he had been brought home from the maternity hospital comes back to her: the beautifully curved bud of a mouth, eyes closed, the blond fuzz of the brows above, wow, what a marvel of a flawless little head, as Mim had never before seen. She muses on how she had been waiting for him to open his eyes.

Day after day she would inspect them. As soon as she came back home from work she would ask: has he opened them yet? She would incessantly talk to him, as the connoisseurs had told her he could surely hear: my love, please open your eyes and give me a look, I need you to see me. But he cannot see yet, the others would break in, especially the women around, who seemed to know everything about such things, he can't see anything yet, mother dear, wait and have patience. When then, Mim kept asking. Well, let a week or two pass, came the invariable answer. One whole week! She cannot say when exactly his eyes began to focalize, but what she knows is that ever since Alex was born she has been spending her life wheeling around him.

And look what has happened now to his beloved mouth, whose flimsy skin has parched broken leaving the red flesh gleam bare into the pale morning light, soothing dawn light, thank God. He is breathing with more ease now, peacefully at last, and the new day will set in and help them. It will help Alex, Mim, and her mother. Her mother is watching over him next to her, but it was Mim who had insisted on taking Alex with them to the seaside in spite of his only one year and a half of age, it was Mim who had been swaying him on a swing on the beach in spite of a weakened sun and a cool late afternoon breeze, Mim and only Mim was to blame. She had taken a picture of him on that day: a sweet dot of a scamp in the blazing sun, his cap low over his squinting eyes, with a nose as little as the point of a needle and a rosy little flower of a mouth, upper lip raised in wonder at the camera.

What if Anton had been right after all? What if having a child means something different from what she thought. What if love means care and care again, loads of care and less enchantment, also better timed lessons about the world. Anton, where on earth are you? Were you here now, you would damn well give her a good bickering: Mim, what have you done? Her own mother had only told her: you've found yourself with the baby on the seaside and simply forgot how little he is; he's just over one, dear. Thankfully, Alex is better now and Mim has a vivid image of herself scampering about town on the day he was born.

29 BRAGA

She alone and the car, a discreet drizzle having set out to melt in silence the heat emanating from the ground. The vapors had already cleared away letting room for the invigorating late afternoon breath, and for the sake of its instauration Mim had got out of the car. "Please lock the doors, I'd like to wait for you outside," she had told Anton. He had left to fetch some sugar and lemon, as his home was only minutes away. There it is, the apartment block he had pointed to earlier and where he is right now climbing stairs, up to the glass door hiding his mother in the lit kitchen. On their first night he had told Mim his mother was behind that door and it was well after midnight.

There are a few other cars in the parking lot, scattered mostly towards the opposite end, all hood stuck into the lengthy hedge on the margin, under a high dome of vigorous green foliage. Beyond the hedge there spreads a carpet of turf, shrubs caching little pink dresses of shy flowers, further away other flower beds and more shrubs, as far as the nearest apartment building, whose belt she can see from here, some window on the ground floor, some lit room, a kitchen maybe. A light is out, but through the leafage Mim can guess new pale lights camouflaged by curtains, new rooms, and other people gathered peacefully in front of TV screens. She alone, next to the car, while a gauzy motley tapestry is being woven all around her feet. Look at her feet, girdled in fine straps of an amber undertint. It is exactly the color of that nectarous drink, *braga*, which is a pity they no longer make. It was like milk made of fermented grain, the most refreshing quasi-sweet beverage, so coarse and pure, and a little sharp-tasting, like an ancient brew. With a glassful of *braga* sliding down her throat she would imagine herself in the opening of a whitewashed small hovel, eyes squinting in the sun, simple cereal cakes awaiting her in the coolness inside, forgotten there on some clay tray thousands of years before. She used to take great pleasure at her own image chomping on such ancient imaginary cakes as though on humanity's past itself.

A familiar image comes back unawares to her. It is that of the little courtyard where, as a child, she happened to join in Coloianu's wake for a few years in a row. She was so very little and could not understand how come this Coloianu repeatedly died every year, sometime after Easter, she gathered, as the party of children used to dress him in colorful pieces of egg shells. Her cousins and the other children, all older than her, would take him to the grave, which was a sewage drain on the corner of the street, and all that procession horrified her, the thought of them throwing the thing down the drain, her wondering what would come of whatever was concealed under the motley carcass. There was loud laughter, lots of hustling and elbowing, and a highly clamorous cortège to the corner of the street that would hail old folks out of their homes to watch and be infused with infectious liveliness. She was the only one who could not laugh, since she was busy trying to grasp the meaning of the whole ceremony. Nonetheless, she relished every minute of it, she loved watching them revel, and that to such an extent that she had come to pray that the next after-Easter would arrive sooner, hoping her parents would again take her to her cousins' place and let her stay there for a few days. She enjoyed as much the aftermath of the procession, when the whole entourage would gather in the back garden, where tiny cookies and *braga* were served. *Braga*, which tasted so weird at first, was the customary beverage at the event. She exulted in having discovered a new taste and soon came to like it a lot. She looked forward to drinking it again, could hardly wait for summer to come and pass, then autumn, then got caught in snow games and carol singing and the ceremonies around the Christmas tree, with candles and presents and all, 'Oh, Christmas tree, oh…' Her father would always open the ceremonies by striking up '*O, tenen Baum*,' trembling with happiness and singing on, while looking the whole family in their eyes, arms floating in the air towards the giant tree all aglitter, meaning how joyful his kids were. Her father's voice touched her deeply, while her mother's high tones intimidated her, and she used to gape at them both in awe, as had not that room which they all called *beyond* turned into a wonder hall where, on top of everything, Father Freezy, or *Mos Gerila*, was going to alight? What with the Father Christmas watch and with many other events and adventures, time seemed to pass gaily for them all, yet she could not forget that taste she could hardly wait for. Well, after the red-painted eggs, the yellow and the green ones, she would drink *braga* again. As she grew up she asked her cousins where they bought it, then she began to look for it about town. She could rarely find boza, but when she did, she was extremely satisfied to enjoy that beverage. She felt older by now and proud to be able to find the tastes she craved for on her own.

It was only in those fabulous times past, when the town was teeming with merchants of all nations, that *braga* was flowing on all roads. It was then when Bulgarian vendors used to shout their sheep's milk yogurt from door to door. 'It was so stiff that you could slice it with a knife,' her father would say every so often. As he was a boy, one such vendor once cut out a crescent-shaped slice of yogurt for him outside the gate to his house, the very wooden gate through which Coloianu's cortège went out in their procession. 'My mouth was watering like crazy as I watched him slicing it; I had been running and was glowing with heat, and that yogurt surely cooled me.' Ah, Turkish vendors would shout out their delicacies on the streets, be it nougat or kebab, the Greeks used to keep luxury shops and cinema halls, and what a parade of elegant ladies, with no match in the whole country. Our town once was the national fashion hub. This was how her father's stories went.

Coloianu, or Calaianu, was long gone, and Mim has still not fathomed its mystery. The spotty pattern on the asphalt now is waiting for the steps of the strange man she has met in the train station, her delicate ankles rise elegantly from fine sandals specially for him, and she knows well how this dress buttoned all the way down at the front compliments her waistline. Although she had admired herself in the mirror before leaving, she is aware of the fact that some of the initial freshness of her beauty has been lost on her way here. Any speck of dust, any puff of air, and the waiting for time to pass, have all been rubbing some of it off, to say nothing of the mute apprehension that accompanied her throughout the journey. Eyes glued to the endless expanse of fields the train was passing by, she had been probing this inexplicable feeling, as though her fear was at any time ready to find expression through some imaginary mouth formed out of those continuously moving visuals. Sheer panic had raised a kind of wall inside her as the train cut through the outskirts of the city, which brusquely dulled the flawless appearance in the mirror back home. She had felt the skin of her face blanch and parch, then a vacuum at the back of her head, where she knew pain was going to accumulate, to then rise to her temples, her forehead, in an attempt to suppress the ascension of her traits and distort the distances so well balanced on her face in the light of her home, at the prospect of this very date with him, the first one.

It is still hard for her to believe how tired and ugly she had been when she had left home on the day she met him. She was so utterly reluctant to go, but she had to, as she needed the course books she had left at Aunt Ana's. The woman was at her relatives in Mim's town, looking for a house to move back to the site of her childhood and of her love life with her first husband. Therefore Mim had already removed most of her things from Ana's house, except for the studying stuff. But she no longer felt like going back there to prepare for the summer exams, so she needed to bring her books home, too. On her way to the station the thunderstorm that occurred could not hinder her advancement, so dead set she was on leaving that house. Well, ugly as she may have left home that morning, she somehow managed to drag that man after her along the train platforms. Would she have the same power now, Tomina wondered, at her arrival in the very same station one week later?

But what did that man look like? She had been so assiduously struggling to reconstruct the features of his face mentally, but to no avail. It seemed she had lost that image, although there was some impression left, maybe just the storm, the rain. She could feel a strong ambition growing inside her that he would like her, that he would keep meeting her, over and over again. Only that this required a lot of hard work from her part. Anyway, she was about to see him again on the platform any minute now. Would she recognize him? Trying to solve this quiz made her nervous, yet how curious she was, oh God, to see what that man actually looked like. She had abandoned herself completely to his mind and will, as in a dream, but the truth was she did not really know him. Well, let her get a glimpse of him now, if only just to figure out what might have inspired that urge in her to replicate the meeting with the stranger in the station. There he is, he really looks weird, her senses had not been wrong. Dispersed figures, the crowd, children, the platform, the columns, and all of a sudden a statuesque frame clad in smooth garments of soft natural colors, blonde straight strands of hair, the white forehead and two eyes which she imagines to be round. Yes, she remembers, his eyebrows are round, dark and round. There is no one like him, no one like the man who had kept her with him one night and one day as a kind of parcel he had promised to take to its destination, as that was the way things happened, all because of the storm, which had stopped all trains. This time he will get to see her elegant self, hair dried, luggage light, just her purse and a small traveling bag with notebooks, course books and a few clothes. She had been a lot less than dazzling upon descending from the train, since she was still apprehensive. So badly did she wish he would like her that in the very moment their eyes met all color dropped from her face. And God how awkward she behaved, downright silly she could now say. Now she feels like laughing at the two of them stiffly upright in the middle of the platform, hi, him taking her bag from her hand, neither of them seeming to know why on earth they had met again. After all, were Sundays not the blandest days of the week? Their representation among those columns struck her as tasteless and dumb as compared to what they had lived in that very spot a week before. There could be no replica of that.

This very sprinkle of rain, so delicate and fancy, appears to be falling in a world completely different from that one. But here he is coming back with a white plastic bag in hand. "Aren't you cold?" he asks, no, not at all, and she comes back to the present. She finds the place fairly nice, holding both of them in a sort of outdoor room, so she wonders what is with that vehicle inside, his car. He comes to life too and joyously takes a lemon out of the bag, then a tin of sugar, and places both in turn on the roof of the car.

"And here's some cheese pie made by Mom."

"Does she know you're here?"

"She does, yes," he promptly replies. "Why?"

"Does she know who you are with?"

"I've told her I'm with a new friend of mine."

"And hasn't she asked if it's not the girl from that night?"

"Oh, yes. What else could I tell her, it's that girl all right."

"Isn't she going to think laughingly at us dating here outside the car?"

"I've told her we're somewhere in the neighborhood and then we're going to have a ride together."

Tomina is seeking to visualize the woman behind the kitchen door, a stern face maybe, or maybe not at all, taking into account her son's soft features. She must be as powerful as he is, enigmatic and inscrutable. What might she be making of her, the girl her son had brought home in the middle of the night?

"I said," he resumes, "Mom, if a girl Tomina calls, put me on the phone right away."

"What, you've told her what my name was?" Tomina secretly prides herself on that, barely able to keep her lips in place. Is she the tiniest least important for the man in the station?

"Why should I not have? My mother knows everything."

"So does mine."

"See?"

Although she cannot tell whether he likes her or not, she at least appreciates his most natural behavior. Plus, mentioning her name to his mother is a sign he has not ruled out dating her again.

"You never called me."

He gets serious and, eyes fixed on his tight lips, Tomina understands that, although that phrase was dropped in as a factual remark, some kind of discontentment is lying on the asphalt between them and she is the one who should bend down to see what it is. So he had been waiting for her to phone him. The thing is she would never dare ring up a man.

"It just didn't occur to me I could call too. Think, what might your folks have said?"

"This has nothing to do with my folks, you are with me."

His words sent a frisson of surprise through her body, he had really taken things seriously, a pleasant thrill that brings back to her the way he kissed her goodbye that first night, and how they did not part at all, afterwards.

"My folks are people like any other people," he continues, "normal people who tend to their own business."

"I would've called you, believe me, I wished I had been able to call you, only that I didn't want to disturb."

"Mim—" He seems to be trying to bring her back to the real world. "Why on earth would you think I gave you my phone number?"

This makes sense and has her thinking. Therefore he would not have felt pestered and stalked by her phone calls, had there been any. Quite very much the other way, he would have been pleased.

"I will call you," she promises full-heartedly.

Why should she think that phone calls from women repel men, and who or what can impede her being a suggestion maker, or a decision maker, so that she should be the one who knows what comes next? She then considers what they, men, might feel while dialing a number and waiting for the receiver to be picked up at the other end of the line.

"Mim!" She startles. He then announces he is going to unlock the car, he does so and comes back to her holding a thin bottle in his hand. "Here it is." He impishly raises the trophy up in the air. "Havana Club, do you like it?"

"I'm not sure, I hope I will."

As he places the bottle on the roof of the car, she realizes she is holding the plastic bag, wondering how it had ended up in her hand.

"Ah, I forgot to bring glasses."

Mim is just waiting there for his next move.

"I know." A solution has just occurred to him, so he opens the car trunk, rakes about in there for a while, and comes out with two plastic flasks, asking her, "Do you know what these are?"

"I don't. What are they?"

"Distilled water flasks. You'll see how I'll make us some fine glasses out of them."

He created two tall tubular ones by cutting off the neck of the two bottles, then meticulously sliced out a wheel of lemon for each, added a little sugar, poured the liqueur, everything while she was standing there like a fool witnessing the whole process and feeling increasingly stressed, tormented by a dumb dilemma: should she mingle in the procedure or not? She took the glass he handed her. "This is yours."

"Thanks."

They both went on to wet their lips on the aromatic, sweet, yet surprisingly strong drink. He had a cassette playing on the stereo in the car, and so they lingered for hours in the parking lot, the car all doors wide open, and the music, and Havana Club, the sugar and the lemon. Late into the night he comes up to her, takes the plastic cylinder out of her hand, places both glasses on the tall improvised table, turns to face her, rests his arms on her shoulders, and then they start swaying their bodies together. They were spinning millimeter by millimeter near the car, from whose inside music was feebly tempting to spread high above the gloaming created by street lamps. They would retrieve their glasses now and then and lay them back again, to resume the dancing. Thinking back, Mim now muses he simply did not know what to do with her on that night, whereas she was dawdling in his arms rather puzzled and tensed, waiting for his intentions. The lingering got her jaded, the drill under the fine spray of rain, among the columns of the trees, and lawns and alleys, with all the lights gone from the people's windows, and just one lamp post nearer to them, which she felt was their lamp post. The sense of night was creeping through the fantastic canopy above, descending upon them like an alleviating veil, in total peace. She would have liked the car to turn into her bed at home, and the light of the street lamp to go out, the music to stop, her body to lie down and her thoughts to doze off. She was sitting an exam the following morning, so she had brought course books with her to go over some stuff again. They were right at hand in her traveling bag, but the whole exam thing seemed so out of her world now. So did the little yard and her room at Aunt Ana's, as though they all existed on some other planet. As to the two of them swaying face to face on the asphalt under the leafy dome below the stars, she had a funny perception of them growing smaller and smaller, seemingly diminishing to dematerialization, some distant world oddities.

She did not say she had to leave and go to Ana's place to sleep, he did not say that either, probably waiting for her to do so, therefore they both left it with time to solve, time, the great attendant of being. So time lapsed till they started to feel themselves again. What they talked about is foggy to her. From time to time they went to sit on the car seats, then they remembered there was pie in the plastic bag and ate it. While everyone else was sleeping, they were partying hidden among the blocks in the quarter. He came back to liveliness and started smiling again. Anton his name was. Strangely enough, Tomina did not call him by his name, so when she needed to tell him something she would wait for a moment to catch his glimpse. She was simply shy to utter the name *Anton*, which sounded so very lofty to her.

When it got too late after midnight for them to be able to decently go anywhere, also because of the police night raids, they extended the car seats and turned them into their bed for the night. "Let me show you what a nice comfy couch I can come out with." He did everything. Tomina just lay down on the improvised bed, all dressed up as she was. "Are you comfortable?" Not really, smilingly came her truthful answer, while her body was making efforts to adjust itself to the slightly uneven line of the upholstery. She was at a loss for what to do, thinking that maybe she should simply close her eyes, in spite of being wide awake by now. When he finally got in the car to lie beside her she was relieved not to sense the least bit of rancor in him for having to bunk like that in the car because of her, when he lived only a few steps away. For her to creep again into his room, in a strange house, was inconceivable, and she had made that clear to him.

He flung his frame right on top of her. In the dim light reaching inside from the street lamp she could see his straight tresses drooping towards her face, his round eyebrows, the sallow lips, and a short flash signaled in her mind the existence of his focused pupils, of the brown eyes she had seen reflected from the driving mirror throughout their journey one week before. His eyes effused such power, too intense, she felt, for the confined space in the car. Mim had been mesmerized by that power and she had completely given herself to it. He now glued his lips to hers, crushed them, opened them, and got clean into her mouth. After the initial shock, she gave in to his ardor and lowered her jaw bone, letting her mouth gape open at his will, wide and flaccid, lips gummed to his in an airtight union, a union with the man in the station. They abandoned themselves to the rhythm of the music still playing, in a kind of lascivious dance of the living tissues gliding one against the other, coiling, and intertwining. Soon it all turned into a pleasurable routine, somehow out of time, which explains why she cannot tell for how long. The memory of her neck arching backwards, lower and lower, is still vivid, its own longing for his mouth still very powerful. His mouth responded by drawing lengthy trails from her chin downward, in ever so slow glides, yet pregnant and purposeful, such to make her head go round. He then brought the palms of his hands down to her waist and started to constrict it in a firm circle, all so to her secret joy that he had finally discovered her stupendous middle, now wriggling like a fire tongue. Next, his palms slid up to her breasts, and as they were cupping them their mouths merged again. She could have stayed a lifetime in that sinking state of satisfaction, her mouth completely relinquished to him. Except that he started forcefully pressing his body against hers, with one hand propping her head, while with the other tormenting her breasts in turn. He then went on to explore the median line of her body, as far down as the underbelly, at the gates of disbelief: was that really happening to her? His sturdy legs were clawing hers, his torso bearing down on her, his manhood intent on subduing her. It felt stubborn and cruel against the bone between her thighs, and as he pushed ruthlessly against that spot, a kind of peevish wave got propagating itself from there all over her body. "Mim, aren't you going to unbutton this dress?" Well, she was shy to undress in front of a man. Come on, Mim, he ordered, please, Mim, he begged, while starting to pull at that poor garment which no longer covered much of her body anyway. They both got down to unfastening the tiny buttons, with him from the bottom end. She heaved up her middle despite the burden of his frame, for him to be able to gently pull the dress aside and fling it away, whereupon his mouth rushed at her breasts. His thighs were stern around her.

It somehow seemed to Mim that the man she was with found pleasure in physically tormenting her, as though some evil entity had corrupted his mind, sending him on a mad chase, all alone and hard-bitten, which gave her the creeps, all the more so against the absolute silence. She did not even know who he was, and who could possibly spot them in that maze of alleys, in that void of a place at the heart of the district of blocks. Only God knew how many misfortunes such secluded places had witnessed, and look where she had ended up. She had been beside herself with joy at meeting that weird guy, but could she really tell what he was up to? He could practically do whatever he wanted to her. At this thought panic froze the feeling of pleasure radiating from her nipples, which frozen pleasure sent a hail storm over her brain, telling her she was either mad or not real. "What is it with you, Mim?" There was tenderness in his voice, and worry, genuine worry. She was *Mim* for him, and he had taken her home to her parents on a devious route winding through stupendous country, and he wanted to be phoned by her, this was the man on top of her now. This had been her wish and will after all, that their road story would go on, so here and now the man was doing whatever he wanted with her breasts. Mim's senses melted back into rapture and her mind freed her, all at once.

He tore her legs apart with a force she had never conceived, grabbed her soft thighs with both hands and pushed them aside. Fear, which was not even hers, it seemed, like an invisible wall made him stop short at the entrance, her tensed muscles sending a frosty halo all around them. He sensed that. "Mim, you don't want to tell me you're a virgin, now." Why, oh why should they talk about this, she simply loathed the very thought of it. The issue of a girl being or not being a virgin — agh! She had not wanted to be a virgin, just so. She had wanted to get rid of her damn virginity, get over with this embarrassingly unpleasant, debasing event, or process or whatever one could call it, yet fatefully inevitable, mandatory, yes. She had arranged everything with her ex-boyfriend and had set herself free once and for all. But this had nothing to do with that, as at heart, and in her mind also, she was a virgin. To welcome him into her was going to feel as though she had been born again, or had given birth, or had got married, or had died, any of these life's crossroads, as absolutely definitive.

"I simply do not feel up to it, I need to get used to you first."

"Mim, look at me. This is who I am, can you see me?"

"I can, yes," she says her eyes turned to him, but at the same time purposefully keeping his out of focus, for fear he would catch her glance and perceive such malaise. Just like a child, she now muses, and that was true, she did not consider herself a woman at the time.

She reached her arms for him and pulled his shoulders down to hide her face against his plump chest. Pressing her lips there gave her an urge to kiss the beautiful skin so smoothly stretched on his bulgy muscles, on his sinewy neck, on his searing cheeks, and his mouth. He opened her thighs in one forceful move. Highly stirred up, he began to push them wider and wider apart with grim determination, he needed space to find his way into her, and she spread them as far apart as she could in a kind of exhilarated abandonment. She felt him round and sturdy between her thighs and he instantly darted straight into her, without mercy, full up to the very quick of her. Mim roared with pain. He remained still above her, propped on his arms in an arched position, and fixed his gaze upon her. He had been searching for her eyes in the meagre light reaching down below where they were hiding naked, he inside her. That was one of the few times their eyes had actually met pupil on pupil.

"Did it hurt?" "A little," she admitted. He pulled an inch away to pick up momentum, then thrust back deep into her. This time Mim kept her scream of pain in check, for fear he might stop stabbing her like that. Staring down into her eyes, he asked: do you want more, Mim? She said yes, thereupon the thrusts increased in number. "Come, relax now." He brought his torso down searching for her mouth, and as they were kissing, stopped to whisper into her ear: does it still hurt? No, she moaned. All the pain was gone, throwing open the door for a total sense of contentment, somewhat superior and self-centered, that took her up as in a balloon over the world. If this meant being woman, if this was life, then let it go on in the same manner. Which it actually did. Despite the pain in her upper leg joints, she was valiantly lying widely sprawled to welcome his ramming. She had come to keep only pride alive, nothing more. A suspended pool had been formed between their bodies, a filmy layer of merged perspiration swashing rhythmically, in a dull routine by now, rather discomfiting as well. Tiny globules would drip from the tip of his chin while she was mentally tracing the groove this man above was incessantly running inside her. He went on like that, alternating roughness and gentleness, till he finally let out a long deep groan and came to a stop. She was happy for him, for having taken him there, which gave her a sense of self-worth. It felt as though she had passed a test, that of her own womanhood. Full of gratification for what had just happened inside her body, she could feel the trails of pain in her. Deep down, she was palpitating.

They shoved the car doors wide open. The drizzle had ceased, leaving behind a peaceful tableau of bracing cleanliness for them only to inhale. Not long before sunrise they locked themselves in the car again and made love till the glow of dawn gradually washed out the halo of the lamp nearby. In the cool morning air it was only the mist in the windows that shielded their nudity from the soaring sunlight. With drowsy reluctance they both pulled on their clothes. Mim's body hurt all over, with a whole spectrum of pain overrunning her every bone and muscle, and she could barely move because of the wound in her womb. No one but she could hear its throbbing, which was alarmingly increasing in intensity, just like she had a second heart there, overstrained and pounding for help. Her flesh was radiating an uncanny heat, the skin on her chest and face withered with exhaustion. Her face buried against the chemical-reeking wall of that metal box of a car, she had just been waiting to get out and walk away, as she had to present herself for the examination that day. Now she knew she was not going anywhere in that nauseating condition, adieu exam! It so seemed that she had to face a new strange world, with people like aliens who had begun to get out of their homes. She observed them passing by on the alleys in a to-and-fro glide. A car at the other end of the parking lot started revving its engine, then another one, the sun will soon show up in all its splendor, whereas all she could possibly do was go home and sleep. What on earth had she done? This exam was as good as failed. Never ever had she misbehaved like that, and this was damn serious. What would the world say, the professor, her mother?

She changed into the skirt and blouse she had brought in her baggage, and he sincerely admired her all white outfit, insisting on her going up to his flat to grab a bite. He would not take no for an answer, she could at least join him for a cup of coffee. So be it, she told herself, the worst had already been committed. The glide of the immaculate skirt up her body, from ankle to knees to thighs and on her hips, was her inauguration into the league of people who err and do not give a damn.

30 THE ARTIST

The gold-touched tan of wheat spikes under cloudy skies of his thin hair radiating from the top of his head just like shadows against the blazing light which came from the beady eyes crammed playfully above ruddy cheeks — pure life blood was bursting forth, carrying along happy tales of past lust fulfilled in every heartfelt, wholesome, bona fide way — and his stub of a nose, jollily sniffing around for meaningful life, so witty and wise, clever in every sense of the word that flashed upon her at the moment, were conducting, in tune with the rippling waves sent all around by the sways of his bulk of a bull's head, the energy currents of life and spirit which bore his words to the audience, a mesmerizing continuum of artfully crafted metaphors and parables, at times brightened up astutely by some coarse joke, as greasy as a duck's rump imaginarily jeering and leering, now addressing the left wing, then addressing the right wing, the wings of the audience. They were all seated upright on row behind row of wooden folding chairs, a swarm of butterflies briefly at rest, wings wide spread to accommodate their buttocks, which will afterwards be folded flat and swept away to be put to sleep in some dark recess until the next life, when the otherwise empty chilly hall would be again filled with spirits gathered around some great artist come from elsewhere.

They were uncomfortably pressing their buttocks against the lacquered narrow boards of the seats looking in open-mouthed wonder at him who was conducting their choir of muteness, rekindled senses, rapture, and humor. As how could one help relishing that greasy juice sprinkled around every now and then in the company of his sharp glad eye? In such moments his cheeks would push even higher up against his eyes, as if purposefully squeezing them to yield some tonic sprays that would infuse their pallid bourgeois faces with such genuine secretions. These would bite like acid from their masks, so coquettishly worn. Although the impact would send shockwaves through their very gut, they somehow managed to keep their frozen stances, just essaying futile cosmetic smiles — collective portrait croquis in pale gray, quasi colorless crayon. But not for very long though, as this aggregate mask melted away like celluloid in a voiceless dance, a sea of visages in a stenchy process of fleshing. Soon that juice was no longer acid for them, as what more could it burn. Rather, it was now trickling like a life-giving fluid that illusory fingers would keep rubbing into their skin, whose pores were unquenchable. Above all, were their insides not as unctuous? Secret greases and liquids were ceaselessly circulating among their organs. Although they might have had the curiosity to listen in to their activity every once in a while, they had not dared allow them exude in the open. Well, they were now finally anointed with their own shared oils, so they could freely sweat together in a liberating murmur, just like in Verdi's chorus, eyes fastened on the two pale lips resembling thirsty leeches, which would stretch out into lascivious leers to almost instantly compress and crumple again in a pucker, subliminally enacting the blessing of drinking. Although it was those lips that spoke, they essentially spoke the audience's words. The chorus of murmurs, inaudible as it was apparently, was indeed growing more and more vigorous in the tall hall, in acoustics that made tremble the walls laden with paintings. Mim had the sensation they all formed a body of energies being brushed into the very paintings, a maddening collage of souls running on the same tune, their tune, his tune, the speaker's.

His lips would bulk up as they fed on that energy to bright red. Fat as they were, they would part to let loose words as crude as raw organs, would press together and waggishly wink in the corners of his mouth, just to help everybody present find themselves again. He was the great artist from the capital city, in flesh and blood right there before their eyes, and all the walls were alive with his paintings. Such power resonated all around the big man, that white Minotaur of a man.

The impression of a merciless Minotaur, all light, had for some time made its appearance on the corridors of Mim's mind. Anton, his frame arched in the darkness, iron-firm, like a cloud of power above her, her crazed heart thumping in her head with premonitory insistence that there would strike thunder born out of his confused energies, just like a final stroke of a sword swooping upon her in answer to everything, slashing her in answer to everything, and that only because she happened to be there. She had thought the light-white Minotaur in her intuition had stemmed from that image. It was lurking in the unknown, where both were trapped. And to counterattack and maybe make him leave her in peace, she wrote:

Minotaur, you lie in a painted station, lips and thighs writhing in oil, I go all white with moments furtive and mystic, the stray beast appalled is ever so sweetly hurting my chest as I thrust myself into light to reflect back to you, you massive and eyes and exits…

She thought it was all Anton's power, his anguished screams for not having got to come out and reveal his self to the world, the light in him which, not finding an exit, had accumulated into a terrible monster. And how she had been waiting for him to let her in, and how she had also been ready like a midwife to help him emerge. She figured that, after years, that monster had somehow managed to trace her in some occult ways. But no, it was nothing of the kind, the Minotaur stood for the great artist, or for the two of them together, who knows, twinned into a fantastic creature which was haunting her from another dimension.

They were in that selfsame great conference hall when she first laid eyes on the great artist, seated in state, powerful, massive, and lively. He had started to come to their town quite often, for vernissages and other cultural events. He had recently founded a cultural magazine and was interested in the young artists here, in his native region, willing to meet as many of them as possible, seeking to support and promote authentic talents. He had many friends and acquaintances among the members of the very club Mim had joined. The president had told her the great artist had seen her paintings displayed there, had been deeply impressed, and wanted very much to meet her. He had already selected two of her works for participation in a national exhibition. That sounded too good to be true. Could it be so easy, Mim wondered, no clenched fists, or palms brought together in prayer, neither agony, nor all that grim excitement prior to being invited to a cultural event of such note? 'He wants to see you, as simple as that.'

Mim had indeed been feeling for some time that something was about to happen in her life and the world was going to bloom open to her, that the fruit of her work she had so assiduously grown were ripe enough to go to market. For a long while now she had been taken up with her work, had done nothing else but paint, on weekdays, on

Sundays, during holidays. She would leave home like an automaton and come back likewise, keeping her mind on her canvases. She had taken a fresh look at older works and either refined or modified them completely, according to new perspectives. This process had, on the one hand, opened the gate to an innate spring of creative power that lay dormant in her, and on the other one had broadened her views such that she had developed the courage to reveal a more and more brazen self to the world. The more she discovered herself, the more she became an artist. This fostered a feeling of elation which pushed her to show her paintings to her mother and father, to a colleague at work, then to some friends. They had all marveled at them, and it so happened that one such person understood her wish to make her work public, so she introduced her to the president of the art club. She attended their meetings, colloquies on various themes which were held weekly, when works by members of either the literary section or the visual art section were subject to debate. In the beginning she used to be very shy, all the more so due to the presence of so many critics in the room, those disheartening highbrows in the world of culture. There was a composite group of literary and art critics always eager to jump at one another's throat as soon as the prey was brought into the arena, the one member whose turn it was to exhibit the outcome of their latest artistic endeavors. They were cruel like starved beasts, fighting like pit-bulls over the morsel of art on display. As a rule, there emerged two provisionally opposite wings, pro and anti, then there were the unbiased ones, like herself, and finally the president, the pacificator who would always point out both the good parts and the drawbacks, placing focus on means to enhance the quality of the work of art. They would all bury the hatchet by the end of each session, coming together as a good-humored coterie. In truth, they basically had deep feelings of fondness and high regard for one another and could hardly wait to gather again, as nothing could, to all appearances, give them more pleasure than live life between war and peace like that. Indeed, there was genuine, back and edge living during those meetings, of such intensity that the whole room sparkled with brilliant wit, irony and erudition. Mim discussed in confined circles during breaks and, more often than not, had ample tête-à-têtes with the president, giving voice to her artistic visions, innermost feelings, and process of creation. Every once in a while she would bring over one of her canvases and show it to him, and he would always speak words of encouragement to her. He had come to insist on her accepting to be assessed as an artist during an upcoming meeting. Her work was worth showing, he considered.

Therefore the moment had come, that she had been somehow unwillingly postponing. Reflection on this prospect brought about a whole range of conflicting facets of anxiety. As much as she might have wished to put off that moment, an inner voice was telling her this was exactly what she had been long aching for, the world's eyes. That voice would keep on claiming that her worlds were peculiarly exotic, distinct from anything ever exhibited at the club, and that it would be pity if the others did not see them. Once back home, she would admiringly stare at herself in her own paintings, burning with desire to fill up more fresh canvas, vast spaces of it. Everything was already there inside her, just waiting for the transfer to be made, the all physical transfer into matter, whereas the physical-she was forced to travel far every morning and put up with exhaustion, road dust and humiliation. Even so, at weekends she would lock herself up in her room to live astonishing stories, stories so thirsty to suck in color through bare fabric lips, so thirsty to absorb light through pupils hunting in the great void, whence Mim's soul could be heard cheering wholeheartedly. She forgot about eating altogether. Her mom would call out at her: hey, Tomina, come to table at once, or you'll eat cold food. Poor woman, she would work herself up in a tantrum, but against all the huffing and puffing of her mother, Mim could not have the heart to let that life behind and be wasted. Nor did she sleep enough. She no longer cared about the way she looked. A frightful sight that was, with strands of unkempt hair lolling limp, gloomy circles under her eyes, lips stretched unhealthily thin over her teeth, and skin as yellowish as the wax cheap candles were made of. For all that, light was clear in her eyes, leading straight to her soul, appeased, finally coming free into the world.

Execution day came at last. Her works had been on display at the club for two weeks and discussions were due according to schedule. She dressed nicely that evening and had let loose her freshly washed hair, making an appearance that her club mates had never seen before. Popped eyes were joggling in their heads, wow, was that really her? They had not had a clue that her hair could be so bold and her lips could puff up to such sensuous ripeness. Her heart was beating so wildly, almost like it meant to flee and leave her all alone in the ring with the bulls. Look how they were ready to dig their analytical fangs into her, dismember, pull her apart, and chow down on her, morsel by morsel. Terrified, Mim wondered whoever would be the first to attack. They were all lined up in snarl position in front of her, who, at the moment, could not care less about the rest of the congregation, seated on the hither side of the battle order alongside her. She mostly feared one that went by the nickname of 'the Philosopher', a phlegmatic misogynist who, with just a simple twist of his polished shoe's heel, would emphatically scrunch anyone, no matter how high they might rank, just like they were cigarette butts. When the artist under inspection was a woman he gave the impression it was not even worth applying any body weight at all, so he saved energy and — phut — carelessly dropped the butt. His thick dark hair was always impeccably cut tight and high with a flat top, trimmed into a hem-like line behind his ears, and his narrow goatee, closely cut and stylish to a T, so threatening in its stern black luster. Wicked as it was, that patch of hair was nothing near so evil as what it ushered Mim to: the sight of his terrible eyes which she perceived as two splinters of hard coal freshly slivered in order to be driven right through her. And then there was his mouth, two identical lips in a tight frozen package — he, the brain, used to shift them in defrost mode, just for the thin long he needed to let out his laconic verdict. Lo and behold, they were thawing out right there and then before her petrified heart, as it was exactly him who was going to break the ice therefore and open the proceedings. Mim's heart missed a beat just as the first current of air made ready to push sounds through his tight throat. He began speaking in his typical unperturbed, self-possessed manner, yet what he deployed was some kind of genteel phlegm, way too suave for her to believe her ears. His phrasing was untainted with sarcasm. And where was opprobrium, where was derision, the nitpicking and the scolding? Nothing of what she was hearing pointed to a final condemnation. So her heart came to, somewhat disappointed for the energy wasted on that syncopation, whereas Mim herself, utterly astounded, had practically forgotten to get down to decoding the messages coming forth through the slit opened between the perfect lips across the table from her. It was not too late though for her to focus on the import of his words. He was speaking well of her, even more than that, he was praising her, which did not sound like him at all. Something had to be wrong. He was finally drawing to a conclusion, and that was all about hope, namely that his laudatory speech would not get to her head. Then all the company of critics and artists took turns to express admiration for her work, which ranged from nice appreciative words to pure eulogy. They were in shock, Mim was a veritable dark horse, where had she sprung from, there was hardly any match for her art in point of freshness of vision and uniqueness, at least in the country, her paintings could only be judged within the framework of innovative art of the greatest contemporary artists. They overwhelmed Mim with a flood of praise, expressed in such miraculous words, sometimes maybe ringing too high-flown and elaborate in her ears. All that mattered was that everything she felt was now endorsed by the right people in a position to do so. Saving that endorsement came with a lot more than she had expected the critics to see, or to admit. This success resulted in her being invited to submit works for other exhibitions in town, where the great artist had remarked them, and so he was eager to meet her.

Therefore the very first time she saw him, Mim gaped in wonder at the spectacle of vitality that he was, quick-eyed and hearty-cheeked, and a sea of words rolling forth in languid ripples, one after another, almost like his powerful throat was some kind of drainless magical goblet sprinkling beads of saliva with each kiss of his lips together, some strand of limp hair dangling from his temple like a nosy tittle-tattler. She was absorbing that vigorous energy like nectar that would later give her strength. To her, those droplets splashing about now and then were a sign of continuous flow, a sign that he would go on chanting. And so he did, and she interpreted those strings of words as segments out of an unbounded message addressed to her personally. His puffy white hands would gently brush the air, and then peg themselves in a youthful stance on his hips. It was with those robust fingers that he worked matter, and she imagined them soundly dipped in clays and paints, fumbling for shapes, squirming their way to the core and squeezing out ooze like wine, to dabble in it. His metaphors were alive with fruits and pulps and wines, with kernels he was forever curious to reach, and all his ventures seemed to end with an ecstatic cross — he crossed himself first, and then crushed the core. That was what his paintings were like. Mim was deeply touched. He impressed her at such an intimate level she could almost hear those juices seeping into her viscera. Some kind of passage between them, she felt there was, on a different plane, where he already knew her through her paintings. He actually seemed to scent her presence in the conference hall.

This was how the great artist was delivering his speech, sweeping his glance over the audience. He was now singing the praises of the young artists in this town. He had discovered a few authentic talents, some of whose works he had selected for the upcoming summer salon in the capital city. Mim's feeling he was looking round for her face in the crowd grew, and as his eyes were getting near, her heart was running mute in her chest. She imaged it hidden in her lap, waiting for the beam of his gaze to spot it. It was a poor freaked-out heart, naked and wet, exposed. His lips parted to utter the names of those artists. Mim perceived herself as beautiful on that particular day, all the more reason why her heart might want to lie low. That day she was tall, dressed up in white garments, hair running happily down below her shoulders. That day the lineaments of her face were perfect, her skin stretched with anxiety, and the fire in the great artist's cheeks was glowing just below her eyes, which seemed to gulp in all the light which was flooding the room through the windows. In point of fact, he could not remember all the names, therefore he was only going to mention a couple or so, that was what he announced, and he could not have retained hers, no way, that would have got her to fever pitch. One name, the second, the third one, people Mim all knew. Even as she was enjoying a bit of relief that he had not uttered hers in front of everyone, she heard: Tomina Tudor. That was her, none other but her. Right in the very end he was saying how greatly this artist had impressed him, how she was a whole universe he desired to get to know better, and how it was not two, but four of her works that were going to go to the capital. "Is she in the room?" It seemed to her he had purposefully put off that moment in order to give himself time to gather the sap in his cheeks in a pool of courage before finding a way to see her in the flesh. But whatever was she doing? She should stand up now, tall, white, at the zenith of his pursuit, she like the very apotheosis of quest, of quest as a way of life, *chercher l'âme, la femme*, since what other had he seen in her paintings, if not the woman. Well, he was about to meet her now, so she stood up. "I am Tomina Tudor." She was aware she was all flushed in the face. Her heart had jumped back inside her chest and was shaking it. For a thin while he held her in his glance, and just for the lapse of that very second nothing more budged on his face. His blonde strands themselves, and his lips, and even the pupils of his eyes stood still to let that image impress his retina, and that was her image. How come this was happening just as she had envisaged? If not this had been a recurrent pattern in her life before. She used to dream of something, visualize it, set her heart on it, and all of a sudden, zap, it came true when she least expected. "So, it is you." The light-hearted tone in his voice had got tainted and he grew rather somber and mean and that was all, he had no more words to address to the audience, except for a simple request for Tomina Tudor to show him more of her paintings.

Right now as he is perorating, his gaze is fastened on her. He had noticed her among the on-lookers, so he rolls his eyes throughout the room and then back on her. She is making efforts to keep her vision blurred, since she cannot possibly keep her eyes on the ground like a bashful child when everybody else has their eyes nailed on the speaker. And then, what could he make of that, he could get her wrong. What she fears is accidentally shafting through his pupils, all dilated and on vigil right there in front of her. She hears her name. He is asking for her opinion, and that is on what namely, for Christ's sake, and with that whole army of critics from the capital attending in firing position, and the press. She is at a loss. Whatever should she say? Her voice falters as she mumbles something generally valid, upon which she resumes her seat with no feeling in her legs. What she gathers is that the artist wishes her name to get out into the world, he wants to get the wolves acquainted with the sound of her name, it is common knowledge this is a first step on the way to the top. Each time he had come to their town he had asked her to bring him more paintings, and these were always entering exhibitions, either locally or nationally. No sooner had he arrived than he would request to see her: let Tomina know I'm here, I want to meet her. It was the president of the art club who called her up each time, and she would pretty nearly fly to those meetings.

Her absorption in work had reached a peak of enthusiasm. She no longer minded the daily humdrum, or let the morning worry drive her to desperation, that the bus would be too crowded to take her on. No longer did the late afternoon torture have the power to chip at her enthusiasm and devotion. Undismayed, she would stand lashed by whirls of dust, her neck poking into the road for any chance vehicle to take her back home, where she would get herself a quick clean, a bite to eat, and the relief of being in her room. There she would assiduously prepare for the next descent of the great artist, and only when the news was communicated to her did she allow herself to take a few moments off work. She zapped back into the physical she and enjoyed listening in to the secret process of rejuvenation in her skin, to youthful blood reaching the finest capillaries, she bathed and dressed her body in beautiful clothes, gave herself a once-over in the mirror and got out the door, eager for her destination, where she would find out whatever his opinion was on her latest work.

The artist had promised her own solo exhibition in the capital, but she still had a lot of work to do for that. In preparation, he had already started to gather all Mim's notable artwork in his personal office at the club's headquarters, so that other important persons could see them and make an opinion. She figured it was the dignitaries or bigwigs in the art field or in the media who sometimes accompanied him on his visits. Some figures. Sour-faced and grim-spirited, always wearing solemn dark suits, people who seemed to notice no one outside their clique. They walked and talked as though they had neither aim nor interlocutors. Against all appearances, it was the great artist who had power of decision. He was one of the most outstanding plastic artists at home and abroad. 'You have no idea how powerful I am,' he would tell her, 'it all hangs on my decision.'

"Them, don't mind them arrogant peacocks and their gaudy feathers, it's I who decide." Mim knew that. "But tell me," she would insist, "I want to hear it from your mouth, do I have real talent?" "Tomina, I'm not playing any game here, if you had no talent I wouldn't have walked my legs off to help you." She had imparted to him her dream of becoming a scenographer, in order to have a larger access to the public. "But this only if you really think I am gifted," she insisted. "You can get there, as far as you really want it. It lies entirely with you to do it. You'll have to be hard at it though — tell me, what have you been doing so far? You've been pretty much out of the swim, huh? I was already a name at your age, plus two international exhibitions." In spite of the meaningful silence, she tried to explain herself then. "There was nobody to turn to, I felt cursed with a lot of bad luck and suffered in silence. But I'm all for it now, and at present all I live for is this exhibition."

Every such important event occasioned by the visit of the big shots from the capital ended with a shindig at some posh restaurant. Is Tomina coming, the artist would invariably ask, let Tomina join us, let the girls come. Although she did not have the heart not to join the party, she always had one to call it an early night and withdraw like a Cinderella. She would feel the warmth of his gaze lingering in her wake while others pulled at him, attended on him, asked him questions, or drew him aside for a tête-à-tête, as was he not the very hero of those soirées which were practically held in his honor? They would take him to their bosom or actually snuggle him dearly, while the representatives of the Inspectorate of Culture would all bow and scrape before him, so needy and desperate for his support, the only hope for the town's advancement, no matter how petty, on the way out of nowhere. He was reluctant to show he was aware of Mim's leaving, yet after a few such occasions this came to be written all on his face, in broad limelight. He would turn cup after cup bottom up, sending down his throat their ambrosial content and chanting its praise in spirals of prodigious words which would coil up with cigarette smoke into a billowing canopy, quasi metaphysical. In his verbal alembics Mim could sense pure strong liquor discreetly vaporizing toward her brain. But there was no way she would let those intoxicating fumes get to her, so she was at pains to keep them at bay, and that simply by trying to act natural, at least as natural as the circumstances demanded. She swam with the tide, doing whatever the rest of the group were doing, talked to them, laughed at their jokes, and what with this and that, she came to doubt the assumption that it was on her that the art wizard was zeroing in. And if he really was, then what would the world say? Maybe that she was some star-struck wannabe who lacked real talent and was only invited to exhibitions just because she stood high in the maestro's favor — this or who knows what other Grundyisms. She did not want her name to be tossed about. Perhaps distorted perceptions were circulating in the mise-en-scène, perhaps she was all wrong, perhaps it was nothing but some kind of impromptu Bacchic art, or mere wine and dame jokes the artist engaged in at such parties. Except that, when she participated in those gatherings, Mim did not think herself a woman. In fact she cringed to consider the thought that those mature men might take her for one, in the anatomical sense of the word. In their company, she rather felt like a schoolgirl, a schoolgirl who strained after praise for her achievements. And good conduct. Fleeting whisperings and vulgar scraps of hearsay of all kinds had been accreting at the back of Mim's mind ever since a child, like a chorus of wicked genii which she would constantly shoo away. She did not want to know about the grownups' world, but now look how that fleece was being spun into a thread which grew stronger and stronger, so sharp as to cut her mind into two: the grownups' world was different. It was uncanny. Obstinate, impregnable Mim would act like a fetus in the face of such adversity, unwilling to part with the environment in which she was naturally gliding along, unperturbed. That was why she resisted riveting her eyes on the great artist and was always mindful to leave in good time.

Saving that on the latest occasion it had been him who, not long into the party, started to his feet, walked to where Mim was seated, took her by the hand and made a nearly formal announcement: I'm leaving. He left behind two parallel rows of hollow-mouthed masks, frozen still in their tall-backed chairs, facing one another in a very icon of perplexity. All were there, those who had been looking forward to blowing some favor in his ear or to touching him up about their own artwork, those who had been working their butt off to formulate pompous home-made speeches, those whose canvases were lying in the trunks of their cars either sticking out from rigid folders, or rolled up in scrolls ready to unfold before the maestro's eyes. Those feasts followed the same small-town pattern: the art wizard as a central figure kissing the cup at the head of the table, fantasizing, telling lewd jokes or summoning up funny episodes in his life, while a never ending Indian file of various other personages was sweeping in slow motion toward him, looped around his throne to give voice to their pleas, to then trickle away along the other side and only come to a stop in order to resume their seats, where they would remain put to gourmandize, raking their brains to figure out whether or not the artist had understood, and if he had, was he not likely to forget?

He was obviously well oiled on that occasion. They must have been giving him to drink in some nearby village which he was so proud to have visited, as what fine wine he had drunk there, ruby-red, strong, and so damn life-giving. And as he was pulling her away through the door, what was she to do but ask where to. To have a private chat. What would the others think? The others, what others, I don't give a crap about any of them. At this, an involuntary trickle of laughter escaped her otherwise straight mouth. He could not even get a good hold of her hand, she thought, as his was glazed in sweat and rather plump, making hers repeatedly slip out of his grip. The fact was she was not well at all, utterly embarrassed, but how could she help smiling inwardly at his clumsy staggering which, damn, was interfering with his grim determination to drag Tomina Tudor along. On top of all that, some sort of sidekick was straggling on the artist's heels. When they reached the car, the chauffeur opened the doors for them, and that tip-top adjutant was the first to pop in, seating himself in the front seat. The artist waited for her to get in at the back of the car, than flumped his heavy frame beside her. "Where would you like me to drive you, sir?" "To the hotel, of course," the great artist promptly replied. That sounded ugly into Mim's ears. Her thought instantly jumped back to the table fellows they had just parted company with. She could almost hear their malicious gossip going round. They must be speaking bad things of her, the woman, the only one to blame. The image was so vivid in her mind of women's mouths spitting venom, sending loads of it whishing through the air to reach her, and of men's mouths sneering and jeering, in as far as, when it comes to art, men are worse than the devil himself. Nonetheless, she strongly dismissed the impulse to bolt away. They were fully grown up people so they would have a talk together, all right. He was not perchance going to chop her up. As to the others, let them think whatever they might.

Mim supposed the chat would take place in the hotel's lobby, so she sat on a settee there, observing his massive frame swaying on stalling feet as the hanger-on asked the receptionist for the key to the maestro's room. No way, no, how could they talk out in the lobby, the artist rejected the idea and grabbed her hand on the instant, steering away. The elevator, out of the elevator, the hanger-on unlocks the door. Just let me know what to bring you. A bottle of mineral water, Tomina, do you want coffee, see if the young lady would like some coffee. No, thank you — she was smiling dumb, what on earth was she doing there? The underling noticed her uneasiness. Their eyes interlocked, she gave him a pleading glance, and added she would like some fruit juice, whatever kind.

Mim thought of a change in tactics. She pretended she had understood they needed to discuss the details in relation to her forthcoming exclusive exhibition. No sooner had that other man closed the door behind him than he went straight to a couch by the window, on which he reclined, closing his eyes, so he might not have paid attention to what she had said. But he soon seemed to wake up from his snoozing and jabbered something, skip that now, he coerced her into silence. The next second she was at it again, questioning him about her art, begging him to tell her what he really thought, but all he did was talk about power, his power. Tomina should only get at least forty works ready and leave the rest for him to deal with. He was clearly not in the humor for that sort of stuff and she figured he must have had enough of it, what with the army of inspectors and activists and with the cohorts of art teachers and artists who kept on at him with that type of discourses each time he alighted in town. Come here, he told her. He lay there, sprawled on his side, with his generous abdomen at rest, his bloodless eyelids limply drawn over his eyes, while between his two thighs brought out into full relief by the creases in his pants, a hump was silently rising like a small Dobrujan hill, making the room too narrow to accommodate Mim's thought that the truth lay probably there, that the truth was by some chance lust for life bulging like dough between the robust legs of a man on whom others hung for success. And even as this thought of hers was constricting, his eyelids turned pale pink, and suddenly he jerked up on the couch. "Come sit next to me, why in hell are you sitting there?" On a chair at the large table in the middle, that was, where she had clumsily seated herself in the meantime, not knowing how to flee the Minotaur's abode without stirring his anger. She was hard put to it to join him on the couch. "I'm better here," she said, trying, through her eyes, to work him into her way of seeing things, in that particular case the table as a better place for discussion. "As you wish," he said curtly and dived in the typical poetic blabbering, a kaleidoscope of fresh kernels, and apples and pulp and aromas, all of young maidens, the color in their cheeks and the smooth skin of their well-rounded thighs. Somebody knocked on the door. "Come in", "Yes," they said concomitantly. It was a waiter with a tray — where's the coffee, I haven't been told, a coffee then pal, OK boss. He was slow in scrambling to his feet. "If you won't come over, what else can I do?" She went to help him up and he rested the palms of his hands on her shoulders and twisted her around to face the large window. A slit in the curtain formed a curious scenic background, opening a resplendent column of brightness against the diffuse light sifting in through the nut-brown shade of the fabric. The dazzle instantly scared her pupils so small that the irises glowed like sapphires in the penumbra.

"God bless my soul, what eyes you have!" he exclaimed. She took in his eyes then and noticed they were also light in color, if it was not just a luminous illusion. She observed his swollen eyelids, and his lips seemed to be swelling up too, as though to match his florid complexion. After a shake of his massive head and a dangling of his fine tresses of hair, he made for the table and said, "Let us sit." Didn't you order coffee, he went on to say, no, thank you — thereupon came his coffee, and the waiter went right back out. He plumped himself on a chair and took a sip. "Come, sit here on my knees." She gave in to a smile. "No, I won't," she said facetiously. He clasped one of her hands and pulled her to him, positioning her on his knees. "Like that," he said. Never in her life had Mim even dreamed of sitting on the lap of an art mogul, thought at which a sense of relieved bemusement rippled across her and she felt literally swept off her feet by a vast tide of beatitude, yes, anything can happen to anyone in this life. At the very same time she was irritatingly aware of the burden of her own physique, which felt stiff and uncomfortable like hell on the man's thighs, so bloody wider and wider, so bloody hotter and hotter. Danger was looming, so she was raking her brains for means to unglue her body from that foreign flesh and pelt back to her chair. It was fated to her, she awoke to the conclusion that she was fated to annoy all the men who could protect, support, or befriend her. Why had she not made herself uglier, so that he would leave her alone and only help the artist in her. If there was any. Now she could no longer be sure. And that was her one and only interest. "You know—" she heard herself say. "I wish I could achieve something justly. If I really am talented as you said, great, but if I'm not, I don't want you to help me." She did not know whether to continue or not, and what more could she say. He had been keeping cool and distant for a short while, to let her spill the beans. But then he broke the silence. "You do have talent." His words came out slowly, in an absolute tone. Only now did Mim let the strength in his phantasmal alembics permeate her, drop after drop of that liquor of power she had been always fighting so shy of. Now that she had her answer she felt like giving him a kiss, a thank you kiss. He somehow guessed her urge and turned his cheek to her, in a fatherly manner. She gave him a peck and dashed back to her place.

But even as she touches the seat of the chair it strikes her that she could, what if she did uncover herself and traveled naked on the asphalt of life, what if she felt the currents with the nibs of her nipples, the bitumen with the pores of her soles, and the fresh coolness, between her bare legs. Another old wish of hers comes to the surface, to go skinny-dipping in the sea at night. Now she can do it, let her have a taste of it now or never, let her stride naked on highways. Or maybe later, later feels better.

There is rapping on the door, so she presently springs back to her feet and rests standing just like a schoolgirl caught out in some inappropriate act, only to take in a most mundane picture, that of the underling, who was addressing her with his eyes — he had come to rescue her. How reassuring, she chuckles in her heart, since her hopeful thought had instantly conceived of the man spreading the good news that nothing indecent had happened in that room. Knock-knock again, another two turn up, banquet fellows who have left the venue, as what feast could that be in the absence of the great artist, in whose honor it had been organized. "So, what now?" she questions the artist, a little confused. "Tomina, all I said holds true, so get your butt to work. Look, I'm now taking with me everything I have in my office at the club." He is adding them together. "But why don't you sit down, dear?" "Thank you, but no, I must be leaving now, it's late. I have to be up early tomorrow." "Tomina," he chanted her name while signing to the others to sit at table. "Let them bring in some wine," he orders, then relapses into a lyrical state, "Tomina, please stay to drink a glass with us." Her face booms into a warm smile and only kind words rush to her lips. She says, "I appreciate that, I'd really love to, truly, but I don't drink, thank you." Doubting the kindness of what she sounded like, she makes for the door in small reluctant steps. A picture flashes in her mind to cheer her spirits, of the whole congregation of revelers filing in a termite-like transfer to that hotel room, where the feast will finally come to fruition, and what bustle and clamor. "I'll be waiting for you to return. Till then I'll do nothing but paint. I'll be seeing you, have a nice ride back to the capital." Saying this, she continues her advance toward the door looking repeatedly over her shoulder, irises each time gaped full right into the column of light. From her angle of sight, there zoomed out a spacious room, something more like a long banquet hall, with the great artist in mid-way between the large glass wall of the window and the departing Mim, reclining on a chair that was too small for his formidable stature, his irises dim in her tracks, sniffing like dogs, set between eyelids fully opened by now, eyes so heavy, weighing so heavy on the lower lids, making everything in the room slowly sink into the ground, until nothing was but a stately hall with the column of light indicating to Mim the way out. He remained as though hung on a thread Ariadne had forgotten in there.

That was the last time she spoke to him. She soon came upon a new path in life. Yet another time, Mim reinvented herself and took off, leaving everything behind. He continued to ask about her whenever he came to town, her former colleagues at the club told her — where is Tomina, tell her to come. In spite of his summoning her up with each announcement of his arrival, she was never there, except for that one time when she attended his lecture at the vernissage of his personal anniversary exhibition. How could she go, when she was all set on leaving, preparing for a new existence? Tomina as the great artist knew had disappeared, but that was just for a while, as she would come back some day to complete what she had left pending. The image of her bunch of paintings lying waiting in some corner in the artist's office, gathered so meticulously by his artful hands, would not leave her. Oftentimes she would feel a gentle brush by her temples and she knew it was them, her paintings crying for her return. They would keep whispering into her ear that perhaps she should have bathed in the sea along that silvery moonbeam in her imagination, and perhaps it would have done her good to pace the median of the highway, stark naked and free.

31 MYSTIQUE

Her vigorous hair is falling into a cascade at the back, she knows. What keeps her transfixed is the shimmering strands which drape down between the base of the statuesque neck and her shoulders, the perfect frame for her tall, flushed cheeks. All her eagerness is encased there, between the columns of hair and the thick tresses above her brow, just like under an Egyptian wig. Everything falls into place, the glowing pink at the bottom of her eyes, the elegant edge of her long nose ending in slim triangular nostrils, and the mouth, stilled right at the proper distance below. Regally set, the gems of her eyes send forth mystical glints of an ancient blue, a terrible force below the shower of golden tassels. It was shining, her hair was bathing in gold, for all that, retaining impenetrable depths. As she stood mesmerized in front of the mirror, her small face was reflecting light from just the right points, and there was this sweet slyness about her lips which was turning them sublime. What she could read on them was sweet life. That was *Mim*. The stranger in the train station called her Mim.

This exact image will be gliding along with the train's pulling into the station. Frame after frame rolling in a row, and among them, this exact still. She will descend from the train car just like a still picture, her neck stretched high to let her hair fall straight down, if only there will be no wind to spoil this perfect image of her, on which she so badly wants his eyes to zoom in. She prays God for a favorable entourage of words and gestures, of fragrances, and even of her own thoughts. The slightest impression of discomfort, any hint of disharmony can change her facial expression in a shot, and the miracle is gone. She considers the peculiar fate of her beauty, so fragile, so elusive, dependent on so many things, demanding so much care and life force and happiness. And when she thinks how easy beauty is with other women. They simply are beautiful and that is all there is to it. Carved out in robust matter, they walk the world nonchalantly, sleep tight and long, laugh vigorously, and they do not care a straw. In spite of all that, Tomina is happy to be as she is. Her beauty is like a living entity which visits her occasionally, a vital breath which comes, filters throughout her body to give her new life, and goes immediately away. It disappears as suddenly as it appears, but as long as it stays with her, in her eyes, in the fingers of her hands, in her legs, or in her hair, any perfect human being is dull as compared to Tomina. Yes, she is happy with that, it is a lot more difficult, but how wonderfully exciting.

The fine kohl black line she is going to draw all along the inside of the lower lid will enhance the sapphires of her eyes. It seems their gleam holds stories of times long forgotten, stories about love and death that have traveled like a flash of power across times, through ancient galleries dressed in lapis lazuli and gold. *Antique, mystique*, these are the words that alight in her mind, *-que*, glissando to and fro, *-y-*, cutting deep to the quick of flesh and thought, to the quick of mankind's conscious of forcible weapons crossed above fire, basins cut out in mighty stone scorching prostrate before claws of sphinxes, everlastingness like a column of sunlight running towards an infinity of stars,

God, fearsome fulmination, love. Stop. It is time she unhooked herself from her own stare in the mirror. "Mom, how do I look?"

Her mother measures her up and down from the other end of the long corridor. Her mouth opens wider and wider with each step Tomina takes toward her. Her green eyes stretch smilingly to the temples, while her exuberant mouth tells Tomina that yes, he will be as enchanted by her looks. "Wow, how you've made yourself pretty, my girl." She sounds truly pleased with what she sees, although she does not consider her daughter a beauty. She was not, as a matter of fact. Tomina did not feel herself beautiful when she was with her mother. She would relax all her muscles negligently in her presence, of both her body and face, and would allow tiredness to run like languid lymph beneath her skin, jaundicing it, sucking in any drop of vividness. "You sparkle indeed," the woman stresses this time the word in the middle, prolonging its vowel. "What have you done to yourself?" Tomina shrugs her shoulders, shy to talk to her mother about her beauty. Her mother has no idea she is beautiful. Only others see her as such, and that is because she reveals her beauty to them, which is due to whatever gets into her out of the blue, like a cloud enveloping her to sublimate her features and to set the pupils of her eyes aglitter for others to see her like that.

The only time her mother could get a glimpse of Tomina beautiful was as she gave herself a look-over in the tall mirror in the vestibule, just before getting out of the door. It was then when the usual 'I don't like the way you look' was replaced by exclamations of wonder and awe, as it also was upon her return, throughout the recount of her outing. Strangely enough, this kind of story telling would maintain her traits alive until the very last word. Once this uttered, they would collapse, there was nothing left to prop them up, and her makeup turned into a heavy mask, dry and dusty. Then her mother would say: come on, go wipe off your makeup, it is late. As she spread cleanser all over her face and rubbed and scrubbed, a sense of the ugly awakened in her and soon acquired voluptuous dimensions, which prompted her to hover around her mother, reveal herself in her true likeness, look, this is the real me, not the dazzling princess who turned heads at the ball. Come, go to bed, her mom would again shoo her away. That awful sight surely gave the poor woman the creeps, also due to the greasy layer which brought into full relief all the sharp angles and the deep shadows on her pitiable face. Go away, her mother would then go on to entreat her dearly, all simpering, we can talk tomorrow. And she did go, but always came back a few times more. Thank god her father was asleep and did not see her like that. Come now, go to sleep, Tomina, her mom kept at it, now shaking with laughter at her prankster of a daughter, that chameleon-like wonder wisp of a girl who, once out the door of the house, conquered men's hearts. On the other hand, whenever Tomina dared as much as simply imply that she was not happy with her own looks, her mother would start ranting in a huff: you are always underestimating yourself, I do not want to hear any more of this nonsense.

Now it was one of those just before getting out moments when her mom, her dad, and herself were all gathered under the light spot in the vestibule. Her father was choking with emotion, his loving gaze fixed upon her from the frame of the living room door. His almandine eyes of a whitish blue were misting up for the simple fact that his daughter looked beautiful and was leaving home on a date. His darling daughter was also going to battle, and how he was proud she would certainly return victorious. She was sitting her first exam of the summer session the following day. "Good luck, dear Daddy's girl, come back safe!" "Hurry, or you'll miss the train," her mother urged her out, then added, "Tomina, take good care, and mind them both, the exam and the boy."

32 PIETÀ

For Alex's first Christmas, Mim recreated the world under the tree for him. A fantastic miniature world with tiny wooden houses and families of folks brought together from old sets of games and toys, or various cutouts plastered on cardboard. Utterly incredible for her to be the selfsame person who shouted his cries down — shut up, child, for God's sake — desperately pressing his tiny face against the floor as if their only salvation rested upon stifling his squalling.

They were all keeping ducked to the ground in the hallway, hearts ticking like crazy in their chests, while the roaring rattle of machine guns was unbearably louder and louder. The terrorists were climbing up the stairs towards them. There was rumor that they usually picked themselves up a top floor apartment as vantage point to overlook the whereabouts and from where to shoot. And where should they find a better strategic position if not in a ten-story tower situated right next to a military unit? Just like the very block of apartments they lived in. They had been shooting up the neighborhood since early that evening, with dull sunken sounds of gunshot at first, which came to resound

253

frighteningly up the staircase in their building, ascending closer and closer to their landing. The rat-a-tat-tat was blasting into their eardrums when Mim commanded everyone, mom, dad, brother, brother's wife, to throw themselves flat on their bellies in the middle of the hallway, the only place in the apartment that had no doors or windows. Mim had a vision of sparks flying off their brains. Right then the sound came to a still — the terrorists must be on the fence about which door to choose to shoot their way in and take over the location. She already imagined the brutes storming in and pouring a hail of death upon the whole household, all shot dead, and that was the end of them. And the newborn was crying and yelling and screaming. As hysterically sharp as her orders might be, whispered in urgent grimness, Mim could not make him stop. How could hysteria make him stop, she now realizes, poor thing, awoken into a world so dark. Literally dark, as they were heaped on the floor like cockroaches in the shadows, hump next to hump. "Pray it will not be us." She braced up to convey that to them curtly, in tune with the rhythm of her heart beats. As she finished saying that, a sense of liquid pity flooded her all over, the purest feeling of pity for the newborn, and, as if under orders, a tide of balmy moisture exuded through the pores of her skin. That was pity as balm.

The squalling had ceased. Quite so. Mim was saying a prayer for Alex silently, oh, God almighty, please save this child. They kept frozen in that position piled up on the floor, holding their breaths, as the firing rumble subsided. It finally came to a definite halt. Mim had a hunch it was somehow for Alex that they all had been spared and could not stop thanking him inwardly. She eventually detached herself, just like the whole family, from the black abscess of fear. It was over, the terrorists had retired, they had probably received orders to move on and terrorize other quarters, other human beings.

Where in hell would these terrorists hide during day time? Every night they would torment the locals, inflict anguish on them with such savageness, only to leave them alone by day, as though granting them a respite to get out from the blocks. Night and day, two disparate worlds. Warfare nights full of mystery, peril, death, harrowing fiction-like nights so hard to accept as true. Was this really happening to them, was this really occurring in their town? Rat-a-tat-tat, went the thunder of shotguns, tracer trajectories split the night sky like lightning, helicopters were approaching! Total darkness down where the military unit was. People were hiding there on the lookout. Mim could almost visualize them lying in ambush, ready to counterattack, ducking, squatting, or maybe prostrate on their bellies, perspiration surreptitiously being squeezed out of their infants' souls. They were all mama's sons. Sweat was lying in wait at each entrance to their each man's pore, in a cold pellicle, like a shield against terror, the very barrier of their conscious of lads brought up in some good people's households. That could not be, why would that terror have picked them up, why would fate have chosen them to put to fire and sword the manhood of their nation's pacifist blood, so appeased, self-conciliated, and long dormant. There were no two ways about it, it would irrefutably happen, the ridge of the worlds is right here at the gate of their fearful pores, so their bodies will rise, from their elbows and knees, and will fling themselves forward with a battle cry. They will charge forward at command, under hypnosis, just bodies that will leave their minds at home, in the distant farmsteads spread on hills and valleys beyond mountain ranges, in those bucolic lands Mim was dreaming of, like the Zarand Realm, where the dear sun's gilt sprawls out in its glory on everything, turning sheep's fleece to a gold tint, the blades of shepherds' knives, and the hazel of women's eyes… The recruits would leave behind everything that was. They would throw themselves on the other side of the world, under orders. Those in command know the ways, you — go there, you — stay here, under order. Fire! Yessir! That was what they had sworn, to say they understood. And did the poor boys ever get any sleep those days? Maybe they took turns to snatch a wink, all camouflaged. There was time of war and the entire unit was under curfew. Not the faintest twinkle came from down there, but Mim could guess their existence. She could see them stuck together in the darkness, their perspiration shy to ooze out and run.

33 BRAZEN

The car is gobbling up the road carrying her, a desperate passenger who does not know where her stop is. Where in this large world will she find a way out, where will she eventually discharge this matter within her, incandescent with so much running and meandering? What will the light blazing covertly in her chest change into, and when, oh when will Mim finally spread on canvas the turbulent lives she used to conceive in the grottos of so many white nights under the cover of her child's comforter? Is it already too late for that, and if there is still time, where shall she begin? It is high time she put in the hard work, it is high time she got down to forging the matter, to sweating. Sweat is the only way out to freedom, and the very first step is the step out of this four-wheeled machinery, out of this mere means of transport passingly carrying her frame.

But where shall she get off? She always has to get off, get on and then off, set out on a journey and then arrive somewhere. She is burning with desire to grasp something, at last, with her bare hands, to clench her fists, to feel the robust pulp of life with the flesh of her hands. Tools and means, an assiduous refrain of noises becomes audible in her mind. The whole world comes alive with a multitude of smiths and artisans toiling in a vast planetary workshop, bodies bustling about in ceaseless motion, wriggling and squirming to dislodge themselves out of cold blocks of matter, people polishing shapes in a trance, people rasping themselves against matter till beauty is reached, a global congregation of souls exerting their forms upon objects.

What is a fetus, if not a shapeless conglomeration of cells, and what about its thoughts, its first impressions? Nothing is ever lost, nothing at all. Everything is variable to contact, accumulation, and change. It is all natural for people to get hold of a chunk of matter and torture it in tune with their own evolution. It is the quest for their very first thoughts, so they strike it and melt it and punch it with the fists of their first rebellions, and then caress it with the fingers of their first delights. They dream and strike, with the determination only love can foster, to discover their purpose, to discover themselves and reflect themselves back to the others. People forever toiling have started to populate her dreams lately and now she feels she understands why. You cannot expect the world to receive you as a gift unless you search yourself back to the moment of your own conception, totally free of shame. Shame, this lacquer with which we coat all the crude surfaces, is unknown in dreams, as much as it was unknown to the naked squatting around the first fires. Shame is a social institution.

She casts an oblique glance at the grim visage to her left, the man at the wheel, the man full of secrets whose eyes get wet at discovering the secrets of great artists, the man who is sulking unnoticed for not having time to pursue his own quest. 'I should have made art, Mim, this is what I was meant for.' Could Mim have been able to ease his pain? At least that was what she used to think, but he would not allow himself to fall in her trap. The fool, Mim would have died to see the beauty locked deep down in him. This was what she had been fighting for, a sign from him so that she could unveil her own self. She will unroll everything she has on canvas and, who knows, some day he might come across a trace of love from her. Look at him, a mountain of cogitation, uncounted fears blocking his ways to people. The coward has chosen the making of the inanimate construction, all concrete and so cold. It will be cold for him in there. The twisting, vile thoughts will forever smother everything that is good in him. Look at him, effigy of grimness driving Mim away, just to get rid of her, the sly little being who, against the firmness of his gates, had managed, shy as she was, to slink in the terrible darkness. There was tenderness and compassion there as well, and even tears, just as she had imagined, wonderful powers which no one else could have guessed, with the exception of his mother maybe. He knew what Mim had seen there and she wonders if he considers her a sinner for that.

Well, Anton is dead set against shame, against the shameless shame which interferes with everything that is beautiful. He is a truly admirer of the human body as nature's utmost work of art. Parents are wrong — she remembers his words and re-sees his peeved countenance in response to an old man's indignation in the face of a nudist on the crowded beach. Poor man, fate could not have played a more ironical farce on him than prompting him to express his protest to Anton, an advocate of nudity. She was afraid he would turn and rend, and she prayed he would not burst into one of his tirades. What he did instead was take it all on her: I can't bear the sight of them, dumb freaks, ashamed of a man's body, why in hell do they stare then, they are not invited. Quite contrarily, Mim was a lover of mystery, she was after unexpected effects created by the symbiosis between garments and the human body, with its shapes, and poses, and odors. Making art on the human body fascinated her, all that amalgam of draping fabrics, creative tailoring, textures and colors, makeup and movement resulting in stunning spectacles. 'Where did you get these bourgeois airs from,' Anton would enquire keeping an inquisitive eye on her, 'what are you hiding?' Don't you ever do this or that — all natural thing that was, he would blabber on. Wow, how he would have engaged in nude dancing, as he dreamed of a type of art that would completely expose the beauty of the human physique in motion. He would not blush to unveil his body with such nonchalance, but why then would he be so stern in shielding what he had beyond that?

Well, why is she so timorous, so self-conscious? Living with Anton has made her ask herself these questions. She is a liar, since only God knows how shameless she actually is on the inside. Anton is right, after all, she is a hypocrite and a *bourgeoise*. Damn shame, this membrane surreptitiously growing around us along evolution, out of who knows what primeval expression of life, perhaps out of the very living together of two conscious entities within one and the same body. Ha! Soap bubbles, this is what we are, a world of soap bubbles. Only that, when we collide, when there is contact, a common mouth gapes wide and there you have the utmost act of brazenness. All these intricate thoughts exhaust her, but who on earth should find answers, if not ourselves? This pursuit may be sinful all right, this innate eagerness for a destination, yet this is the only way we can be and give. And when she thinks other people like her are striving for the same answers, God only knows what they see. Lash Your scourge upon us, God, on us who are trying to reach You through these ways, as are we not perchance more sinful than thieves and murderers, than those guilty of incest or fornication? *Superbia*, the deadliest sin of all, came rather late to Mim's knowledge. And does her search for herself not mean falling into this sin? Asking for it, looking for it with candle light in hand sounds like a suggestive phrase — at which thought she lapses into smile.

She will embark upon a definite, sustained,

overwhelming venture, as never before. She will start cutting out canvas to measure, strain the pieces burst flat within wooden frames, get them ready to accommodate the long restless worlds within her. And she will lovingly look for the specific shades and tints in her visions, blending them to the end-effect of the crude truth about her brazenness, so the others will see. Anton, the man who is presently driving a vehicle, will let her off at some street corner, the very spot from where she will set out on a journey back to her own childhood, her parents, back to the world.

34 BROTHER

Enough. They have had enough. One night, two nights, three nights closed up in their own home with heavy furniture barricading the door. They no longer make solid furniture like this — her mother's words echo in Mim's mind. Quite so, the very entrance door, typical to all residential blocks, was incredibly frail, just pressed board with veneer glued onto it to look like oak. Allegedly, the socialist family does not need a proper, orthodox door, nor do they need full milk or a really hot bath, for that matter, to say nothing of God or ideas or other such things. A veneer-venerating people, worshippers of particle board, miserable flag-waving paraders, that is what they are. Enough, starting as of today we are going to reverse roles and give chase to them. Let us have a good look at them, what the heck, they cannot be other than people like us. They keep in hiding, the beasts, just as the townspeople do at night. They must be lying close, so let us get out and track them down to their lairs, let us be the hunters by day. That was what Mim decided before that night's retreat, to go after the enemy empty-handed.

"OK, let us be going, girl." The quiet side of her

brother rose to life, valiant. "Let's flush them out of hiding, I'm ready."

"Very well, then," She went into a fit of laughter, and of shaking. Her body was shaking with joy and impatience. The blister broke open, that membrane of fear in which they had been wrapping their home for the night had snapped, let them peel it aside at once and get out.

They removed the massive wood cabinet that was blocking the front door. "Mom, Dad, we are getting out," they announced their parents from the doorway, stretching tall their spines and broadening their shoulders. They pulled on their bleak communist jackets and in no time entered their boots. The TV was on. Against everything, it had also been good for them to stick together in union, protected in their cozy and warm abode. The central heating had been on again, just by miracle, and that was one of the top daytime topics in the neighborhood. It had been really restful, so homelike, just like folks of old by the fireside. So reassuring indoors, with the monitor focused on the people outside, the brave, the daring ones, those who were dying, those who were shouting, those who were fighting, either for an ideal, like the cannon fodder, the manipulated — she now realizes — or just to seize the moment and grab hold of something. No matter the reason, no matter the purpose, they were all out there. The two Tudor siblings were coming out in the cool evening too, to know what that was all about and do something.

"Where are you going?" Taken by surprise, their mother let the dishes in the sink and came over in the hallway to see them. My knights, my Teutonic knights — the faint smile on her lips was seemingly whispering, legend and adventure — her eyes were sparkling. Yet the woman herself uttered out loud, "You're not going anywhere."

Their father turns up too. On the threshold of the living room door, his fragile frame is shivering lightly, more and more visibly, then tricky shuddering unveils his shy teeth and he lapses into half-suppressed laughter.

"So, you're going out." The powerful emotions in his voice made the last word almost inaudible. His eyes were hazy with sudden joy, therefore they would not hide anymore. And how he was proud of his offspring, from whom he had been expecting salvation three nights in a row. That rat's condition was no longer for them. It had been the children who had saved the household by barricading the entrance, and look how it was them again now who were airing the nest.

"How dare you laugh?" Mom was overtly vexed, as why her husband should encourage them to go. "Sakes alive, now you're crying, or what?" She inspected his blurry eyes, then turned to the kids saying, "Dear me, children, you're not in your right minds anymore."

"I've had enough," her brother snaps between clenched jaws. "We'll have a look around and maybe we'll catch the bastards."

Their father has second thoughts. "You'd better stay at home, dear Daddy's children." He is breathing heavily now, with worry and remorse, what had he done, how could he have rejoiced at seeing his children ready to go? As anxiety was settling like a veil over his eyes, he timidly asked, "Are you going downtown?"

"I won't have you go there, I won't hear of it," Mom shouted in her most authoritarian tone. That made Mim flinch with reminiscence from the time they were little, when she was the supreme commander.

"Shall we go there?" Damian enquired firmly, with an implication that he was prepared to do that if necessary.

Many people had been shot to death in the city center the previous night.

"No," Mim said and twisted in place to face her mother and try to temper her down. "Mom, we are only going to check things out around our block. We have to find out who these brutes are, how much longer do you think we should carry on like this? We might find others downstairs willing to join us. And I think we'll do the same every night from now on, so we can sleep peacefully."

"What if something happens? You're out of your minds, I tell you, and you've only heard what these terrorists are capable of."

"They are not shooting at this hour, don't worry. Theirs is a late night show. Let us at least figure out where they could be shooting from, they must have left some traces, right?"

Damian broke in, blood boiling in his head. "So what, let'm shoot, let'm shoot me, and get this over with." His eyes were flashing fire. His hidden self was all out in the open.

The little one, Baby, as Mim had kept calling him ever since he was born, was hiding a whole world under the permanent mask of muteness, a deep world which she had never explored. She had been on a mad chase after Anton's world instead. Every once in a while though, Damian's secret ego would shake her up with sharp blasts soaring tall to the skies, like reversed thunder striking to infinity and not low down close to any human being nearby. The people who happened around were mere witnesses gaping in awe at the fountains of lava which they only waited to cool down, in order for them to resume their daily chores, conversations, or whichever routines. These outbursts of Damian's would soon leave them just like short strange dreams do — thank goodness we are awake. With time, something like an underground pool of frustration had been accumulating, caused by his lack of daring to expose his innermost, peculiar way of feeling the sounds, the people's glances and gestures, which translated into a kind of perception through fascination with the world, with the intimate rhythm of life against the vast plains of perplexity within him, all hues merged into a whitish-gray primitive color, swept across by beams and sparkles of his mind in search of meaning. And there was but one unique answer, the force of life, to his permanent wonder and ecstasy. It was from this that his force stemmed. Yet he was shy to show it to the others, maybe for fear they would be blown away. And why should he have bothered, after all, since showing required a lot of effort. It might have also been difficult for him to find forms of expression, they were not at hand. Awareness of his own power was lying latent in him, and splinters out of this hidden mass would glint rebellion. Rebellion against all masters, commanders, trend setters, any authority of any kind. The seeds of rebellion had been planted early on in his childhood, once he entered school life. Dumb, still as a statue, unblinking, apathetic. They would shout at him and there was no response, they would hit him and there was no budging. He was just waiting for the authority to lose steam and eventually give up. The very notion of educator, of teacher, completely contradicted his outlook on life. He was a free being. Free to sense the world, to understand it and learn about it on his own. Mim was late in comprehending this child's drama starting with his first school year.

The two of them had been spending a whole life together until then. They would get up in the morning and eat, then gambol throughout the day, living all kinds of stories about knights and princesses rescued by them, stories of valiant warriors on battle fields, of adventurers and daredevils ambushed by banditti. Damian always played a double role, the villain in the beginning, and the good guy in the end. They would set out on imaginary expeditions across seas or along raging frothy rapids, sometimes the frail of her on the verge of falling down some ravine or cataract, with him infallibly the rescuing hero. Other times they would take quiet journeys through fanciful hinterland, with him at the wheel sitting on the bottom step of the polished granite stoop at the entrance of the old stately house in which they were born, and her on the upper step behind him. In wintertime there were sledging expeditions. Theirs was a fairly large sled, with backrest and side rails, looking very much like a sleigh, so Damian played the horse, Tomina, the damsel, then they reversed roles, with him a boyar, or the fairy-tale Kai kidnapped by the Snow Queen. They would build peace dwellings only for two, amid flowerbeds in summertime, with pungent earthy smell of turf flooring, and in winter carving their cubicle in the banks of snow freshly piled up by their father's early morning shoveling for paths, the lengthy path leading to the other end of the courtyard and then bending to the left, where their summer kitchen was, and next to it the mysterious, huge, two-roomed storage house, under whose floorboards they pictured long buried treasures. But in that remote backyard there was something even more mysterious, the chicken pen. Within its confines, at the side adjacent to the huge wall towering over the entire household premises, there was a tiny shack made of stone bricks, looking rather like a monk's cell, which Mim imagined to contain a kind of gateway to some unknown world beyond, or to another time. With her mind's eyes she could see a dwarfish door concealed in that back wall, through which you could, if you really wanted, worm your way out on the other side. Yet she had never even as much as got into the chicken's enclosure. Maybe she did not want to.

Therefore winter was a time of sweating work at their igloo in the mountain of snow in the yard, and that must be the reason why she was never cold as a child. Once the shelter finished, they would climb up and cuddle together in there. Freezing cold outside, wild lashes of blizzard gales, howling wolves, while the two of them were comfortably protected against any harm. They enjoyed exerting themselves for real while playing. Sometimes, for instance, they would range all the chairs in the house in rows of seats, and both acted bus driver and conductor alternatively, simultaneously substituting for passengers as well. She cannot think of anything they have not been passengers on. There were race cars and trucks and rafts and boats of all kind, and planes shooting off to the skies. When night came, Tomina, the elder one, would make up amazing stories to stuff the little one's head with. She even created a series for him, whose protagonist she would drag across all recesses and crevices of the world. However, about half way through his first year at school, Damian lapsed into silence. Her lively playmate had vanished away. Thankfully, he managed to get back to his former self during vacations, especially the long summer ones, when they would resume their travels in lands of their own concoction, which seemed more real to them than everything that happened around. It is only now that Mim interprets his muteness as a refusal to bend, to crush his inner world in order to comply with the outer one, that of norms and regulations. Hard as they might try to subject him to their norms, by yelling or calling him names, or even by beating him, Damian would not grant them access on the secret plains he was roving.

What he did abandon to the mercy of others was his physical body. First of all he did so in the face of his own mother's impetuous temper. She used to beat him. No sooner did she arrive home from work than she would start her inquisition. She would give him a smack for this and a smack for that, for doing this or that silly thing about the house in her absence, for not having done his homework, for having got a bad grade. Gauged against Tomina's brilliant school performance, his poor results were driving her practically mad, so the woman would knock him off his feet in a fit of fury and start landing a hail of blows and punches on his inert, insensitive body. And that was just the preliminary. Getting no response out of him, she would then aid herself by grabbing the simplest implement at hand, usually a flyswatter, driving slap after slap upon him as he lay grounded, still unresponsive. Infuriated and completely out of her mind, she sometimes ended up throwing kicks in the sides of his body. She would keep on like that until she finally came to a halt for lack of breath, and of hope, demoralized, defeated. Her mother's arrival came to make Tomina's flesh creep. She could hardly believe it was their mom, who once used to enlighten their faces with joy when she stepped through the door. With each blow Damian got, her heart would shrink to her throat with pain, petrifying the flow of life in her eyes, lips, and nostrils, and she would stop breathing in prayer to God to make that day's torturing session stop so that she could draw in some air again. Tomina herself had once got a slap with the damn flyswatter, one single slap, and it hurt beyond words. God, how much pain that wretched child's body must have endured. But his soul would not be corrupted, no way, it stayed strong, unsubmissive. Their mother suffered a lot too, because of her beating him, because he would not react, because she had taken the way of despair. It was a mercy that, after a couple of years, she realized there was no point in going on like that and tamed down, reconciled to her fate. With their mother back to her senses again, Tomina felt a lot more at ease, even though there were times when her eyes still darted fiery glints, or when her countenance turned bleak all of a sudden, or when she let out screams so high-pitched as to pierce their eardrums. She would shout at Tomina for not keeping her things in good order — look how Damian is orderly and meticulous, she repeated. 'Tomina!' she would summon her by shrilling her name from another room, and Tomina presently reported, to hear more or less the same domestic phraseology: what are these doing here, pick them up right away and put them back to their place.

They set out on their hunt for the elusive terrorists that evening. Well then, go have a look — there was no stopping them, their parents understood. "But let there be no mistake about it, you have no business going downtown," their mother concluded. A few other fellows joined them, friends of Damian's, determined, stout lads in the neighborhood — yeah, sure, let's do it. Yet the most valiant of all was Mim, she was the group leader. They inspected all the collection rooms at the base of the garbage chutes on the ground floor of the three high-rise buildings near the military unit. In fore position, Mim was the first to kick open each wing of the metal gates in turn, banging them forcefully to the walls. Nothing dubious unrolled before her eyes at a first glance, except for garbage, so she went on to look behind the doors, and then prowled her way to the center of the room, with the rest of the company straggling behind her. Soon their conduct somewhat turned from pioneers' daring to that of seemingly rightful settlers, as awareness conquered ground that nobody alien had been foraying the premises. They would shove their boots probing into the mounds of garbage — not here either, bro. "Go ahead, comb the whole chamber," Mim would command, then remember to thunder away against whoever their enemy was. "God forbid I should get hold of one of those now, or I'll tear them to pieces." She had a feeling nothing could stand in her way to carrying that out, being practically convinced she would be able to kill an armed *securist* bare-handed as she was. The palms of her hands felt a lot larger and her fingers like steel, while hatred was blowing hurricanes into her arms and legs.

She could sense his shadow — beyond the mountains of filth hid the image of the important art critic from the capital city whose presence at their club's meetings was quasi permanent. What if, she thought laughingly to herself, she should bump flat out into that guy now, he little and squat and lying so low. She was concomitantly being called forth to challenge from the darkness by another phantom. The traits of a particular face, as though painted in sludge, were taking shape on the grimy walls. A narrow face divided by the thin bridge of a nose so evil, which cast its devious shadow over the Majorcan lips below in a rictus as terrifying as to suit only representations of the devil, the vilest of grins also darting from the livid lids so tense above those hollow eyes, gray, the fabled blue eyes of the Securitate men. This image came back to her, propped on that tall neck of an observer's, the very face of the man who had put all the honey and vitriol together in his voice to summon her on the phone to the Securitate quarters in town. Just in order for them to have a talk, but it was mandatory. She went.

In contrast to her expectations, it was all but a laughing matter. Then she got the whole picture: those people could not be farther from the real world, they were living in stories, in adventure fictions, just like Damian and she used to when they were little. That guy kept prattling about various scenarios of terrorists and spies and counter-spies who kept a close watch on them, Romanians. Wherever they went and whatever they did, he meant, they were in danger of being contacted. Mim had once told a Turkish naval officer in the street what the time was and they knew about that. It was them, therefore, who spied on people. He also mentioned something about the Red Brigades, which was enough to make a cat laugh — red, dumbhead, are they not leftists like you, she laughed inwardly, barely able to keep a straight face. Their infantile silliness was beyond belief. She admitted she kept correspondence with someone in that country, so what, she studied Italian. Many of her fellow students corresponded in a whole array of foreign languages and she did not think there was anything wrong with that. It seemed she had come there to listen to a series of amusing anecdotes. But that until the moment when the two worm-like lips that were dancing their slimy dance on the man's face dropped in the topic of the art club she was a member of. That brought everything home to her and her thought jumped right to the top critic from the capital. Art critic like heck, the tick, the contemptible parasite. So it was that kind of art. And that was the *securist*'s little game, picking her brains about the activity of the art club. "What are you talking about at your meetings?" That capped the climax. Mim retorted promptly, "I would have you know that it's all about art, sir, we only talk about art there, and that's flat." Her blood went up to her head and she flew into a rage. Her face on fire, she sprang to her feet and began blurting out in a wild staccato, with little oxygen plucked up after each syllable, trembling as she had never before trembled, with fury and indignation — the shock she had received was felt by far more powerful than fear: I would thank you not to bother about my business; I didn't really know what this was all about, that's why I'm here; had I had the slightest idea you summoned me for this absolute nonsense I might just as well have stayed at home. She took her leave in as a civilized manner as she could and went straight out, cheeks still burning, picturing that ridiculous character as flat as a poster behind her. Villains, damn bastards, she was babbling in her mind trying to cool down as she made for the exit, so it was all true, the wretches were really playing at spies and detectives in their sick minds. They were sick, she thought reassuringly, and were trying to attract others in their silly games, other sick people like them, as who could make better stool pigeons, who could possibly buy their espionage scenarios, be they even real, but the retarded and the mentally insane? Normal people did not believe in detective stories, so the *securists* needed to resort to the opposite type.

Well, if she were to come across that poster now, Mim thought rubbing her palms — he only lived in the neighborhood, as she had seen him around a couple of times carrying a shopping bag, poor devil, so if she were to bump into him, she would make him one with the mass of garbage. All the more so for she had just remembered the greasy voice on the phone only four nights ago, which she knew was his. A voice that had spiked her like steel wire all the way down from head to toe, rasping at length in her chest in slow mode and with such heed, to rend the torture unbearable. It was her birthday and the voice said happy anniversary. Mim asked who it was, but no answer came from the other end, just harrowing, persistent silence. She knew it was that man, it was them. They finally had some work to do.

She did not find him then, nor did they find any other perpetrator. There was no trace of terrorists. That time normal people were led to believe in stories, while the *securists* had awakened to reality. Just for once they were occasioned to do a real job, following a well-made plan, with a precisely defined objective. Mim and her fellow combatant climbed back up the stairs to their apartment tapping each other's shoulder, bursting with the tonic stamina of a mission accomplished. From that night on, they no longer barricaded themselves in their home.

Anton also had a brother, and just like her and Damian, although they lived under the same roof, they led separate lives. They too had once been inseparable, on the mild green hillocks up north. Anton's brother was as fair-haired, as tall, and he had the same faint colored lips, a little flatter and a slight more extended. However, his face lacked the rounded dark eyebrows of his brother's, and his smile was nothing near as playful and lively. The overall serene expression rendered him rather plain. Taller features, yet bland and bereft of the contrasts on Anton's face, with eyes of a pale blue, so quiet and so even.

Mim did not exist for Anton's brother. When she first saw him seated at the large oval table in the dining room, as she was passing by at Anton's hand to his room, Mim wondered who that man was who did not even seem to greet her back, no matter how anemic and merely deferential her own greeting may have been. He did not like her, or he was maybe envious of his brother bringing his date home so often. Not even when she was first invited to dine with their family did he seem to notice her presence. He kept eating in silence, somehow permeating the atmosphere with his dispirited disposition. Mim felt it was because of her, the intruder. She once asked Anton why his brother was always like that. That's the way he is, don't mind him — Anton had bluntly closed the topic. It was only too late, toward the end of their cohabitation, when his brother had begun to drop a smile now and then, to Anton, when they joked together, and soon even to her. Yes, he had begun to take heed of Mim. The two brothers would reel out old memories in her presence, farcical episodes set in their native land, where they had been frolicking and capering and tumbling down hillsides and chasing each other. He had even come into the habit of visiting them in Anton's room, which used to keep the status of undisturbable privacy. The three of them would chat together and laugh, and Mim felt extremely contented to see the brothers reunited, feeling things were about to settle down for the better in that household, in a spirit which had been long lost. She also prayed Anton would not put a stop to it someday, in his typical, abrupt manner — enough is enough. What with so much chatting and with so many childhood memories, some untold anguish came to surface. Mim found out that her man hurt because the other brother was better loved by their parents. He was convinced they had always loved the first born more than they loved him. This is not true — Mim tried to alleviate his pain. How could he believe such a thing, when she could only see how dearly his mother uttered his pet name, Antonush, and how proud Mr. Arvinte was of him? Above all, he was the younger one, was he not, and no one in the whole world could have a smile as winsomely sweet as his, so how could he possibly not win them over, over his brother. Anton tried to make things clearer to her by giving her examples from the family's past life, and present life, showing her she hardly knew anything at all. She decided to watch more attentively everything that happened around, to see for herself whether or not Anton was at least partially right. Maybe he was, possibly, she could not tell for sure. What she observed, though, was the constant competition between the two brothers as to which of them achieved more or better, which could make their parents more proud. But Mim wished this would not impact her serenity, and she wished Anton would not take things to his heart so easily. She wanted so badly that the two brothers would be good friends.

Before long, Anton's brother confessed he would very much like to find a girl like Mim to be his date. Exactly like her, he would accentuate on an almost daily basis, looking now into Anton's eyes, then into hers, as though trying to convince them to lend a helping hand in the search. Take her, then, Anton mischievously retorted one day, to then immediately sugar the pill with a smile between shrugging shoulders — can't be done otherwise, if you mean 'exactly'. Anton's brother was an engineer and a brilliant mathematician and he longed for a pretty, sensitive person to brighten up his existence. That was all there was to it. His pursuit had already begun, feverishly so, which could be felt by everyone in the house. He was dead set on finding a woman whom he could bring home to his family, embittered by the fact that the younger brother had beaten him to it. And soon his wish materialized in the person of a spruce small woman, who permanently kept an upright posture as if she were made of steel. Everything about her visage was plain, her ashen complexion, the simple features, hair of a dull greyish-brown, which was bobbed very short. The only striking exception resided in the lower half of that insipid face, which presented the eye with man-like strong jaw bones, as perfectly square in shape as Mim had never seen before. Her wide, firm-lipped mouth flashed such fearsome canines one might think ready to grind stone. Quite paradoxically, there was a gentle air about that woman when she spoke. In a rather whiny tone, she somewhat managed to express firm opinions. She was a doctor, fond of internal medicine and literature. Quick of mind and well-read, she was a truly sensible woman who knew perfectly well what she wanted out of life and would not allow anything or anyone to stand in her straight way to whatever her target was. She was quite the opposite of Mim: outspoken, unambiguous, assertive. She had definitely conquered Anton's brother.

Elena shortly gained Mim's respect too. Mim admired her for the two apparently incongruous facets of her personality, for both the steel and the sensitivity which enabled her to retreat, in her spare time, in a parallel world, that of books. Elena was always on her guard, closely observing the world around her. Nothing seemed to go by her hawk's eye. 'Why are you acting like that?' she would curtly interrogate Mim hissing through her teeth as soon as Anton departed. 'Why do you put up with his behavior?' she would insist in his absence. What do you mean? — Mim could simply not understand what was wrong with Anton's behavior. 'Oh, come on, Mimi, you really can't see…' And she would whisper yet another piece of advice into Mim's ear. It was clear Anton had smelled her out from day one. He had seen Elena's menacing fangs and started loathing her the very first moment he laid eyes on her. 'Mim, I don't want you to listen to any of Elena's crap while I'm not around, let there be no mistake about it.' How come he knew Elena was telling things to her? 'Mim, do you want to lose me?' he would threaten her. 'Who are you listening to, her or me?' Mim got to the end of her tether. A mute war was being waged between the two, all through her medium, leaving her completely confused. What beat hell was that truce came with Mim losing Anton for real. And that was also because of Elena, just as he had predicted. She had been like a wedge driven into their common trunk to split it apart.

Thanks to Elena, Mim started to see everything from a different perspective, and for her, everything meant her life with Anton. Although he was looking for a home for them, and had even taken her to see one, although the whole household seemed to be singing an endearing cantata to her whose ears were surrounded by whisperings of augury that Anton was fervently preparing a big surprise for her — you will soon see, Mimi, Mrs. Arvinte would impishly foretell with a smile larger than usual, although the event to come was so important that Elena herself had been imparted the secret in spite of her late arrival in the house, although life in that habitat seemed to be running toward an imminent grand change with everyone murmuring to its rhythm, Mim herself had started to sing a new melody, very timidly at first, which she hoped would get in tune with theirs, with Anton's. She was gradually trying to change, into a better, stronger person, she thought. Pick that up and give it to me, Anton would drop a casual request, absorbed in whatever his activity was. Pick it up yourself, came back her answer. "Bend down and give it to me, Mim." "No," she said. As if she did not care a bit. But she did, she cared and hurt a whole lot, while trampling on love just in order to regain her dignity and be like Elena. It sometimes hurts like hell to keep your back straight. "This is Elena again, huh? I knew it. I knew she was trouble when I saw those eyes glinting in her head. Well, I'm not the fool of my brother."

A short while after that episode, the nest broke up. The parents bought themselves a new home, Anton bought his own, while the old apartment, including Anton and Mim's beloved room, was all left to his brother and Elena to live in. They got married, therefore appropriately the elder brother first. It was in the photos taken at their wedding that Mim saw the lady who had helped them all procure new apartments in town. When Elena told her on the phone they were redecorating Mim felt the white paint wiping out her life.

She still thinks back fondly of Elena. Whenever her image revisits her, Mim pictures that short wiry body in a white doctor's coat, thinking how authoritative she must be, a woman of a firm word and a steady hand, in the biggest hospital in that city. Her impeccable uniform, though, will never be able to heal Mim's wound and will never conceal the infinite range of hues that blend into our lives. At the end of the day, wisdom means accepting your own way. And it does not have to be straight, straightness is relative. Mim would not feel herself on Elena's straight kind of way, which, she only now understands, was nothing but blind grimness born out of a less happy childhood, maybe, or out of having to compete early on in her life, as Anton had. It may be wise to take life as a competition, but not on all planes. While for Anton and Elena art was the venting hole on their straight road, for Mim art was the very plain of life, in all senses boundless. On these Champs-Élysées Mim will forever glide her way in an infinity of intertwining curbs and zig-zags, and straight lines as well. She has everything there, while they have one sole road.

It was Elena who revealed to Mim the contemporary literature in their own country, in which she had not been quite interested until then, for she had been living in other literatures, of other nations. Elena kept herself updated on the latest releases and poured over them. She was simply in love with those national writers. 'Here, Mimi, take this and read it.' She would lend her books to read and Mim read them, then the two of them would discuss the contents. Perhaps that was another reason for Anton's jealousy. He and Elena were competing on the plane of releasing tension through art, he through the medium of the great Russian novelists and English poets, she through that of the contemporary Romanian ones, and both of them pouring out their passions on her, Mim. An outsider had turned up out of the blue to steal Mim from him, Mim who was his and only his.

And so it was that Mim discovered the magic of those people who lived among them, right there in their country. Each of them was a whole particular world, just like any other celebrated author. All you had to do was open the book, and there you set out for a new journey. This was how she traveled, at sea, by reading a novel written so neatly, in short taut sentences, as though scribbled in haste: Mr. Such-a-one was so and so. He enjoyed that. He did such and such thing, he thought this, and he imagined that. Mim just took a simple flight accompanying that protagonist, and at the end of the road Mr. Such-a-one would not leave her mind. That short novel flowed so smoothly, like a concert by Mozart, at a lively and well calculated pace, so musical and so mathematical at the same time. The rather down-to-earth Such-a-one took great pleasure in unwinding to music, which was his daily escape. That music somehow overflowed the simple metrics of the writing itself, taking the reader to fantastic worlds in large swaying waves that swept Mim away as soon as Mr. Such-a-one started playing a record. The author would grant her the time to actually relish the tune, God only knows through what miraculous artifice. She pictured that writer to be a tall upright man, of a tall face, mathematically rigorous a person, and covertly musical. She later saw his image in a photo, surprised to find out that he looked exactly like that.

It was again thanks to Elena that Mim found herself dragged along in a dizzying drift through the mind of another apparently banal character, turned some kind of literary medium. To her amazement, that tricky venture enacted her own conviction that once you manage to get in — inside someone's mind, no matter whose — you are in for stunning, unthought-of surprises. All is there, impressions of everything that was and will be, for the simple reason that anyone's psyche is part of mankind's collective unconscious. What particularly impressed Mim was the fresh, prosaic approach which had led her to that selfsame conclusion. She actually went again through the same process of discovery, as though reliving her childhood musings in Ana's little yard, eyes turned up to the skies, long before she had read Jung. People carry those treasures on them without even being aware of it. They tend to whatever their business is, mumbling in silence, talking to one another in their minds, taking in some people here and some people there, their subconscious telling them by far more than they consciously know, telling them everything, if only they paused to listen. Just as well, one can access wider knowledge by probing, down to the most obscure recesses, whatever is wobbling inside the mind of a medium-character, in response to a minute gesture, to the most furtive glance, to a sunray touching somebody's hair. Let yourself go, and you will transcend, at crossroads unseen, the now and the factual, let yourself go through the gates to another mind's world, to another one's soul. A miscellaneous hail is bombarding Mim's mind: *À la recherche du temps perdu*, Cathy, the tiny gate in the back wall of the poultry coop, the open spaces beyond her brother's muteness, the dark opening of the tunnel through which she used to slide, shyly, to Anton's mind.

¿Te gusta este jardín? Her memory drifts back to a novel which had once taken her on a weird ride through the protagonist's mind. She realizes the serene mathematical rhythm of Mr. Such-a-one's story had been just an agreeable drizzle as compared to what she really luxuriates in. Riding with thrills of tastes and whisperings, this is what her nature is compatible with, as though she was restless energy herself, lashing lianas of fabulous rains, whipping with gales, herself dispersed into tendrils so gracefully slender by breezes blown from the edge of the world. Or the sea fretting against eternal cliffs, while longing after the

masses of palm trees which only winds can reach. It is amidst these prodigious gardens where Mim's soul feels at home. A name echoes in her mind, her favorite poet, yes, let her sway in the alluringly savage, transcontinental gardens of his conception. At the interface between the whimpering reverberations of submarine hurricanes and the murmuring of green palms, between thought and light, lustrously tanned, irradiant, wrought in gods' flesh, there emerges Perseus, like a tall saint — Mim visualizes a kind of Perseus. She loves to throw herself, unaware, over the world, and she feels as though that poet were her kin, her brother. That entire amazing fantasy of his poems stemmed out of his childhood years, and it was what he lived then that made him create the world again. Had he not been swallowing everything around through his senses, just like Mim herself does? And what was he, if not a lost Perseus, stranded in time's shine, among all elements there are? Oh, goodness, brother and sister, brother.

35 TELEPHONE

She is lying all curled up in her bed at home. Every time she hugs her knees closer to her chest, she re-sees everything. Tons of rain pouring from the skies, a girl venturing forward up on the bridge against the curtains of water, headed for the train station. The girl was her. Then there was that man she now has something to share with, the strange night in his room, the road journey, that almost fantastic advancement through the crude green of foliage, he and she breaking the day together, he and she witnesses *en vitesse* of daylight gradually rising like dough over the land between the branches of the grand river. There was that city as well, Tomina's first time there, her waiting for the man to come back to the car, where he had left her.

She was almost getting sick trapped inside, and he would not show himself. Everything had started to feel bad, and she thought she should maybe close her eyes and try to get some sleep, as she knew that was what she needed. But how could she give herself over to sleep, when there was so much novelty to take in and taste, when she had just inaugurated a new kind of life, waiting for a man in his car. She began whispering out at him, feeling sick at heart, and physically worse and worse: please come, do not let me locked in here all by myself, come, my man. But all to nothing. Mumbling to herself did not help, nothing which stood in her power could bring him back sooner. Losing all hope, she gave in to weeping. She could no longer bear the pitiable condition she was in. She could not even make as simple a decision as to get out of that car and walk a few steps around. No, she was reluctant to do anything in his absence. Let him come, let him talk to her and smile to her again, let him help her out of there. She would leave it all to him, and would not move until he was back.

But he was so late and this was practically sending her crazy. She finally understood she had to do something about that situation and for starters, get out of the car. She had to make an effort and apply herself to reasoning again, to making decisions on her own. Nothing could help her but relearning how to manage her own body. That stood out so clear in her mind, as though she had not known it before. She damn well knew one could not live without judgement. But now that she felt so proud of the decision she had just made, she realized the practical procedure of safely locking a vehicle behind was occult science to her, which brought her back to despondency. She saw the set of keys. The darling had left it on his seat for her, not imagining she had never before been left alone with a car. She decided to venture out and see how she could manage, so she picked the keys, got out, and slammed the door shut. She immediately checked the door and it would not open. Good. She was shaking with tension. The responsibility for that man's car put too much strain on her nerves, and her temples were pounding for fear she might do something wrong. Having left his property to her care was a sign of trust, and she did not want to break it. The blame would be all hers in case something happened to the car. What if someone stole it? Then Tomina would become the object of his ill will. How stupid of her to give in to so many negative conjectures. All she had to do was check all the doors in turn, and if none opened, then nothing was the problem. She plucked up courage and began the proceedings. Although everything seemed to be fine, she was still shaking. She observed the trembling hand which was holding the bunch of keys. Despite the bulging blood vessels which cobwebbed over the back of her hand, it felt so weak. Those keys overpowered her whole being, and that was only because they did not belong to her. They were strange keys to an object strange to her and she was simply not able to make decisions with regard to something that did not belong to her.

She departed timidly from the car. With each step she took further away, her heart appeared to pound even harder, as though mocking at the slow pace of her departure. She paused to cast a glance over her shoulder, and was taken aback by the multitude of cars crammed one next to another in that parking lot, among which she could hardly distinguish the one she had just left. But there it was, whitish, and so very dear to her. Anyway, she told herself she would not go too far, also due to her difficulty in walking properly. She made her way in the crowd like a marionette, embarrassed with a sense that everyone else was staring at her as they would at an alien. She perceived herself as a white shadow moving aimlessly among the normal people who were hurrying to and fro on errands, while her thoughts were drifting to her feet, which seemed to be making significant efforts to carry her frame along, and to the sharp outdoor air which she could barely breathe in, and to her drowsy eyes, dazed by the bright sunlight. Trudging her way toward an unknown terminus, she was trying to find consolation at the prospect of soon readjusting her eyes to daylight, coming back to her senses, and of never again abandoning herself to another person's will. That was wrong. As the features of her face were plumping back to life, she started to feel her body lighter with every step, and her sense of freedom was regained, freedom to explore a new place swarming with people. She was part of that crowd, and he would eventually rejoin her, so they would be strolling the streets together. She could already feel the taste of that.

After a short while she was on her way back to the car. She scanned the parking lot from a distance, convinced she would presently pinpoint it. No way. Lots of them were whitish, all shades of white. She realized the fool of her had not even looked at the number plate. How could she possibly single it out of that multitude? She spotted a likely one, but no, it could not be that, since it was registered in that county. What she had to look for was an off-white car with a number plate of his town, but, to her utter dismay, all vehicles parked there had local registration numbers. How could that be, she wondered, she had only left it right there. There had to be something faulty, she must have made some terrible blunder, she might have left one of the doors unlocked. She refused to believe a misfortune of such proportion had befallen her. This was downright serious. It was not about some toy, but a whole damn car. Numerous objects she had lost until then rushed into her memory, and what an absent-minded schoolgirl she used to be. Not a day passed without her running back home during a break for some notebook she had forgotten to take. Sweat and panic were once her daily routine. But that did not give her any lesson, as it were. Now she had finally come to her autumn, reaping the fruits of her careless nature. What if, she thought, the business meeting had ended earlier, he had returned to the car, and not finding her there, had left. He surely had a spare set of keys. Why should that man care about her, after all, a girl he had only met the night before in a station? Now, really, what was she to him? Yet, no matter what, could he have had the heart to leave her alone in a strange city, with no money, no baggage, absolutely nothing? He might have dropped her baggage somewhere.

Therefore she should start searching for it, if only some other person had not already picked it up. But what if the car had been stolen, as it had first occurred to her? Well, what was she supposed to do in that case? She would keep searching. She crossed the street in a crazy vault and began to inspect the interior of each car, praying the variant of him having left without her came true. She would find a way to get home, so long, dear man of mine, she was silently humming, as who was he to her, in the first place? She did not even know what his last name was, what he did for a living, what kind of person he was, nothing at all. Was she not blessed nothing dreadful had happened to her, reckless wretch. She was safe and sound, thank God, and she would soon be at home again, and everything would get back to normal. She would have a really nice deep sleep and then start preparing herself for the exam ahead. She surely had to tend to her own business. How it feels good to stick with the right path, to stick to your daily grind, no matter how boring life may get at times. Adventurous detours were definitely not for her.

She had been peering through dozens of car windows and still had not identified any familiar interior. It eventually dawned on her that she had merely perceived the inside of that car as a sum of sensations, the taste of the road, of adventure, the smells, the pleasantly piquant aroma of tender skin touched by sunlight, their breaths, the giddying sense of complete happiness, and the presence of that priest, the priest whom they had picked up on the way and given a lift to a village tucked in the hills by the road. That man knew him and dared cordially drop in a question, 'Your wife?' Yes — he curtly silenced the priest, making him understand that was a closed subject. Hidden behind on the back seat, she wondered if that was not a sign, a kind of benign augury. How come that particular passenger had chanced on the road, to utter those particular words? She still felt so embarrassed only to think of the awkward position she had been in, a girl he had offered to give a ride back to her parents' home. Throughout the journey she had kept silent, including prior to and after the episode with the priest. She had absolutely nothing to say. First of all, questioning people was not in her nature. She would rather listen to whatever they volunteered to tell about themselves. Then, it felt like the faintest mundane action might ruin the miraculous perfection inside the car. It would have been a shame. No, nothing seemed to prevail against the adventure she was living. Also, there was her total ignorance as to his opinion on her, his intentions. Her muteness all during the ride had camouflaged her persistent exertions to enter his thoughts. Her mind had been trying to sense and detect anything that might be coming from his. The reflection in the rear-view mirror of his eyes permanently focused on the road was telling her of power, pure, true, manly power she could rely on. But he was as tight-lipped as she was, which compelled her to cope with the silence on her own. In spite of this, every now and again she would feel a thrill of exuberance run through her chest. Quite a weird trip it had been to this town, up to this very parking lot, and on top of that she was not able to recognize the vehicle which had brought her here. Hope sprang within her as she was peering into the next car in the row, that could be the one, and as she bent forward she heard her name being called from behind — Mim! She loved the sound of it, *Mim*, and it was such a blessing to hear it again, it was him. "It took longer than I expected, did you get bored?" If only she could explain how sick she had actually been seeing he was so late in coming. "No, nothing of the kind, I walked around a little." "Come," he said. "Where to?" "I'll walk you through the town for a bit, and then we'll have a bite somewhere." Good, she thought, she felt safe again, laughing back at all those scary scenarios which had kept her in panic only minutes ago. This time she remembered to glance back and look at the plate number. To her surprise, the car was registered here, in the county where his work place was. She impressed those digits on her memory and told herself she would never ever forget them.

He held her by the hand all along. Mim felt proud to be with a man like him and imagined everybody observed the peculiar bond between them. He acted as though he had known her for a lifetime, when in truth he knew next to nothing about her. He neither asked her anything, nor told anything about himself. They hit the road immediately after dining, headed to her parents' place this time. She had never approached her home town on that route, a long road of fantastic beauty meandering smoothly through wild vegetation, passing age-old hills and villages. They took the elevator to the tenth floor, rang the doorbell, Mom, Dad, this is Anton. Everything in her house developed as a matter of course, they shook hands and smiled, short and simple. Smiles came naturally to her parents' faces when they received guests, her mother dazzling the others with the perfection of her teeth — that was her, she always smiled first and then spoke, and so was her father, except that he was more shy to part his lips. He would only smile instead of speak, if that was possible. Anton himself gave a true smile, as how could one respond otherwise to such welcoming benevolence? Her mom served coffee, Anton explained where they came from and how way-worn Mim was, that she had greatly enjoyed that route, and then that he had to be on his way again. He sipped the last drop in his cup and sprang to his feet, while Mim could hardly believe her adventure was getting to an end. "It's been a pleasure, ma'am, Mr. Tudor. We'll meet again, anyway." He sounded so confident, but he had no word for her. When would they meet again, and where? If they were not going to talk then, she was afraid they would estrange from each other. With every step he took towards the door, her face turned even paler, for lack of power to utter anything. Let him do what he will, she thought, whether or not his will was going to exclude her. "Bye, Mim. Go to sleep, you look awfully tired." She nodded acquiescence. "You said you have your first exam next Monday, so mind you take care. I'm letting you study." With these words, out he was through the door, a bit too hurried, as it seemed, too cold, dismissive. He might have got a terrible scare when he took in her wearied looks. No matter how attractive the freshness and innocence of her rained on face must have looked, now that she had turned ugly the man awakened face to face with an unsightly stranger he did not know what to do with. He had kept his word, had brought her home, and that was that. She had lost him for good, she suspected. She was now paying for that miraculous ride with loneliness. That was what loneliness truly felt like.

Mim stretches her cuddling body and turns face down, burying her nose and cheeks in the bedspread. She has been crying so many times on that bed, only this time hurt is cutting so deep that she is dried out for tears. She itches for some sort of physical pain, so she starts rubbing her face against the coarse hairs of the cover. Fate willed it that she grow unexpectedly soon into the mature woman reflected by the mirror in her childhood. That is life's way, of course. Has she not been grieving since a little girl over people having to part some day? She had sooner not have met him at all. She would rather he had let her alone, and not chased her throughout the station. But he did, and now she is wondering why, since neither the storm, nor the night that followed, nor the car ride seem to have meant anything to him. After having held her hand all along, now, really, he is allowing her time to study. He did not as little as mention ever getting in touch with her again, and how could he, when he did not even ask for her phone number. The most he knew was that she was coming to his town next Sunday, for the following day's exam — will he meet her at the station? A likely surmise, provided that he guesses what train to wait for. Well, now she can hardly study at all. One might think he has shown up in her life just in order to make her fail that exam, her, the obedient girl, who has always chosen the appropriate thing to do, the right path. The first time she chose deviation has left her sick and tired and extremely tense. She is holding on to something whose nature is yet obscure to her. She can feel this blind determination poisoning her mind, it may be the story of the girl in the rain, Mim, and he was the one to have baptized the protagonist. Now she knows, her ambition is that Mim's story will never end. Right, she wishes for the impossible, since it is common knowledge that any story has an ending, or at least turns into something else, good or bad, possibly sad, or banal, but different anyway. The status quo does not resist time, unless maybe in another dimension, there must be a dimension where everything stays, the subconscious, maybe. Whichever that is, there must exist a place of energy that unites all beings in one huge unitary soul. Well, her story will be forever unfolding there, untainted by change.

The telephone is ringing. Energy is vibrating in Mim, longing racing, longing so dire, shooting through smoky uncertainty, a spearhead glinting from various mysterious angles, premonition, him, it is him, against all odds, against the fact she never gave him her phone number. He may have found it somewhere, in a phone book, she does not care how he got it, but it is him at the other end of the line. She jumps out of bed, bangs the door open, and flings herself upon the telephone in the corridor. "Hello." It is a calm, husky voice, a man's voice she has never before heard in that earpiece. "Yes," she answers, heart racing. Although there was little air left in her lungs to utter that word, she did it, and she did it quickly, to cover up her emotion. Now she is waiting.

"Mim—" He says her name in a velvety voice, which falls down and pauses a little in the middle and then rises again. Yet it comes out so natural and matter of fact.

"So you're home," she suddenly bursts out happily. His name is stuck on her lips, let her say it, for Christ's sake, but no, she finds it ill-matched to a cry of joy.

He kept silent.

"I'm so happy you called, you can't imagine just how happy." She feels relieved to have said that. If only he could guess the terrible anguish she has been through. He offers her time, and does not say a word. So she continues, "I thought you'd never call."

"Why should I not call you?"

"Well, I thought you didn't have my number."

"Mim, all the way home there was only one thing on my mind, I couldn't wait to get here and phone you. How could you expect otherwise?"

"Yes, I wouldn't have," she says completely stuck for words, "but you didn't say anything when you left."

"You're such a kid, why, I have your phone number from last night, in the station. Remember I was standing right next to you when you dialed your home number?"

"Wow, you're right," she discovers. "Yikes, you've stolen my number!" Pretty cool she thinks that was.

"What were you doing?"

"Well, I was sitting, sitting in my room and thinking."

"Thinking of what?"

"Last night, the ride, everything…"

"Are you going to sleep now?"

"That would be great. I really hope I'll be able to sleep. What did your mother say — about last night?"

"She said nothing." Mim could hear him smile. "What about your mother?"

"Nothing," she also says.

"Come on, I don't buy it. Wasn't she curious to know how you met me?"

"Yes, I think she was. Well, I'm going to tell her."

No sooner had he got out of the door, than her mother came up to her and asked who that man was, but

Mim has not told her anything yet. She still had to feed her memories on the sweetness of the whole escapade. She just made a promise to tell her, and she will, but right then her ecstasy was beyond words, and her lips could simply not round to articulate any sound. They would extend rompingly to her cheeks to pump them up shining, while her eyes, yes, by looking at her mom Mim was well aware they were driving her crazy with eagerness. The woman almost pleaded, "Come on, tell me, who is he?" "Mom, oh Mom, how perfectly beautiful, please let me play everything out again for myself first, and then I'll tell you," she said, and retreated to her room.

"Mim, I'll let you have a rest, you need to. Mind you mug up on your exam."

"Yes, I will, thanks, but when I think of it…" She is expecting more words from him, like when he will phone next, when they will meet again. She needs to know.

"OK, Mim, I have to go now, good night."

Therefore no such words came.

"Bye, good night," she replies, trying hard to put some life into words.

Why, he has hung up leaving her in the same nasty fog as before. How is she possibly going to cope with all the exams ahead if he keeps her in that state of confusion, permanently waiting for a call which might not even come. Well, this is awful. And when she thinks how calm and composed he is. That is only because he knows, he is so all-wise and omniscient about his intentions, whereas she is being left to wait and see. The next time he calls, if he does, she is determined to tell him how she hates waiting like that. She feels at least contented for the little peace of mind he has granted her tonight, as her wish came true and he called, after all, did he not? He will phone again, she tries to reassure herself, and she must yield herself to his will if she wants some hearts ease. No matter what comes, she should be thankful for what she has now, a beautiful story with herself as protagonist.

She makes for the kitchen. She pictures herself like a comet whizzing along the hallway, cheeks and ears burning with a sudden flare. Her mom must be wondering about her daughter's story in there, and the time has come for her to listen to it, starting with the storm. Mim got in, pulled a chair from under the table, sat herself and said, "Mom, I'm here to tell you, are you ready?"

36 WEDDING

Anti-social, rebellious, a heretic walking the world aimlessly, fruitless, this is the vision she has of herself. She has joined the horde of the unorthodox, turning her back on her forefathers' laws, on tradition, on her family and all the righteous people out there.

Still, how virtuous could they be, the honorable decent people, since it was not out of reverence for the concept of purity, for tradition or for Christian precepts that they praised virginity so highly. No, it was the world's mouth they feared, being the talk of the town. People lived in terror of mortification. To rebel against their piety, Tomina had set her mind on getting rid of this burden. She was eager to get past that unpleasant divide in her life, although she feared it, and the immediacy of which she could hardly stand. Her going through that process was as implacable as death. She had to do it, so she had found the right person to assist her, her boyfriend, who was so much in love with her. The only thing left for her to do was set the date of that mandatory surgical operation. She at least willed herself to wait until after high school graduation, out maybe of some sense of respect for herself, and for her parents, although they would forever stay innocent about this. The subject was taboo in any household.

There came a time when children started showing one face to the grownups, and another one to their peers. The shy mothers' little ones, whom elderly folks took so much pleasure in teasing at their gatherings — before you know it, baby, you will: grow a moustache, be called up to the military, take a wife, itch to get married — were playing totally different roles in their other life, and sometimes maybe they were not just playing at all. Mommy's dear little girl, and Daddy's prize winner, could well act as a woman in her own right in her parallel existence. The only time of intersection between the two worlds was the wedding, a ceremony which in some parts of the country included age-old traditions Tomina found degrading for the bride, downright barbarous. They must have emerged in answer to the community's ravenous curiosity. Tomina could simply not understand the common chin wagging over a blushing bride's virginity. That question would hover over a wife's existence till old age: was she untouched on the day she took her matrimony vows? It was, she thought, as though this should be written all over the place. The answer would anyway come into the wash one day, to satisfy any blood-thirsty mind, and that was usually occasioned by a divorce: the good fellow has washed away her shame, and look at her now, ungrateful shrew.

Mim found wedding ceremonies tiring and boring and hated wedding receptions. The long tables over which paunchy men wetted the bargain ogling the merchandise exposed in full view, a puppet the revelers would very much like to see sprawled right on spot, legs wide spread. Their jokes, the wine, the loud cheers like lashes of whips snapping as if in enactment of the nuptial inaugural tearing, all this repulsive mixture, may have led her to loathe any high-pitched cheering in general. Her mind had transferred all these manifestations of joy into the voyeur's sonic discharge, allowed by tradition only, she surmised. There might be genuine, light-hearted cheering as well out there, yet she brought them all down to the leveling measure of this savage bridal cry. The people's roars and the men's fuddling at wedding parties were no laughing matter to Tomina. What she saw was a kind of mock cheering of encouragement for the groom, which disgusted her. She had decided her wedding would be nothing like that. Instead, it would be a time of joy and celebration for the matrimonial couple themselves, who would generously offer tokens of gratitude, like choice tidbits and liquors, to humbled guests. There would be nothing humble about the bride and groom.

The dance of the bedsheet. Tomina had been clued into that horrific custom in her early teens, by a friend who had developed an interest in wedding traditions and their significance. The girl would scour libraries for books on that theme, pour over them, and then come to spill everything to her, only to scare her to death — listen here, she burbled, have you ever heard of anything more awful? Tomina told herself she had been living head in the clouds, without the least inkling of what people were doing on the face of the earth, of what scabrous games and tortures their minds were capable of devising for their fellow human beings. Night after night that white cloth kept dancing in her imagination, fluttering high from a stick so that the wedding party could clearly see the bloodstain, as proof that the bride's hymen had been intact. At the time she heard that oddity, Tomina tried hard to wrap her mind around that sample of human existence, but she found no room inside her brain for that ritual. She felt like shouting to the skies at her impotence. It was then, she thinks, when it struck her that life was difficult, since everyone, including her, had to go through such cruel, hardly bearable moments. And it was the visions triggered by her playmate's incredible stories which planted the seeds of dissent in her.

Tomina's virginity would not be displayed on any table.

Hers was a quiet wedding. It occurred inside a small narrow room, devoid of pomp or pain. There was nothing like the unbearable pain her friend had read about a few years before, in fear of which Tomina had been living ever since. Spread on a sofa, all tensed, eyes closed, she had been counting down seconds till confrontation time. It was purely pain she waited to face up to and get over with, to set her psyche free. She had been reading about such things herself. Her mother had one day pushed the door to her room ajar to slip a book through the opening. It was one of those fat books stuffed with knowledge, which she laid on the margin of her daughter's bookcase, jabbering in one breath: here's something for you to read. Whereupon she shut the door swiftly and left. The poor woman must have been awfully embarrassed. Mim rushed to grab the book and when she saw what it treated, a wave of liberating jubilation swept through her. Her mom had finally conceded her deliverance. Tomina had been acknowledged the right to enter the adults' world of mysteries. Many a time had they been whispering secrets in her and her brother's presence, many a time had they turned mum when the kids made their appearance, or sent them away to another room — we are talking adult stuff here, it is not for your ears, please go out. Ever since a little girl Tomina had been passing her life under a light rain of riddles, here a secret, there a puzzle, of which some would be lost to oblivion. However, others would come back to her, and she told herself she would find an answer to each of them someday, which actually occurred. As she was growing up, answers came easy to Tomina. And now the day had come her own mother was offering her the source of them all, all on a silver platter.

Once the act of defloration had been performed on her, she could think of nothing else but the bedsheet. She had been worried sick she might leave traces on that unfamiliar bed. Her cortex had gone off in alert mode, urging her to get heedful and ready to send back orders of containment — her blood would not stain the bedding. When the lights came on, she got into a panic, praying nothing was there. Thankfully, the sheet was perfectly clean, but she was now wondering how that was possible. Only that, the moment she scrambled to her feet, she felt a short hot tide between her legs. She went on to pray, this time that she would be able to hide whatever that was, at least till she got to the safety of her house. It was at the same time curiosity that hurried her back home. In her parents' bathroom, alone and triumphant, she gazed at length at the large darkish stain between the legs of her jeans. The psychic torment was over, she was liberated. Only when she next met her boyfriend, although nothing physical occurred between them — neither then, nor ever after for that matter — did Tomina become aware of the instinctual, animal force within her. Her body appeared to have a will of its own which tended to overpower her mind. With Tomina seated on the boy's lap, her midriff would squirm like crazy in his embrace, and it felt like nothing would ever make it stop. For the first time Tomina had allowed her body to express itself freely. It was only then in her room, on her own territory, when she fancied she was becoming woman, and it was there where she bled abundantly, because of the inner spasms. When the boy took notice of that, she rejoiced without a trace of shame. She had, in a way, accepted her blood as a sign of that rite of passage, the wedding.

She came to later regret the whole experiment, the very idea of it, the fact that she had crossed over one important threshold in her life without fully comprehending its symbolism. What she felt was pain like death, for which the dread she had felt throughout her teen-hood was no match. Of course she pretended not to hurt, as she had a life to live. It was through the baptism of that kind of pain that the concept of ritualistic tradition broke its way into Mim's consciousness, her spiritual consciousness. Unfortunately, she no longer possessed a body to suit her newly found awareness. And before long, she was to be filled with such bitterness at not being able to perform this symbolic wedding, in truth, with Anton. Mim's sense of self-offering while she was with him, so inexplicably profound, so archaic somewhat, would have made her the perfect medium for enacting ritual initiation into womanhood. She had come to identify herself with a mythical woman at the very core of this custom, wounded by man for life, for life serving her pain-inflictor, for life yearning after reunion with him. She has a reverence for wedding rituals now, and what she once found barbarous is perfectly acceptable. Few are the things that do not appear barbarous in an ignorant child's eyes. Now she wishes her mother had spoken to her about such things. If only somebody had talked to her, if only her people got rid of the false shame which pervades all space, petrifying their lives.

Her relationship with Stefan was as devoid of meaning as her sexual initiation. She merely roomed with him. Her days were floating impassibly like swans on a pool, a wanly colored pool in the middle of which, though, there was that islet of fire, his body blazing bluish flames of frustration, which she constantly gave a wide berth to. The taste Mim was left with was bitterness again, the bitter disappointment imprinted on his mouth when she rejected him.

She knew life as man and woman with Anton only, that beautiful fragment in anyone's existence, which unrolls sometime between wedding and cohabitation. The feeling of it will stay with Mim forever, as no one could take feelings away from her. Nor could they take away her perception of Anton as a person, her quest to maybe figure him out some day. The corners of her lips rise slightly, to offer her own thoughts a mild condescending sneer —

what life? It may have been just a reaction to the anti-life around. A form of escapism into romantic fantasy, or rather, into sociological experimentation, if not pure foolish ambition. Could it have been a simple penchant for romance of a teenage girl, or masochism, or stupidity? Looking back on her life she can identify countless circumstances when she acted stupid. The only thing she is certain about is that she loved Mim in her story so much. She was in love with herself, not Anton, this is the key. Anton happened in her life only to give her a chance to romantically hurt and then victimize herself, fall in love with herself. She now feels thankful to that weird man for having acted as a catalyst for her love to pour out, all that love accumulated in her, or which she may have been born with. She might be one of those people who are born with this burden of love, and who, not finding a recipient for it, give vent to it into stories. Anton's harshness had directed all the magma in Mim to canvas, so she can only be grateful for that. A new ambition was born.

She is lying on the bed gazing at the walls, wallowing in self-contemplation. Completely stuck. She gives her senses free rein to pick up details around at random, saving her conscious the bother of having to interpret anything. The feeling of emptiness is so delightfully relaxing. Mim will leave everything behind, she will take flight. Let her clear out her inner chambers and give room to new perceptions, to her otherness.

37 FIRST

The Tilia trees, their fragrance and hers together… It smells of Tilia and of Mim — she recalls Anton once saying. They were on the small street where he would park his car every night that summer, that bewildering summer. Her confused senses would sip in the mixture of sprinkling droplets from his lips and the scented particles of limes at sleep on the margin of the perfectly quiet street. Her own breath would she sip back, in elongated time bubbles, imbued with her scent. She could smell it lingering between their nostrils, gently brushing against the stealthy beads of sweat in the air, or sliding down the misted windows of the car. She was wallowing in an abundance of time, and waiting for his mouth felt like eternal blessing. Whenever his mouth finally came to hers, perfumes would fuse into a heady sensation which melted her stiffness away, whereupon like a limp shadow would she slip in among his shadows, unnoticed. She would nestle there, a mere puppet praying he would not chase her out. He was a dark long tunnel, how long she never found out exactly. The next thing she knew, she was outside again, pretending she had not seen anything, never been anywhere.

On the night they met, the moment she felt his hand approaching her middle, she froze — as though in expectation of a cool snake's embrace. It was panic stations, as she did not know what he was going to do to her. He wrapped his arms around her waist, the very stranger she had seen earlier on the station's platform. Although she was afraid, a worldwide pool of quietness made her stay and wait. The next minute he was tormenting her mouth, and she no longer knew who she was. She was in the movies, she thought, she was playing being kissed by a man, that man. When she had glimpsed him in the crowd he had reminded her of someone she had seen before on screen.

Some long minutes later she said she had to go. Back to her empty room, lonely, would have wiped out the storm, as if it never happened. She wished someone would tell her she could not go there, someone powerful, authoritarian. She thought he was the one who should not let her go.

"I'll pick you up first thing in the morning, you're coming with me. I'm sure you'll enjoy the trip, and then I'll take you home."

Tomina was shy to accept, but her inexplicable want to be with him overpowered her shyness. She longed to stay close to that man, and somehow needed to be dominated by him, so she straightened up in her seat, placed both hands on the top of her head, then began to caress her hair in a downward sliding motion, pressing the long tresses against the sides of her neck, where she paused her palms. Her will was gone. It felt so light to let another reason in her place. She swiveled in her seat and glued her back to the door to face him. She could barely make out his face, but a shadow was there against the lucent background provided by a street lamppost on the opposite sidewalk, the shadow which she expected to decide everything for her, what to do in that very moment, what to do tomorrow, what to do the day after tomorrow.

"I really must go now," she heard her own voice say, as if he had been keeping her there.

"Mim—" He seemed to have read her thoughts, and continued, "No, I won't have you go there alone. Come, you can sleep at my place tonight, and we'll leave together early in the morning."

"I can't." With regained firmness, Tomina announced, "I'm getting out, now." Then she opened the door, trembling.

She came out into the silent street, strangely turned their own, as a kind of absolute interior where they could say and do anything. She was amazed at the beauty of it, and at the way in which the name he had given her earlier that night resonated with that setting. She performed one full turn under the lime trees, took in a breath of quiet perfume, then walked to the back of the car and rested her small hand on the top of the trunk, waiting for him to join her.

He approached her with firm steady steps, speechless raised the lid of the trunk, took out her luggage, and started to cross the street in the direction of the gate he already knew by now.

"Come," he said.

Mim followed him across to the green gate, then, nice surprise, he brusquely turned around and went right back to the car, with her hot on his heels. She watched as he flumped the bags in the trunk again and slammed the lid shut, wondering what he was up to. She positioned herself right in front of him, smiling. With light coming from the back, his face was again in the shadow. An arm detached itself from the penumbra, and she saw his hand closing in on her, rising to her face, a beautiful hand of long, straight fingers, so white, she mused, so much like her father's. She felt its touch under her chin, which was gently being guided upwards toward the shadow where his mind resided, and whence she expected to receive all instructions. She conjured up the mouth she had seen on the station platform, its contours, the square jawbones. They were facing her now, and at such close range. Those glowing eyes were fastened on her now, and she wondered if maybe that was not their natural glow.

He was staring down at her when she started at the sound of his resolute voice. "You're coming with me."

Oh, that was pure anguish, she had better not, definitely not, she could by no means dislodge herself from the places designated to her for night time, or life would turn freakishly bizarre. All of a sudden that beautiful night got dark, all the scents ebbed away, and nothing was beautiful anymore. Abnormal was the word that permeated her mind, no, she would not allow herself to slide down where fantasies met their end. She yearned to hear him speak again, tell about himself, about his mother. Quite so, where was his mother right in that moment? Was she waiting for her son to come home?

"Mim…" he whispered her name, making her raise her face to his eyes, although she could not see them. "Look at me, Mim." He sounded like imploring. "I will not touch you, I promise, if that's what you think. I live with my parents, and they must be asleep by now, we get in and go directly to my room, there's nothing to worry about."

"Sorry, I can't do this. I have to take my baggage, please."

"This? What do you mean by 'this'? What's so terrible, for goodness sake, as I really don't understand? Come on, take a good look at me. I swear, OK? Mim, I swear I won't touch you, do you believe me? I want you to believe me, and I want to prove this to you. Come, get in the car, day should be breaking soon."

Why should she be thrown in such a twisted situation, why should she rack her mind for a decision now, instead of sleeping quietly in her room?

"Mim, do you really want me to leave you alone in this

house? Come on, tell me. Everything I've said is true, I swore, didn't I? And if I'm taking you home tomorrow, that means I'll meet your family, isn't that so?"

"What about yours? What will they say?"

"You'll meet them. They're people like any other people, you'll see."

"That's exactly the point. When I meet them, what will they think of me if I come there tonight?"

"They're sleeping at this time, I'm sure, so they won't even know it was you."

"You want me to sneak in like that? I shouldn't dream of doing such a thing, it's horrible."

"That's childish thinking, Mim, be reasonable. You are with me and nothing else matters. My parents, well, what about my parents? Leave them be. You should trust me and that's all there is to it."

If only she could call his name and beg to be understood. Why on earth could she not bring herself to utter his name, Anton, and implore on it?

"I don't know what to say."

He took her by the hand, led her way to the car's door, opened it for her, she got in, then he got in at the wheel, started the engine, and pulled away from the curb.

She was past caring what happened next, yet still puzzling over the strangeness of that feeling, still wondering whether that was a scene in her life's course. When would she get back to the orderly sequencing she had been so used to, morning and evening, night, her mom and dad, Aunt Ana's home, if perchance that had been part of her life? Why should she not, after all, try something different, see what this otherness tasted like? Could life really be as fascinating as what she had read in books? Why, yes, life was way more exciting than fiction, carrying Tomina along in a story in which a man who had found her was actually taking her away from her dreams, into his reality, where she was no longer alone.

There they were, outside a building among many others in a quarter of residence of sparse parking lots, and trees, and hedges, vegetation so silent. They both got out of the car, and he led the way carrying her bags, down an alley among a peaceful population of sleeping residents. She, the intruder, was going to crash somewhere among them for the night, among their monotonous, routine breaths. One landing, the second one, the third, and it seemed they would climb steps forever. He stopped in front of a door, that might be it, she presumed with her heart in her throat. He was turning the key in the lock, but that door would not open, giving her some respite to think she was not perhaps wanted there. Just as she was considering running away, it creaked open, only to scare her even more. The room right in front of her, the kitchen, she thought, was lit. A glass door only stood between her and the bright light inside. Tomina was pinned into place by a broad beam of shame that spanned all over her. She would surrender, it was too late for her to hide, so she would expose her dirty self to the eyes of whoever was in there. With these thoughts, fear was replaced by slackness.

"Mom is in the kitchen," he whispered. "Let's tiptoe to my room, I know you wouldn't like me to introduce you to her now."

Tomina slinked after him through the house, a large room first, then a narrow hallway, the door to his room, and she was finally safe, heart still thumping. She relied on him to protect her.

"Mim," he announced, "I won't be a minute. I'm going to the kitchen to talk to Mom."

"Don't tell her who I am, please." She searched for his eyes to further her begging, and in that moment asked herself what he might see in hers.

He offered a smile and got out. She was now alone in this man's room, a man she presumed had a position of power at his work place, if she were to consider the timbre of his voice and the accomplished diction, his somber, yet quick eyes. His power resided in knowledge. He seemed to be always ready to make decisions, and he knew what he had to do and how to tackle things. Above all, that man was a profound thinker. She sensed in him that type of person who would reason deeply before making a decision, but once that made, it was definitive and final. Then her thoughts jumped to his graceful hands, and it occurred to her that he was a doctor, at which her heart started racing again. Other people's lives relied on his judgement and on his skillful, steady hand, on everything he had studied, and had to be still studying. Her gaze surveyed the numberless tomes piled up on the bed's storage box, on top of the wardrobe, on chairs and tables, apparently on every piece of furniture around. Old furniture, she reflected, démodé, but covered in impressive books. She took a few timid steps to have a closer look — treatises on medicine, she knew it. For each case he had to study thoroughly, as one could not toy with people's lives. His power took on even greater dimensions in her mind. General medicine in several volumes, treatises on skin diseases, endocrinology, genetics — she wondered what his specialty was. Was he a dermatologist, a gynecologist, oh, no, what if he was a gynecologist? That meant he knew everything about her, and Tomina instantly turned little, less, as little as she could get.

He entered the room with two glasses and a jar in hand.

"What are you up to?" she inquired.

"You'll see," he said, carefully laying the glasses on the large table near the window. "This is a drink made by my mother, elderberry juice. Have you drunk that before?"

"Once, I think."

That table was also covered with all kinds of things, from books and booklets to boxes and fancy cups full of pencils and pens and a lot of petty stuff, and a stack of picture postcards in the corner by the window. Other postcards were pinned over a wall calendar, above which hung an unframed painting, a signed oil on canvas board featuring a dream of white and light blue horses on the run. Next to it there was another one depicting a field of wheat. Those were nice paintings. She was pleasantly surprised to discover that he was an art lover.

Liquid being poured into glasses was audible, and then she heard his voice.

"Let's celebrate our having met," he said, handing a cup to her. "Cheers, Mim."

"Cheers." Shy to raise her eyes to meet his, she took one sip and laid the glass on the margin of the table. Then seeing him making for the door again she asked, "Where are you going?" She had a strange feeling of isolation whenever he left her alone.

"Just a minute."

She crossed the room after him and sat on the edge of the bed, a bed of considerable size, with a big box for bedding stuff against the wall. Sitting there in a still pose, she kept her gaze on the two paintings for a while. Then she riveted her eyes on the dressing table that covered this other end of the same wall. It looked very much like the one her parents had in their bedroom, a long squat piece from the center of which raised tall a conspicuous mirror. It was in the huge crystal-clear mirror at home that she had spent most of her childhood, in which she had so many times seen herself beautiful, breathtakingly so, and sometimes also the ugliest of beings. Tomina started in place as he turned up with two cups of coffee on a tray, only to be immediately mollified by the flavor of familiarity which enveloped those objects. His family appeared to be leading a quiet, ordinary kind of life, so similar to that of her folks at home. While nothing seemed to be out of common about their existence, she had a strange feeling that this man, their son, did not quite blend in. Rather, he had the air of one temporarily finding retreat in the midst of this warm, modest household, as though he only came here to rest and to partake of the meals. Otherwise he had a totally different life of his own. Well, that also held good for her. Wherever she made an appearance, people could hardly make out her status, they were curious where she came from and would invariably label her as 'different'.

At university she was believed to be the daughter of some well-to-do powerful folks, and her colleagues had even come to speculate she was some kind of spy nestling in their midst. After the initial shock at being prompted that stupid assumption by one of them, she got down to mentally reconstructing her latest student days, and recognized vaguely a stagnant, stale atmosphere, putrid, she then thought, that her passage had been seemingly dislodging for some time, her passage through their ranks, in the generous space inside the sumptuous building. She was lucky to find that out only in a jokingly playful manner. Still, that funny story acquired painful dimensions in a few days, and hurt her to the quick. It felt as though the whole fresh crispness that she was had been split and infested with worms already fattened in another milieu. Although she soon got past revolt, a dull pain remained, a puzzle unsolved. Why she, of all people, she who never had a clue about what was going on around her, she who, at the time, had no idea universities were allotted *securists*, or agents, or whatever they were called, to spy on students? It was only by means of those 'jokes' that she was clued in on that surprising piece of information, and she still could not believe it. It sounded too fantastic to be true. But then that thunderstorm chanced in her life to sweep all the dirty harm away and cleanse her mind. And it so happened that she came across another citizen of the world who, just like her, could barely blend in the autochthonous décor.

All through that night, or better, what was left of it, Mim lay tense, shrouded in that selfsame khaki dress, which had eventually dried on her, next to that man in his huge bed, thinking back of the storm that had occurred like a grandiose spectacle messing with people's inner and outer lives, mingling them together, mixing them up with nature, the most violent thunderstorm she had ever seen, others had ever witnessed — the voices of the folks amassed in the train station, vibrating in awe, still resonated in her mind. She wondered what namely had urged her forward, where her grim determination to reach the station at any cost had come from, therefore she kept trying to replay everything in her mind, frame by frame — she alone and all soaked up, back plastered to the concrete pillar amidst the pandemonium, that man, the misty atmosphere inside his car, her presence here in the man's room, in his bed. They would set out together in the morning, her life would take a new path. What she used to live in her childhood's mirror would come true, this time all too true. There was a man for her, a man of pale eyelids and broad forehead who was so dear to her without any apparent reason.

She had been praying daybreak would come sooner and it did, they left the quarter as its inhabitants were still sleeping under shelter from the brisk coldness of the morning, the car rolling down to the river they found themselves in sunshine and a heated up interior. There was a long line of cars waiting for embankment on the ferry, which they soon joined, how exciting, they were crossing the river to open new roads on the other side.

38 DEATH

She is floating above a sea of clouds, she Mim, like a carefree soul on top of the world. As a child, almost every night she would dream of herself flying over the street where she lived, over the whole town, in full admiration of the community of youths she secretly admired and with whose standards of age she was so eager to catch up. Mouths agape in awe, they would point up to and wave their arms at her, the little girl in the neighborhood. It was never clear to her what her body was clad in. She simply appeared like a fluttering flame. In the sky, a matter as mundane as clothing was absurd.

She used to daydream too, of flying across seas and countries, getting rich there, and returning to her native town to build homes for the poor. Another her childhood aspirations was to put that town on the map, make it into a kind of capital of the arts full of great concert halls to host international festivals launched and financed by none other than herself. She used to envisage her home town as a cultural hub of the world, and herself as the object of its citizens' admiration and love. Once back in a state of full vigilance, she would get down to sketching architectural designs, town plans, business plans, till her head got into a spin and she told herself she had better spring to her feet and start living her life by the hour.

Right now she is on her way to fulfilling her old dreams, brimming with love for Him who has finally made it possible for her to fly free in His element. God, she feels closer to You and to Your infinite kindness, so vibrant, so truly accessible that she can no longer distinguish herself in the immensity of Your domains, in this ocean of spirit which fuses all color, all thought, and all soul into oneness. She is feeling one with her mother, with her father, with her beloved little Alex, with the souls of those engaged in the petty humdrum below the aircraft's belly. One with clusters of spirits, the Norse ethos, the essence of African swelter, the moist North American deep green, with the ghosts of all those dear to her who passed away, family, celebrities, Isadora, Jimi. Bathing in this vaporous epiphany, Mim identifies herself with space, this boundless energy of love, which will someday bear her back to her family.

God, as You are taking Mim to the world, in all goodness You are bringing her physically closer to You, showing her earthly life in its glory, more gloriously so in the raw sunlight, which she has been in love with since her high school days when, together with her colleagues, did field work on cargo boats. She would climb up to the top deck and would earnestly beg the sun to come full up and take the chill off their young bodies. The metal those ships were made of was so dull and unbearably frigid in the early morning. However, the touch of sunshine would bring the entire boat to life and it suddenly turned from bleak and hostile to bright and protective. Even now, she reflects, were the sun not to shine, were its rays to be blocked by clouds, the world would not seem as beautiful. Inside clouds there are turbulences and a plane trembles like a leaf, and Mim sees death and starts praying it get out of the dark masses, and into the sun again.

She considers the irony of death occurring in brightness, not in the sun's absence, as she has usually imagined. Even so, she recalls it was in full sunshine that little Tomina came close to death once. She and her father on their bikes on a glorious summer day, her first ride about town. She had discovered the excitement of speed on the asphalt of a wide main road and forgot to take heed of such things as intersections and traffic lights. Had her father not knocked her off her bike at the last moment, she would have ended under the giant wheels of a truck which was speeding right across their way at a junction. She was never aware of the menace of death, not even after the incident. She only recalled what the on-lookers said, or her father who, once in a while, would reiterate that. All she felt on the spot was irritation caused by the fall, and her first reaction was that of revolt against her father's forceful action which had put a stop to her swift, smooth ride. Why would he do that, she rebelled, just as she had been enjoying the thrill?

Except for that time, all the other instances in her life that could have taken her across the line have indeed occurred shaded from the sun. The memory of her running along the dark corridor of the landing to the elevator comes back to her. She was in high school and so damn late for the morning classes, so she frantically pulled the heavy iron door open ready to fling her body in, only to find herself face to face with the pitch-blackness of the shaft. The tiny filthy box was not there — just a bunch of cables that she was somehow able to distinguish at the last moment. Why she did not throw herself forward then, as she usually did, she still does not know. Unexplainably, something made her freeze on the brink of the abyss, right at the peak of momentum. When she returned home that day, she froze one more time, agape at the material representation of her nation's ethos. In spite of her rushing back home that morning to take a sheet of paper on which she had hurriedly wrote in huge block letters *danger of falling*, and which she had asked a neighbor to glue on the landing door, its grim metal gray lay shamelessly untainted by any sign of warning. And when she opened the door to check if the elevator was safe again, her eyes met the same murderous blackness. However, she never heard of anyone having fallen to death in the shaft those days. God, she thought, then her people had to be the luckiest on earth, completely trusting their fate to divine protection.

Within the walls of the Arvintes' home Mim could have died twice. Away from the sun, confined in the narrow space between Anton's room and the bathroom. The second time only had she been aware of imminent danger. She had been warned by his eyes glowing gruesome blackness at her. The first time though, Mim had no idea Anton had already sent her set the first steps on the way without return. She did not need to know, or she could have got scared.

They had been thrashing things out the whole afternoon till late into the night, in what had seemed to be a duel of attorneys in a complicated trial with no prosecutor and no defender, Mim versus Anton. She had been insisting on him aiding her in coping with that situation, while he would repeatedly counter any of her pleas — Mim, do not involve me in this. They were sitting in opposite corners on the bed, both gaze lost through the window, alternatively producing lengthy strings of words, at longer and longer intervals of silence, waiting for the day to fade away into twilight, waiting for the sun to ripe red and fall on the other side, and leave them into soothing dimness. Mim had initiated the discussion early in the mellow afternoon light, having waited first for the midday fire to die down, which had been quite a long delay. Something had started to shadow her serene existence, something she perceived to be against normality, and she simply did not know what to do. She was sure Anton could help her. What she presumed was going on inside her body was looked upon as pure catastrophe in the country they lived in, and in Mim's case it was unthinkable. She was the pride of her family. Something like that could not happen to her, she would not allow it, the more so given her terror of giving birth. That savage moment had been surreptitiously acquiring horrifying proportions in her imagination within the web of words woven around her ears since early childhood. It had later bloated beyond bearing in her mind, to the funeral march of urban tales set in maternity hospitals: women let to die with a *securist* at their head substituting for the orthodox candles, women treated like beasts by doctors and midwives, cockroaches, rats, contempt volleyed with disgust upon wombs in contraction, sneers impregnated with sadism, swearing and loads of filthy invective commanding a woman to get her baby out at once.

After 1989 she considered allowing herself to give birth to a baby, but ugly stories were still coming out of maternity hospitals. Women screaming in pain were reminded that it had felt damn good while copulating, and they surely did not make so much fuss. It was a shame to bring a baby to this world. That was why she was so thankful to Alex's mother. She admired that beautiful girl enormously for the courage to act as a woman to completion and go, chin up, to that horror place. Her radiant rosy face on the night before Alex was born comes back to her memory, the perfect features enlivened by the miracle within her which was about to show. Sat across the family table from her, Mim told her then how beautiful she was. The mother-to-be was illuminated by a halo of such diaphanous pride, and Mim was gazing at her as at an icon. Mim, too, is free to have a baby now, as she is headed to a destination where this event is welcomed with happiness and respect.

Mim hated the word *midwife*, and all the other words that came with it. She associated all birth attendants with a cohort of old hags, barbarian witches dancing in a circle around the victim, arms flailing, their puffy hands holding all kinds of torture implements, obscenities raining from their fat tongues. Ugh. This was the picture that permeated her mind the night she urged Anton to help her. By no means would she give birth to a child in her country, never. She had rather die. She would punch her belly, raise heavy weights, bathe in boiling hot water till either that sickness or her soul would leave her body. A week had passed, so it had to be that kind of sickness, and she could no longer postpone action.

This is your problem, so solve it yourself — this was how Anton had begun his pleading. I have nothing to do with this, whatsoever, he would restate now and then. And this, despite her conviction that he was all powerful, despite her having imagined to be under the protection of his power. "Would you rather I hadn't told you anything? Say it, would it have been better," she asked. He was absorbed in thoughts. Mim was observing daylight getting weaker, while exerting herself to muster up courage to open her mouth again and utter the same words, her side of the issue. It was hard for her to believe there was no medicine to interrupt pregnancy at such an early stage. If it existed, she thought, then he could get it. No, he insisted, there was not, and his tone was literal, expert, firm. He pronounced a word whose sound she could hardly bear to hear, that terrible butchering operation which was difficult to accept as the sole solution to her problem. Her mind switched to those women who always appeared happy on TV screens, on magazine covers, or in public, and considered the absurdity of her being excluded from their community. That rekindled her immovable conviction that there had to be some decent way out of that situation, so she resumed, even more heartily, her process of persuasion. It seemed, though, she was by now rather trying to convince herself. And she went on and on until she was blue in the face, and until Anton said something about an injection. "I could, if I wanted, give you an injection, but I don't want to," he said. From that moment on she kept beseeching him to do that, till late into the night. "I won't take such responsibility, I'm sorry, Mim." Please give me that injection, she wailed again and again, staring out the window into the night. How beautiful she used to imagine life outside that window, on the moon rays, on the beams of the street lamps, under starlight. Beautiful life intermittently pointed to, in an indefinite distance, by the shafts flashing from the light house, across the river and far. But right then she had a problem to solve and life had stopped for a while.

As Anton seemed to wish he had never met the girl in the station, Mim suggested a deal. "Look, you give me that injection and I promise you'll never see me again. If something happens to me, I'll say I did it myself."

"Nothing can happen to you, it's not that."

"Why then don't you do it?"

"I made you fail an exam, I promised I'd make up for that and take you on vacation to the seaside, and then I would personally come with you to take the exam again and make sure you pass it, right?"

"Right."

"Well, I have kept my word. And that's that."

That night he did not drive her back to the student dorm. It had got too late. Both agreed he would take her there first thing the following morning, which was a Monday, the beginning of a new weekly cycle. Upon waking up, he said he was after all going to give her the injection, so she had better not go to university that day. "Stay here with my mom," he advised. She could not believe her ears, life was going to flow smoothly again for her.

"I will not have you leave the house, I want to find you here when I come back from work," he insisted from the doorway. That surely was a warm cozy prospect, her waiting for him in the home, him wishing to see her post injection. He kissed her goodbye, see you later.

Mim busied herself tidying their room, thinking that she could dedicate the rest of that quiet morning to reading, alone among Anton's things. She was fairly happy with her life when her body was seized by chills. She blacked out for an instant and then started to shiver, feeling all the cells in her body stirring as though they were going to break apart and shatter her to pieces. When more violent shudders started, Mim realized she was no longer in control. She felt and sounded on the inside like what she imagined might be a train speeding off tracks. The next attack was on her stomach, and she wondered if perhaps that was not an actual blow. Maybe it was because of the milk she had drunk, but why should she feel so utterly sick, where on earth had that plague come upon her from? Then her abdomen got caught by convulsions, shaking to its own deep, grave rhythm. She rushed out into the hallway to go to the bathroom, but collapsed before its door. She raised her hand and grabbed the door handle to help haul her frame closer and finally crawled into that room. Once inside, she propped her elbows on the toilet stool with such confidence, as though that was her only source of comfort. She felt love for that bowl then. Posed in expectation of all her insides to be thrown up in there, she was swept all over by a pure wave of tenderness for its cool, white porcelain, a feeling which is still vivid in her memory. She threw up, but that was not the end of her ordeal. On the contrary, convulsions got increasingly violent, so threateningly violent that she felt her whole body was about to disintegrate. It was then when she got scared to death and shouted for help. "I'm dying," she cried. Mrs. Arvinte showed up immediately. At seeing Mim squirming at the foot of the stool, she placed her hand on her forehead and asked, "What is it, Mimi?" The woman kept pressing her warm hand on her forehead till the convulsions subsided and finally died away, when Mim announced she was going to throw up again. Mrs. Arvinte offered to go make some hot tea, but she wanted her there to hold her. She stayed, and Mim cooled off a little, thinking it was all over. She went back into the room, but some unknown, deadly threat inside her body made her return in a tear to the dear porcelain bowl, apparently her sole salvation. She sat on it and then something gushed forcefully out of her, blood, a whole flood of her own blood. It had to be that, she had not had the time to think of that before, but now she knew it was all because of the injection Anton had given her only a couple of hours before. She heard the insistent buzz of the doorbell, then Mrs. Arvinte's voice, then louder voices approaching the bathroom, swishing of garments in movement, and her wishes jumped to Anton, God how she wanted him there to tell him what had happened, and him to help her. She had the impression one of the voices was his, and the name *Antonush* chanced among his mother's words, then firm steps were getting closer to where she was and a voice said, "Where is she?" On the other side of the door she heard him: are you here? "Yes," she shouted from the bowl in a fit of instant happiness. Him it was, and none other, he had come to her rescue.

He later explained that he had rushed back from work earlier especially for her, he had been speeding home and running himself breathless up the stairs to check on her, to be near her. What he had injected into her was a medicine used to induce abortion in mares, which was banned for human use.

"Now you see why I didn't want to do it. It wasn't easy for me either, Mim, and I gave it a lot of thought. I had to titrate the dose with highest precision. One drop more could have killed you, and God, I didn't want to have you on my conscience."

"So that's why you told me not to leave the house."

"I knew what was going to happen, and I let Mom know, too. I told her to come check on you from time to time."

"What about me? Why didn't you tell ME anything?"
"You might have got scared."

39 THE ENCOUNTER

Hurrying through the dark corridor she is still fighting bemusement, will she come back to her senses, she wonders. She pushes the door open and finally enters the loneliness of the small empty room. Travel bag abruptly dropped to the floor, she flings her dear red sack on the bed and rests standing to think, puzzling over the surrealist sensation she is experiencing. Something quite extraordinary just happened to her. She studies her own image in the shy round mirror. Strands of wet hair are stuck to her face, over her eyes, still revealing a pair of glowing cheeks. She should pause to consider what may have caused such a reaction in her, but not yet, since her mouth explodes with happiness and she finds herself so incredibly pretty. She extends her arms to the ceiling, trying to reach some expression of life that beckons her upwards, to life. Taking off on one of life's thrilling trips seems an offer hard to refuse, and she cannot help considering herself plainly lucky.

But how did it happen? She was so loath to leave home in the morning, feeling so devoid of energy, and looking it too. She had to, though, thinking she would return to her university town incognito, so that nobody could see her like that. She finds herself lolling on the bed, musing. That man will come and take her for a ride, and she will do everything to look her best. She is still all wet, and there is not much time left, so she should spring into action. She unbuttons her dress, slides swiftly off it, gets out of the room, and scurries along the porch all the way to the bathroom.

Hot water is only trickling out of the shower head in a thin thread, but she is determined to make the most of it and feel good. What about scents, she panics, as she has no perfume with her. Suddenly she remembers she could do with a tiny pink spray can she keeps in her bag. It is a youthful fragrance, so sweetly feminine and fresh at the same time, expressing some kind of childish femininity, so much like her. Fervently cleaning herself under the tepid drizzle, she dreams of the aroma of her skin which will remind of faintly scented white camellias. She turns the tap to colder water, colder and colder, but soon realizes there is no time for a Scottish shower. Her mind rests aloof against a mute encounter between time restrictions and the need to indulge in wellness, in all awareness of her crude youth, so fortunately beautiful and rained upon by God's water. An absolutely special man has spotted her in the crowd, followed her, and she wonders whether he had really been in need of some coins to make a phone call. She feels like shouting her happiness out to her mother. Smiling, Tomina urges herself out of the shower.

She runs back to her otherwise poorly lit room, so conspicuously bright now in the darkness of the back yard. She gets into her dress, and leaving it open at the front, grabs the hair dryer, puts it to work, and resumes musing while facing her own reflection in the mirror. Her hair will gradually gain volume to make her look even prettier, although she loves it as it is, wet and perfectly styled by rain. She looks like a child, big eyes sparkling, rounded lips rosy, spreading an aura of light. That light, where from, she wonders, gathering this must be the reason why that man is coming to take her to the disco. He insisted so much, despite her continual refusal, but look how she has finally accepted, and how she is going to dance, and what she wants the most now is him see her dancing.

She is ready. Giving herself a once over in the mirror, she applies the last finishing touches thinking ahead of the scented spray from the little pink can. An expanse of blossoming buds invade her mind's vision, minuscule white ones, and she feels enveiled in fragrant scent of grapevine flowers. She alone walking along a path all white among vineyards, she strolling under a fragrant canopy, she envisions him in her place, she wishes him to smell what she smells, yes, she would definitely want a perfume of that essence, an essence French *parfumeurs* she remembers her teacher of French once said use. She checks the time, she should be going. Hair primped, mouth still, eyes sharp, she buttons up her dress, which feels still damp, fastens the belt band, and declares herself satisfied with that gracefully sportive look that suits her mood. She switches the light off, closes the door behind her, walks along the gallery in the darkness, passes through Aunt Ana's salon, and gets out into the front yard. When she opens the gate, he is there, waiting for her at the curb. She gets into the car next to him.

"The train carrying our friend hasn't arrived yet."

Tomina mimes surprise. "Not even now?" But she does not really care.

"No. So, back to the rail station, we wait for the train, we collect my friends, and then we all go dancing, OK?"

"Yes," she agrees feebly. She is pleased he has kept his word and his friends are going to accompany them. She feels safer like that.

As the car is rolling in silence, traces of light stretch out and intersect in front of them on the wet asphalt. The coolness outside is gradually subsiding with their passage, the great restoration of the city's spirit is being discreetly engulfed in the breathing of the crowds, and its inhabitants already seem to have forgotten about it. The atmosphere is suffused again with the exhalation of people straying in the night, the station, so many of them leaving it, his friends. That train must have finally pulled in, as a girl is joining them outside the main entrance, luggage lying at her feet.

How cheerful Anton was for having encountered Mim. The picture of the station that night comes back to her, the pleasant centrifugal sensation as the car rolled around the roundabout, the all expected, yet frustrating for her, pulling up, the other three people getting in at the back, him barely able to contain himself — this is Mim. He turned around to address to the blonde girl. "You deserve a kiss, dear, you bring me fortune. How would I've met Mim, if it hadn't been for you?" *Mim*, a beautiful name, Tomina kept murmuring inwardly. Smiling had set on her face and would not go away, no matter how hard she might try. The man beside her was jubilant, everything about him told of his triumphant happiness — look at Mim, I have finally found the one.

There was no dancing that night, it was a Monday and the discotheque was closed. The group are climbing steps in the dark, silence everywhere, silence outside the club's door which the boys insist opening. They eventually give up trying, yes, sure, it is Monday. Mim presses her body against the large cold glass staring for a while into the darkness inside. That was the first time she had genuinely not wanted to go dancing, as she had thought she had better wait for some other occasion when she would look better and wear a more suitable attire. However, she felt so utterly disappointed now that she had already imagined herself moving to music, dreaming in darkness, spinning, eyes closed, and swinging her hair.

They went to that place many a time after that. It was

always crowded, music was blaring as they sat at one of the small tables, rhythms would change, and Mim felt that was exactly like life, with so many lights glittering all around, beams of light merging into imaginary roads extending across the whole world, over highways and oceans, through the indefinite illusory matter in the great sky, with she, Mim, everywhere, somehow omnipresent and yet *en vitesse*. They would dance together, he ordered coffee, cocktails and long drinks, he would order again, chuckling like a kid every time he did so. One of those nights things got serious. With one hand he pulled her hair at the back of her head and guided her face right into his, asking, "Mim, who are you?" His eyes were driving dangerous daggers into her pupils. Was he demanding an answer? She thought not, she was supposed to keep mum, tame, submissive, all wrapped tight in coils of rope whose end part was at his hand. It stood in his power to strengthen the grip or lessen it a little, him, him and only him. He was definitely feeling something for her. Something was gnawing at his heart morphing the traits of his face. Deep down, well set granules had begun to fret, colliding with one another in a Brownian motion which caused him to suffer. She had the impression he was hurting, and that puzzled her. Rain, rain, rain, like a watery film flailing and wriggling to warp the length of vowels and mess accents up, a pellicule of rain flailing its way in the darkness, among the columns of light which were dimming, going pale and smoky, till ashen smoke enveloped everything, and in this pasty fluid Mim was sinking. She allowed herself to hang limp from his hand, and it was then when she started to feel pain, physical pain, at the roots of her hair. He let go of her. She had the sensation of a sharp blade cutting deep, it was cutting one world into two, and then the two worlds were coasting away from each other, and she plunged with a sharp cry on one of the shores, which was love, love, love.

That first night they left the club totally dispirited, as

parting seemed to be the only normal course of action. He drove everyone else to their homes, then Mim, back to where he had collected her from. He stopped the car opposite the green gate. In the cool peace, they could almost hear their souls' yearning for the world-shaking energy of the storm. Mim had planned to get out of the car as soon as he pulled over, and without much hesitation grabbed the door handle and pushed the door open saying in one breath: thank you, goodbye. While her muscles were straining to haul her frame out, it struck her that his replica might not be as bland. She was half way out when he said, "Wait—" She froze. "Don't go." She turned her head to show him a lightly surprised smile, which merged into gaping wonder at hearing him say, "What would it cost me—" He seemed to have broken in the middle of some longer question. In an awkward position, with a foot out and the other still in, and her torso switched to face him, she stood, mouth wide open, to hear the latter part. "—to kiss you?" "Nothing," she presently said, out of her inborn generosity. He drew closer, pulled her back inside, put his arms around her, and started to kiss her hard. She stood tense in her seat while he was trailing the palms of his hands over the shapes of her body, recoiling from his more daring moves in a rather vague, delicate manner.

When she broke from his embrace it was so late into the night, and the gate she was supposed to go through seemed so distant, yet part of her knew that was the place where she would feel comfortable. She lapsed into a state of strange sickness and felt dirty, with everything she had on weighing heavy. Prisoner in that stance as she hung from the man, gazing at the small gate, she envisaged herself alone in her room there, then better still in her room at home, she would sooner be lying in her own bed, take a warm bath, brush her hair, take that damp dress off her.

40 AIRPLANE

She never discerned outlines of monsters in the sky, although she reckoned frightening visions were quite likely to come to the eye, etched from the chaotic movement of masses of vapors. She sometimes liked to challenge the shaping of some hideous image, of some terrible entity that would really give her a fright. There were times when she even forced a change of perspective, not at all afraid to dare things that were probably there, some sign of evil omen hidden from her biased, benevolent sight. Now, however, as her gaze is sweeping over the expanse of blue, a strange shape seems to be bothering her, and it is not some cloud formation. It is a vaporous shadow at the back of her mind, the afterglow of her past life, fading away in the free sky. The sense of the word *belfer* glints to her in the distance, Anton, white, handsome, wallowing in well-being so complete that all the others are excluded.

In the leveling immensity a kind of map takes shape, the map of her life, what has happened to her, waves upon waves of different hues, which she could read as a graph of her journey through people, colors and changing directions, colors reflecting light in infinite combinations, mixtures of elements, chromium, nickel, lead. Paradoxically, receiving light from so many random angles appeases her, as they are all there, their worlds merged into hers.

Stefan, scarlet, sweltering crimson, the pink manganese of the baby, the blaze of her mother's garnet and verdancy and dazzling white, her father's ivory and shy azure, she and her brother as kids, both sunny and joyous, Damian later fading away from her, treading his own path, his service in the army, his family life and the birth of the child, Aunt Ana's glowing embers of eyes — all these come in a unitary picture of life and love. Then there are rays of light cutting through other colors, watery pastels of serene existence prior to life in groups, the first years of that kind of life regulated by strict rules, rather dull and neutral in her memory, Tomina's pair of plaits, her rose-colored cheeks, the smalt blue of her secondary school years, the blaring bright hues in high school, the fiery rainbows shot high over a varicolored world, wild mustangs, Jimi and Janis, electric pink, psychedelic plains, Pink Floyd, infinite stretches of water flooded by sunlight, bold flaming colors jarring the senses, shrilling phosphorescence, dancing, semi-darkness, parties and raves, soirées, life gurgling in sparkling bubbles of foam, flesh pearlescent pink, liquid deep red, the wheel of hues dizzying her into light, dispersing her into space, where he is waiting, arms wide open, to catch her. What if he does not, she smiles. The power of love, this silvery railway on which she is sliding off from Anton into the wide world, the warm tints, the smoke, Stefan's passion settling around her like a nimbus, his sorrow heavy as lead, the tear, her green cry to go away, take off, first flight, many others, earth tones and ochres longing for her love from below, thousands whispers, she like a lightning bolt against a blonde amethyst sky, victory, brilliant circles, then sudden airy cerulean, the airplane, arrow of silver, all hues together in a sky of light she is traveling right now. New horizons, new people, Mim is flying toward other lands.

Pallid behind, Anton's face. Let her smile, yes, this time in all peace, let her lips lie basking like indolent thighs in the sun. She remembers herself never quite able to reconstruct the features of his face, never as easily clear as she did her mother's, or Aunt Ana's. Anton's portrait is the sole one that will not come out in all its perfection, not even now, but she knows it exists in each and every color that she has spread on her canvases, impregnated in all the fanciful stories she has created so far, which she is now leaving behind. Piece by piece, she has been subconsciously recreating this portrait all along, only that she has not had the benefit of a bird's eye view until now. As she is soaring higher and higher above the clouds, she feels fortunate to be able to contemplate her life in all truthfulness. She is not surprised at all to find herself in Anton's portrait, this is her. He was nothing but the paintbrush. In just one imaginary stoke Mim has her mouth smile again, light reflecting from Anton's velvety irises, set on her own face.

Anton waiting for her to make a decision not to leave again for her home town at the weekend. Each time it so happened that the same song was playing in the warm interior of the car. A male voice kept pleading, *don't leave me*, and now she understands it was her pleading with herself to stay. *Stay with me tonight*, it was clearly heard between their ears while he was driving her to the train station, and Mim felt herself to be at the same time male and female, she would take both essences with her and leave, stubbornly headed for her parents' home.

Anton rubbing the breakfast butter into her skin on the beach also comes back to her. Four hands together were stroking her body, his, and hers too. 'Your body looks fantastic, shining like that,' he said. But were those not her own words, her own ecstatic reaction to the shape of her unique, lissome body, was that not she, who loved herself to tears? Anton felt dangerously attracted to her, despite his willful belief that he would have preferred her to look different. He had started to give in to her charm, no longer resisting his own feelings. He would sometimes realize that, catch himself in the act of feeling, and would presently panic and just fly into a rage. She herself had started to loaf nonchalantly about in the company of them two. They would eat heartily together, hidden in his room from the eyes of the rest of the family, sometimes sat on the carpet in the middle of the floor. She remembers them once gorging themselves there on walnuts and brown bread and fresh sheep's milk cheese, which he liked to call stomach balm, their heads buzzing with all kinds of cravings, with anticipation of soon making love, in all likelihood in the same spot on the floor.

They ate watermelons in the grassland across the river, at the foot of the forest. Tiny winged insects were swarming around, some crawling on Mim's delicate skin, yet she could not care less, splitting her face above the juicy wedge she was holding with both hands, bending her head now and then to resume gnawing at its belly. All the sticky stuff on her lips and cheeks would go off quite by miracle, without any water at all, so she could go on frolicking among the abundant fruits of that land. It was then when she peed outside in the middle of the night, accompanied by crickets. Squatting low in the tall grass at the back of the country yard, she could see Anton standing sentry at the door of the cottage, in the light of the bulb hanging above. Not knowing exactly where the prude damsel was hiding, he was addressing the darkness, come out at once, what the hell are you doing there? She burst into laughter and — shameful blunder — a high squeaky sound went freely up straight to the skies, only to make her die with embarrassment. The crickets themselves had been hushed up. To her surprise, he started laughing his heart out, he was content. Still cowering on her haunches, Mim was presented with a childlike version of his face, eyes squinting with laughter, mouth as sweet as the ripe core of watermelons, blooming open under the lit bulb. He could not stop, so she started laughing herself, well, she was being natural, just like he had always wanted her to be. He used to lecture her about that, act natural, be yourself, I want the real you, he would try to explain.

In sharp contrast to his demands, she was seeking to achieve perfection. She had been so ardently trying to blend smoothly in any social milieu that her wish seemed to have come true, in a way. Her skin had a pure infant's smell, and her perspiration always gave off a discreet balmy scent. Nothing about her and whatever she was doing came out ugly, and she somehow managed to bestow artistic quality on almost everything she did. She could not conceive of anything outside the harmony of life. Life was for her nothing but music, dance, a graceful succession of floats in a pageant. Anton disagreed with this outlook of hers. His was a more practical perspective — when will I ever see you act normal, just like any other normal human being? That night in the village across the river it was through Anton's medium that she gave free reign to her secret inner wish to be simple, petty and meek, to amble away, practically expendable under the starry sky, and get lost.

Anton, eyes round with astonishment feasting on her, words on the tip of his tongue almost letting her know his mind, shy to, yet finally blurting it out: you are incredibly beautiful tonight. The only time he had told her that. The same Anton staring her down in an examining eye and reproaching her: if only you could see how strange you look. They were on the quay that once. She had been waiting for him at the ferry in awful weather, and the wind had blown her face and hair stiff and dry. They later joined a group of friends at a disco club and Mim felt how all evening he had been trying to keep his eyes away from her, until the moment when, with all the heat and the crowded place and the chatting around, she started to regain vitality and her features a warm glow, and even her hair became soft and supple, all to turn her pretty again and make a handsome young guy in their company unable to steer his eyes away from her. Soon that boy came to sit next to her for a chat, and he rattled on and on, only to make Anton seethe with anger, give her hell on the way home, pull her tight to his body after closing the door to his room, crush her to his chest and ask his crisis question: who are you, Mim? The fact of the matter is this is exactly the same question she has been asking herself ever since she can remember, who she actually is, how it would feel for her to be in someone else's body, what the others make of this world, and how do they see her, Mim?

She is flying away now, leaving behind trails of him, in the paintings abandoned at her house, at the art club, or entrusted to the care of the great artist. With the weakening gravity, the corners of her mouth are free to rise higher and she feels all her features take off in a kind of extension upwards, wedging wider and wider to unphysical primordial happiness. One single portrait of all comes clear to her vision, in the brightest of colors, clear-cut in her memory, etched in her soul, and that is Alex's portrait. To her, he is like a second Damian. With Alex's birth, she has restarted her own life. And she seems to be heading for a new restart now, simply because she can no longer understand the people in her country. The higher she goes, the more pregnant her impression that she is departing from a deluged world. She will return some day to collect all her canvases and bring them together in a fulgent whole, ready to be shown to everyone.

41 LIFE

Mim lying like a discarded marionette on the back seat of the car, the mute rolling into the dark city, nasty pencils of light poking holes into the poor ragged sackcloth that she feels like, singeing her, tearing her to shreds. The fathomless interior of the car with him at one end, engrossed in rigid concentration at the steering wheel. He must be chewing his jaws for lack of clues as to how to dispose of her, should he dump her at the train station?

What a burdensome puppet, so burdensome it had better turn into dust when the car stops and the door opens. The sinking sensation is a little uncanny and she feels all her bones crumble and fall, dragging her skin after them into a kind of hollow in the seat. It must be her heart, which she feels like a boulder in her chest. This is crazy, between soaring and depression, powder and rock, burdensome conscious for a light existence, if only the stars hurt less. Splinters and sparks fly high off her mind, go on a round ride in cosmos, then back hurting her minutely. There is a swarm of ants in her head, black, scraping, digging a tunnel for her. She tastes bland, musty earth, then there is flight again, a spark, countless green sparks, she is actually seeing green sparks, circles, lights, red arcs in the dark sky, far from the sun, jocund scraps from her spirit. Her mind is enacting that idiom about seeing green stars. Therefore that is what it feels like: your spirit is shattered to pieces which spread beyond Terra's mother field at the speed of light.

This has happened to her once before, when what she felt was her inner self took off all of a sudden, and she found herself above the world, at the same time body lying on the floor in her teenager's room. She had her ear glued to the radio set, and her brain surrounded by waves from all distances, everything that was broadcast at the moment worldwide, in all the languages on earth. That time she awoke to a lighter ego due to enthusiasm. She had been exerting herself so hard, so badly had she willed herself to belong to the wide world that a part of her had split off. Perfectly aware of her physical being sprawled on the carpet, of the radio's speaker buzzing in her physical head, she was flying across vastness, could see cities from up there, oceans, dark-green forests. She perceived herself as a rod, so thin a thread that she felt a tingling in the solar plexus, and then suddenly — boom — she blew up to giant proportions, became a circle of red light, then back thread, and circle again, larger and larger. Pulsating like this she felt she was everywhere, she felt she knew everything. Although she knew exactly where her body was, on the top floor of a tower in her country, in a long room, on red floor carpeting, face up, she could not think of going back, she felt too big to get in. She was beyond physicality. Speeds were going crazy, all those voices, all the whizzing and fizzling from all sorts of broadcasters, satellites, she somehow was aware of and understood them in pure silence, when things got loud all of a sudden, with strong physical impact on her head, which was whirring, her temples were thrumming. Hello, she had been away and then — zoom. She was back in the mold. She tried hard that night to take flight again, repeatedly, unrelenting, each time with increased focus, pressing her ear against the receiver more and more passionately. She kept straining herself till daybreak, but to no avail. Disheartened, she began to puzzle over the whole experience. Could it be similar to what those she had read were on LSD felt, did perchance a 'trip' of theirs feel like that? She had taken off out of passion, out of ardent longing to join the world out there, and she knew there had been no hallucinations.

What she is now passing through, though, is a state of profound lethargy. She is reluctant to accept responsibility of her own physical body, as simple as that. Long ago, in her childhood years, she once read in a book that the human psyche sometimes chooses to protect itself against adversity and deep anguish by keeping the person asleep for as long as it takes the circumstances to change for the better. This is exactly what Mim wishes for now, Anton to deposit her body some place, be it the station, her home, or any corner of any street, no matter the town, without her being conscious of that. She wishes she could then wake up and resume life from that spot.

"We'll stop at my place. I'll take you to the station tomorrow. It's way too late now to drive to your town."

A sign from the physical world. His voice strikes signals of urgency on her brain, so she has to get down to decoding the message. She does so, and gives a reply. "OK," she says, presently observing the broad road, the blocks of apartments, realizing they are headed to the district where Anton lives. She thinks it will do her good to have some rest right away.

"I won't touch you. I hope you haven't got it in your head that what I told you at our departure has changed. Everything stands true. I'm too tired, that's all."

"Good," mumbles Mim, and she budges in her seat, at last, yet the move is too sudden for the frailty of her frame, for that boulder of her heart which is drawing her to the center of the seat.

The car turns right onto a narrow street lined by trees. She is relieved to realize it is finally getting closer to a resting place, and as she is taken through a maze of alleys, it strikes her mind that somewhere at the end of the road she will necessarily have to move away from that hollow, get to her feet, flex her legs up on some steps. Thank God he lives on the first floor now.

Throughout that night she lay awake to his right in bed. He kept his body straight, face up, back riveted to the bed in a fixed position, he who would always toss and turn from one side to the other, he who would other times turn round to cover her in his body, arm and thigh closing her in as into a safe, to make sure she was his and only his. 'This is how I like to sleep, to feel the woman is mine,' he would say. For a long time Mim tried to control her breathing and keep it quiet, and she would rather her heart was meek and slow. But she soon could no longer contain them and, against all restraints, they gushed out forcefully in the whole bed between the two of them. The walls resounded with her heart's beats, and her breath began to draw out into sighs so high, her love turned upside down, her anti-love in cosmic volumes, all passing through her throat. This headlong outpour rendered Mim so utterly weak and worried — what will he say? He said, with hateful meanness in his voice: what now, you can't sleep? He was not sleeping therefore, but on a vigil for her. One giant breath bubbled out of her chest, making the mattress shake, at which he went on to say: you thought I wouldn't keep my word, didn't you?

She languished like that till dawn. She rolled out of bed, picked up her bag, and went out of the room. No, he did not need to see her out, she told him back as she paced the long hallway to the door. On the way to the station people's energy was rubbing off on her, little by little, on the street, on the bus, the wide roundabout, the crowded station building, the ticket office. She bought a ticket and, holding it in hand, came back vigorously into her own body. That was an instance of perfect accord between her mind and her bones, muscles, her entire physical being. Oh God, how life in a body is perfection, the ultimate oneness.

42 THE ISLAND

It is him, the very president of the club, once so enraptured by Mim. He is coming straight in her direction and she wonders whether he might have seen her. Is it possible that he can still recognize her, when she looks so different? She may be another person now, but her eyes and her hair, though pulled slick to the back of her head, her lips as well, are the same, of course, how could he not know her, since he had so many times rested his sad eyes on her face.

He belongs with a different world, that is what she has always felt, and there is this *vetust*, old air about him, so very much not like her. He used to belong to books only, and probably still does, highly unlikely to ever engage in the thrilling excitement of living adventures, like her. She has always been an amalgam of books and films and dance, she would lock herself in her room to paint, but when she came out she simply dashed her way among people and places in a kind of morphing spree, leaving behind old worlds and inaugurating others, always a brand new life, always a new Mim. Look at him, art critic, philosopher, writer of fiction too. He used to write just in the way he looked, in plain somber earnestness. His writing was well documented, precise, underlain by a wish for youthfulness and freshness of expression which equaled that of his jocund eyes and of his poet's long black hair. Alert and sprightly, he appeared to have time enough to learn and do lots of things, all sorts of scholastic stuff. This rather short, frail body was carrying an entire encyclopedia in the head above. Look at him, as agile as ever, mouth a bit strained in a linear jovial smile, lower lip a bit longer than the upper one — this must lend his expression that wishful note of youthfulness.

He fastens his gaze on her, and indeed, he is coming right up to her.

"Tomina, I'm so happy to see you again. How are things going?"

What shall she tell him? She is no longer the person he once knew, completely disconnected from that academic circle, that fervent, densely intellectual island, which has been floating further and further away from her. Intense with rhetoric, brimming with knowledge and sardonic wit, it now seems to be coasting back to her from the past, tempting her ears with a bedlam of whisperings, sage words, diatribes. The people there are contradicting one another, explaining themselves, in a tumult of voices which acquire stentorian resonance in her memory. But that was time ago, Mim has just happened here again for a short while, as her life is actually rolling somewhere else.

"Fine, I should say," she answers the poet, reflecting that her current fineness will forever stay obscure to him. "I'm running some errands. You know, tedious bureaucracy stuff. You may not know, but I no longer live in the country."

He has got word of her having established abroad. "Oh yes, I've heard."

"Do you still write?" she asks.

He flashes a mild, pensive smile. "No, not any more. I don't have time for that. But tell me, who still did, after the revolution?"

"What about publishing your writings?"

"Oh, no, I mean I've quit completely. Nowadays you have to seek sponsors to publish. Look who has time for that." He draws a yellowish little book out of his briefcase and holds it up to her view. "The old man writes about our group in here. You are also featured in the book."

"Really?" This stirs Mim's curiosity and she wonders how that man might have seen her, what he may have written about her. She inquires out loud, "How did he manage to get it published?"

"Well, I've already told you. Cooling his heels is his daily routine. He crawls from door to door to beg, and look how he has eventually found some nabob to sponsor him." He lifts the booklet in the air, addressing a warm condescending smile to its drab cover.

"What did he write about me?"

"You won't have any trouble recognizing yourself," he offers for an answer, spreading his thin lips again, this time pressing them against the white narrow teeth in a definitive gesture.

Therefore he will not tell her, she accepts silently, thinking that maybe it is not something nice. May the old gentleman be mocking her being too polished and chic for that men's coterie? She went on speculating that sure, a pretty young girl can readily be taken for a piece of décor, some halfwit idling time away in their middle.

Working herself up into a fury, she comments, "I'd rather he had written about that critic from the capital, the one sent here on a mission to spy on us. I've always suspected him." Having said that, she realizes she had known the truth without anyone ever telling her.

One night the sophisticated humbug of an art critic drove her home after a club meeting. He gave her the creeps. The sunny side of it was that he confirmed her own view that she was made for a different world. All that nonsense about the Côte d'Azur — what are you doing here, the critic rhetorically asked her out of the blue. A smile lit her face as she opened the door to get out of the car and she said, in a most natural manner, that she did not herself know. She somehow felt obliged to give a decent answer, but nothing came to her lips. Her curiosity was up and she thought he might come up with some further clue.

First of all, she still found it hard to believe that arrogant, conceited upper crust had offered to see her home. That monolith of a man, she wondered, who would not even look around him and was so choosy when it came to interlocutors. He would arrive, make a sly entrance, and occupy a seat, always mindful not to catch anyone's eyes. He smoked one single make of cigarettes, very rare in those times. He once happened not to have his packet on him, and when someone offered a cigarette of that make, he kindly refused, saying he never smoked other people's cigarettes. He would always deliver his speech at the end of debates, right before the president's conclusive word. Although he never put life into his words and was never passionate about whatever he was saying, he was pretty adept at contriving long artful sentences in the critical register. He had the air of unrolling ready-made discourses before the audience, or rather of having learned some patterns by heart, which he slightly adjusted to suit the occasion. This was a far cry from Mim curling up in her room and indulging in suffering before letting herself go on the blankness of canvas or white paper. And when she was asked a critical opinion, she first had to 'get into a trance', as she liked to put it jokingly, and then speak. That was why she thought she would never make a good critic. She was always careful not to offend or hurt anyone, and would rather keep less pleasant truths to herself. Anyway, she would never criticize any work of art in front of other people, as she knew too well how much soul artists put into their works, and how they truthfully regarded these as pure

341

gems. It was different though when she discussed in smaller circles. She would get into the groove of analyzing, and a warm cloud would accrue around her as people came to listen. This was how Mim won over the president, whose appreciation and admiration turned her into a special presence at the club's gatherings.

In total contrast, the bigwig from the capital surveyed the whole congregation from a stiff position in his seat, delivered his habitual lecture, and left immediately after that, invariably alone. The atmosphere around him during breaks was utterly devoid of the spirit and the warm-heartedness which characterized all the other groups which permeated the halls and corridors in the building. He was cold. From the moment he showed up an invisible web began to weave itself about the room, which somehow kept everyone under its authoritarian spell, and which would break and dissipate once he left. Mim is sure she was not the only one who had that feeling. Despite everything, Mim had reverence for him. He inspired respect all around the club and nobody understood why. Mim looked forward to his arrival. His attendance during debates was a stimulating challenge for her. She sometimes found herself wondering in what capacity he attended those meetings, as he was neither president, nor a member artist, and neither his status as an art critic was confirmed by anyone. He was a kind of observer. This was the name of the web hanging in the air, and the word began to carry more weight, turned oppressive, set about slashing a deep gash through Mim's conscience, starting with the night he saw her home.

He was offering her a position, that of assistant curator at a museum in town: this means considerable workload, research work, working with archives, so think wisely before making a decision. On an impulse, her interpretation of his proposal could not go any further than flattery, and the interval in between was full of surprise — why her of all people, of all the men in their club, such remarkable intellectuals? She knew men were usually appointed in positions of that authority. Discreet pride began making its way through her arteries to each cell in her body. Inspired by the mute interior of the car rolling about town, it expanded nicely under her skin sending her drudging round the clock locked inside an archive room to become somebody, some important person with great responsibilities, and an adept organizer. She instinctively discovered this inclination deep down among her inborn assets, and decided she could do an excellent job in that field, so she was definitely game for investing in that side of Mim. On the other hand, she kept asking herself with obstinacy why he had chosen her. She was not a man. He probably liked her.

She had always wondered why men came to her, one after another, to engage in conversations with her. She just kept quietly to herself, when she would wake up face to face with one, some man who had been treading on her heels. Of the whole clamorous crowd of agitating, clinging women out there, men would choose her of their own free will. Why on earth they all seemed to come to her, only to put her in a bind. She neither wanted to hurt their feelings, so she was kind and considerate, nor did she want to lose their friendship. That was why she did not have any friends. Fate willed her to remain like a monument in their memories, yet so lonely in real life.

And now the 'observer' himself, what did this one want? Although she had to admit he was a fairly good-looking man, she found it simply beyond imagination that she let herself go in his presence. Besides, if that position was conditioned by some kind of closeness, then he might mean it to be nothing but a provisional one, or a bluff. This inference had already deflated her by the time he pulled up at the curb. But then, just as she was preparing to step out of the car, he threw the bait. Exactly so, she did not really know what she was doing here, when life seemed to be unfolding in all its splendor somewhere outside the confines of that enclosed space of her country, which could barely give her enough air to breathe. So she stopped in her tracks in order to hear some more from that man, to hear what he really wanted.

"I picture you somewhere on the Côte d'Azur, dressed differently. You are not made for this life. Have you ever thought that?"

She was lost for words. Only God knew what the man was after, yet, what the heck, let it be, let herself tell him he had hit the nail on the head. So she said, "How do you know? I'm amazed."

"Tomina," he resumed his act in a kind of ominously soft voice, "that is your name, isn't it…"

"Yes."

"You are a beautiful talented girl, with an air about yourself… so uniquely yours — you have class, you know, and speak foreign languages… It's a shame to waste yourself like this."

"I was thinking the same, that it is a shame. But that's the way things are. Anyway, I've had a wonderful life so far, I've lived fascinating moments, as in a dream. There's not one thing that I regret."

"I believe you, but please tell me: wouldn't you like to see the world?"

"Wow, this has been my dream since a child. I know you have been abroad, I heard you talk about that. You were telling about running into our club mate in the south of France, then you two chanced to meet again in Rotterdam the following year, or something like that. Well, that's wonderful memories, about meeting in various spots in the world like this. Someday, who knows, I might be able to share similar memories." She sighed.

In the silence that followed he was meticulously preparing something. He got a cassette playing in the background, a saxophone's shrilling sounds soaring above a metropole all aglitter in the night, a warm night just like the interior where they were, cars, street lights, shows, a spectacle of a world. Mim saw herself gliding away into that world through the looking glass in her childhood, she felt an urge to let herself go, as life felt like a naughty chimera that swept you off your feet. Mim whizzing above skyscrapers aglitter with diamond sparkles, above light-flooded entrances to theater halls, stiletto heels and tiny rhinestone purses, women's long hair shining against milk-white skin, dazzling flawless skin, glaring light coming in blasts, show windows blatantly defying the darkness, snap-shot, snap-shot, curt stills rolling at dizzying speeds, and again on the saxophone's sensuous tunes, Mim glided back in, between the car's door and the light-eyed man, a good-looking one, the observer.

"I can arrange for you to be sent to work on the Côte d'Azur. You can speak French, is that so?"

It just did not ring true in her ears, so she took his words as a joke. She said in a long breath, "*Bien sûr, j'aimerais bien travailler sur la Côte d'Azur.*" She then let out a languorous, subdued ripple of laughter.

"And you speak good English too, don't you?"

"That's true, yes, I can speak several languages. Languages have always been my passion. But I don't understand, what is all this about?"

"This is a serious matter, so think it over."

"A serious matter," she repeated. "OK then, I'll think about it."

She got pretty nervous. That guy seemed to know a whole lot of things about her. The notion of observer kept cutting. It was like a saw job, getting deeper down into her conscious, till it got to another notion, a lot more frightening, the word whose sound and implications her fellow countrymen feared so much wherever they were, in a queue, at their work places, in their beds at night. It was those observers who were everywhere, hundreds of them, thousands of eyes and ears, and one of them was so close to her in that narrow corner of his car, wanting something from her, wanting her to become one of them. Despite her nervousness, Mim slowly gave in to a vain feeling of self-regard and appreciation. The sly facet of her personality came to the fore, and she recalled how, as a child, she wished to become a spy. She used to imagine that she would make an excellent one. No one would suspect anything at all, she conjectured from her duplicitous behavior toward her parents, who did not have the tiniest clue that their daughter lived in parallel lives. No one ever suspected that little girl's exceptional, thrilling invented life. One particular moment came back to her, when she had discovered she was the same star sign as Mata Hari. That was the only time so far that she had caught a tinge of the sweet slyness lying deep in the recesses of her mind. A soft ripple of laughter spread from her chest to her lips and she told herself that, after all, she could take the plunge and play that role too, as life was practically open to anything.

Lurking in the shadow, the observer was keeping a close look-out for her reactions.

"Fine," Mim uttered more like a prolongation than a close, stretching her elegant neck backwards.

She was beginning to sense hidden feminine powers grinding ounce against ounce within her, making ready to puff out as powder, powder to enshroud in a spellbinding cloud the negotiator himself. In the very process, she caught a vague whiff coming from the man that maybe he had rushed into things, and too untimely so, that maybe the confidentiality of his proposition was not completely safe with her, as she had the air of not taking it seriously, being a bit too childish as it seemed. In truth, Mim was not sure what the whole thing was really about. She could not trust her imaginings to be the real thing one-hundred percent. So what did he want from her? If he wanted this, then he could not have made a more hilariously bad choice, as her stomach simply rose against such things. She hated the very sound of the word spy.

Anyway, she thought there was time enough for her to think things over in the days to come, and decided she should draw the line and call it a night, so she said out clear and strong, "Thank you for driving me home, good night."

"Wait, shall we not set up a date to meet at the museum? Just come and see what this is about. Will tomorrow be fine with you?"

"Ah, you mean the job at the museum, well yes, tomorrow then. Is it OK in the afternoon?"

They set the time and she did show up outside the museum the following day. However, he did not go any deeper into the issue than he had already done. He explained that the person they were supposed to have a talk with was not there, some other time, then. They walked their way back to the city center through a park, Mim telling him that, anyway, she did not consider that position suited her. There was no more mention of the French Riviera. She never found out for sure what that man's plans had been with her. On the night of her birthday anniversary, exactly one day before the terrible events in the capital city broke out, someone called to give her their good wishes, in gruesome, slow-paced syllables which froze the blood in her veins. She instantly knew, and she still knows, that it was one of them. They left her in peace after that. She was finally well out of it, as everything changed in their country, or at least so it seemed. Mim had proof they were still out there doing their dirty business, stalking people, very hard to be stopped. Her mother received only half of a letter she had sent from abroad, then another one with only three photos of the five she had enclosed, and many other letters from her were never delivered, and that was throughout the 1990's.

As she first made her way along the French Riviera, old scenes of her own imagination flashed in her mind, her two countrymen meeting at a bar there by chance, then herself speaking a variety of languages on that strip of land, just as the observer's deceptive discourse had inspired that night. She was smiling, there she finally was. I am here, she kept telling herself, breathing in the atmosphere suffused with moist, glittery particles. As soon as the car had crossed the border into France, both the air and the sea acquired a new quality, solar and salty, so distinctly different. That was another world. High above, coming from Italy out of the road tunnel dug into the mountain, Mim felt light blue butterflies in her stomach. The car then meandered down in larger and lower curls, gliding happily toward the sea. The Côte d'Azur was exactly as she had imagined it to be, a long narrow whitish-gray ribbon which pulled you forward with it, past restaurants reclining on hillsides among olive orchards, through a maze of gardens suspended on rooftops, along perfectly trimmed lawns and shrubs, on both sides leaving behind oleanders and orange trees, and then descending smoothly to the sea, gliding along the shore amidst a warm azure, so musical, of hap-pi-ness. That ride feels like floating. With the foam of the waves so close, airplanes in the sky, bateaux à voiles, silvery ships, fishermen further off in the distance, the perfectly straight line of the road cutting through wide expanses of golden sand, hotels so near, hotels so far, flat stretches of land as far as their windows which reflect sunlight like glasshouses, palm trees everywhere, and by night fall, your soul simply bumps into reality and you stop dreaming, as you are there.

What should she tell the philosopher she has just met, what shall she begin with, when there is a whole life to recount? He is mumbling something about spies, they had been spying on him, the meetings of their artists' circle had been under surveillance.

"Sorry, you were saying…"

"Yes, you heard that right, my apartment was being

tapped."

"You mean your telephone?"

"No, I discovered the whole scheme when I had cable TV installed. How do you think they'd been listening in on me: from the apartment below, through the socket to the building's collective aerial cable."

"We all were surveilled. I always wondered what the role was of that guy who drove all the way from the capital to attend our meetings on a regular basis. He was there on a spying mission."

"Right," he says pressing his lips together in total agreement.

"They phoned my home to give me a fright right on the night of my birthday anniversary. The following day the well-known events occurred."

"Is that so?" he asks, seeming to reflect deep on her words, his mouth gaping in disbelief.

"As true as the day is long. Only that I knew nothing about that illegal party. I heard the leaders were arrested those days, they had been followed. The curator of the museum was seized in the capital city, wasn't he, and our other colleague, right here in town, on that selfsame date. He kept running into that critic of sorts while overseas, it is pretty obvious why. I had no idea he was the leader of the party, I found that out after the so-called revolution."

"The meetings were held at my place."

"Ah, you were also a member, I didn't know."

The scholar straightens his shoulders and offers a tight-lipped smile. "Founder member," he says bursting with pride, thus introducing his other persona to her.

"Well, it's all this that the old gentleman should have written about in his book."

In truth, Mim has never seen that elegant dapper man as being old, although he had been retired for some years by the time he joined their club. He had been an actor and had an impeccable diction and manners. She once glimpsed him in the street during another one of her visits in town, but was convinced he did not know her. The fact is she has never imagined the man ever took any notice of her, and that is why she is dying with curiosity to see what he may have written about her.

The president's lips soften and his gaze rivets on her again. Out of tender consideration for him, she visits his eyes, waiting for him to say something. He makes as though he would speak, and then would go his way. He is a busy man now, an education inspector.

"You were very dear to me. I want you to know that."

That sounded like a seal on her soul, and she says, "I know."

The president is departing, briefcase in hand, straight dark locks billowing behind. She cannot appear in the book any different than the way he has always seen her.

The island brimming with spirit flickers once more in her vision, only to fade away in his wake, whisperings weaker and weaker. Full back into urban-scape, Mim decides she has to find that book. Well now, dear sir, let us see how you pictured her.

43 TRAIN STATION

She could return home tomorrow, so she had better retrace her steps back to Aunt Ana's. Try as she might, though, this storm is carrying her along, and she truly enjoys the feeling. The bridge over the train rails is only a few more steps away, and she will be on the platform in no time. Let it rain on her, now that she has ventured out in this weather. She will not go back, happen what may. As she is climbing the iron tread boards to the deck, the wind feels like a wall against her breast. Were anyone to see her, they would think she is out of her mind, but there is not a soul outside. She considers again taking shelter back in her little room, while still carrying on, undismayed. That room is emptied of practically all her stuff, so cool and so desolate, as dismal as the whole house, with Ana being also away. She is between the devil and the deep blue sea. Should she go back to that bare bleakness, or confront the elements in order to rejoin her family? She pushes forward, determined to conquer the bridge, step by step, against the fierce gales.

Never before has she known such violent fierceness of nature. Water is running in rapid streams down her hair and face, drenching the dress on her, if that can still be called a dress. With that garment turned into a watery film itself, Tomina can feel the deluge directly on her skin, no longer frigid and strange. Her body blends like a spear of water into the downpour, giving her a singular feeling that she herself has become rain. She is on the top deck now. Mesmerized, she is gazing into the grey light which is cleansing her eyes, imagining this grandiose miracle as likely to unite people's souls. The sky's mystery opened up to her, the cascade of rain she feels one with, and her high position up on the bridge, all mixed together form a bewitching field around her, fated to lure her closer and closer to the train station, and she knows she will not stop until she has reached it. Proud to be offering herself like this to the madness of rainstorm, she pities everyone else, who hides themselves in their homes.

In the station, wonder of wonders: throngs of people gathered together on benches lining the main platform, waiting rooms packed to the full, hustle and bustle around the information desk, and her train hardly likely to ever leave that night. She dumps her red sack and the travel bag at the foot of one of the pillars and plasters her back against it, starting a stare play in the subdued, bizarre light which is flooding her eyes. She is quietly observing the sea of faces spread before her as at a mute funfair, to which the participants have been summoned by the drums and trumpets of the thunderstorm, none of them knowing when exactly they are going to leave for their destinations. It is a predicament they all share and Tomina rejoices to feel so many people united in such an unexpected way. Her hair, all soaked, still feels like streaming in the shape of rain, from the top of her head down below her shoulders. With water and wavy tresses trickling over her eyes, she has the impression she has got out of the bath directly here in the station, caught in a film still for people to stare at. She can feel her pupils being flooded over by the irises all agape to absorb the gloam in the distance, which seems to attract all the glances upon her, as though she was a vacuum at the hub of the fair. This has come like some sort of answer to her being driven here in spite of everything — you could say these people had been waiting there for her arrival. She glimpses a face of indefinite age at the pillar opposite to her and fleetingly labels it as strange, just as she turns around to pick up her luggage. She drags her bags to the nearest pay phone and calls home: Mom, Dad, the train is delayed, I will keep waiting just like everyone else, there is an army of us.

Their breaths mingle together in a warm cloud which is felt hovering in the air among them, gradually, and so very unwillingly, dulling away the pristine coolness brought by the rainstorm. This human warmth is pure caress to her senses. Only now does she realize the storm has ceased. There is nothing left in its wake but them, passengers, amassed in that station as on a busy international airport. And they are so cramped, so compact a mass, that none can hide from the others. She elbows her way through the crowd to the other end of the platform, and lays her luggage on a bench next to a pay phone there. People chat fervently and smile while waiting, looking very much like extras on a film set. The actress in Tomina is reveling on the quiet, and she almost expects to hear a voice calling *Action!* She thinks this is the ultimate public place, and train station at its best. Quite surprisingly, everyone seems to have forgotten of their trains, and nor does any of them give the faintest sign they are ever going to part and scatter away. They are simply enjoying a great time together.

Trains have been reduced to mere excuses for convivial small talk, and Tomina's is rumored not to circulate until the following morning. Consequently, she rakes up a couple of coins and just as she makes for the nearby phone she sees a guy, arm stretched ostentatiously to it, ready to drop a coin. But he decides not to. Instead, he invites her to use the phone. Please, he says ceremoniously, then gives in to a genial smile. Ah, it is the strange guy she had glimpsed in the crowd, and he is flashing a smile so much younger than she could have imagined. She smiles back — thanks, I'd rather you phoned first; let's see if it works. When her turn comes, she announces her mother that the train is hardly likely to leave that night. Immediately after that she returns to where her luggage is. But who shows up again, if not the guy at the phone. He needs to change a bill for small coins. Sure, she promptly helps him with some small change, and he uses the apparatus again, only to join her some seconds later, and start a chat. Her attention is drawn to his entrancing, mature, velvety voice, and to his educated diction, purposefully perfect. She, a student, Tomina, waiting for a train which is highly unlikely to leave that night to take her home to her parents'. He, accompanying some friends who are meeting someone at the station. So, you are not leaving anywhere, understands Tomina. No, he resumes, one of my friends is waiting for his girlfriend to arrive. He points to his two mates who are throwing wondering peeks from behind columns.

"I could give you a ride home, but I have to be in another city for a meeting first thing in the morning tomorrow."

"Thank you, but no, it's OK. I'll wait for a little while longer and if the train's not—"

"I'll take you home tomorrow," he cuts in wholeheartedly. "Anyway, there's no way you can leave tonight."

She admits it to herself that he is in all probability right. It is already late, so she will phone her parents again and go back to her room at Aunt Ana's.

"I wanted so badly to get home tonight. I'm wet to the skin and have no clothes to change, and I just hate it to be like that."

He nearly sweeps her off her feet. Without second thoughts, he grabs the handles of her two bags and flings off, with her trailing on his heels. He is proudly strutting his way with her red sack in one hand and her travel bag in the other one, determined to demonstrate his friends in loud ostentation that he is no less than hell-bent with regard to this girl he has just met. His parade seems to be begging for raised eyebrows and questions of the type what on earth has got into him. Indeed, Tomina can glimpse the two young men smiling between their shoulders.

"So long, guys," he calls out joyfully as he goes past them. Bursting with happiness, he then addresses her behind his shoulder. "Look, we're going to ask one more time at information, I'll do that, and if there's no train, I'll drive you to your place, OK?"

There can be no reply to such enthusiastic determination, none other but total submission. Laden as he is, he jostles his way to the information office to get the latest about that train. Well, its departure has been postponed till morning. Tomina brusquely wakes up to reality, wanting to know what the man next to her looks like, how old he is, what he does for a living, and how he has come to carry her baggage throughout the train station. Quite so, she does not have an inkling of who that man is. Yet it feels festive, their having met feels like fête.

ABOUT THE AUTHOR

Viviana Ioan was born in Braila, Romania. Passionate about visual arts and the art of the written word, in her early teens she was a correspondent member of the Psychologists' Club led by Radu Cimponeriu. She also took a drama course at the Art School in her native town. A Master of Arts in English, between 1985 and 1990 Ms. Ioan was involved in the literary circles *Mihu Dragomir* and *Panait Istrati*.

In the 1990's she left Romania for a cultural and linguistic European 'pilgrimage' and eventually settled in Italy. Upon returning to her home country, she decided to take up residence in Bucharest, where she currently teaches English at a national college of arts.

Her published work includes poems, poetic prose, and fragments from her novel *Traveling: roman sensual*, all in the literary magazine *Luceafarul*. She continues to write her novels, as well as articles on her personal blog, vivianaioan.com, under the concept *Next Woman*.

17948788R00209

Printed in Poland
by Amazon Fulfillment
Poland Sp. z o.o., Wrocław